"Taut and chilling, *Hands of Darkness* keeps you looking over your shoulder, yet James has filled the story with hope, reminding us that the Light of Love can destroy the Lure of the Serpent. Another powerful, gripping story that will keep you up long into the night!"

—Connie Mann
author of *Angel Falls*

"Stripping away the blinders and ripping away the curtain, Heather James exposes evil for what it truly is—the dark and sinful spawn of Satan himself. But ultimately we are shown that the darkness, no matter how thick and deep, can be overcome with one single ray of light. With great tact, and a whole lot of wittiness, James has penned a thrilling, edgy novel that can be shelved beside the best crime novels of the biz."

—C. J. Darlington
author of *Ties That Bind*

"I've yet to meet another author who pens such a strong, courageous, and snarky heroine and puts her in the middle of such distress! If you love suspense with tones of dark humor, don't miss Heather's books."

—Jordyn Redwood
author of *The Bloodline Trilogy*

LURE of the SERPENT · BOOK 2

Hands of Darkness

A Novel

Heather James

Kregel
Publications

For my sisters,
Erin and Megan

Hands of Darkness: A Novel
© 2014 by Heather James

Published by Kregel Publications, a division of Kregel, Inc.,
P.O. Box 2607, Grand Rapids, MI 49501.

ISBN 978-0-8254-4292-6

Printed in the United States of America

14 15 16 17 18 / 5 4 3 2 1

Evil Sings

Ibelieve Evil likes to sing its little lungs out. It first pitches its tune soft as a canary, melodic and beckoning. Once it knows you're paying attention, the roughness factor goes up exponentially. Like a sledgehammer to the gut or an ice pick to the throat. Yes, I realize that sort of roguery isn't akin to singing, but I also know the Devil doesn't fancy himself a tenor as much as he does a thug.

I

And that's that.

I wish she hadn't fought back. Layla shouldn't have done a lot of things. It was a snap of anger but more than that. I knew it was a bad idea to date someone at all, let alone someone who reminded me so much of Mom.

What kind of loser am I who has let his own mother do this to him? I've hated her for years and I think she likes it that way. I sat outside Mom's house earlier tonight, after Layla broke up with me, when Layla said she didn't see herself with someone with so little ambition and drive. That what we had was fun and loose for a while but she was getting to the point in age where she'd have to be serious in her choices and she didn't envision being serious with me.

My voice betrayed me and said words like <u>reconsider</u> and <u>I could try</u>, but in my head I was already envisioning wrapping my hands around her throat and squeezing until her eyes popped. For years I had fought the urge to do it. To do it to anyone when my mother came at me the way she did. At some point the phone rang during Layla's speech and she turned her head and I could see the back of it and that made more sense. I'd take something, anything, and give that head a big whack. Then she'd drop down and shut up for a change.

I never knew who was on the other side of that call but the way she spoke and acted during it made her seem more like my mother. When she was done and turned back to me I could tell something had left her face and she wasn't going to be nice about it anymore. I should've smashed her head in right there before she finished with me.

"Honestly, David, nothing you could do would help. I'm only saying this because I truly want you to seek help. I think you are . . ." She trailed off, using her hands to monitor the pause, making little circles that wrap within one another and I really wish I had something nearby to whack against the middle of her forehead. I didn't care any longer that she'd see it coming.

"Broken," she finished. Her eyes widened as she looked away. "Really broken." That extra emphasis was something I knew I'd make her pay for. She kept talking. "I really wish you wouldn't shoot up with that stuff. I mean, how much muscle do you need? You must know the side effects, right?"

That was an area she should've left alone. It was the only thing I've ever done for myself and she was trying to take it away after I had only tried it out a few months earlier and the muscle mass was something I'd always be proud of.

"And then," she said and I couldn't believe she was still talking because it was no longer whether I'd hurt her but how much I'd hurt her. She rolled her eyes. A big roll. "Honestly, I think your mother has a lot to do with how much you're broken." She blew out a huff of air. "Look, I wasn't going to say anything, but I ran into her at the mall not too long ago and you know, she started talking to me and then before I knew it, she's buying my lunch, but David, that woman is horrible. Despite what happens between us from here on out, please listen to me as a friend—you should distance yourself from her. I hate to say this, but it's like she can't even stand you and wants to torture you with it. She even told me to run away from you, that you are a—" She paused and I held my breath. "Loser," she whispered. I felt the backdraft of anger. Years of it.

That's the moment when the snap came. At first it felt like I was sleeping and then a floating hand came near my ear with fingers ready and gave a SNAP! to wake me up. Loud so I knew I was up but still confused, panicked and swinging when there wasn't a reason to be like that.

The only thing that saved Layla at that moment, right when the snap came, is I still blamed someone else more.

I found myself sitting in my car, staring at Mom's house in the dark, and I realized it was more than a hand snapping its fingers. It was a snap in half. Me. It reminded me of those glow sticks. They're one thing when you pull them out of the package. Sleeping. But then someone gets their hands on it and SNAP! You have something new in your hand. The smashing and mixing of everything inside, burning together.

And that's what Layla and Mom felt to me, burning together inside me. They lit me on fire and they'd pay. For years I'd fought the urges, Mom always knowing, somehow knowing, what I was thinking and she'd say that I should just go ahead and do it, be a sociopath like my father, even saying his full name to me as if it would mean something more venomous that way, a man I've never known until recently.

But then she'd shake her head and rethink it. "Don't you do it, you good-for-nothing piece of filth, or you'll be just like him and that will be the end of me!" I never really thought about doing anything, except when she said it like that.

The words had claws at first, then they had nothing, and all the time I still wanted her to love me so I did nothing because maybe I could turn her. But could I? No. Why hold it in any longer?

A golf club. That's what I had. Mom had given me the set for my twenty-first birthday and said if I couldn't figure out how to be a normal man by that point in time, then she was done with me for good and I was hopeless. Even if I didn't use them, she said that if they sit in the corner of my apartment, then it might confuse a potential wife long enough for her to see past my "creepiness" factor. That's how she put it. That was last year.

I couldn't escape the feeling that if I hurt someone, something would light inside me. Like the glow stick. A snap could mix everything together for what I was supposed to be. All I had to do was get inside my mom's house and bash her head in because I don't know what I'll be forced to become if she's still in the picture, still making me pay. Then it could be over. The urges would leave. As long as she's around, she's around. She made visits when I was dating Layla. Mocking me, teasing me, wondering if I had made Layla ditch me by now and if I'd made her go running because I was a sick and rough freak like my father, calling him by his full name. Always calling him by his full name.

I already knew she had lunch with Layla. She said she could tell Layla had her doubts about me and maybe she'd have the good sense to dump me so that I could finally hear it from another woman other than my mother that I need help on being a man because of where I came from and how I behaved.

But that's the part I hated her for the most. How I behaved. As if there was ever a choice for me to be okay when she did the things she did, hated me the way she did, made me suffer the way she did.

I can see now it wasn't possible to escape this. My mother had a choice, but I didn't. She could've had an abortion, she could've given me up for adoption. She didn't have to keep and raise the son of a man who raped her. I think she did it because she wanted to make someone pay. Not him, not my father, because she didn't want the press and trial. That was her answer one day when I was twelve, screaming and crying that I couldn't take any more, her words, her neglect, her anger.

She transferred the hate to me, to protect the crime of my father. She's lucky for that, in a way, because when I stood above her with the golf club, her snoring on her bed like a big-chested freight train on silk sheets, I wondered if I shouldn't learn from her. Transferring the hate. She was smart. Successful. Lied through her teeth to protect the secret of where I came from and how much she hated me, but she managed to keep it all together. There could be something to this transference. If I killed my mom, they'd come for me quickly. Being her son would certainly mean a police visit, even if they suspected nothing at first, they'd get me. If they visited me, they'd get me. Mom always said I wore my guilt on my face like the stupidly kicked dog that I was.

So I backed out of her room and went to find Layla. That was the only time I was glad Layla never told any of her friends or co-workers about me. It'd be harder to track me down since she treated me like a ghost.

She got a few hits in first. My eye has some swelling that will show for the next few days. I'll just wear a hat and lay low. At first I hit back only to get her to stop fighting me. And when she was lying there, her head slumped over but still breathing, I thought about taking her one last time. But then that would make me my father and make my mother right about how I'd end up just like him.

She had always said it like it was her own prophecy of cruelty but I could see the fear in my mother's eyes if it were really true. But I had already come this far. Might as well as long as there's the possibility it will look worse on Mom. How will she be able to keep the layers of lies now if I am caught? How would she be able to smile and continue with that sort of press?

I don't want to get caught, no. But if I do, that would be something worse than death for her. And my father. Could he really be worse than her? Maybe I'd find something in trying to be him for a change.

And that was that.

One Bigot and One Ugly Tie

Andrew Doss looked at me as if gold bars were about to drop from my mouth. That's what he had paid me for so I suppose he had a right to do so. I sat with him at counsel's table in a San Diego courtroom, having been hired to do his jury consultation.

"Drop the old lady," I said.

He nodded at the recommendation.

That should've been that. I say to drop the old broad, he agrees, and we move on to juror number thirty-who-cares. But Doss's second chair for the trial, the real party cracking the whip upon Doss's derriere, wasn't buying it.

"Why would we do that?" Ben Levy asked, his tone suggesting he didn't believe a lick of what I was saying or doing. He'd been like that from the get-go. It was Doss's first time up to bat with a big case like this, but Levy was a legend in his own mind. He insisted on taking second chair to help young Doss. He had said it was to provide guidance, as necessary. But the way his eyes regarded Doss whenever Doss wasn't looking, I figured it wasn't for mentoring as much as it was for being an overbearing head-master. He wasn't going to help Doss; he was going to remind him every step of the way that Doss's career couldn't afford to screw everything up. At least, not utterly.

Apparently, that included shielding Doss from the likes of me. Levy had already accused me of performing a sideshow palm-reading act. I wasn't the type to get offended from the mouthing-offs of people I don't care for, so I let that one slide. That was, however, his one and only free pass. And now, he was starting with me again.

"Well," I said, lowering my voice and leaning toward both Doss and Levy, "suffice it to say, she's a bad seed."

Levy scoffed. "How so?"

"She's got an ulterior motive for being here. Don't know what it is yet, don't think any of us need to know what it is, but whatever the reason, I'm convinced she's not a fan of yours." I pointed to Levy. "So, either way, you should skip her. You have enough challenges left and we're thinning the jury pool."

"She doesn't like me?" Levy asked. "What abracadabra formula are you basing that one on?" He was trying to sound important, mighty, and sardonic all at the same time. I didn't want to answer him. What was the point? He was going to disagree with me anyway. It seemed the perfect time to drop the charade with him and simply light afire the anticipation of any future working relationship between us. Let it burn, baby, let it burn.

Besides, I had to use the restroom. My soon-to-be-born son, Owen, was taking a nap on my bladder. At that point in my pregnancy, one spoke to me snidely at their own risk.

"Well, *I* can barely stand you as it is," I answered Levy. "But more to the point, that old lady curled her lips at the mention of your name, right after Doss introduced you to the jury pool as co-counsel."

"What do you mean? Only at his name?" Doss asked. Then he appeared to mull over something. He looked quickly at Levy, then to the old lady. It was probably the third or fourth time he had done that since I started talking about her. I figured she knew she was our subject matter, yet she acted pie-in-the-sky giddy, making little hushed comments to the young woman to her right while the attorneys conferred during the pause in *voir dire*.

If the young lady hadn't been worth her time for the last three hours, then why was she important now? At that point, my initial reason to get rid of her seemed irrelevant. She was just plain shady. I wanted her gone.

"Are you suggesting," Doss continued, "that she sneered at Levy's name because she thinks he's Jewish?"

Levy grunted. "I am Jewish, you idiot," he said to Doss. Then he leaned back in his chair and raised his eyes overhead to the boxed light set illuminating the courtroom. He let out another grunt.

"Well, no, I can't say for certain that's the reason," I said to Doss. "I only said she sneered when you introduced Ben, that's all. I'm not willing to classify her as a Nazi right here and now; I'm just saying she gave a disgusted look. And it wasn't like an 'Oh, I've been sitting here in this chair for too long and my granny panties are riding up' type of sneer. Nor do I think it was from anything else that would indicate frustration or distaste in general, like the courtroom being too stuffy or someone's perfume too strong." I shook my head for emphasis. "I am certain she doesn't like *him*," I said, pointing to Levy again.

"And, who knows," I continued, "maybe it's because she recognizes him from somewhere, but won't fess up to it. Maybe he stole her parking spot at the grocery store. Maybe he didn't help her cross the street when he was a boy scout. It could be any number of things," I said. "It could even be because of that horribly ugly tie he decided to wear today."

The sound of Levy's chair snapping back up cracked through the courtroom, echoing off the wood paneling and tiled floors. The pen in Levy's hand suddenly took the appearance of a tiny ballpoint arrow that I was sure his aged and overly soft hands could fling to the spot between my eyes. I took my yellow legal pad and stood it up on its edge in case I needed it for protection.

Doss bore a look of confusion, like the little fawn that had yet to learn that momma deer and daddy deer are, in fact, blown to smithereens in the forest. That is, if you let human nature play out long enough.

Perhaps Doss did need Levy to help him with this trial more than I realized. I guess I didn't want to see it, didn't want to see the usefulness behind the snarky second chair.

Doss was still caught up on the bigotry angle when he said, "I want to believe society is beyond that," rubbing his hands across the tabletop.

"Not at all. We are not beyond this by any stretch of the imagination. In fact, many men wear ugly ties on a daily basis. I'd actually call it a pandemic."

"Oh, for the love of . . ." Levy mumbled. His whitened knuckles said he wanted to snap that pen in half, but those hands—as I had mentioned— were quite soft and unburdened in every sort of ultradelicate way. When I got a better look at them, I decided he wasn't really a threat to me. I let the legal pad fall down.

Doss tapped his fingers. "So, cut her loose, huh?" he asked me.

"Yup."

Levy leaned near my face. I felt his hot, panicked breath coming at me. It smelled of rank bitterness, as if his only breakfast was a cup of black, cheap coffee, and a case of acidic nerves and self-doubt. Yet, I still enjoyed it. It meant I was going to have my way because he wasn't as tough as he pretended to be.

"It's a potential three-million-dollar verdict and our client is only what—five, seven years younger than that juror you want us to cut. Not to mention that our client was butchered on an operating table during a routine procedure. One that this juror, herself, might need in the near future. But you want us to get rid of a textbook empathetic juror?"

I scooted my chair away from him. "I'm not a fan of repeating myself." I left it at that.

It was only after we were nearing the end of the day that Doss cut her loose. I think he had meant to all along, but figured he needed to, maybe wanted to, play by Levy's book. Most lawyers have to grow the requisite backbone as the years progress. The experience mounts and the burn marks from more cunning adversaries leave a lurid trail on one's backside that helps the process along.

When I walked into the hallway to head out for the day, I found the old lady Doss had excused from the jury pool still there, her back to me as I exited, and commiserating with a younger guy who had gotten cut five minutes after she had. I overheard her say, "It was that Jew lawyer who had it out for me and now I don't get to be on a jury. I think that fatso pregnant woman is a Jew too. They both had it out for me."

I could've corrected her on the points that, one, I wasn't Jewish, two, being a bigot is a lousy, cowardly sort of life, and three, unless you favor being backhanded, you don't call a pregnant lady fat. However, by that time of the day, I was feeling less tactful than usual and realized if I started into it with her, things would go south quickly. It'd be just my luck that she'd have some sort of heart attack and die. I mean, talk about a crapshoot for a Tuesday afternoon.

Besides, Eddie had made me promise I wouldn't start any epic battles of wit and tongue with anyone until I was no longer incubating his child.

My ankles throbbed. I tried to look down at them, but . . . Perhaps the bigot had gotten the fat part right. Good grief.

I had been doing jury consulting for months now, having turned to it after the State of California decided to take my bar license away. The state apparently frowns upon mothers of molested and murdered daughters that hunt down pedophiles and throw a bit of angry cowgirl justice upon them.

That's another one I have to chalk up to *live and learn*.

My daughter, my Corinne, had been killed about a year and a half ear-lier. The lead investigator on my case at the State Bar compared what had happened to my daughter and my response to it the difference between apples and oranges.

If there were a pear around, I would've chucked it at him for saying such a thing. He was lucky in that regard.

The State Bar Committee was especially condemning over the fact that I actually blew one of those pedophiles away. That part, if we're being particular, was done in self-defense according to the criminal prosecution and dismissal of my felony charges, so it's not the official reason they disbarred me. As far as the records are concerned, they hooked me on the part where I was unlawfully carrying a firearm. Lawyers, I tell you.

Still, if they could've seen the whole picture as I knew it, they would know I really didn't care that they stripped my license away. Being an attorney was no longer for me. Sure, I'd do the occasional jury consultant job because it paid well and I seemed to have a knack for reading people, but when I was chasing down those pedophiles, it was as if I were a wolf pup having my first taste of blood.

I hadn't told Eddie about this—I hadn't told anyone—but something in me still craved it. I wanted the hunt. I wanted justice. I wanted the sickos and demon incarnates to slither back to the pits they had come from. I wanted to lock them up and feed the key to some drooling jackal that barks and snarls for their fill of putrid flesh and bones.

No, it wasn't a butterfly and rainbow type of job aspiration, but it was still the stuff I thought about in quiet corners and on long drives, always wanting to get my feet back into it. What could I do about it though? Nothing.

I was a disbarred attorney with few options at my door and that *Dateline* episode about my escapades didn't help much. I would have pre-ferred it if they had either vilified me or put my name up in red, white, and blue, surrounded by sparklers. Instead they did both, leaving it up to the viewing public at large to decide whether or not you'd want me at your child's birthday party, whether I'd be the life of the party or the dope who ends up toppling the birthday cake into the flower bed.

One would think that the driving sense of security most of us have to protect our children would applaud my actions—less pedophiles on the street is a good thing. But because the *Dateline* episode included the part about me being able to identify a pedophile based on how foul and toxic he smelled to me, the situation was like those nutjobs who run across the outfield of a major-league baseball game. Yes, we see you. Yes, you're giving us a moment of entertainment. And yes, we still think you're stupid.

So, jury consulting it would have to be.

That's what I thought. Until Brian Thatcher asked me out for lunch.

TWO

The Forsaken Life: Burn

If I didn't have at least another day, maybe two, ahead on the jury selection, I would've hopped on the 6:15 p.m. Amtrak back home to Eddie. Back to Fresno. This was notwithstanding the fact that I promised Thatcher I'd meet up with him. I hadn't seen him since he left Fresno a few months ago, and before that only sporadically since we solved my daughter's murder together. I preferred to take credit for that one on my own, but the fine print only records the detectives working the case and I was no detective.

Thatcher got his dream promotion from solving my daughter's case, and from a few others I had been involved in with him during that time. He was now a task-force commander with the San Diego Police Department. He even had to say good-bye to his girl back in Fresno. She wanted more if she was going to make the move, and Thatcher had his mind set on moving alone, likely thinking that his new career would be his all-in-all. It made me think that those old days he enjoyed so much—the television-inspired machismo where the handsome young detective slid over the hood of his sedan and then kissed the girl—were over. He was a boss now. He'd have to take the long way around to the driver's side. The boring way. The boss's way.

He was also being stupid. What good is the pursuit of success and dream jobs if you don't have someone who has your back the way Eddie has mine? I guess I didn't know all the details, though. Maybe Thatcher's girl wasn't an Eddie, the one you go the stretch with, come what may.

This traveling business without Eddie around was killing me. Amongst other things, he helped me behave, not to mention that I had a dull yet nervous tingle going on inside of me. Like I'd most certainly

need the comfort of his hold by the time I was done with both this particular consulting gig and whatever Thatcher said he'd wanted to discuss
with me.

He had asked me to stop by his station since I was in San Diego, saying it was for a bit of old business and that he'd take me out to lunch.
Business. It was a strange sounding word coming from Thatcher, but I
obliged and went to meet him at the station.

I figured San Diego's police headquarters would be some sort of tower-
ing white building out of *Dragnet*, or something similarly imposing and
impressive. Instead, it looked like your typical cookie-cutter executive
building. The location gave it a bit of flavor though, if vagrants and pros-
titutes were your thing. I parked my rental car on the street in the only
spot I saw left, in front of a row of meters that went on and on like some
robot of a man standing in a hall of mirrors.

I tipped my satchel upside down in hopes for some loose change.
Thirty-eight cents in all. The pennies were worthless. Meters weren't that
cheap of a date. I waddled to the front of the meter, ready to put the
quarter and dime into the slot, only to find that a thoughtful citizen had
jammed a mangled wad of bubble gum in there.

"Great," I muttered. Looking around, I concluded again that this was
the last spot on the street. Maybe my car and lack of meter feeding would
go unnoticed. But still, what brazen fool doesn't feed the meter this near
a police station? I thought about leaving a note, telling the meter maid I
would've entered my coins if it weren't for the bubble gum impediment. I
also thought about leaving the coins on the windshield wiper, right where
she'd slip the ticket.

A homeless man walked nearby, pushing a wobbly cart, his mobile
storage unit du jour. It wasn't the *thump-whump* sound of his laden-down
cart that got my attention at first. Rather, I felt him looking at me, his
gaze boring into me. When I turned to face him, he was taking a good,
long look at my belly. "Looks like you had a big lunch," he said, guffawing
at his own remark, forming the hint of a smile.

His jaw moved rhythmically, as if he was chewing on something, but I
saw nothing in his mouth.

"Yes," I said to him, putting a hand on my belly. "If this is the result of
a lunch, then I ate a baby."

He dropped his smile and shut his mouth. It slammed faster than a
front door on a rogue bee. He also let go of his cart handle, the cart rolling

a foot away before it got caught in a raised crack of sidewalk. His head shook at me as if I were ghastly and debauched.

"That ain't right, lady," he said. "Why would you eat a baby? What's a baby ever done to you?"

"You can't possibly think I'm serious." I put my hands in my coat pockets, one of them still clenching the coins I had originally intended for the gum-filled meter.

"I tell you, I don't know. In my time, here on these streets, I've seen some stuff."

"I'm sure you have," I replied. "But I thought we were playing with one another." I pulled my hands out and laid them on my belly. "I'm clearly pregnant, not consuming babies."

"I *was* playing," he said, "'cause that's the way I play. I see a pregnant lady and I say she's had a big lunch. She laughs or she ignores me and that's the way it goes. In all my years I've been telling that joke, no one ever says they've done eat a baby. What's wrong with you?"

My head drooped. "I don't even know where to start."

His smile came back, but he stretched it too far. His lips cracked a bit and a tiny piece of skin hung down near the corner of his mouth. "Hey, I guess you okay. You like to laugh some, don't you?"

"I have my moments."

"It still ain't funny to talk about eating babies," he said. "Not in these parts, anyway. It's no joke."

I fought a sudden urge to close my eyes and mentally process a rewind, erase, and rerecord of the entire conversation. Starting with the inappropriate baby joke and ending with the fact that I believed this homeless man just confessed—at least by inference—certain and unthinkable terrors available to him on the streets.

"I apologize for my bad joke," I said.

"That's okay. Hey, so you got any money to spare?"

Last I checked my accounts, I had a spare few million. Well, not spare per se, but it was one heck of a nest egg if I could liquidate it. That's if he was asking generally, but if he meant in my possession, then I only had the thirty-eight cents for a meter that wasn't able to take it.

"Here." I reached back into my pocket and then dropped the coins into his hand. "I wish it were more."

"Thanks." He smirked. "People like you, dressed in your fancy suits, usually have the most but part with the least."

"You're kidding me," I said, feeling my brows furrow together. "Are we talking about giving you the only change I have on me right now, or are we venturing into the realm of social commentary?"

"Both, eh?" He smiled again. "Ha!" He was missing most of his side and back teeth. "I'm just saying lots like you don't want to part with your money 'cause you thinks we're going to buy booze and more booze."

"Are you?" I asked.

"With one quarter?" he mocked, holding the big coin just under my nose.

"What if I had a twenty?" I asked.

"Do you?"

"No. But what if I did and I gave it to you?"

He let his mouth start moving into that successive chomping gesture again, five, six times. "I'd buy booze," he said.

"At least you're honest."

"You'd buy booze too. Life's hard out here."

"Yes," I replied. "I'm sure it is."

I pointed across the plaza to the police station. "I'm going in there. I'm sure someone has donuts. They're cops," I said, smiling. "Want me to get you some?"

"Nah. I gotta keep moving this morning. If theys find me stopping out front the police station, theys think I'm gonna rat them out."

"I'm sorry, what?" I asked.

He smiled again at me and nodded, like he knew something I should have. Then again, maybe he was just a homeless guy and it was only the typical banter of a forsaken life.

"What's your name?" I asked him.

"Why you want my name? You ain't gonna send me a Christmas card."

"I'm Evelyn. I ask for names when I meet a new friend."

"We ain't friends."

"Then give me back my change," I said, but not meaning it.

"My name is Burn," he said.

"What's your real name?"

"I just tolded you. You call me Burn."

"It's an unusual name. How did you come by it?"

He shook his head. "Nah."

"Nah, what?" I asked.

"You going in there?" he asked me, pointing at the police station.

"Yes." I was going along with a change in subject matter.

"Then you worse off than ol' Burn and you don't need to worry about my name."

With that, he grabbed his cart again and shoved off. I turned to face the station.

II

The smell and the sight made me sick and even though I was there to cover my tracks, I spent more time worrying that I'd leave traces of myself everywhere else. My sweat, my hair, and the several times I wanted to spit out whatever seemed stuck in my mouth. Dirt. Digging down to her made the dirt fly right into my mouth even though I didn't bury her deep the first time and I wasn't digging too good on account of my nerves.

I was less nervous when I put her in there. But I couldn't leave her like that. If anyone found her there, they'd do whatever they do, the cops, and they'd find that I got to her. I've seen the shows.

Walking around the first few days was the hardest. I went back to work right away but it felt too heavy. It was a mix of feelings I didn't know how to deal with. My brain says it was an accident. I had been angry and I lashed out. It was either going to be Mom or Layla that night and Layla just had the tough luck that it was easier to rationalize striking at her.

It was still an accident. My head said if I hit her, I'd feel better. The rage will shut up for a change. All these years, holding back. All these years I've wanted to deck Mom, but you don't hit your mom, that's what she said. That's what she said when she pushed and pushed and pushed. "What are you going to do about it, little boy?" Push, push, push. "Can't hit me because then you'd be a loser like the man who planted you." Push, push, push.

When I got old enough, big enough, I hit the wall, inches from her face, and was sent away the next day, locks changed. Four days after my fifteenth birthday. I would've been on the street if she didn't have her career to protect. But since she needed to protect herself, I got a nice dorm room in a local private school. I told people my family was from Pittsburgh. Locals didn't live in the dormitory. They went home with their parents at night.

I got stronger and stronger so that not even a changed lock could keep me out if I felt like it, but I rarely did. It was peace without her. More so when she cut off the funds when I graduated. Good. On my own. Working like a man, a real man, not having to depend on her, and I thought it was all over.

But it wasn't. I can see that now. I can see how much I still hate her and how she ruined me for life.

Stupid Layla. STUPID LAYLA! Just had to meet her. Just had to be so much like her. Just had to tell me I didn't measure up.

And now she's measuring down, stinking up the soil.

I was doing work at one of my places, taking a break, and saw Mom. She didn't see me but I could see her. I almost wanted to smile. Like a great burden had been lifted, and I suddenly had power. I could crush her skull with the power of my hands alone but chose not to. I have her life in my hands and she doesn't even know it. I also have the power to humiliate her. To grind her with shame. But the lift didn't last long.

She was standing in line behind a younger woman, young like me. Pretty. So pretty it angered me because I felt an unexpected elephant on my chest and an impotence in my pants because I suddenly realized that that girl was a girl I'd like to be normal with but nothing like that could ever happen again. Not after Layla, not after Mom. Especially not after I realized how good it felt to set Mom up for the humiliation to end all humiliations.

If I did this right, I could go down in history and her being my mother, it'll be like she's raped all over again but by the world, the world that's watching. And then I hear, "You can do this. You were made for this. Prove it to everyone." I don't know who says these things. It's like an inner voice of the real me, the me I'm supposed to be. And they're said nicely, with respect, and I've come to like the sound of respect.

I did some reading on things and that's why I went back where I buried Layla with a few jugs of compound that will get rid of anything I might have left on her.

I'm thinking about a next time. Whenever I think I'm messed up for doing these things, for wanting to do these things, I hear that respect again: It's not me that's messed up, it's those women. The haughty ones who have big plans for their career and don't have time to be bothered with what I am. I mean who. Thinking they can toy with our feelings and tell us we're not good enough men to know how to be a man.

I always thought my father must've been some sort of coward for what he did to my mom, but maybe I don't know all the facts. I don't necessarily feel the thirst for taking women like that, and with Layla it was different because I already knew her.

But it's like my dad says, with some women, there's only one way to show them who's who and maybe he's right. He doesn't know who I am when he talks to me like that. He doesn't get it at all. He only thinks I'm a follower of his interests and that he can talk to me like that, with bad, bad stuff when he thinks no one else is listening.

He told me not too long ago that he felt a strange connection to me, that he could tell me things he'd be too scared to tell anyone else, because he could tell I had similar interests. I was repulsed by that at first, but considering Layla and what I want to do to that other one . . . if only he knew.

That's when I was feeling proud about it, right when I was pouring the compound over Layla and hearing it slosh around her slumped, filthy body. It splashed on me and that meant the end of those pants.

If I did this again, then I'd have to find a better way to do it. But Layla can stay. Good-bye, Layla.

THREE

The Earth Revolts

"You're pregnant!" Thatcher said to me when I arrived on his floor, his eyes widening at my belly.

I shook my head in disbelief. "You've known I was pregnant for what . . . seven months now? In fact, you were there in the hospital with that whole Gordon Racobs thing when I found out." I was about to remind him of the other two occasions I had seen him since—once early on in the pregnancy and then again before he left Fresno—but I'd been married long enough to realize the futility of pointing out the obvious to men. Especially regarding the processing of pregnancy issues and the collective fodder they simply classified as "chick stuff."

"Oh yeah, right, right," he said, faking recognition. "But the last time I saw you, you weren't so—so . . . " he stuttered and then stopped to motion a wide—a very wide—circle.

"So help me, Thatcher," I said, "if you finish that sentence with any other adjective apart from *radiant, ravishing,* or the like, I'm going to talk to you about mucous plugs for the rest of our visit. I'll even pull up some pictures on Google and show them to you while you're trying to eat."

He looked at me confused, a small wrinkle pinching in the middle of his forehead. "I don't even know what that is," he said.

"Oh, you will," I assured him. "Just keep it up, and you will."

I looked around his floor, feeling a heaviness and severity in the surrounding air that was recognizable to me. It was like running out of gas on a darkened, back road. The slap of the moment still stuns you a bit even though you probably saw it coming.

I could feel the . . . what's the word . . . *misgivings* of the place.

"Do you have criminals up here?" I whispered to Thatcher.

He gave me a funny look. "What do you mean 'criminals'? Do you mean *suspects?*"

I scoffed. Criminals, suspects, what's the difference? This was, of course, the reason I never practiced criminal law.

"I mean criminals," I replied. "People you've already arrested. Are they up here?"

"No," he said. "If they're not already at the central jail, then anyone who has been arrested is down in holding."

If there weren't any criminals up here, then the intense air I was feeling was coming off the officers and detectives themselves, like a film of grit upon one's face after a dust storm. It was the first of many times I'd come to realize that in the world of crime solving, of wading around in evil and neglect, everyone, and I mean everyone, comes out a bit uglier in the end. I looked at Thatcher. He still had that sandy blond hair, bangs down to his eyes, and that impossibly young looking skin and an easy smile. Yet, it was still there, that harder and roughed up look. Like he had been thrown against the school-yard fence by the beefy, yellowed-teeth kid, but was coming back to fifth period as if lunch was all about nonfat milk and soft, white bread.

His slight tarnish could've been the stress of his new job, or maybe it was the grit that liked to flock to the shiny guy simply because it could. Might've been both and probably was.

The entire floor looked like a sea of cubicled coffins. The lot of plain-clothed detectives could just as easily have been an underpaid population of telemarketers but for the accoutrements on their waistlines—holstered guns, leather holders for handcuffs, and their badges.

I let him lead me into a glass-enclosed room with a medium-sized conference table in it and a dry-erase board shoved up against one of the walls.

"Would you rather me jump right to the point?" he asked.

"Always."

"Okay." He took a seat on the edge of the table while I sat in a chair. "Would you ever consider working down here as an investigative consultant?"

I felt a knot in my throat and it wouldn't budge. It was only after a few more seconds that I realized the clump was from a lack of breathing on my part. Hadn't I just been thinking this, about getting a chance to work with the police again?

I took a slow breath in and found a spot on the table to focus on so he'd think I was acting aloof.

"What do you mean?" I asked. "Like being a cop?"

He laughed. "You, a cop?" His laughing continued as he got up from the table. He took a seat in the chair next to me.

I leaned forward and said, "It's a strange thing, but I almost feel like I should give a swift kick to your shin right about now."

His smile dropped, but not as fast as he scooted his chair back from the table.

"Relax," I said, withdrawing from my position of attack. "Eddie has me on a strict nonconfrontation pact."

I could actually hear the boldness of laughter rising back to Thatcher's mouth. I cut it off with a sharp look. "But, I have a long memory and won't always be pregnant."

"Fair enough," he said, scooting his chair back toward the table.

"So, not a cop, but what?"

"That *Dateline* episode—"

A pitiful groan escaped my mouth, interrupting him.

"Hold on," he said, "let me finish."

"I'm listening. But barely."

"My boss saw it," Thatcher said. "And then he gets this notion that you could do for us what you did for the department up in Fresno."

"What I did for *you*," I corrected. "You were the only one who really let me play," I reminded him.

"Yeah, well, my boss asked me if I could get you to come on board with the Crimes Against Children team, but I said last I knew, you had lost that sense of smell."

"Never existed." I barely wanted to go into the explanation of it all.

He shot me a confused look.

"It did, but it didn't," I amended. "I've gone to a lot of doctors since. Psychiatrists, neurologists, and pretty much anyone else who has the capacity to write a prescription to make my brain softer than it already is. And they all seem to be in agreement. The consensus was that my so-called sense of smell was a psychosomatic response to my head injury, when Robert Bailey smashed my head open. They said best-case scenario was I adapted a finely tuned ability to recognize a pedophile when I saw one, because at that point in time I lived and breathed solely to find Corinne's killer. So, when my brain triggered around a potential pedophile, a contrived sense of smell came with it to make sure I didn't miss what I was looking for. Or, whom, I should say."

"But you were right," he said. "Each time you were right. How do they explain that?"

I didn't want to go through what I truly thought, even with Thatcher. There's a wide berth of forgiveness with brain pain issues and at the end of the day, if you could chalk up strange behavior to such, then the other kids might want to play with you again.

Still . . .

Between God and me, I had a bit of a hair-raising inclination that it wasn't *all* part of a psychosomatic response. What if it had been a gift from God Himself, to bridge the gap between the pain of losing my child and my certain descent into self-implosion?

Without the hope that I could catch my daughter's killer, I would have very likely driven myself into a thick, old tree at the thought of my own impotence. No brakes. No tread marks. It was one thing to wake each morning with the overbearing guilt that if you had managed to watch your child just a little bit longer, with a little bit more earnest, she'd still be your little girl. Add the flippin' futility of knowing her killer could spend the rest of his life running around as a free man . . .

I didn't really know. I suppose I had thought such things to make myself feel warmer inside, holding on to the belief that God may use His right to amaze us even when we're the only ones who know what He's done.

All the same, the part about the sense of smell being gone was true. I no longer had a personal need for it anyway. Corinne's killer had been caught, although he's still awaiting trial. He's been in county lockup for the duration, but I'm still offering a Bundt cake with a nail file in it to the first lowlife who does him in on the inside. Yes, I feel guilty for admitting that but no, I'm not in a hurry to change my tune.

I looked at Thatcher. Like he said, I had been right about all those pedophiles. But that was then and this is now. Would I really be of any use at this point? I shrugged. "What did you tell your boss?"

"Like I said, I told him you didn't have the smell anymore and that hunting down pedophiles was one of the last things you'd want to do."

"That's true. It's a noble cause, to be sure, but it would remind me too much of . . ."

I couldn't finish it. How would I ever be able to? I let my head fall to my chest, to cover that familiar tingling and slight heat signaling tears headed my way. But lowering my head only made it worse and, before I knew it, one had rolled down my right cheek. I left it there in case Thatcher became cognizant of my pain by virtue of the fact that I was wiping something away. As it were, he might not have noticed at all. I turned my chair away quickly and that tear fell somewhere. I don't know where. By the time I looked back in his direction, Thatcher was leaning forward, crossing one arm over the other on top of the table.

"Sure, sure," he said. "I promised I'd ask, but what you just said made me think of something else. What if you worked on my team rather than the Crimes Against Children? Even if you don't have the smell, you're one heck of a people reader." A mischievous smile crept upon his face. "Not to mention the fact that you push peoples' buttons like nothing I've ever seen. I mean, I'm constantly amazed I can tolerate you."

"Ditto," I sneered, although I wanted to chuckle.

Working with Thatcher again. It was definitely a notion worth considering.

When Thatcher left Fresno, he mentioned his new job had something to do with serials, high profile, and high volume cases. All the undesirable messes the city wanted tidied up before the pitted cauldron of depravity bubbled up and spilled over on this seaside city.

After all, San Diego should be perfect. San Diego *was* perfect, at least judging by the lead stories on the news and in the paper about puppies in drainpipes as opposed to a constant proliferation of hard crime.

"I could bring you on board as a consultant," he said. "Nothing fancy, and no, you won't be a cop. Definitely no firearms, and you'll very likely not be able to do much when I'm not by your side. For lack of a better phrase, I'll have to keep you on a leash."

"Like a pet." It wasn't a question. I knew what he meant.

"And you used to live down here, right? You're familiar with the area?"

"Yes. I lived here during law school."

"Well, do you want me to show you what I've been working on?" he asked as he stood up and walked over to the dry-erase board.

It was blank, so I wanted to quip that it meant Thatcher was working on nothing, but then he grabbed the board from the top and flipped it over so that the side that had been at the wall now faced me. The images on it pummeled me like an angry, drunken sailor packing a punch that was vicious, sloppy, and wholly unconcerned about the consequences.

"Oh my gosh," I muttered, my hand going up to my mouth in horror and disgust. I quickly stood and turned my back to Thatcher and his board of horrors.

"Sorry, geez, Evelyn, I'm sorry." Thatcher came over and put his hand on my shoulder. "I guess I should've given you a heads-up first, huh?"

"Yes!" I shouted.

A heads-up was a definite plus before a pregnant lady unwittingly beheld photographs of murdered naked women taped up on a board. Thatcher took me by the elbow and ushered me out of the room and to his nearby desk. "Here," he said, "sit down."

With my eyes closed, I tried to find my bearings. "I am vaguely interested in working with the police again, and especially with you, so I'll give you a few minutes to tell me exactly what you're doing here and what use I'd be. Tell me everything before I change my mind."

"Are you sure?" he asked. "Because we could go do lunch first—"

"Just get on with it, Thatcher!" I barked.

Thatcher spoke of someone they considered a lone perpetrator, a man who had already raped and killed three women. He said rape wasn't a rare crime in a city the size of San Diego, typically done by the likes of men acting on impulse, men who are easily seized by the police. Then they had the rapes turned homicides, similar to the current case. Even with the majority of those, they were almost always done by men acting in the heat of the moment, leaving behind plenty of evidence.

He gave some examples. He even went as far as saying those cases incorporate what they considered a "run-of-the-mill rape/homicide."

Run-of-the-mill. That's the world we live and procreate in. Awesome.

I was feeling sick. Nauseous. A day in the life of demons. First that board of horrors and now Thatcher seemed to be reveling at the stupidity of certain monsters. Just because some are easy to catch doesn't mean there isn't a mother out there weeping for her butchered daughter. Or her son-turned-abomination.

"But this case," Thatcher said, pointing back toward the other room where the dry-erase board stood, "is not run-of-the-mill. This guy doesn't kill on impulse, or to cover his tracks, or even because he can't control his anger. I think he does it because he likes to kill. And hurt them first."

Though I could no longer see the pictures on the board, they were still before my eyes. The images had been burned into my memory forever. Naked women with puffy and bloodied faces, sprawled out on the ground. When someone dumps a dead, naked body on the soil, the earth revolts. It spits and twists, insulted at being forced into having a part in the grisly scene.

"And unlike your impulse homicides," Thatcher continued, "this guy doesn't start planning the cleanup once the dirty deed is done. He goes in knowing he's going to kill and knowing how to cover his tracks. Each of the rape kits came back with residue suggesting that he also wears a condom.

"Of the three victims, there is only a slight deviation in their attacks. The women had all supposedly been alone, and taken in dark areas. One notable difference is with victim number one. She was at a bar down in Pacific Beach with a date. First date sort of stuff. Witnesses told us that she was sitting at a table when her ex showed up, all strung out on meth. They start to fight in the middle of the bar, he's going ballistic, she shoves him back, and then he balls his fist back like he's about to knock her on her rear. The date told us all of this part. He said after the ex brought his fist back, he looked like he gave it a second thought and then dropped it.

"Then the victim begs her ex to take the argument outside and the date said the two went through the back, where the bar has an alley. It's just a place for dumpsters and deliveries. Once they left the bar, neither came back. When the date went to check on the girl, no one was in the alley. He said he assumed the two made amends and took off together. Next morning, we find her body. Dumped over in a wooded area off the freeway, over by SeaWorld."

"So, where's the ex?" I asked.

Thatcher shook his head. "I tracked him down a day later. He's trash. Even during my interview, he was completely strung out. He'd probably been awake for forty-eight hours, but I don't think he's a killer. The victim's nose was broken when they found the body. I asked him if he had punched her and he said no."

"Did you look at his hands?" I asked.

"Sure, but I'm telling you, the guy was a mess. He had cuts, scrapes, bruises, scabs, you name it. Everywhere. Even if he did punch her, his past involvement with her and his meth issue would've probably meant two things: One, he wouldn't have used a condom and we would have found his semen. And two, there's no way this guy could organize a trip to the grocery store, let alone a rape, murder, clean up, and body dump."

Thatcher said that from that point on, there were no other witnesses, no one had come forward to say anything about any of the three attacks, and the bodies didn't have any trace evidence on them that would link them to their killer.

"I'd blame your crime-scene geeks if they can't find anything on the bodies," I said.

"I don't think so. All the women had been thoroughly scrubbed with a bleach and antibacterial compound. Inside and out," he added.

I shuddered in my seat. Tell a woman "inside and out," and we all know what that means. I shuddered again. "I'm sorry, Thatcher. I need some air, or water. Or something." I stood, needing to leave.

"Lunch?" he asked.

"How about a barf bag?"

III

I followed her just to follow. Everything was ready and I had it all planned except for the part where I grab her. Layla was easy. She knew and trusted me. For others it would be an issue. How to get them to come with me.

But there she was in the alley. Out cold. I didn't do it but I will do the same from now on. It's smart. I'm amazed at how simple and smart it was. I should have figured it out earlier.

Once I got her she didn't put up as much of a fight with me as Layla did since this one was already hurt. Right before the end I asked her if she'd be embarrassed to introduce me to her friends. She looked at me like I was stupid, like the way my mother did when I asked her for something when I was a child, and it was good-bye for her.

They're all worthless.

My dad talks more and more about urges like he knows I'm letting them all out. I hate that he's right about that stuff. I wonder if he'd be as disgusted with me that I take it all the way with women as I am with him that he's probably been planting this stuff in my head since I first started having talks with him a year ago, when he thinks I'm nothing more than an easygoing stranger. When the urge comes again I'll go see what my mother is up to. She's predictable. I know where I can find her and that way I can find others like her. There are always other women to fill the need.

FOUR

An Old Friend

Jennifer Ness used to be my roommate during law school. We met in Contracts class, first year, and she got my attention because of her ridiculous outfit. I had worn simple flip-flops and cutoff jean shorts. It was San Diego in August, circa 1998, and I don't have to defend myself any further. But not for Jen. She came prancing into that classroom looking like she had just plundered a Neiman Marcus manne-quin, making off with its starched blouse, skintight pencil skirt, and four-inch patent leather heels. When she sat down next to me, my first instinct was to flee. But because all the other seats had already been filled, I stayed put. The only thing left for me to do, therefore, was be acerbic and hope she'd find a new seat the next day.

"You're looking mighty fancy today," I had said to her. "Did you forget we're not in a courtroom yet?"

"You have to look the part," she replied. It had a snotty ring to it, but I supposed I deserved it.

"I do look the part," I said. "I'm playing the part of a poor, malnour-ished first-year law student. Whom are you playing? Queen of all?"

"Sure. And you are my subject," she said, her eyes locking on mine, the rigidity of her face displaying her nerves of steel. "First royal decree: Keep your nasty attitude to yourself because I can't get to another seat. These shoes are killing me and I might've just ripped my skirt when I sat down."

I wasn't sure if I wanted to pull her hair or laugh at her. Ultimately, I decided to go with option number three, which was to like her. I leaned into her. "I'm sorry," I said, meaning it. "I just have to know, though. You do realize no one else is dressed to the nines for a Contracts law class, right?"

"I don't care," she replied.

"Fair enough."

It wasn't long after that we decided to become roommates. The arrangement worked except for one point of contention: she'd study for hours while I perfected my golf swing and socialized. And for that, I still got better grades than she did. Not by much, but I think it was the amount of my effort—or lack thereof—that truly ticked her off. We had a fight about it once toward the end of our second year. She professed the unfairness of it all, asking how I managed to get my grades if I didn't devote the same amount of time she did to studying the textbooks and case law.

"I do study," I answered. "Just not the way you do."

"What other way is there?"

"I study the professors. I talk to them. At length, actually. I've asked every professor we've ever had what gets an A in his or her class."

"And they tell you?"

"Of course they tell me. They're law professors. And law professors are madly in love with themselves. You just have to ask them the right question. 'How would *you* write an A paper?' And they spill. They always spill."

"Seriously?" she said. "That's your trick?"

"How's that a trick? Like I told you, I'm still studying."

"Studying people, not books."

"People give so much more information."

Now that I thought about it, I bet Jen found it amusing I had turned to jury consulting. She'd instantly be able to recognize it was right up my alley. And, unless something had changed in the last few weeks, she was still in the back caves of her tremendously large downtown San Diego firm, doing the recluse book stuff like Bankruptcy and Estate law. I would never say this to her face, but the different paths we took after law school sort of solidified the differences in how we approached our studies. She was still stuck in a room studying books after all, and I was still trying to milk people for information.

I hadn't seen her in years, not since I married Eddie. She might've been at Corinne's funeral, but if she was, she never made her presence known. Then again, I was in no condition back then to keep tabs on anyone. When I sent her an email yesterday that I was in town, she offered to take me out to dinner but I wanted something a bit more low-key. We agreed to meet up at her condo in University Town Center, just northeast of La Jolla. A doorman in the lobby greeted me and asked me my business.

When I told him who I was there to see, he said "Ms. Ness" had already told him I would be arriving.

When Jen opened her front door, she threw a quick hug around me, being mindful of my protruding belly. "Evy! It's so good to see you again." She looked down at my stomach. "May I?" she asked, stretching out her hand to touch.

"Yeah, knock yourself out."

"Can I just say," her hand was making tender little circles near the top of my mound, "that I'm over-the-moon happy you're pregnant again? I'm just so inspired that you're doing this after all the pain you've suffered."

I gave her a sheepish smile, hoping that this was as far as we'd go on the subject. Corinne had been gone just long enough for me to feel comfortable about moving forward, but not so long that I wouldn't break down and cry if someone—someone like Jen—needed some sort of personal closure in broaching the subject. Yes, yes, I thought, you'll feel like a better friend if you bring it up, shed some tears, and then go forward, but I won't. You can go there and recover in a matter of minutes, but I'll be there for the next several hours, and uncontrollable weeping isn't on my agenda for tonight.

Jen ushered me inside her place and closed the door behind me.

"I can't even imagine . . ." she started but then trailed off for a bit. "I still break down and cry when I think about—"

Fan-flipping-tastic. Here we go.

I put my hands up to stop her from talking about it any further. "It's okay, Jen. It's still pretty fresh and I'm trying to be a big girl, but honestly I'd rather discuss other things."

"I'm sorry," she said.

"It's okay."

"I'll tell you what," she walked into the kitchen and positioned herself in front of a cutting board with a lime on it, "we'll talk about other non-weepy things and have fun. I only have, what, a few hours with you?"

"Yeah," I said, pulling out a barstool that had been tucked under her counter. "My train leaves in the morning. Back to Fresno I go."

"Fresno," she muttered, slicing off two rounds from the lime. "Wow. I still can't believe you chose that over San Diego."

"Have I ever mentioned that I made more money in that Fresno firm than you do at your fancy, high-rise firm down here?" I asked, giving her a smirk.

"Why yes, you have mentioned that," she said, cocking her head at me. "In fact, don't you include that as part of your signatory line in your Christmas cards too?"

"I think I lead off with it, actually."

She chuckled and then dropped one round of lime into each of two filled glasses. "Here," she said, handing me one of the glasses.

"Ooh, lime slices in water. This is a bit pretentious. Even for you," I said, taking a drink.

"Don't get too excited, I filled yours from the tap."

I took another drink. "And yours?"

"From an untouched glacier in Alaska."

"Of course."

"Of course," she repeated. Then she smiled and furrowed her brow at me. Classic Jen. "You know it's coconut water, right?"

"Yes, the coco-nutty component was my first clue. Thank you for spoiling me." And I meant it. Old friends trumped new ones any day.

"You're welcome. Now, can I give you another hug? I've missed you, you know. It's been so long. But, if I remember correctly you have quotas or something on physical contact."

"A quota would imply I allow at least a minimum."

"So . . . no?" she asked.

On my way out of her condo that evening, I noticed she had a running band used to strap a phone or MP3 player to her upper arm, tucked in a little basket near the front door.

"You run?" I asked.

"Yeah, I just picked it up as a hobby. It's great. Just me and the ground. All the stress seems to melt away."

"Outside or in the gym?"

She guffawed at the question. "I live in San Diego, remember? Of course I run outside. It's always beautiful."

"Alone?"

"Oh, don't start with me," she said. "I don't want to end this visit with a lecture. I've heard the speech from a bunch of people, and yet people still run every night and live to tell about it. I'm careful. I promise."

"But, Jen," I started, trying to hold in a rush of bad thoughts surrounding me—the fear, the panic, the absolute acquaintance with pain. Was there really a safe place anymore? Were any of us ever wholly safe?

She saw my composure and softened. "Oh, Evelyn," she said. "You're right. I'll . . . I'll find a running buddy. I will."

She wasn't being sincere. I could tell. But she had drawn a line, and I could tell that too. She had meant it: no lectures. The only thing I could do was pretend I believed her. Then again, there was Thatcher's criminal on the loose, raping and killing women.

"You better," I told her. "You need to," I added, my hands balling into little fists and wondering if I should tell her about the killer. Thatcher had made me promise not to breach his confidence and discuss the case with anyone other than Eddie. But I had to, didn't I?

Jen casually shook her head at me, almost as if she knew I was about to start the lecture anyway and thus chastising me for it.

"I'm serious, Jen," I said, deciding to walk a thin line between what she needed to know and what Thatcher would allow me to say. "I can't go into too much detail about it, but I know from a very reliable source that there's someone on the prowl in this city. You shouldn't run alone."

"Oh, there's always someone on the prowl," she said. "It's the world we live in. I know. But like I said, I'll find a buddy."

IV

Layla was because I was angry, that second one from the alley was to see if this was something I needed. Was I the messed up little turd my mother always accused me of? I only finished off the second one to see if it was an antidote to everything I've stuffed down or if I'd finally be repulsed with myself. When Layla said I should get some help I don't think she understood how her dying would be all the help I needed.

It's not normal. I at least know this. The way my mother has lived her life isn't normal either. She lived two lives and so can I.

I didn't want it to be this way but it's a strange comfort to know that a part of my father has seeped into me. I've been thinking of a way to let him know that I'm his son and perhaps what I've been up to will help him not be able to deny that I am his. I don't know if he'd deny it at all, but in case he did, maybe we could bond over it and I'd finally have someone else who could appreciate me.

Something in me has taken over. Even though it seems hungrier than I want it to be because I still fear getting caught, it's still the only thing I've ever known that doesn't betray me. It tells me I'm worth this and the women are nothing but worthless.

I got two more. The first one worked at the bank. Didn't think a scrawny bank teller was a good choice because she wouldn't put up a fight. I like to let them know that even if they try, they are no match for me. I'm too strong. Too big and not a loser at all. My physical strength is my measure of being a man, even Mom can't deny that. She always said I was too small and runty, like a good-for-nothing. She can't say that now.

I thought of passing the bank teller up but the scene was too good to leave empty-handed. She had a nice car parked in the back of the lot, far from everyone else. Easy to grab. I parked right next to her and she had to pass my vehicle to get to hers. She was the first I tried my own punch with. I heard her heels clicking as she walked the parking lot. I stood between our two vehicles right at my back tire so she couldn't see my feet as she approached.

I punched her square in the nose and she dropped cold just like the one from the alley.

I had her locked up nice and neat and did to her what I only really did so my father and I will have something to talk about. I waited for her to wake up so I could do to her what even my teeth trembled to do to Mom. But as soon as she woke up she started blubbering. I told her to just try and take a swing at me so I could show her I'm not a nothing. I even accidentally called her Mom when I said it. It had to end quickly after that. Especially since she was so soft. After all of it I couldn't help thinking that she could've been one who might've felt sorry for me instead of scoffing at me so the night felt like a waste.

The next was a number cruncher. I followed her for three days waiting for her to be alone and prime. Nothing until finally she went to check her mail at eleven thirty at night. I came up from behind and when she turned, I punched her.

When I picked her up to take her away, I ran into one of her neighbors. I let her face go into my neck and I cradled her. I mumbled that she'd had too much to drink. He told me to party on.

When I got her back, I realized she hadn't survived my punch. I'll have to scale back on the next one.

These last two were disappointments. I need something more significant. What does Mom call them? Legal eagles.

I want to find a legal eagle and make her pay.

I made a stop at the courthouse and saw one I liked. It wasn't my usual rounds but I wanted to see one in action. Her style was different from what I like and she was older, but she held my attention. It was only when she turned to the side that I noticed she was pregnant.

I thought no. I'd let her have her child and maybe she won't yell at him and tell him he's worthless. Then he wouldn't have to be me.

FIVE

Leaving, the Not So Uncowardly Way

Eddie was clean-shaven when I returned home.

"Why?" I asked. "I loved the beard!"

His hands went up to his face, rubbing against his smooth, shiny cheeks. "I wanted the baby's first impression of me to include my whole face."

"Yeah, that's sweet and all," I brought my hands up alongside his to pat his baby-smooth cheeks. "But let's face the facts, shall we? Owen's first impression is going to be of my milk supply, not your face."

He nodded, showing a little surprise at the way I phrased it. "Still, he'll eventually get around to looking at my face and I want him to see it in the raw."

I leaned against the side of the couch for a moment, putting my hands down on the high back of it and trying to take some of the weight off my feet. It was unmercifully hot back in Fresno. San Diego didn't have one-hundred-plus degree Septembers. Somewhere in the back of my mind I cataloged that as yet another reason to consider working for Thatcher. It meant we could move away from the heat.

Eddie wrapped his arms around me and nuzzled against the back of my head. I wanted to turn fully into him and return the sentiment but my belly prevented it. Instead, I made a half-turn so my side pressed up against him and kissed that hairless cheek. It was a shame a man's beard wasn't like a favorite pair of shoes. Put them on, take them off, just like that. Of course, I'd prefer the beard always on, even if Eddie had been squawking of late about the love-hate relationship he had with it. About a month earlier, he actually had the nerve to compare its constant pruning and shaping akin to a woman's makeup ritual.

Oh, Eddie. Sometimes he knew nothing.

Although, he did shape and sport a beard the likes of which I've yet to see on other men. I let out a desperate sigh, wanting Eddie to put that beard back on, forthwith.

"Eddie," I said, sliding my hand to the lower part of his back and giving him a tight embrace, "your beard *is* a part of your whole face. You've been wearing it for almost two years now, and I got to say I'm a huge fan."

He put his hand up to his face, in the spot my hand had just left, and looked pretty pleased with himself and his beardlessness, despite my vocalizing otherwise.

"And did I mention that the beard makes you about ten times more virile as far as I'm concerned?" My fingers found the top of his waistband against the small of his back. I slid them in and then moved them around and forward until I got to his front button enclosure, about five inches beneath his naval. "And by virile, I mean sexy. Hot. Sexy-hot," I finished, tugging at the top of his jeans.

Eddie looked down at me, one side of his mouth turned up in a playful smile. "You make a very valid point, wife." He put a small kiss on the bridge of my nose and then added, "Don't worry. It's just a first impression for Owen. After that, I know who I really need to impress."

"That's right," I said, perhaps a little louder than I should.

There was something in my back that was pinching from our awkward holding position, so I gently pushed myself out of it and straightened up. "I want to go change into some comfy pants," I told him. "I barely slept last night and the train home was horrible. Some woman with a level ten voice carried on one mindless cell phone conversation after another, seemingly to everyone in her contact list. When I shot her a look of disdain, she stared back at me with an expression that said, *What? This is my inside voice!*"

"You didn't throw something at her head?" Eddie asked, smirking again.

I looked at him seriously. "I thought you said I'm not allowed to do that anymore. Besides, you know those trains. Everything is bolted down."

"Why not take her very own cell phone and then use that?"

I feigned some tears of joy and then leaned into him, big belly and all, and gave him another kiss. "Oh, baby, that's why I love you so much. You give me the greatest ideas to work out my frustrations on others. Throwing her own cell phone at her. That's genius!"

He smiled and chuckled once, then a look of intensity ran across his face like a storm cloud blocking the sun. "Wait, we're kidding, right?" he asked, holding my chin so he could look right at me.

"Well, maybe you were . . ."

"Evy," he said, his small grip on my chin tightening slightly.

"Of course I'm kidding."

"Okay, good." He released my chin. "I just have to make sure. You remember our pact."

"Daily."

"Then great. I'm good."

After I changed, I went to the couch and sprawled out. I could eat dinner here, sleep here, I no longer cared. Eddie would eventually help move me into the bedroom for the rest of the night, but for now, I'd stay here.

My eyes closed and it felt good, like a sudden release of all my synapses. I was home and could relax. But then I felt Eddie come up, hovering. At first I thought he was going to curl up next to me, but then he clapped his hands together and said, "All right, let's go."

I only opened one eye to look up at him. *Go?* Go where? I had just gotten home. I stared at him with my squinted eye. "Let's go?" I asked, repeating him. "Is that your abbreviated version of let's go get you sprawled out on the bed so you can be more comfortable for your nap?"

"Um, no," he said, extending his hand out to me, an offer to help pull me up and off the comfy couch. "It means we need to leave or we'll be late."

My eyes closed again and I rolled over, giving him my back. I felt his hand on my shoulder, giving me a few gentle nudges.

"Come on," he urged.

"This joke became unfunny before you even started it," I said.

"Sorry. This isn't a joke. We have a Lamaze class. It starts in twenty minutes."

I reached for a throw pillow and put it over my head, shutting my eyes tighter. I was willing myself to pass out. In some fantasy part of my brain, I kept thinking that if I didn't write the date of the Lamaze class down, talk about it, or even encourage Eddie about the idea, it'd just go away.

He'd insisted we do it this time around because we hadn't when I was pregnant with Corinne. I was always "too busy." Then I ended up having Corinne by Cesarean anyway, so it didn't matter. Eddie said he hoped that wouldn't be the case this time, so we needed to get our practice in.

"No," I whined.

"Yes," he said, pulling the pillow off my face. "You promised."

I turned over to look at him. "Doubtful," I said, snide. "I'm not dumb enough to promise things I don't intend to pony up."

"Well, you never said no."

"And I never said yes, either."

"Your silence meant yes," he said.

"All right, now you're just lying. Me, silent?"

He let out a quick sigh and then folded his arms across his chest, staring down at me.

Uh-oh.

"I want to do this," he said. The tone of his voice had changed. Eddie was a pretty amicable guy. Yet, every now and then when it really mattered, he put on his steel-toed-boot personality and that was that. The Lamaze business was no longer a suggestion or wish. I would have to comply. I knew, however, I still had wiggle room to let him know I wasn't happy about it first.

"I know you want to do it," I started, "but you're not the one who the classes are for. So, don't you think *I'm* the one who should want to do it?"

"Why wouldn't you want to do it? These classes are to help women ease into childbirth."

I scoffed.

"How is that funny?" he asked.

"Because it won't make childbirth any easier. I'm pretty sure the process will come at me the same way it comes for most women: with screaming and thrashing until I pass out or curse my existence. Those classes aren't going to make the actual pain go away so it's a waste of everyone's time. I mean, they ask women to sit down, all spread-eagle on a mat in some smelly rec center, and pretend to be in labor while practicing breathing techniques."

"Uh-huh," he said. "And how is that a waste?"

"The whole pretending to be in labor business. Can't replicate it, so why practice it?"

"So you already know what to do."

"Yes, I told you about my so-called 'birthing plan' last time you asked me about this."

"Remind me."

"I'm going to freak out and writhe with pain until I pop. And then boom, we have a baby."

"That doesn't sound like a plan."

"I don't judge the plans you make for your business area, so I don't think you should be making party plans for mine."

"This is ridiculous," he said, pulling me off the couch. I let him. I was getting ready to wrap up my tirade anyway.

I told Eddie about Thatcher's job offer.

I think I already knew he would say yes. It was only a month ago when Eddie hinted around about a change, saying we'd never have a better go of our lives—since Corinne was no longer with us—if *better* didn't also include *different*.

We could only take so many long-way-arounds to the store, or church, or even the mall, trying to avoid spots that reminded us of her before we realized that the destination itself held those memories too. I thought Eddie would be above that sort of avoidance, but for my sake, I was sure glad he wasn't.

When I told him about the possibility of moving to San Diego, I could actually see his shoulders rise again, lifting above the burden. They lowered slightly again when I told him what I'd be doing if I went to work with Thatcher. They didn't go as far back down as they had been, so I still had a bit of winning in the equation.

We had just sold our other house, the one we had raised Corinne in. Between the profit on that and the money I had accumulated from my case winnings and jury consulting over the years, we had enough to make the move and live comfortably. We figured we'd invest in a small business in San Diego sooner or later, but at the time Eddie seemed perfectly content to postpone his career as a telephone pole climber in order to tend to Owen while I gallivanted around with Thatcher for a few short hours at a time as the situation warranted.

Eddie opined that my work would be for the greater good and that's the main reason we should do it. That might have been true. It didn't negate the fact, however, that I was certain he desperately wanted out of town and would jump at any opportunity not to look like cowards while doing so. I knew this because I was looking for a reason too. Except I didn't care if people thought we were cowards to leave the place that reminded us of our dead child at every turn.

It hurt. I hated hurt. Plain and simple.

V

This one will be the toughest.

She'll put up a fight I'm sure of it. But that's not the problem. It will hit close to home. Close to Mom's world and she might suspect something but it will also be the worst sort of humiliation.

This one even went to church and I followed her there. I wondered if people knew what I'd done. Of what I will do. But no one knows anything there. That's what I was told, by that reassuring, respectful nudge inside of me. Lives in there like someone who has my back and gives me the confidence to fulfill my destiny.

I hated how the last one died before I fully took her. I punched too hard. I won't pull back as far. I won't hit as hard. Wouldn't want to jam that bone in the brain. I think that's what happened. I'm no doctor but I've seen it on shows.

This new one actually knows my mother. It's going to be a lot of fun. I don't think Mom has even told people she has a son. Just like Layla never told anyone she had a boyfriend. What am I to them? Nothing.

What will Mom's friend be to me? Everything. I have a good feeling about this one.

SIX

Dancing in the Fire

Three days until my due date and the last of the boxes were finally unpacked in our new home. "Home" is a bit of a stretch though, considering its shoebox size. I figured the term "bungalow" would be more appropriate. That's what happens when you decide to move to La Jolla Shores, a few blocks up from the beach. It's either the sixteen-million-dollar home on the sand, or the shoebox for a cool million.

Eddie said we were cozy and comfortable in our little place, although we both agreed that nothing about spending a million dollars on a tiny home is cozy or comfortable. We'd sold our Fresno home for more and, well, Fresno is no beach so we tried to see the silver shine of it all, even if we couldn't fully open the master bedroom door because it hit the foot of the bed.

"Just think of it as going back to our roots," Eddie told me. "All this living large in huge houses is a new thing, and look how family values are breaking down. It's because everyone has their own wing or room to disappear into, rather than enjoying each other's close company."

I patted him on the chest. "Yeah, you keep telling yourself that, pioneer boy, when you notice that our closet is so small, there is no room for your clothes." We had to make several adjustments because of the size. Even days after the move, I kept opening the hall closet door, hoping to find the other thousand square feet of the house.

All the same, it was a place to start over with the upcoming baby and, frankly, the ocean was good for my soul. For the first time in a long while, I didn't feel like a thousand unblinking eyes were looking at me and feeling sorry for me. Oh, and the judgment.

In the back yard, Eddie found the holy grail of his recent unemployment status: a metal detector left by the previous owner. It was lying against the trash can, near the back gate.

"I can't believe they left this beauty behind," he said, his eyes aglow with delight.

"Given its close proximity to the trash can, and the fact it can't fit inside said trash can, I'd argue the previous owners were trying to throw that beast away, not bestow it upon you as some sort of housewarming gift. A fruit and cheese basket, yes. A metal detector with a splintered handle and a bent spine, not so much."

"No, no," he muttered, picking it up and inspecting it from top to bottom and clearly not seeing the ugly pores and zits of the thing. "I bet you they didn't even realize they left it. It was practically hidden."

"In that case, let's ship it back to them, forthwith. They are probably crying because they can't find it." I reached my hand out to touch it, but thought better of it. "I know *someone* will be shedding tears if this thing stays here."

"Bup, bup, bup," he said, quieting me. "I'm keeping it. For a million-dollar purchase price, I'm going to go out on a limb and say this bad boy was included in the amount. Besides, I've always wanted one of these things."

"What for?"

"Well, the obvious sort of screams out, don't you think?"

"Hmm. No. I've learned over the years that your 'obvious' uses are different than mine."

"What is your obvious use for this?" he asked.

"To throw it away," I said.

I heard a snicker coming from the other side of the fence. Leaning forward a bit and peeking through the slats of wood, I saw portions of what I assumed was our neighbor. I shifted left and then right to get a fuller image between various slats. It was a woman, bending over something on the ground. She had on a straw hat with a lilac ribbon, her shirtsleeves rolled up to the elbow, lime-green gardening gloves, and a canvas of liver spots between the two.

"Hi," I said.

Eddie spun toward me to see whom I had just addressed. I pointed to the lower portion of the fence to give him the general vicinity of our neighbor.

She groaned as she straightened, her voice sounding strained and meek.

"Hi there, you two," she said. "Are you the couple who just bought the place?"

Eddie hopped up on one of the supports of the fence, a beam that ran parallel to the ground, and lowered his hand down on the neighbor's side to introduce himself. "Hi," he said as I watched his shoulder rise and lower, shaking her hand. "Yes, we've just moved in. I'm Edward and over here is my wife, Evelyn."

"I'm Marguerite, but you can call me Mag," she said. "Honey, can you get up on the fence too?" Mag asked me.

"No, sorry, I'm nine months pregnant. I'd just bounce right off. But, I can walk the five feet to the driveway and say hi." I motioned for Eddie to get off the fence.

"Yes, that is rather practical, isn't it?" she said.

Mag wasn't as old as her spotted forearms suggested, but since her wardrobe pointed to a love of gardening, I guessed she'd been out in the sun for years. She told us she was excited to have new and permanent neighbors as the house had previously been rented out as a vacation destination, people only staying for a week or a weekend at a time. The metal detector was something the prior owners had stocked as a vacationing amenity.

"So, you heard us talking about the metal detector, huh?" I asked.

She laughed. "Yes, I did. I could tell by the way you two were discussing it that you'd be a fun couple. I like fun couples. Opposites attract, you know. My husband and I were like that, but I was more like you," she said, pointing at Eddie, "and my husband had a sharp tongue on him just like you," she said, now pointing at me.

Eddie thought that was sky-high hilarious. My nostrils flared.

"Oh, calm down, you gorgeous girl," she said to me, flicking her wrist while the fingertips on her large gloves jostled back and forth. "You must be a delight. That's why I was chuckling at you. I love people who say what they're thinking. No candy coating and wasting everyone's time. Just as long as they're not mean about it. You're not mean about it, are you?" she asked me.

My head whipped to Eddie, staring him down to make sure he didn't answer on my behalf. The two of them thought that was even funnier.

"Well, I guess the both of you have my number," I said. "If you'll excuse me, I'm just going to go chase kittens into dark alleys and all that other fun stuff."

Mag was still laughing but now holding her green-gloved hand over her mouth, trying to stop. "If my Frank was still alive, he'd join you. Oh, what a delight," she said, finally able to compose herself. "Dear Evelyn," she said. "I really don't mean to make fun of you. You just remind me so much of my late husband. If he were still here, I have no doubt you two would've stayed up hours into the night talking about how ridiculous the world is."

Hmm, that did sound like my kind of evening.

She extended her hand to us again, stretching to me first. "I'm so very happy to meet you."

I took her hand, squeezing it gently. "I'm sorry about your husband."

"Don't be," she said. "We had our life together and I was loved. I couldn't ask for more."

I looked at Eddie. He was smiling at me. I winked in return.

"He passed on about five years ago now. I didn't want him to go, of course, but he needed his respite. Even in retirement, he was pestered, plagued really, from the pain that followed him throughout his career."

"What did your husband do?" I asked.

"Oh, he was a detective for the police department."

My jaw clenched. I had just filled out the start of my personnel file at the station that morning. A cold chill ran through me. Not the sort that just races up or down your spine, but the kind that radiates through every artery, letting you know you've just been claimed by a fear that's going to stay for a good long while.

"What a coincidence!" Eddie said, turning to me and then back to Mag. "The reason we moved down here is so Evy could take a part-time consulting position at the downtown station."

"Is that so?" she asked, looking at me. "Now I really wish Frank was still alive. The things he'd tell you, Evelyn. But that would be dark matters, wouldn't it, Edward? You and I could talk about lighter stuff. We still can, can't we?"

She started a barrage of chitty-chat things at that point, every now and then giving me a stabbing glance of something unspoken but essential to my hearing anyway. And while her voice was saying pleasant things like how the neighborhood is quiet and the weather nice, her stabbing glances spoke of something else—a message meant only for me. I think I heard an inner tinkering, a whispering really, that went with it. It could've just been my imagination. It said, "Beware." And, "Beware," again, because you can't hear it enough times.

Beware when you dance near the fire that he has built. Those that dance have burnt and scorched skin, crackled and pinked and scarred over and over again. Their faces writhe in an open-mouthed scream, and they suffer though they have yet to suffer the worst. They are altogether damned.

Mag's voice came in and out of my awareness but she was still talking about fluff while I felt lost in a journey of fright. All because she inferred that her husband's death was a gift to escape a career similar to the one I was about to enter.

She talked about the price of eggs and milk and the fact that stores should call fresh bread "fresh bread," instead of "artisan bread" because why gussy up the truth when the truth is perfect as is.

It was then that I second-guessed my decision to take the job. Not the sort of second-guessing that spins and picks at a thought, where I wondered if there's something better for me down the pike. No, no, it wasn't silly like that. It was more like, "My God, my God, what have I done?"

The knot in my stomach tightened. But it was too late. I had already said yes to the job and it was the type of yes my soul was holding hands with, with greedy, interlocking fingers.

I put my hand on my belly, feeling worried. I felt pain. Maybe she had seen the fear on my face because she started talking about her dead husband again. I must've missed the transition because I was stupidly daydreaming about a hellish bonfire.

"But you know," Mag added, "I'm proud of him for putting himself out there. Scars will come, but it helps to have a God who heals. That was Frank's motto. He figured it was better if he was on the receiving end of inner turmoil rather than someone who protested God didn't exist. How do they heal after an injury? How would they get better if they only relied on themselves and what they think they know?"

"Aw!" I exclaimed, my eyes widening as I felt a savage pull in my lower abdomen. Mag and Eddie looked at me.

Mag said, "It's not that great of a revelation dear, but I appreciate your enthusiasm all the same."

I shook my head, grabbing onto Eddie's sleeve.

"What is it?" he asked.

"Owen's coming."

VI

NO! NO! NO!
What was I thinking?
NO!

SEVEN

Someone Is Always Wilting

Y ou did it, son. You redeemed Wednesdays," I told my new-born, Owen. His eyes were opening, closing, taking it all in as the delivery room lights dimmed. He was born at 12:10 a.m., a Wednesday, in early October. He had a full head of gorgeous dark hair. He seemed to have my darker eyes, too, but it was hard to tell. In my heart though, I knew. It was one of those graces: my son wouldn't be too much a reminder of Corinne's brief life.

My face scrunched up though, contemplating something else.

"Oh, goodness gracious," I cooed at Owen. He was trying to land the backside of his fist into his mouth. "Your sister was the most obedi-ent, obliging thing ever." I bounced him ever so slightly, to feel him, to take some sort of internal measure of his every ounce and inch. "So, that means"—I tapped his nose—"you're going to drive me toward madness."

The back of his fist wasn't working for him any longer. He let out a little squeak, his face turning red. Then a pained squeal. The red in his face ballooned all over while the creases in his forehead turned white. His body flexed, rigid. I turned him to my breast and he simmered down. He still let out a small wail every few seconds, just to stick it to me I think because I hadn't anticipated his need sooner. Or, maybe because the entire millisecond it took me to get him started was a millisecond too long. So, *waaa!* Take that, Momma.

I couldn't help but smile. It made sense, really. If Corinne embodied everything that was Eddie, then Owen, oh, dear me, Owen had no idea he was feasting off the breast of the person who gave him his personality.

Having Owen finally in my arms, I could almost taste the first drop of a tomorrow that wasn't perpetually steeped in the regret of yesterday. Not that there wouldn't be days I'd cry and moan at the sheer pain and agony of losing a child, but there was an honest to goodness joy now. Something tangible to look upon and hold. A gift to remind me that something blooms after a fire scorches the forest bare. That's what I thought I was looking at when I stared at Owen. He was the bloom after the engulfing heat, after the burn. Owen was settling down as he nursed, his tiny fist resting right where my heart was beating under my skin.

Something beautiful really does spring up from the ashes. Something always does.

"Wednesdays," I said to Owen, and to God, too, "aren't the only things you've redeemed."

About seven thirty in the morning, my cell rang from the rollaway table next to my hospital bed. It scared the ever-loving daylights out of me since I had only been asleep for three hours at that point. Neither the ringing nor the quick jerk I made affected Owen. He continued to sleep soundly, cradled in my left arm.

Finally, the phone quieted. A beep and off it went to voice mail.

I settled back down, turning into Owen's tiny body. I wanted to take the beanie cap off his head, to get another look-see at that gorgeous black hair, but felt a chill in the room and opted to leave it on. As my eyes closed again, inhaling the scent that is unmistakably the essence of a precious little thing, the door to my room opened. I looked over my shoulder and saw a duo of nurses coming in, each rolling a cart.

I grunted. I didn't care how audible it was either.

"Time for the poking and the prodding," I whispered to Owen. "And I'm sure someone will inevitably stick something up either one or both of our butts."

"That would be me," one of the nurses said, offering me an apologetic look. I felt a twinge of guilt because I was relieved the nurse who fessed up to the rectal prod was the one pushing the plastic bassinet cart.

"Sorry, baby," I said, kissing him on the forehead. "Welcome to a world full of cold injustices and rubber-gloved hands."

The pediatric nurse held her hands out to take him from me, but first I whispered to him, "That doesn't mean you can't scream your head off when it's happening."

My checkup was probably as bad as Owen's. I was also sick of having to throw my modesty out the window during the constant onslaught of hospital personnel. At one point during labor, I was expecting the janitor to come in and shout, "Now, that's what I call ten centimeters!"

My cell rang again. I huffed. Might as well answer it. It was Thatcher.

"Hey, sorry to bug you. I called earlier and left a message. You got a minute?" he asked.

Where to begin? "Let me start with I've just had the baby and end with explaining to you that there's a nurse here using gauze and some sort of sterilizing liquid down by my lady business."

The nurse's head popped up. "It's a maxi pad, actually."

"Did you hear that, Thatcher? It's a maxi pad, actually!" I gave the nurse a thumbs up.

"You're a sick, sick woman, Evelyn," he said. "I think you may have ruined any idea I had about creating offspring, but still, I want to wish you and Eddie a heartfelt congratulations on your new son."

"Thank you, and you know, even if you were to call me on any normal day at seven thirty a.m., I'd probably figure out a way to be rude about it."

"I don't doubt that, but I really needed to talk to you," he said.

"What's wrong?"

"I'm sorry. Forget it. I didn't realize you just had the baby. I'll call you back in a few days."

"Try a week," I said.

"I'm not sure I can wait that long."

"Oh, for the love of—" I bit down on my lower lip to prevent myself from saying anything further. I took in a steep breath through my nostrils, then released. "Just tell me what it is, Thatcher, and be done with it. You've already violated my sanctity of childbirth, so let's get it over with."

He sighed. That meant he was gearing up for it. The big IT. With him, it never mattered what it really was, only that IT mattered to him and he was going to talk about it and twist my arm until I felt as impassioned about it as he was. It was laughable most of the time, but not on this morning.

"I think he's going to strike again. Soon."

"Is this your gut talking?" I asked. "Because really, it might only be that your gut is hankering for a jelly donut."

"No," he said, the higher tone of his voice signaling his offense. "Statistical probability."

Notwithstanding the fact that the last time Thatcher had uttered such a highfalutin phrase, he was making fun of the person actually using it, his words hit me. I had only been playing earlier about him interrupting the sanctity of my childbirth, but now it had actually been pierced by the filthy, plunging horn of some beast. Statistical probability was right. It would be soon.

But not today. Thankfully, not on Owen's birthday. I just wanted this one day to feel that all was well with the world. Rejoice! I was a mother again. A mother again!

One day where the world let me be. One day before it slapped me in the face yet bent in gently to whisper, "Enjoy it while you can, precious, because don't you know that someone is always wilting?"

Six days later, my phone rang. Thatcher. My eyes played a trick on me, though—that or the lack of sleep from having a newborn—and I could have sworn that it was Thatcher's number all right, but not his name. No. Instead, it said: Statistical Probability. Or at least that's how it looked to me.

"He struck again last night," Thatcher said. "Our guy. Got another woman."

I could hear, feel even, my heartbeat bouncing in the back of my throat. This wasn't something a mother wanted to hear after she had just birthed her child. I thought of the selfish thing to do: tell Thatcher to field this one without me until Owen was twenty-two and I could finally suffer being away from him for a few hours to dance with the filth of the world. Why oh why had I agreed to do this?

Yet, I felt compelled to listen. *Filling the gap,* I could've sworn echoed within my ears. *Be there for Me,* it added.

Thatcher continued, "This time, Evy, she survived."

Boom, boom, boom! went my pulse.

All I could think was how this woman—though mercifully alive—had endured the worst night of her life. I wondered if she even knew that she wasn't supposed to live, that it's not the way the monster's playbook was scripted. My heart ached.

I had just taken those last six days, basking in the grace of God through the gift of Owen, feeling that his arrival into my life was the first piece of flowery brilliance that shoots up after the pain. Yet, somewhere nearby, a woman was in the middle of the flames. And she wasn't done burning. She still had to do that flesh-on-fire deal where one truly realizes that hell is alive and well here on earth. I had been there. I wasn't able to walk out of it the same.

The door to the bedroom opened and Eddie hovered just inside, looking at me. I looked down at Owen, sleeping in my arms, and by the time I got back up to Eddie's eyes again, my own had filled with tears. He came quickly to me with his arms out, to take Owen. But I held on tighter, unwilling to give him up in this moment of unplaced panic. When Thatcher's voice started again, I realized it was wrong, sacrilege even, to be holding Owen whenever Thatcher got around to more details. I nodded at Eddie and he scooped Owen away, and I felt the loss.

Thatcher said, "I get that you've just had the baby, but I'm not too wise on that . . . stuff. So, I have to ask anyway. Can you come along and interview the victim with me?"

"Where is she?"

"She's at the hospital. Scripps. Are you in any shape to do it?"

I sighed, falling back on my bed and letting my head burrow into my pillow. "Thatcher," I started but then stopped. An entire conversation came at me within the folds of my mind, compacted with a slew of excuses, but there it was again, that nudging: *You are needed.*

Yet, I didn't feel worthy. I didn't feel qualified. I didn't feel safe.

But that's never really been the point, I suppose.

"I'm not sure I'm ready for this," I told Thatcher. He was walking a few feet in front of me, nearing the elevator on the first floor of the hospital. The newest victim was two floors up. I was only shuffling along at best, the sound of my flip-flops dragging over the hospital flooring. I had tried on a few pairs of shoes but none of them fit my still swollen feet. Thatcher looked at me now and then as I dawdled behind, giving me weird looks. At one point, his brows furrowed, pinching up with a bit of white from the blood flow ceasing smack in the middle, and I wondered if he was going to ask me if I was walking that way as a leftover from childbirth. That wasn't it, of course, but I reasoned with myself that if he did muster the nerve to ask such a thing, I simply had to scar him and tell him that yes, I was walking that way because I broke something in my southern hemisphere.

By the time we were in the elevator, the doors closing in on us, anxiety rose up within me and I couldn't place its origin. Was it because I wasn't ready to face the music, this waltz that spun me into a place of crime and wayward morals? When the door opened on that third floor, I knew there was no turning back. I'd have to work this case. I knew of no other way, and I was certain that both Thatcher and Eddie would force me to remember that.

When we got to the victim's room, Thatcher flashed his badge and the nurse quickly scooted out the door. The woman in the bed had her back to us and a blanket pulled up past her shoulders. From her posture alone, I could tell she wanted to disappear. My guess was that she wouldn't care if she disappeared via the blanket, the bed, or even the darkness of the room that swallowed her, so long as she simply sank away.

The pounding of my pulse got the better of me. Something was up but I couldn't put my finger on it.

"Ms. Ness?" Thatcher asked, directed at the woman lying on the bed.

"What did you call her?" I asked him.

The woman turned her head to acknowledge us.

The room let out small bursts of a crackling sound paired with the illusion of flashing lights. I grabbed the doorframe to my right for support.

EIGHT

Alive, if Possible

Evy," she slurred through cracked, busted lips. "What . . . what are you doing here?"

I felt a searing pain in my side. I thought my innards were convulsing while the rest of me tried to stay calm, thinking about how to answer that.

Was the right response, "Because it's my job now?"

But no, this wasn't simply a job. This was a tragedy. This was my friend lying in a hospital bed, raped and beaten to a bloody pulp.

Oh, but God, thank you God, she was alive.

This monster's victim number four was Jennifer, but she was still alive.

"You two know each other?" Thatcher asked, looking worried.

Jen turned her back to us again, rolling slowly like someone who didn't want to let the bed creak loudly beneath them. Except I doubted it was the bed she was worried about. More like a creaking spine or rib cage or those pulverized cheekbones. I didn't know if she turned because she didn't want to field the question or because she wanted to go back to that sinking away business.

I nodded to Thatcher, answering his question in almost a whisper. "We were roommates back in law school. I visited her the day after I saw you at the police station, when I was in town picking that jury."

Thatcher whispered back to me. "Are you up for this then?"

I pushed him away. It was more like a nudge, but he got the point. I took several quick steps until I reached her bed and sat down on the side of it, my hand going up to her shoulder. She tensed and shuddered as if I had jolted her with electricity. My hand recoiled and I let it rest in my lap. My weight on her bed made the mattress bow a bit. A portion of her back lay against me, but she left it there. It made me realize it wasn't me she was resisting, at least not generally, just my hand. It made sense. Hands had been her enemy last night.

Thatcher approached and I motioned for him to keep his distance. "You're lucky to be alive," he said.

I rolled my eyes. The terrors and nightmares had to subside first and only then could she fathom such a thing as luck. Jen seemed to agree in this regard because she made a few quick sobs and then turned toward us, letting more of her body, her midsection now, rest against me.

"Sorry . . ." she started and then stopped. "I'm trying to process everything."

"Don't apologize," I said.

I was shaking my head at Thatcher when I saw Jen's hand move. She was attempting to wipe a tear away from a face that now looked like a palette of black, purple, and deep red. There was pus and blood and I didn't know how she could differentiate those elements from the tear that escaped her swollen eyelids.

Her finger only got as far as touching under her eye before she winced in pain. The wince caused yet another pathway of pain and she splayed her hands in further agony. That's when I noticed her hands.

I had never seen such a thing. I would've thought someone had driven over her fingers a time or two. Her knuckles radiated the same color scheme as her face, and that was in addition to the swelling that stretched down to her wrists.

She had fought the monster and had done so fiercely. A part of me wanted to soar. She was an underdog and had overcome. At the same time, I ached for what it had cost her.

"Oh, Jen." I was unable to add anything else. What else could I say? I balled my hands in my lap, resisting the urge to touch her. It then occurred to me that I still hadn't answered her question as to why I was in her hospital room. We also hadn't officially started the interview. I could almost feel Thatcher's angst cross the few feet between us to shake me, saying, "Let's go, let's go, let's go!"

I looked at him and gave him a simple nod. At some point, we had to proceed.

"Ms. Ness," Thatcher said. "My name is Detective Brian Thatcher and you already know Evelyn."

Jen squinted at me with the better of her two eyes, the less puffy one. I could tell from her gaze that she hadn't forgotten her question from earlier.

"I took a job with the San Diego Police Department," I answered. "Consultant, they call me."

She turned her head more into her pillow. "I forgot about that," she said. "You emailed me."

She lived nearby so I told her once we were all settled in, I wanted to have her over for dinner.

Dinner. It seemed trite now. Let's start with a healed face, body, and spirit. Then dinner.

My head sunk thinking of something. The last time I had seen Jen came barreling back, of when I wanted to pitch a bigger fit about her solo running and didn't. I wasn't certain, but I felt like a bit of me would die if Jen came around and told us her attack had happened during one of her runs.

Why hadn't I forced the subject? Why hadn't I simply betrayed Thatcher's confidence and told her every bloody detail? She wouldn't have told anyone, and it might've made a difference.

I wasn't sure that running alone was what prompted the attack, though. The other women were taken during various activities, from being passed out in an alley to checking the mail. Yet, that familiar turning of my gut, the one I felt when I noticed Jen's running band in her apartment, came back to me the moment Thatcher identified this victim as Ms. Ness.

I wanted to ask, to make sure, but what was the point? Whether it had been on a run or if it could have been avoided, that wasn't going to make a lick of difference now. She'd still be here. Beaten, tortured, and violated. Alive, but a small comfort that was at the moment.

"Are you on this case because of me?" Jen asked.

"No, I was on it before. This guy was the person I was tell—" I stopped. I was about to tell her this was likely done to her by the same sicko I'd mentioned at her apartment, the reason I asked her not to run alone, but again . . . what was the point?

"Officially," I said, "this is my first day. I'm finding out that this guy took his fourth victim at the same time that I'm finding out the fourth victim is you."

"Four?" she said, groaning.

"If you don't mind," Thatcher interrupted, speaking to Jen, "I want to ask you a few questions." He grabbed a chair that had been tucked away in the corner of the room. "If you could, please tell us where you were when you were taken."

Jen opened her mouth, but then closed it, looking at me and letting pain wash over her. The heart-hurt kind.

She *had* been running. I knew it was only a matter of seconds before she announced such to Thatcher.

"I should've listened," she said to me, her voice scratching and her eyes closing. She was trying to sink her head farther into the pillow but the bruising all around her face seemed to prevent her.

When I looked at Thatcher, he was confused.

"She was running," I said. "Near the condo, right?" I asked. I wasn't expecting her to say yes, but she would've said no if it weren't true.

"Can you tell me where, exactly?" Thatcher asked.

She said she had been running along a greenbelt tucked between two rows of single-family homes. It was just off the 5 Freeway in University Town Center, a few miles from her place. Her typical jog was from her front door to the 5, then turn around and come back.

I knew the greenbelt she was talking about. It's a community area, about a hundred yards wide and a mile long. There was a sidewalk winding through the middle for anyone who wanted to use it. On each side of the greenbelt, there were plants, shrubs, and trees to separate the common area from the private property of the homeowners.

Jen had been nearing the end of the greenbelt when she heard someone cry out for help. She looked but found no one in sight. The voice called out again and she realized it was coming from behind a cluster of tall shrubs. It had been a female voice, she specified, adding that she wouldn't have gone in if she thought a man was back there.

"Once I got into the middle of the bushes . . ." She paused to do another pain-filled swallow. "There was no woman there, but a fist came out of nowhere and hit me in the nose.

"The doctor told me it was broken. When he hit me, I remember buckling over, everything going blurry and almost black. Then he picked me up. That's when the real panic set in. He was taking me somewhere. I tried to scream but he had his hand over my mouth and kept pushing up on my nose and it hurt more when he did that. I saw all those stars they say you see when you get hit. It made me want to die. I just wanted to lie there limp as long as he'd stop pressing on my nose.

"But I knew I couldn't let him take me away so I kept trying to scream. I must've blacked out at one point. Next thing I know, I'm in this dark box."

"What kind of dark box?" Thatcher asked. "How big was it? Like a storage locker? Could you move around in it?"

"No, but yes," she said. "I only knew it was big enough to move around a little bit, and that I really couldn't see much of anything else."

She had more to say. Much more. But she turned on her back and let her head follow through with the turn, looking out the window in her room. Thatcher opened his mouth to say something, but I held my hand up to stop him. She needed a minute and Thatcher needed to learn patience. Typically, I was just as impatient. But not when it was my friend who needed the minute.

"It was the size of your typical walk-in closet, if I had to give it a size," Jen finally said. "I could move around in it a little, but I remember crashing into the walls a lot when he started shoving me around. When I first came to, I couldn't really make out anything except for a light to my left, on the ground. It was shining in my eyes so it felt like a spotlight. I think it was only a small light, like a reading light, blinding me when I was lying where he'd put me. When I stood, I couldn't see anything else because the light was only a spot on the floor. Everything else was black or gray. No windows, nothing on the walls," she said.

"Did he say anything to you?" Thatcher asked.

"Lots of things. Horrible things."

"What was the first thing he said to you?" Thatcher asked.

She let three mousy sobs escape. "He said, 'Would you introduce me to your friends?'"

NINE

Playtime

He pulled me by my ankles, out of the small light, and strad-dled my chest. His knees were pinning my arms down."

"How big was he, would you say?" Thatcher said. "Over two hundred pounds, under two hundred? Over six feet? Under? Could you see his face?"

I turned my head slowly to Thatcher. What sort of half-baked questioning tactic was he using? Interrupting her and then barraging her with questions? I looked back at Jen and found her staring off at the wall. I rose and went to Thatcher, leaning into his ear so Jen couldn't hear us.

"How about you save your questions 'til the end? That way she can get it all out first before you bog her down."

He leaned back in his seat, giving me a stern look that said, because this is how I do things, that's why.

"I don't want to forget to ask anything" is what he actually said, under his breath.

"Then flip the page on that notepad of yours and write your questions down so you don't forget them. When she's done talking, you can go over your questions like the good little detective that you are."

I don't know what I was thinking. Who was I to tell him how this was done? In a snap, I recognized my method: I was being protective because this was my friend and I really should've insisted on giving that lecture about running alone. I let her down and was determined not to do it again, even if it meant clashing against Thatcher.

He raised his finger at me, about to tell me off or put me in my place, but thought better of it and put his hand back down. "Fine," he whispered.

"Jen," I said, finding the same spot on her bed and gently molding myself back into it, "go on, if you can."

She nodded, just barely.

"He was a big guy, built," she said, her eyes drifting over to Thatcher. He didn't see it because he was already writing things down. "He had a face like a refrigerator. Big, rectangle thing."

I heard something that could have only been the sound of Thatcher's mouth opening. When I turned, sure enough it was, but then he closed it.

"White guy. He never put his face near the light so all I saw was a darkened shadow of his face, but I could see a portion of his lower legs at one time during the fighting. He was wearing shorts and brown boots, the kind that lace halfway up the calf. His legs were smooth, like they were shaved. He had on a long-sleeved shirt and wore gloves. I didn't really see much else. My eyes were constantly watering. Every time I tried to look to the right or left, I saw stars all over again. And except for when he was actually—" She stopped and gasped for air. Thatcher and I remained quiet, and the only sound in the room was Jen struggling for composure.

"When he was . . . raping me, was the only time his head got near the path of light. Even then, he tucked his head below my chin and I could only see the top of it. He was bald."

I made a conscientious effort not to show my disappointment. I wanted more detail so we'd have something solid on the guy. I was certain Thatcher did too. Heck, I'm sure Jen probably wished she had more to give.

Even with the comingling of blood and pus and all the black and purple, it was still possible to see the tears on her face.

"I knew I couldn't win. I knew there was no escape," she said.

I heard Thatcher's pen scratching furiously. At least he was keeping quiet.

"But then I remembered something," she said. "You remember, Evy, don't you? It was that self-defense class we took all those years ago. Remember? In law school?"

"I remember." There was a date-rape scare on campus back then and the dean had brought in a self-defense instructor for all the female students.

"Two things came back to me," she said. "One, don't willingly go to the second destination, away from the location where you encountered your attacker, because the second destination is where they kill you." She scoffed. "It was too late for that though," she said, the sarcasm biting deep.

"But you didn't go willingly, you know that. He knocked you out."

"What's the difference now?" she asked.

"Remind me of the second thing," I said to her, hoping to yank her back into where she was going.

"The second is fight like it's all you have left because it really might be all you have left."

"If you ultimately go," I added, "you don't go down as a consenting victim."

Her head made a little nod.

"And there's a better chance you'll get the perp's DNA on you," Thatcher added, pointing the tip of his pen at her knuckles. After he said it, he dropped his head and went back to scribbling on his pad.

Jen's eyes closed. "Yeah," she said through a breaking voice. "They've already swabbed them and took whatever was under my fingernails."

"Did you get him good, Jen?" I asked.

Her lips quivered. "He blocked a few and called me a weak and disgusting legal eagle. He kept pushing me back into the walls. Slamming me actually. Then I landed one on his cheek."

She broke into a sob, and turned her face away from me. A moment later, she said, "I didn't hit him hard enough. I know I didn't. It's just . . . it's just not in me. I don't hit people. But it stunned him for a bit. Either that or he was still mocking me. All I could feel was this sense of rage in front of me. I wanted to make him pay so I hit and I hit and I hit some more. I could tell he was shielding his face after the first hit because after that I was landing blows on what felt like his forearms. I hit until I felt like I was going to black out again and it was silent.

"For the tiniest moment—" She interrupted herself with a chuckle. I could tell it hurt her in more ways than one. "When it got all quiet and I couldn't even hear him breathe, I actually thought I won, Evy. I thought I had done it. But then it was like this suppressed wind was let loose and it was coming from him. He punched me in the stomach and when I was bent over, trying to suck breath in, he backhanded me across the jaw."

I could tell she was getting toward the end. Her whole body was engulfed in a slight but steady shake.

She looked back at me. "Don't think less of me," she said.

"Why would I?"

"Because I stopped fighting him at that point. I just lay there for him, pretending I was gone because I figured that was what was going to happen anyway. They may say to fight like it's all you have left, but sometimes dying with a little less pain is also what you have left to give yourself."

My eyes welled up. I tried blinking the tears away. I even looked to the ceiling hoping my tears would just drain back to wherever they were escaping from.

"I didn't want it to happen, but it seemed inevitable. But then, when he was"—she choked back a sob—"inside of me, I realized that it was the perfect time to let him settle down, and then maybe I could get more blows to his face if he thought I was done fighting."

"That was smart, Jen."

"It didn't really matter though. He still raped me."

"But it does matter because you're alive. Especially if they get his DNA off you."

My comment made Thatcher twitch with a follow-up question. He blurted out, "Go to the part where you got away."

"I guess it was just a bunch of punks," she said.

Punks? Do tell.

"I had gotten a few hits in while he was raping me and he punched back. My breasts, my ribs, wherever he could hit me. Then the place we were in started shaking, like an earthquake, and I heard muffled laughter coming from outside. I even heard humming or singing, or maybe music. I don't know.

"He was cursing by now and had stopped hitting me. He shouted, 'Go away,' to whoever was outside. That's when I struck him good. I got his teeth." My eyes were drawn to her hands. I saw a gash on her first knuckle.

She took another moment, crying. "That's when he gave me another hit to the face. I felt like I was choking on a gush of liquid and figured it was my own blood. I kept trying to breath but I couldn't, everything kept closing in and the interior was still shaking. He got off me and I heard something unlatch, then a cold gush of air.

"I heard him yelling at someone and then the sound of running, like on gravel. I still felt like I could hardly breathe but I knew enough that my escape was wherever the air was coming from. I don't know where I found the strength, but I told my brain to make everything on my body work. I followed the fresh air and it led me to a door. I was elevated on something and I jumped down and started running. It was a parking lot, or it looked like one."

"A parking lot?" Thatcher said. "Were you in a vehicle?"

"I don't . . . I don't know. I guess it could've been. It sort of felt like one when it was shaking."

"Did you look at it once you were out?" Thatcher asked.

"No, I just ran into the wooded area."

I looked at Thatcher. Woods in San Diego? Maybe I had been sticking too close to the beaches all these years.

"Police found her in El Cajon, at a senior citizen's recreational center. Not an old-folks home, but a big building where they can gather during the day and play bingo. Stuff like that. Anyway, it abuts a wooded parcel. Also part of the center's property," Thatcher said, apparently seeing my confusion.

"I don't know how many steps I took," Jen continued, "but I do remember when I fell to the ground. It hurt. I landed on my face." Her fingertips went slightly to her busted nose. "I think I blacked out again. I don't know. The next thing I know, I hear crunching around me and I know it's him. I recognized his breath."

She huffed. "It sounds funny, I know. That I'd recognize him by the sound of his breath."

"Not at all," I said.

"I just knew it was him and that it was all over. I thought he was standing right above me. I closed my eyes and prayed for it to end quickly. But then the crunching seemed to back away. I waited, but nothing else happened. All night like that. It was cold. I was shivering and waiting to die. The night would do it or he'd come back and get me. I couldn't go any farther."

"But a security guard found you?" Thatcher asked. "He said he heard you calling out for help, just after dawn."

"I was so cold. I didn't care if it was him that came back. I just wanted to be warm again."

"You're lucky to have escaped, Ms. Ness. If this is the guy we think it is, his intent was to kill you. But I think you already knew that."

Thatcher clarified a few final details. When we went to leave, he said, "Oh, and one more thing. We're going to put some officers to guard your apartment building because my guess is our man is going to come back and try to finish you off."

"Thatcher!" I shrieked.

"What? It's true. We need to take precautions."

"Truth and delivery are distinct but cooperative parts of relaying a message, Thatcher."

"Can you two leave now? I'd like to try to sleep," Jen asked.

"Sure," I said. "Sorry."

She suddenly grunted, trying to prop herself up and looking at me. "Evy," she said, sounding surprised, "you had your baby."

"I did," I answered softly. I watched her process it.

"When?" she asked.

"About a week ago."

"Hmm," she muttered, laying back down and looking up at the ceiling for a moment before turning away.

TEN

When Punks and Elderly Collide

It had to be a van or something like that, right?" Thatcher asked me.

Jen's details hadn't yet evolved into a clearer understanding of what had happened. The biggest pebble in Thatcher's shoe was his inability to understand why Jen hadn't turned around to look at what was behind her as she fled for her life.

"She still should've looked back," he said. "Why wouldn't someone look back?"

"Isn't that the part in horror movies where the victim falls down because he or she tripped on a tree root or something? All because they looked back?" I asked.

"Yeah, I guess," he said, letting off a single chuckle.

"Asked and answered, then."

"She should've looked back. That's all I'm saying." He apparently was accepting his new status of being a broken record.

"Well, let's get a homicidal, raping, face-punching maniac to 'play' with you for a bit and then we'll see if you find it prudent to look back once you've finally broken free."

"You and I would both look back in the hopes to get something to nail the guy and you know it."

"No, I don't. And that's why I wanted you to drive me to the crime scene."

Three days had passed since Jen's rape. It had taken me that extra time to get a decent pair of pants on if I was being honest, but that's not the story I told Thatcher.

The parking lot of the El Cajon Senior Citizen's Recreation and Rehabilitation Center was where a security patrol had first heard Jen's pleas for help. He found her almost three hundred yards out. The crime-scene guys had already processed the area after the attack, and Thatcher had the digital images they took, saved on the tablet he was carrying with him.

We went to the rocks where Jen had fallen. Maybe she really had looked back at that point in time, which might have been the reason for her fall. She hadn't said it was the reason, but I don't think it would've mattered anyway. I remembered that night because it was the first night Owen decided to get colicky. I had been up plenty that night, taking it all in. It had been a dark one with a sliver of the moon hanging loosely in the sky. I don't know why but I remember finding it eerie at the time, hoping it wasn't a bad sign for Owen's colic. Little did I know back then that the omen wasn't for him, but for Jen.

The rock formation she fell into provided a perfect cocoon if you didn't mind stone as your walls and pillow. Still, I didn't know how Jen could simply fall into the middle of it. Trip upon one side and smash her face, yes, but then she would've had to crawl up and over about three feet to get in the middle. Her memory was bound to be a hit or miss on that night. It seemed logical that she'd remember more of how her attacker smelled and grunted than how she managed to hide herself in a rock crevice. He'd stick out more in her mind because he was the problem while the rocks were her solution.

The blood from where she scaled the rocks was only visible in the pictures; the rocks themselves seemed to have been scrubbed down by either the tech guys or their clean-up crew. The dirt in the middle had been stirred up to hide the bloody evidence too.

Thatcher was sliding through the pictures on his tablet. My glance went back and forth from the pictures to the real deal in front of us. It was clear that while the rocks could've shielded portions of her body, they couldn't have shielded all of it. Not enough for a killer to be duped, especially one that likes to take precautions against leaving evidence. I'd hazard to guess by his standards, a girl left alive summarily suggested an epic failing. He'd be motivated to find her. I replayed in my mind how Jen said she'd heard his footsteps come almost all the way up to her, heard his breathing, and then he walked away. This guy seemed bent on killing women. Why did he leave her?

"Maybe he did see her," Thatcher said, interrupting my thoughts. He was holding the tablet against his outer thigh now, his opposite hand propped on his side. "And he figured she was already dead, so he left her. That's what he would've done anyway if he followed suit. He'd dump her at a site and be done with it."

It was possible, I supposed.

"But Jennifer never mentioned that he touched her again."

"Why would he have to touch her again?"

"To see if she's still alive. I don't buy that he just assumes she's dead by sight alone."

"He strangled them all," Thatcher said. "Not including this last victim, of course. Your friend. Oh, and then there was the victim before this one. Coroner found finger bruising around her neck, but said she was already dead from the beating."

Choking. Splendid. I guess I hadn't bothered to commit that detail to memory. My hand went for my own neck. My brain was starting to feel like it was stuck in a rut of bad thoughts: Been there done that, been there done that. This job was stirring up all sorts of memories I didn't want to deal with.

I cleared my throat. "Still, he seems more hands-on to me. Simply eye-balling to see if a woman is dead isn't going to cut it."

"Okay, so he doesn't see her."

"Yeah, but . . . but I don't get it," I said. "I mean, I'm glad she's alive, but I don't get it. This is a straight line from the parking lot. She said she could hear his footsteps crunching along toward her, so wouldn't he be able to hear her? And then she said he stopped. Maybe to listen. He hears no footsteps so the obvious is to look around and then even more obvious is to look in this rock area. Even if the rocks hid her from first sight, why wouldn't he take a closer look? This guy has been leaving nothing behind on some heinous crimes. We have to assume he's more diligent than this."

"What are you thinking, then?"

I turned to him, looking intently at his face as something was occurring to me, something I think I had seen earlier when we arrived. "The lot," I said, walking back to it.

Thatcher followed behind and when we both stood at the edge of the paved surface, I motioned for him to give me his tablet. I flipped through endless pictures until I saw the one I wanted.

I tapped on it, making it zoom in. "There." The triumph rang in my voice.

"There what?" Thatcher asked, squinting his eyes at the image even though it was blown up and in focus. "It's just the empty parking lot the way the crime-scene department found it that morning."

"Yes," I said, shoving Thatcher's tablet back at him. "How it looked *that* morning. Open your eyes Thatcher and look at it today."

He did but his face didn't show recognition. He wasn't getting it. In the picture, there were no cars because it had been early in the day. Now, at about midmorning, there were about twenty or so cars huddled near the front door. The area I was pointing at was still vacant.

"Donut holes, Thatcher, come on!"

"No, I'm not hungry yet."

"No! There. Look." I pointed more exaggeratedly at the circular tire treads across the lot. One, two, three times around. "Remember the 'punks' Jen said she could hear, the ones she said he chased off? That's how the door opened. That's how she made her escape. He opened the door to her prison because of what she called 'punks.' In other words, teenagers. What if her attacker didn't chase the teens off the first time? What if they were still trying to cause trouble when he went looking for Jen? It would explain why he didn't complete the search if he knew those kids were still nosing around. Choose the lesser of two evils, right? Allow Jen to escape or get collared by a bunch of kids."

"You think those kids came back here and did the donut holes?" Thatcher asked.

"Could be. Actually, yes, I do. Consider it a territorial thing. I bet you the kids who did the donut holes are the same ones that provided the distraction for Jen to escape. If so, and if we find out who did the donut holes, we find people who could give us a vehicle description and tell us what the guy looks like."

Thatcher sighed. "That's nice and all, Evy, but that's putting a lot of hope on some teenagers we might not ever be able to track down."

I lifted my hand and rested it on the top of Thatcher's shoulder, giving it a little jostle. "You need to be more schooled about the propensities of others."

"What's that supposed to mean?"

"It means that if teenagers were here the night Jen was attacked, causing a scene in the lot, and then there are these fresh donut hole skid marks in the same parking lot three days later, it's safe to assume that not only is it the same teens, but they'll also be back. Teens are like coyotes. They run in packs and stick to their territory, hitting the same fun spot over and over. It's like *Westside Story* minus the cuffed denim and a sudden inclination to burst into song and dance before a fight."

"How do you suggest we get ahold of them, then?" Thatcher asked. "Wait here until they come back? *If* they come back?"

"Oh, they'll be back. They'll come under the cloak of darkness, but they'll come back. If they saw what we think they saw the night Jen was attacked, they won't be able to stay away. They'll want more action to talk about at school."

"I guess I could get an unmarked car to wait down the street at night and see if they show. If so, we'll bring them in for questioning."

"He'd only need to be here from ten at night until about two in the morning. I'm going to go out on a limb here and say they're high schoolers and that they need *some* sleep. They'll be in bed by two." I turned away from Thatcher and headed off to the Center.

"Where are you going now?" he called out to me.

I looked back. "To check out the inside of this place," I said, pointing. "There's got to be a reason this guy chose this place above all others to do his deed. Something other than the ability to roll a hand grenade around this joint at six thirty in the evening without hitting anyone."

If I had ever thought the movement of a post office or department of motor vehicles was something that made me want to pluck my eyes out and toss them in the sand, it's because I had never asked permission to take a police-sanctioned tour of an elderly center. We weren't just nosy pariahs, we were nosy pariahs with Thatcher's badge and gun and no intention of joining the twelve fifteen salsa-style ballroom competition.

That explained the bunch of cars out front on a Sunday. This was the world of prune juice and joint pain, but by goodness, if they could breathe they could enjoy a salsa competition.

Thatcher and I went through at least five different people—all with varying degrees of wrinkles and limbs to favor—who kept asking, "What do you want again?"

I guess we shouldn't have expected any more structure than we were met with. The whole place was more like a glorified clubhouse than an actual organization, and I surmised that by the time the seniors got themselves over here—whether it was in their own car or one of the small retirement village busses I had seen outside—it was party time. Not answer-stupid-questions-from-strangers time.

When I had finally given up doing things the official way, and we were asked by the sixth person the now-infamous question, "What do you want?" I pointed to Thatcher and said, "He's here to change the batteries in the smoke detectors. We're a part of a fire safety squad."

The gentleman in front of us nodded, but then looked at me, wearing a puzzled expression.

"What do you do then?" he asked me.

"I hold the ladder."

"Yes, of course," he said, his eyes lowering to my chest. "Because you're top-heavy."

Thatcher whipped around for a second. I could hear him stifling and choking on a riot of laughter that desperately wanted out. I, on the other hand, simply sneered without comment. Was the old man being practical or a pervert?

Truly, I didn't want to know.

The old man nodded again and said, "Help yourselves, kids. There's a ladder out in the storage yard on the west side of the building. Batteries are in the top drawer in the kitchen, down that far hall to your left. We appreciate the assistance, although I didn't know the city sent people to change batteries in smoke detectors these days."

"Oh yes," I said. Thatcher had turned back around and was drumming his fingers against the sides of his legs, a typical act of his when he was uncomfortable. Clearly, he didn't approve of the play-acting. "We wouldn't want you guys being trapped in a fiery building because the smoke detectors didn't go off."

He scoffed, waving us off. "That won't matter anyhow. Everyone is so old in here that even if the smoke detectors are going off, we'd all be burned to a crisp on account of how long it'd take us to get our rears in motion. And then, our luck would be that the person closest to the door would fall and break a hip and there'd be a pileup till tomorrow as we all start catching fire from the last of us to the front of us, that darned invalid at the front who first blocked the way."

My eyes narrowed at him. It somehow helped me see the little sparkle in his eye. An unmistakable glint of the fun he was trying to have with me. "That's pretty graphic," I said, smiling at him. "You've heard of that happening before?"

"Nah. I'm simply a fan of using my imagination, just like you." He winked at me.

"Do you know why we're really here?" I asked.

"Oh, sure. I heard you the first time you asked Bob over there. Don't know why he didn't say yes to you. Then again, he was in the Navy, that one. Never rose above the rank of petty officer, and I guess it's never occurred to him to make a decision on his own unless it's approved by someone else. I was thinking you two would eventually grow bored and start exploring the place on your own, but when you didn't, I decided to come over here and see you up close so I could get a better view of the perkiest bosoms this place has seen in quite some time."

"All right, sir," Thatcher said, turning my back to the man and guiding me along. "We're going to take you up on what I'll interpret as permission to take a look around."

When we were about fifteen feet away, I said to Thatcher, "I think I'm actually going to barf."

"Do it later."

"Okay."

Thatcher used his tablet to take pictures of the rooms. One, of course, was the dining-turned-dance hall. Then the foyer, the kitchen, an exercise room, a nurse's area without any nurse, and the big rec room, which was divided between a television viewing area and a large cluster of four-seater tables. Next to the tables were two cabinets full of games.

"Any ideas on why our guy would come here, specifically?" Thatcher asked.

Nothing jumped out at me, nothing about the building anyway.

"Other than the fact he might have picked it at random because it provides him privacy at night when the center is closed, the only other thing that would draw him here is—"

"One of the senior citizens," Thatcher said.

"Have someone stake out the lot at night and find those teens," I said. "It'd be better if we had a picture first before we asked these seniors if they just happen to know a particular murderer."

VII

I went back to the center on Sunday and saw cops. I figured they were cops. I wanted to see what was happening and if anyone asked, I'd say I was there to see him, my old man. Every time I feel this internal crushing, like I ought to know better about what I've done and I could've done more before I caved into this hate, I want to burst with the thought of coming back here and pulling him aside and saying, "Look at me, we're the same, father and son, only I'm fully realized."

He's got his own stories of what he did back in his days and he only wants to talk about his stuff if he even bothers to talk to me at all. I know how he sees me but I want it to be different. It'll never work with my mother, not now. He's the only thing I have left. But I'm only the help. That's what I am to him. Unless he's been drinking and thinking. Then I'm in his club where we talk about women and which ones can bear more of our sort of attention.

I might've said something to him, about what I've been up to, but I couldn't because those two were there. I never even got out of the car.

Only one of them looked like a real cop. He had the badge on his belt and his weapon harness stretched across his back. But he sissied it up by carrying one of those small computers in his hand.

The girl didn't have a gun or badge but she seemed tougher. She looked familiar. It might've been the legal eagle from the courthouse but that girl was pregnant and a lawyer and this girl wasn't pregnant and is with the cop.

Was it the same girl? She could have had her kid and it might be the same girl. I wanted to test it and go in. I'd walk right past her and see. But that's stupid and I can't afford any more mistakes after that one was lost from me.

ELEVEN

Crash into Darkness

Two weeks later, Thatcher beckoned me to the station with news they had found the teens from the parking lot. First, I had to meet his boss since he was the one cutting my checks, as measly as they were. The captain was a diminutive man with an even more diminutive hairline, a man who also sported a baby-pink complexion.

Unbeknownst to me, the captain had called a meeting not only of Thatcher's division, but for all the units doing those nasty crimes like murder, sex stuff, and, my least favorite, crimes against children. The captain had apparently called the meeting to introduce me to everyone.

Splendid.

I think the proverbial junk hit the fan when Captain Diminutive—the smallest big cheese ever—suggested that if I managed to add the level of contribution he hoped I could, then I would be lent out to different divisions as needed. Considering Thatcher seemed to be the only cop-like creature I could tolerate, and even that was hit or miss, I wasn't a fan of the idea of turning me into a walking, talking lending item. Not to mention the fact that I didn't really play well with others. It didn't seem like the time to clarify that with the captain, however.

Someone from the middle of the room mumbled out the phrase "medicine woman," followed by gruff chuckle.

"There's no medicine-man business going on here," the captain said, looking at me. He had heard it too. Of course he had. It was only wishful thinking to hope it was all in my head. I stood there feeling naked.

I was standing to the captain's side, a few feet back. "In fact," he added, "there's nothing laughable about this at all. The FBI themselves have behavioral analysts and that's the part we're asking Ms. Barrett to help on. Aside from the fact that as a civilian Ms. Barrett helped our own

Lieutenant Thatcher collar a couple of pedophiles up in Fresno, she has also worked as a jury consultant. From what I've heard, she's never lost on a jury she's picked. Is that right, Ms. Barrett?"

He looked at me again. "Yes," I said, "that's correct."

"That's what I thought." The captain looked out at the officers. "That means Ms. Barrett has both a talent for and a history of picking the right people for the task at hand. We're hoping that translates to picking the right perpetrators for our crimes down here. I've put her with Lieutenant Thatcher for now because of their history of working together but, like I've said, if the arrangement works out, all you'd have to do is put in a requisition for her to be assigned to any particularly pressing case of yours."

"Uh—" I started to raise my hand to try to take this circus train right off its tracks. It wasn't only that I didn't want to work with anyone other than Thatcher, it was that I didn't think I could *trust* anyone but Thatcher. This might've been a new stop for me, but I was abundantly aware that my freak-show label accompanied me in the same fashion that the Ringling Brothers elephants take their stroll down Main Street. They might do it quietly, but it's hard to miss that it's happening.

"Don't worry," the captain said to me, interrupting whatever words I was trying to push out next. "You don't have to say yes. I, myself, wouldn't allow you to work with some of these blowhards," he said, eyeing the room and chuckling to himself. His solitary laughter was like the best joke ever, but told in a morgue.

With that, I laughed.

Of course he thought I was laughing with him, and that likely meant he figured me the only one in the crowd warming up to his humor.

A female detective with giant teeth stared her boss down with an air of smugness. It permeated through the room. I looked at the mug she was holding, her spare hand dunking a tea bag into it. Over and over again, when I could tell that the liquid in her cup was already a dark copper. She continued to dunk that tea bag in slow motion because she was trying to sell something. An ambiance about herself, a free giveaway. Of the exact contents I couldn't be sure, only that it was in the realm of her pitching what I like to call an "I don't give a turtle turd" demeanor.

She finally let the tea bag string fall against the side of her cup, hanging limp but close. "So, Captain, can I clear the air then, and announce that I'm one of those blowhards that doesn't want her working with me?

Excuse me," she let out a planned chuckle, "I mean that I'm one of those blowhards *she* won't want to work with."

A few laughed.

"Yeah, that's real funny," the captain said, turning to another detective sitting close by. "And she wonders why I haven't given her a promotion yet."

There was a tiny snicker in response. It was beautiful because it was mine and she had heard it.

The captain looked at me and gave me another smile. It made me consider him again. He was too short, mousy even, to have been an effective skull-cracker, the likes of Thatcher and other detectives in the room. Men who had a physical prowess that beckoned command. Yet, he was the captain, the boss, and when he smiled at me that last time, I realized how polished and groomed he was, wearing a terribly expensive suit even for his captain's pay.

That's when it dawned on me that he must've had a thread of mean running through him. It seemed to be one of the few explanations behind his job advancement. The mean streak wasn't anything overt like kicking people in the shins, running away, and cackling like a troll. Rather, it was a covert type of viciousness, as if he'd weasel up to people he planned to use and discard. I could see how he was the type that spent a lot of time gathering up stones and laying them just right to have others trip and gut themselves, falling upon their own swords.

I made a mental note to be suspicious of anything he asked of me, including being reassigned to another detective. Unless Thatcher was misrepresenting something to me, it was Captain Diminutive's idea to bring me into this fold. If so, I needed to remain cognizant that I might be yet another stone in this man's field of planned follies.

When it was over, Thatcher led me to his desk.

"You said you found those teenagers," I said to him. "Tell me what they said so I can be on my way. Today was enough fun for a while. You'll be lucky if I step back in here within the fiscal quarter."

He sighed. It was a slow, painful one, his hand making its way through his hair.

"Oh, relax," I added. "I only mostly mean that."

"No," he said, "it's not that. It's about the teens. They aren't going to give us any information because they're dead. It's a tragedy, it is. Did you hear that news story about the three drunk teens who spun out into a streetlight, the whole car going up in flames before anyone could pull them out?"

I nodded. I had made Eddie turn off the television when I saw the story the week before.

"Well," Thatcher said, "we just put the connection together today. Those three teens are the same ones who unknowingly saved your friend's life. They were even bragging about it that night your friend got raped, typing it out on social media."

"What did they say?" I asked.

"Only that they interrupted a guy's 'screw session in the old-fart parking lot.' I don't think they ever knew what was *really* happening. Later, we found another witness who said he was with the three the night they made donut holes in the lot, but not during the time they interrupted the rape or, obviously, when they plowed into the streetlight. That kid said the others were talking about how a guy was chasing them down after they interrupted him, which is why we know it's the same kids."

"Did they give any more details? Like whether it was a van or truck or the guy's appearance?"

He shook his head. "From the sound of it, it wasn't an information session but rather a joking session."

I sighed. "I wish those kids could've lived. I mean, for obvious reasons but also because I wish they could tell us more. You sure that one witness doesn't know more?"

"He said one of the boys was taking pictures on his phone while the other two were rocking the truck."

"He said *truck*, specifically?"

Thatcher nodded.

"And? Where are the pictures?"

"Two words: Fiery crash."

Of course. What teen goes anywhere without his or her phone?

"Great," I muttered.

I called Jennifer's cell. Nothing. Her home, same thing. I doubted she'd be back at work, but I called anyway. When I got patched through to someone at her office, I ended up talking with a chatty secretary who said Jen would be off work for the next six weeks, on medical leave for back surgery.

Yeah, let them think that. Good for Jennifer. Still, it worried me I couldn't get ahold of her. The silence unnerved me, yet I understood. I remembered how it felt to have my space invaded when all I wanted to do was curl up and die. But because it had been almost a month since her attack and she hadn't returned one call or email, I couldn't shake the anxiety.

I had been meaning to pay a visit anyway.

When I entered her lobby, I avoided eye contact with the doorman. My game plan was to pretend he didn't exist. Otherwise, he'd do that whole calling up business, and I didn't want to hear Jen tell me no.

As I passed him, he called out to me, asking me what I was doing.

"Trying to bypass you," I replied.

He chuckled as if it were a joke. I wasn't trying to be funny.

"Who are you trying to visit?" he asked, still smiling.

"Jennifer Ness," I said as I turned and walked back to his counter.

When he heard Jen's name, his demeanor changed as if I had plucked one of his pretty-boy tail feathers out from his rump. Rather than calling up, he summarily told me Jennifer was on vacation, healing from back surgery, and that I'd have to come back when she returned.

"Lies." I leaned against his countertop. It was granite—beautiful, expensive, and cool to the touch.

"I'm sorry," he said. "What did you say?"

"Well, I didn't mumble it, did I?"

He was no longer finding the situation humorous. At least we were both on the same page now.

"Are you calling me a liar?"

"Hmm," I started, letting my eyes wander off to the fountain out front, bubbling from the top and splish-splashing near the valet stand. "Not really," I said. "I'm simply pointing out the fact that you've ushered a lie, in particular. Though that technically makes you a liar all the same, I'm willing to overlook that classification if you'd be so kind as to call up to Ms. Ness and let her know her friend Evy is here to see her."

He took a step back, centering himself with a wider stance, lifting his chin to me.

Oh, mercy, he wants to fight. I wasn't in a similar disposition. The day had been a total failure up to that point. My embarrassment at the station, the dead teenagers, what was next? Was it too much to ask this guy to just let me have my way, thank you very much?

"I could call up, ma'am, if she was home. But she's not. So I won't. It's like I said earlier: check back *in a few weeks.*"

When he was finished saying it, he regained that step toward his counter and lowered his head, pretending to work on something else. Maybe fake delivery logs, or a requisition to soundproof the front door of some recluse in the joint, or maybe even a notation for Jen that she should be happy he deterred some annoying sarcastic chick from the big E-N-T-E-R. "You have a good day now," he said.

There were a few ways to go with the situation, especially since I already knew my own goal ended with me visiting with my friend that afternoon, despite what peacock boy had in mind. However, I didn't want to be too severe with a full verbal attack because I was sure he was just a messenger doing Jen's bidding. I had no doubt she spilled a little of the beans on her attack to persuade this bouncer in a silk shirt and tie to send all interested parties away.

I heard an elevator arrive over to my right. Jennifer would let me in if she knew I was here. Surely, she was turning away the masses, not me. I dashed to the elevator, Mr. Doorman on my heels, yelling at me to stop.

Coming off the elevator was a young guy, college kid I figured. He had large headphones on, his head hanging low, and bopping to whatever music blasted into his ear canals. I raced behind him and did my best to make the shove I gave look as accidental as possible. He and the doorman collided but because the young one turned his face to catch a glimpse of me, presumably trying to figure out why I had been so cruel in shoving him, one of his jumbo headphones sailed into the doorman's face.

The temporary scuffle and disorientation gave me enough time to hit the button for Jennifer's floor and impatiently wait for the door to close. I watched the young man apologize to the doorman, point his blaming business in my direction, and the doorman giving me a stinky—an oh-so-stinky—glare.

When I got to Jen's front door, it was slightly ajar. For a moment, I paused in fear.

I lunged forward but as soon as my hand got to the door, I heard her voice from inside. "I'm sorry," she said. "She's like that sometimes. Most of the time. I'm so sorry. If you have to go to the doctor, I'll pay. And then I'll make her pay me back."

My hand pushed the door open slowly. I peeked inside but all I could make out was her silhouette. She was standing in the dark with a phone to her ear. She must've been talking to the doorman.

Oops.

Jen turned to look at me. I couldn't be sure with all the lights off in her condo—the only light pilfering through was coming from the hallway. "Here she is now, Dave. I'll speak with her. I'm sorry again. Thank you for everything. Good-bye."

I heard the beep of the phone shutting off. She set it down on an end table.

"You busted his lip, Evelyn," she said right after she groaned, letting her shoulders sink in exasperation.

"He's exaggerating. And it wasn't me, per se. It was that young kid's monster-sized headphones. I didn't think he'd smack the doorman in the face with them."

"Yet blood was drawn, all the same."

"No. The blood embellishment is *his* version of the facts."

"Come in and lock the door behind you," she said.

I did, and that was the end of whatever light there was. Amidst the darkness, the air was thick and stuffy. It was as if there hadn't been any ventilation for a while. If homes could take on their owners' moods, this one was pushing up daisies. Yup, I'd been in this pit too. Whatever Jen had brought back from her ordeal had been getting down and dirty in here; it had been breeding, and it had sucked away all the liveliness and goodness that had once lain within her walls. A sad, sad affair. Likely even the silk plants had torn up their roots and the weevils in the flour had taken their nasty selves and marched on to a better gig.

This was yet another reason I liked to put fault on the Devil for all the pain and hurt in the world. When he strikes, everyone wants to shrink from the light. If you ever find yourself standing in a hole, and the hole is dark—creepily and fearfully so—it wasn't God who put you there. When God gets invited to the party, He comes in with the only thing He has. He comes with light.

Jen needed some hope and light in this place, although I very much doubted she wanted to hear it. It was like telling a weary traveler he needs to take a cool dip when he finds himself standing in a scorching desert. He's too tired to do anything but look at what's ahead, and he only sees the cracked and dusty earth as far as his eyes will let him. Yet the pool is right there. Just turn around.

But when a man's gaze is set on his own path of destruction, good luck with the obvious. Jen must've not only had black-out curtains, but probably nailed them down to the window frames. The depth of darkness was likely caressing her and telling her what a pretty, pretty dolly she was, but for me, this crap had to go. I knew the entry way stood right off from the kitchen, so I reached to the inside wall and flipped the switch my fingers found. The kitchen lights went on as one of Jen's hands fluttered up to her face.

"What do you want, Evy?" she asked, shielding her eyes.

It wasn't the words, but rather the disgust in her voice that shocked me, offended me even.

Then again, I had been treated worse by people I liked significantly less so this I could endure. "Some tap water, if you have it," I said.

"I don't."

The light in the kitchen didn't quite reach into the living room. I narrowed my eyes, squinting to locate her again.

"Where are you?" I asked.

"Lying down on the couch," she mumbled.

"I'm going to sit down with you." I took my coat off and hung it on a chair nearby.

"Maybe you should ask me first," she replied as I came around to her, lifting her feet up at the ankles so I'd have a place to sit. I sat down and let her feet rest in my lap. My eyes started to adjust to the dimness.

"That's ridiculous. Why would I ask? You'd just tell me no."

She curled her legs up so that her feet were no longer on me. "Is that like it's better to ask for forgiveness than permission?"

"Not at all," I said, turning toward her. "I usually don't ask for forgiveness." I smiled. Then I let the smile drop. Things weren't the same. Perhaps they wouldn't be for a while. Maybe never.

"Why are you here?" she asked again.

"Clearly, you think it's to torment you, so let's go with that premise. How am I doing?"

She sat up quickly, turning her face to me. "You're doing great," she said, a flare rising in her tone. "First, you verbally attack my doorman, then apparently you used one of my neighbors as the weapon to attack—"

I grimaced and interrupted her. "*Attack* is such a strong word, and has such an air of malevolence to it. I wasn't acting in malice at all."

"What would you call it then?"

"Means to an end."

She sighed, tossing her head back in frustration.

"Okay, fine," I said, "it was a frenzy of sorts, and yes, I did initiate the frenzy. But I'm telling you, there was *no* blood."

She stayed quiet, having pulled one of her feet into her lap, fidgeting with a toe.

"Well?" I asked.

"Well what?" she snapped back.

"You started off with a 'First,' so what's the second?" I asked.

"Second what?"

"Point, I presume. A second point."

"Why are you here?" she asked, her voice soft, but hollow.

"Are you tired of asking that yet?" I asked.

Her head sank.

"Yes, see? You know why I'm here." I put my hands down on the couch cushion beside me and leaned in closer to her. "So then, what do you want to do? Would you rather cry on my shoulder, watch some TV, go out and get a coffee, or do something else?" I slapped my hands together, suddenly thinking of something else. "Oh! I know! I'm sure one of your neighbors who is still at work has an antsy dog. Let's go kick on some doors until we find one. And if we do find one of those poor little abandoned mutts, we can kick on the door some more. If we're lucky, we'll find a terrier or a Chihuahua that might even pass out from all the excessive barking, shaking, and tinkling on the floor."

I saw the corner of her mouth go up. I bent over a little to make sure it was what I thought it was.

"Ah-ha!" I said. "We have a winner. Let's go. Come on, let's go terrorize some pooches."

She let a small chuckle escape, but then fell back over on the couch. That small, terse chuckle had made a quick collision into tears.

I got down on my knees in front of her and then hugged her as she lay flat upon the couch. A minute went by. A few more passed, each tick of a nearby clock keeping some sadistic beat with her pained cries.

I figured I'd probably just have to let her cry it out until she fell asleep, but then she said, "I'm pregnant, Evy."

TWELVE

An Ivory Room Without a View

The funny thing about ivory towers is that you don't realize you're living in one until some hoity-toity landlord hands you an eviction notice. When Jen told me about her plan to end her pregnancy, it was my notice to vacate.

Jen and I had once shared a similar stance on abortion. This meant we had been bunking in the same tower. It also meant she, too, got the boot, although there's a large part of me that believes she left on her own accord.

I wondered if I should remind her about the last time we had this discussion—in that ivory tower, of course. The question on whether or not she'd ever have an abortion, even as a result of rape, didn't require mulling time. No, she wouldn't.

But now that Jennifer was telling me she was pregnant and wanting to end the pregnancy, she pretended the question didn't exist. And me? I was being quiet about it because I felt like that fine line between theory and practice had just sucker-punched me in the gut. What a little coward I could be.

I should've asked her what the value of having convictions were if we kicked them in the gutter when we needed them most, but a lecture wasn't appropriate at the time. We had real-world Evil sink its claws into us.

I had a child taken from me, murdered.

Jen had been beaten and raped; she was carrying her monster's child.

Either our belief systems were destined to be cut down, or they'd bear the scars of abuse but be sturdier for it. For Jen, I hoped it was the latter. Experience told me it was easier to look at oneself in the mirror if that were so.

When I did talk to Jennifer about my piddly opinion, it was brief. She replied by saying it was easier to view absolutes when it absolutely didn't affect me. I found that rather brilliant despite the fact she was missing the bigger picture.

"You don't understand. We make all these rules, God gives us all these precepts to follow, but then we're supposed to follow them even when the unthinkable occurs? Why do the rules have to stand when the worst of the world has so clearly won?" Jen said.

I moved my hand to hers. She didn't shy away but I felt a slight twitch in her fingers and then it was gone. It made me think she had at least considered dodging away.

"Jen, what frame of mind do you think your rapist was operating in? One where he considers rules, or one where he shucks them?"

"It's not the same."

"No, it never is once you get the taste for having it your own way."

"It isn't like that. How would you feel if it had happened to you?"

My eyes widened. Where to begin? "I kind of have a skewed vision these days on the 'to have' and 'have not' aspects of children, as I'm sure you can imagine. I don't really see the possibility of saying no to a life, even one conceived by a monster, when I'm constantly worried a monster is going to devour them anyway."

A rough sigh came out of me. Only after it had passed did I realize I'd been holding it down in my lungs for a while, bunched like a little ball of shame I didn't want to let go of.

"If I'm being completely open here, Jen, I guess I don't quite see the benefit in determining my life would be better off if I terminated a rapist's pregnancy, when my personal experience is that even the babies you want get snatched away from your arms in the blink of an eye.

"I'm sorry I'm not standing behind your decision, but you're asking the wrong person to say go ahead and do it. I'm coming at you as someone who thinks one of the few differences between your rape and the rape of my daughter is that you survived. And, yeah, you're carrying a monster's baby. But that baby is yours too. I don't know what the piece of filth looks like but if your child happens to be a girl, and she gets your blonde hair, I really don't see how it works out for the greater good if the earth has to say good-bye to yet another beautiful little blonde who will never reach adulthood.

"I say have your baby, or at least carry it full-term and then have it adopted. I know this won't make me popular with you, but please understand that I truly believe that life, that God Himself, allows some of the worst to happen to those of us who are able to make the best of it."

She wiped a tear away. I had been hiding my face, my own tears.

"Even if that's true," she said, "it's blatantly unfair."

I laughed a little. It was wholly sarcastic. "Yeah," I said. "That's yet another slogan we should put on matching shirts."

The night trudged past me with record and mind-numbing slowness. I couldn't get much sleep, my mind stewing over things such as my friend being impregnated by a demon, ivory towers, a monologue about the preservation of life from the likes of me—a woman who's killed a man—and the teeming, bubbling pits of unfairness.

Knowing how scarce my sleep already was on account of Owen's feeding schedule, my inability to drift off was that much more painful. Though my body reached for sleep with grabby and hungry anticipation, I couldn't do it.

The next morning, I was back at the station.

On my way in, I saw the same homeless man I had seen that first time. Burn was his name, a name I wasn't apt to forget. I had given him my meter change because the coin slot had been jammed with gum.

Burn was now standing in front of a different meter, giving it his full attention. I approached him slowly, his back to me. I came around to his side but he didn't look up. He was still busy with the meter, his nose only two inches from it. I walked closer, realizing he was up to no good. He was trying to put his own piece of gum into the coin slot. His gum didn't have any give, any pliability, so it was an unsuccessful operation. It must've been a piece he picked up on the street or under a bench, one that had been hardening for some time.

He was still unaware of my presence, focused on getting that gum into the slot. I watched him bring the little pebble of gum up to his mouth where a pasty, almost white tongue poked out a bit. He licked the gum, trying to soften it.

His gesture made the corners of my jaw tingle in a sickly manner. To think about where that gum had been and what it had been exposed to made me queasy.

"Do you want a fresh piece?" I asked him.

He tilted his head a little, looking at me with one eye while he squinted the other, trying to block out the sun rising in the sky behind me.

"Buzz off," he said.

"If you knew anything about me, you'd realize that's an invitation for me to stay for a long while, rather than simply walk away."

He stood straight and looked fully at me, using a hand over his eyes to block the sunlight.

He took several seconds to get a good look at me. "Hey, well, *do* I know you?"

"Not really," I said. "But we met a couple of months ago when I couldn't put my coins in the meter because someone had wedged gum in there."

"Don't look at me," he said, shaking his head. "I'm innocent."

"You don't look innocent. Looks like you're shoving the gum in there right now."

"That's 'cause I got the idea from some lady. She gave me her coins so I figured it might be a good gig. Go on and blame her."

"That was me."

"You shove gum in meters too? Geez, this is more of a racket than I first figured."

"No, no," I said. "I was the pregnant lady who gave you the coins."

He looked down at my midsection. I had already lost all my pregnancy weight. "You used to be pregnant?" he asked.

"Yes. As you can see, I've had the baby. Had him almost a month ago."

"Oh!" He took the hand he had been using to shade his eyes and gave his forehead a gentle hit. "I'll be! You're the baby eater!"

Of course someone was walking by at that exact moment. Her eyes skipped over us quickly but she didn't break stride. Dirty homeless guy equals a quick walk-by.

I considered Burn anew. I figured he was safe enough to speak my mind. "You know, that's an unfortunate name you keep calling me and I'd appreciate it if you stop using it. My name is Evelyn."

I had told him that the last time, but since he didn't recognize me I doubted he recollected the part where I clarified what my real name was.

"You're no . . . what did you say it was?"

"Evelyn."

"You're no Evelyn. That sounds like a fat old lady's name."

"Well, what kind of name is Burn?" I asked.

He blinked in rapid succession, three times. His face twitched in shock.

"You know my name?" he said.

"Yes, you told me your name last time we met."

"And did I tell you why they call me Burn?"

I shook my head.

"That's good then. Some days I tell more than others and then I regret it. Don't ask me. I don't want to say. Besides, I've been aboned—no, that's not the word . . . atoned. I've been atoned for what I've done. What do you think of that?"

"It depends what you've been atoned for."

"I don't want to say."

"Well, how is it that you've been atoned?" I asked.

"'Cause they're the ones who told me to burn it and the blame falls on them." His eyes became glassy around the edges while his pupils dulled, as if they suddenly realized they'd been dead for quite some time so they had better start showing it.

"Who told you to burn it down?"

"I ain't allowed to say!"

He must've figured he'd been too loud that time because it was the first time he'd looked around to see who might be listening. There was no one within earshot. After the one lady had heard about my baby-eating, no one else had come close.

"Was this a long time ago?" I asked, trying to keep the subject alive.

"Not long enough," he said, going back to work on the gum, shoving and jamming. The tip of his tongue came out once more and he rolled the hard piece of gum around like it was the tastiest piece of treat there ever was.

"Are *they* the ones who nicknamed you Burn?"

He squinted up at me again, the one-eyed wonder. "Mm-hmm."

"What's your real name?"

"Burn suits me. I always get first in line at the shelter suppers if they all scared of me."

"You've got a story to tell."

"Baby Eater, you ain't telling a lie right there. Hey, I'll take you up on that free gum."

I didn't have any. Wasn't even sure why I offered something I didn't have. Maybe it was solely to get him to stop sticking his tongue on that thing. But Thatcher or someone else inside might have a piece. I'd definitely ask, even if it was aiding and abetting gypping the city of a few bucks or so over the course of a week.

"I don't have any gum," I said. "But I think I can get you some. If I do, will you tell me about what you burned."

He sneered at me. "You're one nosy lady." He swatted at something, but I didn't break my gaze from him, fearful I'd miss something.

"Well?" I asked. "Will you?"

He only looked at me for a second before he swatted at something again. "Nah," he said. "I don't know. Ask me again next time."

THIRTEEN

Going Back to Amble

As soon as Thatcher spotted me charging to his desk, he closed whatever file he was working on and tucked his pen into his pants pocket. Then he stood. He looked as if he was about to tell me something but I opened my mouth first.

"You told me that sadist wore a condom each and every time," I barked at Thatcher. His head jerked back, stunned by my disposition. "Yet, here's my friend, victim number four," I shouted, "pregnant!"

Most of the squad room looked at me. I didn't care.

"I- I-" he looked down and rubbed his eyebrows. "Is she sure it's our guy that did it?"

"She doesn't sleep around if that's what you're asking."

Thatcher blinked. It was a slow movement, almost as if he were processing something.

I let out a sigh of intermission, moving past Thatcher to steal his seat since he wasn't using it now. My arms dangled from his chair and I got comfortable. I didn't want it to appear as if it'd be an easy task to get me to vacate the spot now that I had taken it.

"You have no idea how I'm trying to control myself right now because I originally came in here to yell and knock coffee cups off people's desks. I can't understand how Jen got pregnant when you specifically told me that the guy wore a condom and that Jen's rape kit didn't come back with any DNA."

Thatcher snatched up his cup and moved it out of my reach. Silly Thatcher, I thought. I didn't mean you.

"I didn't say there wasn't any DNA," he answered. "I said we couldn't find a match to anyone in our databases."

Perhaps he *had* said that. All I remembered at the time was that we were no closer to putting an identity to the guy than we were before. If

Jen had to go through all that and still managed to live, it seemed like the earth would have at least sifted itself to leave one shiny gold nugget to bring this man to justice. Was that so much to ask? Surely even the rocks themselves begged to cry out, *Foul play! Foul play! We tire of bearing the blood of the slain!*

"And we're lucky to have what we have," Thatcher added. "With all the other victims, the only thing that survived the bleach washing was trace amounts of latex and spermicide that coincide with condom use."

He broke into a slight smile. "So, not only did your friend manage to escape before the bleach wash, but now we can say his condom broke." He put his hands down on his desk and leaned toward me, his smile growing. "We finally have a survivor, but of all the survivors!" He chuckled once. "We got the one and only victim where his condom broke!"

"I appreciate your fervor, Thatcher, I really do," I said, "but Jen isn't in as much of a happy state as you are over this news."

His head drooped a bit. "I'm sorry," he said. "It'd be great if we could get a sample from the baby. Is she going to end the pregnancy?"

My nose crinkled at him. I didn't want to start this again, especially not with Thatcher.

"What?" he asked, seeing my expression.

"Ask me again later. For now, what do we have to do to get a DNA match?"

"Find a suspect and get a sample."

"Well then, why aren't we out there finding suspects?" I asked, swinging my arm toward the row of windows to my left, a series of squares that looked out to one of the dumpy portions of downtown.

"Why do you always assume we're not doing anything because nothing is happening?"

I scoffed. "Did you even hear the words that just came out of your mouth?"

"Whatever," he said. "You know what I meant. What else do you want us to do? Should we run around in circles so we give off the appearance of being busy until something new actually does come up?"

I started swiveling back and forth in Thatcher's chair, making a wide swinging motion with my knees while my feet stayed planted on the floor. "You know, in my other profession we called that due diligence. We didn't run around in circles, per se, but we did amble. That way, we didn't miss anything that would've otherwise been overlooked during the first pass through. Hence, the phrase *due diligence.*"

"If you do it right the first—" Thatcher started.

"No one does it right the first time, Thatcher." Hearing myself say it was like a little pluck of fine-tuning. *No one does it right the first time.* No one. Especially not killers.

Thatcher ignored my sudden preoccupation. "In that case, and if you're going to waste time and backtrack, why not run and get it over with faster?"

"More billable hours with a slow, careful amble," I said, smiling. Then I let my grin ease back down. "Since we have the new DNA sample, whether we run or amble, we need to go back around the track."

"You're just saying that because you weren't on the case earlier, and you want to make sure people didn't screw anything up."

"Correction"—I lifted my index finger—"I don't need to 'make sure' people refrained from screwing anything up. I feel obligated to fix what they *did* screw up."

"You know that includes me, right?"

I stood and put my hand on his shoulder. "I wasn't going to say anything, but . . ."

"Why not just come out with it and accuse me of being incompetent then?" The middle of his forehead was folding in on itself as he brought his eyebrows together.

"Don't be ridiculous," I said. "I don't want to anger you this early in the day because I need you to drive me somewhere. Well, actually, it's because you're the only one of the two of us sanctioned to carry firepower. I could drive myself, so really it's only the firepower toting."

He shook his head and sighed. I interpreted it as his acceptance of defeat.

"Where to today?" he asked.

"Take me to that meth guy."

"The who?"

"The meth guy, the ex-boyfriend of the first victim. The one who popped her in the face and left her for the rapist."

"I cleared him for the rape and homicide."

"Yeah, but he punched her."

"Allegedly."

"Blech," I muttered, letting my tongue out as if I had tasted something repulsive. "You're sounding like a defense attorney. Isn't there a hose-down cell for that sort of behavior in this place? Like where some pimply, power-hungry recruit turns the fire hose on cops who start talking about due process and corroborating facts?"

"If there were," he said, "you'd be the first—"

"Don't even finish that sentence, Thatcher. I've had much less sleep in the last week than I'm letting on, and you don't want to be the reason my crazy button is activated. Now, take me to the meth head because I want to talk to him."

Thatcher bent toward his desk and opened the top left door, pulling out the pen he had earlier put in his pocket, and tossing it in. I noticed the drawer contained a stockpile of small notepads and pens. It gave me an idea about the homeless guy, Burn.

"Didn't I already tell you that his story was he didn't punch her?" Thatcher asked. "He had slight bruising on the back of his hand, but he had bruising, scabs, and scrapes everywhere. Guy was a total mess."

"Tit, tat, I don't care. Where is he? I want to talk to him."

"Sorry," Thatcher said. "He's gone."

"What do you mean gone? Where?"

"I don't know. We told him to stay put. And now he's gone. Once we got the perp's DNA sample from your friend, we checked in on him to get a sample to see if it matched. You see?" he said, giving me a moon-faced smile, his eyes squinted together into little slits. "We aren't totally incompetent. We did circle back. A little."

"To what avail?" I asked. "You just admitted you couldn't find him. You don't have his DNA sample, do you?"

"No."

"This is why you *amble* around the circle, Thatcher, not run to it," I said. "Come on. I only have a couple more hours before I have to give Owen his next meal and then I'll be done for the day to spend time with my family. Let's find this guy."

"If I tell you I don't know where he is, and I say I can't find him, what makes you think *you* can find him?"

"Because I'm abundantly more resourceful than you are."

"Stay in the car," I said to Thatcher.

"No way," he said, throwing his seat belt off and reaching for the door handle.

"I'm serious."

"So am I."

We were parked two buildings down from Meth Head's, aka Jared Brown's, last known address. It was on an ugly, smelly street in Pacific Beach. On a bygone day—I'd hazard to guess eons ago—this place was a happy, sunny place with beach bronzed little families and wood bungalows sitting atop their garages. There would've even been room for a small side yard with a little table, a tree, and a well-used swing.

I imagined certain money mongrels came in, buying up the majority of homes, kicking the nuclear families out on their rears, and entering the land of woe and underinsured rentals. The side yards got replaced with two additional apartments, one stacked on top of the other, and both nothing more than semi-evolved lean-tos against the original structure. Garages converted to common areas where occupants could shove quarters in coin-operated machines, and, of course, a place to store their bikes. This being Pacific Beach, there was a gaggle of rusty bikes, flip-flops, and body boards as far as the eye could see.

It was ten in the morning before Thatcher and I pulled up and hardly anyone was milling around. If one had been inclined to rise early and surf, they were already back in their beds and drooling on bare pillows—the pillowcases already in use as makeshift drapes over windows. The emptiness of the neighborhood at that hour made me assume that most of the residents were still sleeping off whatever they did the night before.

I had known a few folks back in law school who chose to live and party Pacific Beach–style. In case I haven't painted the picture vividly enough and gilded that blasted lily to kingdom come, those folks were the idiots of the class. "Can I see your notes from Criminal Law? I had a . . . uh . . . uh, family emergency and missed a bunch of classes." No, moron, you can't have my notes. Put the weed stick down and focus in on reality.

Thatcher told me Jared Brown used to live in one of these units, the tan-and-white-trimmed building up on our left. Last Thatcher checked, Brown was sharing the place with a girl and another guy. Brown was the third wheel while the other two were shacked up, working nights at separate bars.

Goody hoorah. Gainful employment was a plus with this crowd.

My plan was to get one of the remaining roommates to spill their little guts about Brown's whereabouts. Thatcher remarked that if the roommates knew where Brown was, they would have already reported it to him since he had asked so nicely and all.

I wasn't so sure.

"It's better if I do this myself," I said. "Everything about you screams cop."

He gave me a snubbed look.

I patted his forearm. "It's not a bad thing, but let's face it, if those roommates have anything to hide, even in how much they claim they make in tips, they're not going to tell you anything because of your cop-ness."

"Cop-ness?" he asked. "And what do you plan to do?"

"I'm thinking the real estate agent bit. It's classic. Especially if a renter is involved. It should be very informative. Renters will spook easier if I mention the owner is thinking of selling."

"I'm not a hundred percent sure about this charade."

"Try not to get too hung up on it. I'd rather not have any issues of personal guilt before I finalize the many facets of my character."

He shook his head at me. "It's also not safe to go by yourself."

"Well, I can't have you come because then you'll bring all your cop-ness with you, won't you? I feel like I'm repeating myself here," I said. "Besides, you can see me from the car. I'm just going right over there. I'd say look for a sign that I'm in trouble but really, if you see me flailing or running, that's pretty much an indication to help."

After closing the door and walking a few feet, it occurred to me that I needed a prop. I had seen something in Thatcher's car that might work. Once I got back to the car, I grabbed it from his back seat but he tried to stop me again.

"Why are you taking that?" He pointed to the portfolio in my hand.

"It's a prop for the real estate agent gig. I need this to look the part."

"I don't like this deception," he said, nervously drumming his thumbs on his steering wheel.

"When did you get so boring?" I asked.

He huffed. "When I became the boss."

"That's a tragic truth, isn't it?"

Before I closed the car door for the second time, I said, "By the way, Thatcher, next time you go out and buy a portfolio, stick with brown or black."

"Why?"

"Because this," I stopped, holding the bright-red portfolio closer to his face, "is a chick color."

"Red is not a chick color. It says bold and original."

"Yeah, bold and original chick." I slammed the door.

The apartment I wanted was on the top floor, over the garage. I went up the stairs and stopped at the landing. There was a badly chipped, scratched, and dinged surfboard leaning precariously near the front door. Either the occupants were too lazy to set it straight or they were being terribly clever. One swift thump against the inside of the wall and that surfboard would clobber any unwanted solicitors. Myself included. I made a mental note to keep an eye on the teetering board. The other outdoor decorations included candles burned down to nubs in the necks of empty beer bottles, cigarette butts galore, and a rusted hibachi knocked over on its side.

There was also a portion of charred wood siding on the wall. It still smelled of fresh property damage and liability. To me, at least. To others, they'd say it smelled of burnt pine. Since the fire-damaged portion was close to the tipped hibachi, my money was on the little cooker being the culprit. Well, the avenue of burn, that is. The real culprits had hands, lived inside, and I very much doubted they were firing up hot doggies when the fire happened.

The door popped opened, startling me.

"What are you doing?" a small female said, accusing. She had disheveled hair—true and through bed head—and stood before me wearing a tank top and cut off sweat pants.

"Or, you could lead with 'Hi, how are you doing?'" I said. "Anyway, good morning. Did I wake you?"

"What do you want?"

Some manners out of you, I had wanted to say. "My name is Dana Patrick and I'm a real estate agent for the owner of this complex. You know the owner, right?"

I asked because I needed to know if making up the owner's name would blow my cover.

"Um, I guess, well . . ." she said. "We make our check out to a property management company."

"Right." I was only half listening, needing to concentrate on perfecting the ruse as fast as I could. "The property management company works for the owner, as I do. At any rate, the owner is thinking of putting this place up for sale."

I paused a moment, wanting to let that sink in and give her a bit of panic about a possible move in this woefully renter-crowded city.

"If he sells, we still get to stay here, right?" she finally asked.

I crossed my arms over Thatcher's chick-red portfolio, holding it tight, and giving her my best pouty look. "Can I be honest with you?" I asked.

She nodded. I could see a humbling effect wash over her. I had just struck gold. She had opened the door defensive, but was now waiting for me to hold her hand through the conversation.

"Someone has to pay for that damage," I said, pointing over to the charred siding. "Perhaps the reason the owner wants to sell this place is because he doesn't want the continuing liability of all the property damage. He wants to make it someone else's problem, you understand?"

She nodded again.

"Also, it's been brought to his attention that the property management company isn't being as strict as they once were about unauthorized tenants living in the units. You had one, correct? A Jared Brown?"

It was her first glint of skepticism. I had slipped by being specific about a name. I should've left it vague. How would I have known an actual name? I should've kept referring to him as "the unauthorized tenant" until she gave me a name.

"Hold on," I said, grasping for an explanation before she demanded one. I opened Thatcher's portfolio and leafed through some sheets. They were blank, but she didn't know that.

"Yes, Jared Brown." I tapped my finger on one of the sheets. "That's the name. I have it right here." I closed the portfolio back up. "Another tenant in this duplex issued a complaint about three people living in this apartment, when only two names were on the lease."

"Berg," she hissed through clenched teeth. "I hate that loser. She never stops complaining."

I gave her a sympathetic shake of my head and then said, "Jared Brown, though, was he living here or just visiting?"

She turned her head to the side and let out a sigh. "He doesn't live here anymore. He was my boyfriend's friend from college or whatever, and when his girl kicked him out, he crashed here for a while. Three months, I think. I don't know if that's visiting or living, but I swear, he's gone now. It's just the two of us now."

"Gone where?" I asked. "Will he be hard to track down, do you think?"

She proffered that skeptical look again.

"Because he did the hibachi damage, right? Because if he did the damage and then bailed, perhaps the owner can go after him rather than making you pay for it."

She nodded, slowly at first and then with full vigor. "Yes, it was him. He did it. We asked him to pay for the damage, and that's when he bailed."

"Figures," I said. "But how about you let us make that our problem rather than yours? All the owner wants to do right now is get this siding fixed so he can find a viable buyer. If there's any information on where I can find this other tenant, then we can chase him down for the cost of the damage. Otherwise, it's going to be tacked onto your rent."

I could tell she still only trusted me about fifty percent, but money talks. Always. If she could pass off the cost of a bill, even a nonexistent one, then she would. She huffed. "He's staying at one of two places: either back at his old stomping grounds in La Mesa at his parents' place, or there's this drug clinic in Fashion Valley."

"Drug Clinic?"

"Yeah, he seemed shaken up about what happened to his ex." Her arms hugged her chest, as if a cold front had swept by. "She was raped and murdered. So sad."

"By him?" I asked. Just to make sure.

Her face contorted. "No way. He's a total loser, but he wouldn't kill anyone. Anyway, that started him on his cycle."

"What cycle?"

"Use, clean up, use, clean up. That cycle. Some of the clinics are too nice around here. If you ask me, it just makes it easier on losers to make drugs a lifestyle."

The comment made me rethink my initial opinion about this young girl's prospects in life.

"So, I take it you stay drug-free," I said. "Good for you."

She shrugged. "Yeah, you know, I need my job, so I stay away from all that stuff. But if I ever win the lottery or something like that, I'd totally start using probably, because I wouldn't have to get up for work." She laughed it off. I'm sure there was more truth in that than humor and in any event, I decided not to rethink my initial opinion of her.

As I walked back down the stairs, she called out after me, "Since I helped, can we stay even if the owner sells the place? I don't want to be evicted!"

Then don't burn down your rental, you numbskull.

VIII

Stupid teens. I left a twelve-pack of beer in the parking lot for them. I knew they'd come back. They looked around for maybe five seconds to see who left the beer. They wouldn't have been able to see me if they tried because I was hiding in my car on a nearby street.

I'd been back there a lot. I told myself I didn't really know why, but I did. I wanted to take care of those teens. I wasn't done with what I had to do, of what my reassurances told me I had to do, those deep down reassurances that come at me when I find myself sitting on the edge of my bed, rocking back and forth, ripping my hang nails off with my teeth and letting the blood dot.

"Sick freak, sick freak, sick freak," I'd hear as a memory in my mother's voice. "Stupid weakling, stupid weakling, stupid weakling," would come too. I flexed my biceps. I had taken care of the weakling part. Looking down at my bandaged cuticles, the sick freak part resonated, more so than the memories of lifting the girls up one last time, dead, and chucking them out the back of the van. Still, the cuticle chewing had to stop.

And the stupid part? If I let those kids go to the cops without intervening, that would be stupid.

A cop car had been coming and going for three days. It came to look around and the rest of the ritual meant that I had another hour and a half or two to take care of the teens before the cops would come back. Wasn't sure what the cops were doing or why they were doing it but I wasn't going to be stupid again and be in that lot when they came back around.

The boys came ten minutes after the cop car left and I watched them drink the beer. Three teens had three each and they put the extras in their pockets. The music in their car got louder. So did their voices. I could tell they were getting drunk. When it was about time for that cop car to come back, I revved through the lot and tried to smash them around a bit. Only to scare them because they angered me by interrupting that night and for making me nervous they'd rat me out. If I scared them enough, they wouldn't come back and the cops wouldn't find them here. It was luck that the teens came so soon after the cop left that night, and that this was their first time back.

When they saw me coming the first time, they got out of the way and I braked right before I hit one of them. Then they got their wits, jumped in their car, and sped down the road. I wasn't the one that killed them so I won't feel bad about it. They were the ones who chose to drink. They were the ones who chose to drive crazy. They didn't make it past that fourth turn. I thought about helping but then I'd be showing my face and that wouldn't be smart so I let them be.

I went back to my hiding place on the nearby street. I saw the cop car come and go again. He wasn't interested in anything.

I sat there hiding for two more hours to see if anyone would come with sirens for the teens. I'd be able to see them if they came my way. No one did. Must've come from the other direction because I was sure they'd come. Can't miss a wreck like that. It wasn't my plan for them to die but it tied up a loose end.

The only loose ends left are Layla laying in her grave and the legal eagle who got away. The cops are watching her and the center. I'm trapped. I can't do anything unless I'm sure she can't tell them who I am.

And the teens no longer can say who I am.

I'm also getting hungry again for it. If I do it again, I'll be smarter, better, and it'll take my mind off the failures. I need to set my sights higher like on that cop lady because I can't get her out of my mind.

FOURTEEN

A Scab upon a Scab

A day later Thatcher asked if I wanted to come down and observe the questioning of Jared Brown. A few uniforms went on a scavenger hunt and found him. He hadn't been in La Mesa, or at his favorite meth clinic either. But another client of the meth clinic felt magnanimous with the officers and gave up information on Brown's exact whereabouts.

Brown had been bunking up with some mushroom-popping hippies in Ocean Beach. The 'shrooms were to take the edge off the meth withdrawals, he later rationalized. I didn't have any personal experience with this. I liked my brain cells just the way they were.

Thatcher brought me to a closed door at the station. It was small and cheaply made.

"Is this where you guys store the vacuum?" I asked, half-sincere.

"Very funny," he replied, his hand on the doorknob. "This is one of the interrogation rooms. Brown's inside." He started to twist the knob and I held out my hand to stop him.

"You're letting me in?" I asked. "Like, *in* in?"

"That was the plan," he said. "It's this or you can always go in the video room to watch on a screen. But since you're the one who put it all into motion to get him here again, I figured you'd want the honors."

I thought about it for a moment. "I'm in charge then?" I asked.

He smiled, letting go of the knob. "Technically, no. But I doubt that ever stops you from assuming you are."

I gave him a gentle, knowing nod. He was right.

"So, I'm sort of in charge then?" I asked.

He rolled his eyes. "Sure, if that makes you feel better."

"And I can use my own techniques?"

"Lawyer techniques?" he asked.

"Only the ones I'd employ out of a judge's presence," I said, giving him a wink.

He looked at me, seemingly unsure about what I had meant. "Fine," he said, "just start out easy. The guy is already defensive and twitchy."

"Meth twitch?"

"Probably. But twitchy in general too."

I nodded. "Okay, I'll behave." Thatcher hadn't moved to get the doorknob again, so I reached for it and gave it a turn, letting myself in as he followed.

Brown was sitting at a small wooden table, one hand fidgeting in his lap, the other tucked under his left thigh. Both feet bounced as if he'd had one too many cups of coffee, but I very much doubted the cause was so benign. Even his face twitched every few seconds.

"What's up, Twitchy?" I managed to muffle the sound of Thatcher's exasperated sigh as I pulled out the chair across from Brown, dragging it against the floor, away from the table.

Brown slapped his hands on the table, his eyes wincing shut at the sound he had made. "Don't call me names!" he screeched. My mind flashed to Burn and how I didn't like his name-calling.

"Did your ex-girlfriend call you names?" I asked. "Charlene, wasn't it?"

His fists tightened, his knuckles turning white as he leaned forward against the table, his hands getting closer to me.

Thatcher—who stood behind Brown—was biting his lower lip and giving me a nervous look, as if he feared Brown would attack me.

Oh, please. I know what I'm doing. Almost. I was about seventy-two percent sure and that was a decent enough chance for me. The remaining uncertainty, though, caused a tiny ball of nerves to sit at the bottom of my stomach. When I was questioning someone in a courtroom, I never really worried about the consequences of pushing too far. If I did, opposing counsel would open their big mouths and bark some objection, the judge would mutter yay or nay, and then it was over. No matter how far I went, there was always a sense of decorum present. Civilized squabbling, if you will.

Here though, even taking the meth addiction out of the equation, who knew how far I could go before someone snapped and attacked. The police carried guns inside their own precincts for a reason, right?

I concentrated on the room for a moment. It appeared to be a crossbreed of a temporary employee's cubicle and a forgotten storage room. The tail end of furniture miscreants seemed to end up here. Understandable considering the environment, but the general flavor of the interrogation room—from the meth freak to the cramped quarters—affirmed that I was *not* in a courtroom.

Thatcher was eyeing me, his head cocked. Probably wondering what I was doing, what I was thinking.

"Calm down," I said. I was looking at Brown, but speaking to Thatcher. Thatcher obviously didn't take my meaning because he shifted his weight three times in rapid succession, getting even antsier.

Brown cranked his neck to see Thatcher standing behind him. "What's going on?" Brown asked. "You guys going to do that good cop, bad cop thing on me?"

"That's quite cliché, Mr. Brown." I put one hand up on the table, but also leaned away. I didn't want Brown to think he owned the table. If this was my show, then by goodness, this was my table too. Still, I didn't feel like getting throttled so early in the day.

"In fact, it's so cliché, I'd hazard to guess you watch as many cop shows as Detective Thatcher does." I looked up at Thatcher. He hadn't found it funny. Pity.

"Further still," I said to Brown, "if that *were* the game we were playing, then I'm afraid you'd be in for a world of hurt."

"Why's that?" he asked casually, already looking distracted from the conversation and picking at a scab just below his right eye.

"Because we," I motioned first to myself and then to Thatcher, "would both be the bad cops."

Thatcher chuckled once.

Brown worked the scab off, flicked it on the table, and let the fresh wound bead up with blood.

"Agh!" I cringed, wrinkling my nose and then holding a hand up to my mouth to prevent myself from vomiting. "Man!" I spoke through my fingers, "Are you serious with that?" I suffered a gag reflex and then sprang up from my seat. "Hold on," I said, leaving the room just as Thatcher came around and stood beside Brown. I came back with tissues from the ladies' restroom down the hall. I flung them on the table. "Didn't your mother tell you picking makes it worse?"

He shrugged his shoulders, dabbing the blood with a balled tissue.

"Oh, wait," I said, "you do meth, so I'm guessing you don't care what your mom says."

He shrugged again. I thought I'd get a bigger reaction out of him on that one, but his eyes drooped. He was looking down at the floor. I saw thick, black eyelashes curling upward on one eye, and a bare lid on the other, the same eye with the bloody scab area. He had probably plucked them all out. Crazy, crazy stuff.

"All right. Let's go back to your ex, Charlene. You were mad at her. Why?"

He shook his head.

"Are you saying you weren't mad at her, or you don't want to answer?"

He slapped his hand back down on the table again. "Why am I here?" he demanded.

"Oh, I'm sure Detective Thatcher has a laundry list of violations. I can help fabricate some extra stuff, too, if it's necessary."

"Who the frick are you? Why do I have to answer you about anything?"

"If you don't answer her," Thatcher said, "you'll answer me."

"And let me guess," Brown said. "I don't want that. Ooh! Scary."

I laughed. Thatcher scowled at me. "What?" I asked. "Come on. That was funny. It was the way he said it. *Ooh!*" I laughed more. "And did you see his jazz hands when he did it? Good times," I said.

Brown smiled, too, soaking it all up and then looked over at Thatcher, to rub it in I think. When I saw that he was distracted, I dropped my smile and gave the table a quick push, making it collide with his rib cage. "*Ooh,*" I said. "Is *that* scary?"

Brown jumped out of his seat and lunged at me. I was only worried for a moment because by then, Thatcher had him face down on the floor, his knee in Brown's back. There was hardly enough space in the room, but Thatcher managed to get Brown down, even leaving a little room for me to get close too.

Thatcher nodded at me, letting me know he'd hold him there for a bit. I moved to where Brown's head was and squatted down, sitting back on my calves.

"You know what I think?" I asked Brown. "I think you bit off more than you could chew when you convinced Charlene to date someone like you. I've heard you weren't a loser addict when you started dating, but you turned to it anyway so it proves the point she was too much woman for you. And then, you figure if you can't have her, why not punch her in the face, break her nose, and leave her in an alley to let someone else finish her off."

"I didn't hit her! And I didn't know someone was going to kill her!"
he said. He even started to well up a bit. Pain from the memory, not
Thatcher, I figured.

"Well, it's sort of a de facto liability, but it's still all yours," I said. "And
you want to know why I think so? If you followed her to the bar and got
mad when a guy was pawing all over her—so mad that you punch her
lights out—then why would you leave her in the alley, all alone? I mean,
odds are that someone would come and rescue her. And if that happened,
he'd be the hero and that would make you look even worse. You couldn't
have that, could you? So I don't think you just popped her and walked
away for good. I think you went back."

Thatcher shot me a look. I ignored him.

"Not because you cared," I said, "but because even if you hated her,
you didn't want to be a bigger jerk in her eyes than you already were. I'm
not saying you were going to apologize, or help her get medical attention
from smacking her around, or anything else nice and gentlemanly. But
still, you couldn't just leave a situation set up the way you did, making
way for some other guy to be her hero."

"Shut up," he whined. "And get off me!" he yelled to Thatcher.

"He's not going to get off unless you stop thrashing around. And not
until you tell us if it was you that hit Charlene," I said.

"Fine," he relaxed but then gave it one more shot to break free from
Thatcher's hold. He failed. "I hit her," he said. "Let me go."

Thatcher pulled harder. "You going to sit still?" he asked, giving him
a shake.

"Yes!" he shouted.

Thatcher got on his feet first and then brought Brown up, pushing him
back into the wobbly desk chair at the table. Thatcher pointed at me while
speaking to Brown. "God knows how tempting it is, but *she* is off limits.
Don't even lean toward her, do you understand?"

Well, chivalry isn't totally dead. Even toward little pills such as myself.

"Can I go now?" Brown asked. "Are we done?"

"What makes you think we're done?" I asked.

"Because I told you I hit her. It's not like she's around to press charges
or anything, so I want to leave."

"No, no, no, little Meth Head." I shook my head at him, trying to
drum as much condescension as I could. "*I* already knew you hit her. But
let's assume you didn't rape and kill her; that doesn't mean you don't feel

guilt over setting the whole thing up, knocking her lights out and leaving her for the guy who'd eventually finish her off."

"If you don't think I'm the killer," he yelled, "and you don't care if I hit her, then why am I here?"

"I already told you. Because I want to know whether you went back for her. Did you? Yes or no?"

"Yes. But she wasn't there."

"What did you see?"

"Nothing," he said. "I just told you that. She was already gone."

I let my face fall into my hand, letting out a sigh.

"Describe the alley and everything around the alley. What else did you see?" I asked again.

"Like other stuff? I don't know what other stuff you want me to say."

Thatcher chuckled. He must've figured I was about to shove something at Brown again. Maybe a chair this time.

"Yes, other stuff, or stuff that is other, whichever you prefer," I said. "People, cars, dogs. People walking dogs, dogs chasing cars, what have you." I relaxed back into my chair. "So, you know, *stuff*."

He shook his head. "Nothing," he said. "I saw nothing."

"You're at a bar in Pacific Beach, and there's not so much as one other person in the alley, a car, or even one teensy, tiny thing that is related to a dog chasing a car, lifting its leg, or even sniffing another dog's butt?"

Brown leaned back in his chair and let his head fall back, eyes closed. I wasn't sure if he was thinking, irritated, or opting for a power nap.

His head popped back up after a moment. "Oh, a delivery truck, I think."

Thatcher and I looked at each other. Brown had just corroborated what the friend of the dead teens had said, about one of them taking pictures while the others rocked the truck.

"What kind of delivery truck?" Thatcher asked.

"I don't know. It was white, though."

"Big? Small?" Thatcher asked.

"Medium? I don't know," Brown said. "It was at the end of the alley."

"Lights on or off?"

Brown looked confused.

"The headlights and taillights. Were they on or off?" Thatcher clarified.

"I don't know."

"Was it parked or moving?" Thatcher asked.

"Parked, I guess."

"Are you sure it wasn't a van?" I was thinking about how Jen said it felt like a large van.

He thought about it for another second. "It was no van. I think."

We never bothered asking Brown to give us a DNA sample. He had left his picked and flicked scab and bloody tissues right on the table even though there wasn't too much of an implication he was the rapist and murderer. Thatcher was right about Brown not being able to function through any given day, let alone under the fragile and maniacally driven house of cards a sociopath has to keep. But it didn't hurt to exclude him, conclusively. Burn the field to chase all the snakes.

I wanted to burn this field and that field, and the other one down yonder until I smoked that snake out. The one who was slithering closer and closer to his next victim.

IX

She has a husband and baby. A boy.

I don't know. I still want to.

How would the boy turn out if he had no mother? Maybe better. I've been watching her after I followed her home. It's different, different surroundings because of her family. My mother said I wouldn't know the first thing about women but I know one thing. This one isn't the same person inside her house as she is outside of it. Seeing her holding that baby and even sitting next to her guy makes me feel something I don't want to. It makes me feel that I'm wrong. But then I hear it again, that it's just nerves about Layla and the others and I haven't fulfilled myself, cleansed of all the hurt and suffering as is my right.

I wasn't done mixing yet. My light, my chemical reaction, wasn't done burning. And that's why I've come to depend on the reassurances from that voice. It's what a man needs. It's what I've always needed. The voice inside gives me the courage I need to be fully realized, the strong enough man.

Each time I hear the words, I think less of my mother, and even less of my father. I don't need him either. I'm better than him. More fulfilled. A reassurance of late was that some of these same reassurances were given to him, my father, but he didn't take it all the way like I do. I wonder why.

I could almost see the answer in front of me, because he wasn't that bad. That bad as me. And then, I tell that part of me to shut up because it's the worst part of me. The weakling.

And then I see her again with the baby. She's holding him against her chest and trying to close the shutters. It's getting darker and the lights inside went on fifteen minutes earlier. The shutters close for only a second and then reopen, but he did it. Her guy. She closed them again. They did that back and forth before she crinkled her nose up, pointed outside, to everything but not me, and he folded his arms across his chest.

If it was me, she'd be dead by now. That's where the power came. Dead when they thought they were better than you and you were nothing and worthless and not to be listened to.

But he closed some of the shutters, not all, and she walked away, bringing the baby up to her face and kissing him. Again and again. She stopped only to walk back to her guy and give him a peck on the cheek as well before she turned back to kissing the baby.

That's when I felt the stab inside of me. One because I was seeing something I've always wanted and I hated that kid for it. Two, because that woman was right. I was the reason you close your shutters at night, but she didn't force her win.

But the reassurance said go ahead and poke at that one. See if she caves to you. She won't. Unless you make her.

FIFTEEN

A Geography Lesson

I went to my back yard just as night was falling. The air was soft and melodic, tempting me to fall in love with the life of the day even though it was almost over. I took a deep breath in and before I knew it, my arms were up in the air and I was reaching for the sky, stretching my back, and trying to feel a little taste of freedom in the confines of our dinky little property.

I closed my eyes and listened for the ocean. The sound came because the tide was high, thrashing closer against the beach. If I stilled my mind enough, I could almost find myself tiptoeing to a place where the very nature of our broken world hid itself, even if for only a moment.

I reached for one of the patio chairs and eased myself into it while looking at the pink-filled sky in the west. It was a peaceful moment until my rear crunched upon a conglomeration of sharp and ragged items.

I jumped back up. None of the lights outside had been on, but once I leaned close enough to the seat of the chair, I knew the culprit's name. Eddie had managed to cover the entire seat cushion with keys, metal buttons, chain pieces, and coins. I went to the next seat, and then the next, pulling each out from the table. He had covered all the seat cushions with the same junk.

I darted back inside to find him. He was sitting at the counter, marking something off on a calendar.

"Listen," I started, my hands waving in all sorts of animation, "that stupid junk collection of yours out there needs to disappear."

He didn't look up at me. He slid the tip of his pen across the days of the calendar.

"I can't live in this cramped little place and still make room for your metal detector junk. I just sat on some of it and I probably have tetanus. Tetanus!"

He circled a date, put the pen down, smiled, and then walked over to me. He took me into his arms and planted a kiss on my cheek. "Shh, shh, shh. No more."

"But you—"

He put his finger to my lips. "No, no," he said. "I understand. You had me at 'stupid' and then again at 'tetanus.'"

I couldn't help but smile. At least, that's what I was doing on the inside. On the outside, I was furrowing my brows at him. I broke free from his hold. "I'm not done venting about this."

He sighed, then nodded. "Fine. How much longer do you have left?" he asked. "Ten? Fifteen minutes? If it's more than that, you might have to follow me to the bathroom."

I growled.

"Oh, careful," he said. "I'm going to make that the start of your venting time."

My arms went up to push at him, but he grabbed them and pulled me into his chest. This time, he put a kiss on my mouth, trying to pry it open with his own. I refused, wriggling free. He found my reluctance amusing and chuckled, pulled his face away.

"How about," he said, "we do a CliffsNotes version of this soon-to-be argument? I'll give you a summary of what I think you're going to yell at me about, and then I'll skip right to the part where I promise to fix it. Or, how about I tell you that you're totally right and I totally suck? That way, we can skip to the part where I'm down on my knees, begging for forgiveness, and swearing off my silly behavior. Which, let's face it, will return in two or three days because men never change."

"Fine then. Yes," I said, trying to pull off my best air of benevolence, "you may proceed with the part where you're on your knees. And then, would you care to schedule this fight again when you—as you've so aptly predicted—do it again?"

"Sure," he said. "Pencil me in."

I went to my phone and cradled it in my hand.

"What are you doing?" he asked.

"Putting it in my calendar. Like you said."

"Speaking of calendars," he said, smiling. "I want to show you something." He took me by the hand, walked me to the corner area, and pointed down at the calendar he had been messing with when I came storming in.

"See the square for today's date?" he asked.

It had the words *Six Weeks* written in blue ink.

"Yeah," I answered. "Six weeks for what?"

He let go of my hand and flipped back to the prior month, pointing to another date in early October, the date of Owen's birth.

"Wow, You're not wasting any time, are you?" Eddie had been counting down the days from when the doctor told us we could be intimate again.

"You know, I don't want to seem overly anxious about it, but yes," he said. "I wrote this date down awhile back, but hadn't remembered the exact day. Then, when I saw you out there in the back yard and you did that thing where you arched your back—"

"You mean stretching?"

"I like to call it arching, but yes. And the cherry on top was when I saw skin." He lifted his eyebrows a few times in that Charlie Chaplin sort of way. His face dove into my neck for a few quick pecks, but I pushed him away. Only a little.

And then, not at all.

"There has to be a common denominator here," Thatcher said, looking at his board of death and horrors. I had my back to it. It still bothered me to look at it. What would it benefit me, anyway? Even if there was a nugget of information to be found on those shots, that wasn't how I knew to play my skill set.

Let me see someone face-to-face while I ask them questions, and I'm much more contributive. Otherwise, no, I don't want to look at dead bodies. It only served to remind me of two things: the Devil is at the door and he doesn't bother knocking.

"They all either live or work near La Jolla," I said, giving Thatcher the answer to his query.

I heard Thatcher's footsteps as he approached from behind. He came to the side of his desk—where I was again making myself quite comfortable—and sat on the corner.

He nodded at me. "You know, you're right. I did a map of where they all lived, and then one for where they all worked, but nothing lined up. I wonder though . . ." He stood and went back to his board. "Here, come look at this."

"Nope," I said, pocketing a few of the notepads and pens I found in Thatcher's top drawer when his back was to me.

"Oh yeah," he said from behind the board. "I forgot." I heard the peel of tape and then Thatcher was back with two maps in his hand. "Okay, let's look. They don't all live in La Jolla, and they don't all work in La Jolla . . ." He started but then drifted off as his eyes narrowed, trying in earnest to put something together.

"If they don't live there, then they work there. They're all accounted for," I said.

"You haven't looked at the map yet."

"I don't need to look at the map. I remember seeing it in the file. After I skipped the gory pictures, of course."

He shook his head. "Why didn't I see this earlier?"

"Because you're a newer transplant who lives on the east side of town, and I live here," I said, pointing to the La Jolla area. "When I hear or read something that has to do with where I live, I tend to pay attention."

"I still should've seen it."

"Maybe," I said, "but I bet you don't even know what some of these areas are called. What's this one?" I asked, pointing to a star he put on his map.

"Where your friend lives."

"Yeah, but what's the neighborhood called?"

He shook his head.

I pointed to another and then another. He didn't know any of the areas surrounding La Jolla.

"Maybe that's why it didn't click for you," I said. "When your reports say victim one resided in Bird Rock, or victim two worked in UTC, did it occur to you those are still parts of La Jolla, generally speaking. And these maps—" I held one up. "Why did you make them so big?"

"So I could see them better and put my marks on them."

"But look how far they make these neighborhoods seem from one another. You could get from here to here in less than three minutes." I traced a route with my finger.

I leaned back in Thatcher's chair, letting my legs stretch out. "Regardless," I started, "it isn't enough of a common denominator. I mean, sure, it's a little better than saying they all live and work in San Diego proper, but La Jolla is still a big area. I thought we were looking for something much more specific. Let's say, for example, where he's finding his victims. And for that, we should really focus in on Jen. She doesn't have an exciting life. I know that sounds bad, but it's true. Just like I didn't have a life when I was working in a big firm. It's all work and no play. Since she's at fewer places on any given day, it will be easier to narrow down."

"Let's start with jogging, where he got her." Thatcher sank his hands into his pants pockets and rocked back on his heels.

"Did the others jog?" I asked.

"I don't know," he said.

"Sounds like we should amble around another circle, don't you think?"

SIXTEEN

Visiting the Bereaved

I had to make calls to the victims' families. It was the only way. Yet even the thought of it was putting me through mental hurdles. Their pain was bound to remind me of the worst days, weeks, months of my own life. Suffering through grief had its special, merciless way of tormenting you.

Does the world stop for you? No. Does it hurt like the seven pits of hell while it's happening? Yes. And all you can think of is the pain and then wonder when it will stop and when it'll finally let you go numb.

I had kind of, sort of, almost forgotten what it was like to feel that gnawing torture until today, when I had to call those families. The inquest was to see if any of the other victims had done an occasional jog in the La Jolla area. The first call was to Charlene's mother. She resided in Des Moines and could barely push out anything in syllabic form on account of her hemming and hawing every other second. She sounded adeptly shocked at the reality of it all, as if she had only learned about her daughter's death yesterday rather than a few months ago.

I let her go for upwards of twenty minutes. Go ahead and be shocked. God knew I still was, and that's what had sent me into my rehashing about all the haunting torture that day. I figured if the shock went away, if I got my wish and went numb, then my daughter's memory would sail up into the sky like a vapor. As it was, I still had days where I thought someone would pull up into my driveway, honking like a crazy person and brimming with enthusiasm, shouting, "Look who we found, look who we found!"

And it would have all been a big mistake, right?

I'd still have my daughter, wouldn't I?

Life wasn't this cruel to make it real from here to forever, was it?

No, no, and yes. So, yeah, I let the mom of victim-number-one hem and haw all she wanted, and when she had a particularly long shot of blubbering, I said a silent, little prayer. A plea, really. *My God, oh my God, save us please.*

When all that was over, Charlene's mother managed to get through the explanation that she had just finished sorting through all of her daughter's belongings a week prior and there were no sneakers or anything of the like found in the lot of it.

"She was a naturally skinny girl," her mom said, letting out a deep breath that I could tell, even from almost two thousand miles of separated phone coverage, was wistful. "And so young," she added. "Girls like that don't have to worry about running."

But they do have to worry about monsters, I wanted to say. Then again, we all had to worry about monsters. Fat, skinny, short, tall, ugly, pretty, cautious, or careless. The lure of the serpent is such that it doesn't matter how he finds you, only that he consumes you.

Victim-number-two's mother was in San Jose. She said she wouldn't have known one way or the other whether her daughter, Tamara, ran inside or outside. I asked her to try to remember or to supply any bit of information about her exercise habits.

She replied with a snarky, "Does it matter?"

Of course it matters, you . . . Breathe, I told myself.

"Yes, it might. We're trying to narrow down possibilities on where your daughter's attacker first spotted her."

"Okay, fine. I'll say she ran. She was very health conscious. She liked to be fit. Who really knows if it was running she did, or Jazzercise, or whatever everyone's doing these days. There you go," she said. "Whatever everyone else was doing, that's what Tammy was probably doing."

"So, are you or are you not sure about the running?" I asked.

"Who knows?" she replied.

Breathe. Seriously, breathe.

"I don't mean to be abrupt with you," I said, "but pulling things out of thin air isn't the way to catch a killer, so please don't make up answers to placate me."

"Listen, you know what," she said, her tone wavering in anger, "I don't know what you want me to tell you. I don't know what she did. She left here at eighteen, hardly called, never visited, I hear next to nothing for eight years, and next thing I know someone is trying to dump a casket on my door and telling me I have to bury my daughter. And *you* want to know if she ran. Who cares if she ran?"

Click. She hung up.

"Well," I muttered aloud. "I care."

I felt sorry for that one, as well. She, too, was my sister in loss. She, too, had a paw in the pain. I think, though, she wasn't the sort to wait for the numbness. She was the one sinking her teeth in for that disastrous chew almost immediately, going through her own flesh and blood to taste her freedom.

Good luck with that. Then you'll be down a daughter and a limb. Splendid.

Last was victim three, Krissy Milhelm. She was the only one who had relatives in the area.

At some level, I knew I possessed the right to tell Thatcher he should've been the one to make these calls, and also the one who went to Krissy Milhelm's folks' home up in Poway, a suburb in San Diego's north county.

All I would've had to say to Thatcher was it was too hard for me; it stirred up too many memories. Yet it made me feel a solidarity I hadn't experienced since losing Corinne. As painful as it had been to hear the crazy in the other mothers' voices, it made me realize I wasn't alone.

Besides, Thatcher would likely have messed it up or said something stupid. At least that's what I told myself to push through my fear of breaking down in tears.

Each home in the Milhelm neighborhood was a replica of the one before it. The roof material changed, as well as the color of the outdoor shutters and overall paint color, but nothing else seemed to vary. Even the front lawns seemed to follow a rigid geometric formula.

When I arrived at the correct house, a sigh escaped, pushing itself through my clenched teeth. My personal anxiety couldn't have been worse if I were paying a visit to a drill-happy dentist.

Solidarity of grieving be cursed. This still hurt.

Going up their front walk, I heard shouting from inside. I could tell it was something along the lines of a domestic dispute. A woman's voice, shrill and reaching, rang through the solid structure to my ears, only a few feet from their front door.

I couldn't be certain what the problem was, only that she was quite upset. She bellowed, "Why?" and "How could you?" and "You don't understand."

I considered going back to my car and taking off but I knew I wouldn't have the resolve to come back later. I put my hand to the door and knocked. The shouting stopped at once.

A moment later an older man opened the door, his face looking like he had just slammed his fingers shut in a drawer and was trying not to show how much it had wounded him.

"Hi," he said, sounding hollow. "I'm sorry, but whatever you're selling, we're not interested. Sorry again," he said, closing the door on me.

"Hold on, please," I said right as the door was about to click in its latch. "I'm not selling anything. I'm with the San Diego Police Department and I'm here to ask you a few questions about your daughter."

He reopened the door, letting out a pained exhale. "Today's a bad day," he said. "Can you come back tomorrow?"

Out of courtesy, my answer should've been yes, but I didn't want to do either the drive or emotional preparation for the task again.

"It will only take a moment. I could just speak quickly with you if you like."

He stepped over the front threshold and closed the door behind him, both of us now standing outside. His hand did a slow sweep down the side of his face and he looked over his shoulder and through one of the front windows. I figured he was looking for his wife, to make sure she wasn't around.

"Honestly," he said, looking back at me, "I can't talk to anyone right now because I'm worried about my wife. I have no idea what she's going to do at this point, which is why I need you to come back tomorrow. I've never seen her like this and . . . and . . ."—he let his head sink, shaking it back and forth, bearing regret—"she's simply not handling our daughter's death. And I don't mean not handling it well, because how could any parent handle it *well*. I mean she's not handling anything. I'm afraid I inadvertently pushed her over the edge today by doing some laundry."

My head cocked to the side, confused.

He rubbed at his face again. "Krissy's laundry. Our daughter. I thought I was helping." His eyes watered up and his bottom lip quivered. "I knew Beth wanted to save her stuff. Put it in boxes and what have you. And Beth, you know, God bless her, she's always been so good about laundry. Likes things clean and smelling clean. I think that's why Krissy was twenty-one and still living at home." He gave a subdued grin at a memory far, so far away now. "No one else was going to keep her clothes as clean as her mother did." He wiped at his eyes. I wanted to sink with him into his grief. Or hug him. I was too much of a weakling to do either.

"Since Krissy died, though, Beth hasn't been able to find the will to do even a single load. So, I've helped. I don't mind it. But today, I decided it was time to put all of Krissy's clothes in those boxes, for safekeeping. She had some things left on her closet floor, her dirty pile, so I washed them, and boy oh boy, was that ever a mistake."

I bit down on my lower lip to stop it from shaking alongside his. Maybe even to bite on it so the pain would remind me not to cry. "Was your wife not washing her clothes because the dirty clothes, even if they're dirty, still smell like her?"

He gave me a pained nod, the shape of his mouth wanting to turn to agony. His tears fell.

"Even you get it," he said, a sob escaping. "Why am I so stupid for not having realized that? My wife told me that's all she had left that smells like Krissy. I can't take it back now, can I? I can't take any of it back."

His breakdown made me think of why he was really crying. It wasn't over a load of laundry or that his wife was upset with him. It's because Evil had come and left its mark in their lives. Forever.

I hated the darkness and I hated how its filthy little fingers were in everything we did, felt, and touched. He's a greedy one, that Devil. His thirst for us is never satisfied and never quenched, even when he succeeds in picking us off one by one with rape, murder, pedophilia, pornography, drugs, and any other facet of destruction that strikes his undignified fancy.

I put my hand on the side of Krissy's father's arm. "I'm so sorry. Truly, I am."

The question I had for him was only three words: Did Krissy run? But yes, it could wait, it would have to, until tomorrow.

SEVENTEEN

A Page-Turning Moment

Before going back to the Milhelms' house the next day, I decided to stop by Jen's. I had a last-minute idea to bring Owen along with me to introduce him to Jen, but considering she was still in the throes of doubt regarding her own pregnancy, I didn't want to press things too hard. As much as Owen made my world alight with stars and sunshine, he might reopen some wounds for Jen. Besides, even though I wasn't planning to go to the station that day, something in me felt Owen shouldn't be a part of my visit to the Milhelms either.

Jen's place had one window shade open, and only partly at that. It was still a good start and an improvement from the shroud of darkness I had found last time I visited.

"How did you get past the doorman?" she asked, stepping aside to let me through her front door.

"Well, a fine howdy to you too," I replied.

"Sorry," she said. "Hi. Nice to see you. But seriously, how did you get past him? I mean, I would've let you up anyway, but he didn't call. You didn't pull another stunt, did you?"

"Define stunt," I said.

"I don't want to define stunt."

"Then my answer will be vague and ambiguous."

"I'll object," she said.

"I'll overrule."

"You can't. You're not a judge."

"I am in my own mind."

She smiled at me. It was a reaction that made her bloodshot eyes brighten a bit, made them look like something other than pits.

"If you can at least assure me you didn't hurt anyone or break any laws," she said, "I don't actually need to know the specifics."

"I'm shocked by your lack of faith in me but I'll appease you and tell you no, I didn't hurt anyone or break any laws. However, in the interest of upholding my stature in this world, what I did was apologize to your doorman this morning."

Her face crowded with disbelief. "And that worked? He let you through even though I specifically told him no visitors?"

"Ah-ha!" I exclaimed. "I knew you were still shunning everyone, myself included."

"No, no," she said, looking away from me, "not you. Like I said, I would've let you up." She walked into the kitchen and pulled out two coffee cups. "I still don't know why he wouldn't call first, though."

"Because he was rendered speechless by my method of persuasion."

She stopped paying attention to the cups in her hand for a moment, seemingly stunned by my comment, and let them clink down on her countertop too fast. The sound startled me.

"What method?" she asked.

I pulled out one of the stools at her counter and took a seat, slipping my jacket off as she poured the coffee. "The method of a large bag of BBQ chips and a six-pack of Diet Dr. Pepper."

My eyes stayed on her, counting down each second of her hanging jaw—three, two, one, and yes! Her mouth closed.

"How did you— What made you—" she stuttered.

I took a prolonged sip of my coffee, smacked my lips together when I was done, and then said, "I'm that good, I tell you."

Her initial shock gave way to annoyance pretty quickly. "Tell me," she said, matter-of-fact.

I pointed to her refrigerator. "Your Christmas list. One entry says"—my fingers went up in air quotes—"'Dave the Doorman.' I saw it when I was here last."

I took another sip of coffee. "I knew I was running the risk of it being the wrong doorman, but alas, it wasn't. Either way, I think anybody would appreciate a bag of BBQ chips and Diet Dr. Pepper. They say it tastes like the real thing," I said, smiling.

"Does it?" she asked.

"How should I know? I don't drink that stuff," I replied. "But there you have it. Mystery solved. I still thought he'd call up here and get your permission. I came bearing gifts not to sneak up on you, but as a peace offering to him for last time."

"You've given up sneaking past doormen, then?"

I shook my head. "Are you kidding me? It's even more of an adrenaline rush than pretending I'm Dana Patrick, the real estate agent."

Her brows furrowed.

"It's a gig I do to get information out of people."

"While working with the cops?"

"Yes, but I did it before too. I'm doing all sorts of things now that beat taking depositions and drafting motions."

I wasn't going to tell her there were things that were immensely worse too. Like seeing dead bodies and waiting until parents stopped crying so I could ask them a simple question about whether their daughter ran or not. Not to mention feeling like a useless imp because you can't find the man who raped, impregnated, and had meant to kill your friend, the one who had just poured you a fine cup of coffee.

"But taking depositions—at least the ones you and I have done—don't usually involve rape and attempted murder."

"That reminds me," I said, even though her comment didn't remind me of anything, "is someone from the department still coming around or calling to check on you?"

She shrugged. "I guess. This woman calls every day about the same time. If I don't answer, they send a patrolman to come and check on me." She let out a sarcastic laugh. "You can imagine, then, that I don't miss that call very often."

"Well, if he *is* watching you, maybe it would be good if he saw a cop car coming by every now and then."

"Maybe, but I don't think he is. I have a feeling he already knows where I live and work, and that's how he knew about my running path. So, if he hasn't come back to finish me off by now . . ."

I wanted to remind her that that was the same mentality she bore when she went for a solo run after I begged her not to. But what kind of insensitive beast would that make me? Normally I didn't care about showing that side of me, but with Jen, I did.

I wanted to change the subject and ask her about the baby, wanted to ask her if she had made a decision about the abortion, but then thought better of it. Something to let be for now, while her feelings were likely jumbled.

She looked back at the memo pad on her refrigerator, the Christmas gift list, but when she faced me again, she was crying. My first response was panic, thinking I had done or said something wrong.

"You're good at noticing things. Like my Christmas list. I bet you would've noticed if someone was watching and following you," she said, wiping a tear as it fell. "I bet you would've noticed if someone was hiding behind the bushes. And I bet you would've never gone into the bushes by yourself. Never even been out jogging alone."

Something twisted in me like a knife to the gut. "Don't give me that much credit," I said.

"But it's true."

I shook my head. "Even if it were true now, which I can't say it is, I think you're forgetting what happened to Corinne. I'm the last person to give a lecture on the requisite vigilance needed to spot monsters."

She went back to staring at the memo pad, or maybe just the refrigerator. Or maybe nothing at all except the memory of the darkness of a place where she had been hurt, nearly destroyed. Yet God and His universe asked her to keep treading. I could only hope that Jen believed that too, that it was God asking her to go on, not only me.

The task was a brute, though, even if doled out by her Creator. Well, I think she still thought of Him that way. At any rate, the chore ahead of her, of living, of the humming along, and keeping your chin up baby, oh . . . that stuff required conquering the likes of breathing, eating, and walking upright. All those inane things that appeared as Olympic feats when your sense of self and safety in the world have not only been burned, but the ashes have been kicked and thrown in your eyes over and over again.

"I'm sorry," Jen said, her voice dropping low. She must've been apologizing for Corinne, for my loss of her. I couldn't think of what else she could be apologizing to me for.

"Don't be," I replied. But then again, sometimes being sorry is all we have to give when our methods for comfort run bankrupt in every other regard. Pity may seem weak and cheap to some, but I say it's the last ditch effort when words and actions won't put the pieces back together. Perhaps, then, I should've let her be sorry for me. I know I felt sorry for her.

Jen looked over at me and then her eyes lowered to my shirt. "You've spilled coffee on yourself," she said, trying to form a half-smile. "It must've been from all that bragging you were doing, pretending to be clever in knowing what I had planned to get my doorman for Christmas."

I was already wiping at the stain on my chest. "I never pretend in that regard," I said, winking. "Now, if you can point me to the bathroom, I'd like to take care of this."

She motioned to my left. "Use the one in my master. The guest bathroom has no towels in it right now."

"Sure."

I went down the hall to her bedroom, which had an open en suite bathroom inside. The only door to close was the one that led into her bedroom. This was a hidden bonus for me because closing the bedroom door gave me more leeway to gauge something. Jen seemed to be doing a bit better, but how was she spending her days? Surely, I could find clues to her state of mind in this inner sanctuary. It couldn't hurt to do a bit of snooping.

Her bed was a mess, but that was no surprise. I didn't think either one of us had the constitution to be uptight over wrinkled bed linens even in the best of times.

I went over to the toilet and lifted the seat. Her lack of wanting to make her bed said nothing to the fact that Jen was an absolute stickler about a clean toilet. Random as it was, I remember more than a few roommate brawls on the issue.

The bowl was clean, but I noticed there was a self-cleaner attached. It told me nothing as to whether she'd maintained the wherewithal to keep up on her favorite task.

I opened her closet next and found her dirty clothes hamper. It reminded me of the unpleasant task ahead at the Milhelms. A pile of dirty laundry had sent poor Mrs. Milhelm over the edge, and also represented a heaping dose of guilt that her husband would likely never shake.

I spotted an empty hanger on a nearby clothes bar, grabbed it, and used it to stir up the contents of her hamper. There was hardly anything in it except underwear and the occasional T-shirt. Even today, for our indoor coffee date, she was wearing a pair of gym shorts and a T-shirt. This part was not her. She was typically too glam not to have even a shred of decent clothing in her dirty clothes pile.

Leaving the closet behind, I looked at the bed portion of her room again. That's when I saw a glimmer of hope. In the far corner of the room, on a cream-colored, armless chair, was a blush-colored silk top and a black pencil skirt.

I heard her approaching, her footsteps dragging against her thick carpet. I darted back to the sink but before I could turn the faucet on, she opened the door.

"What are you doing in here?" she asked. "I haven't heard the water go on once."

Of course! That was quite stupid of me. I would have been able to keep her at bay longer if I had bothered to follow through and actually turn the water on right away.

"I was fixing my hair."

"You've been spying, haven't you?" she asked.

I opened my mouth to deny it.

"Don't bother," she said, holding a hand up. "Just tell me what you're looking for and I'll help you snoop."

I let out a sigh and propped myself up against her sink. "That's why I like you, Jen," I said. "There's no pulling one over on you. You and Eddie are unique to me in that regard."

"You're mistaken," she said, looking around to make sure I hadn't messed anything up.

"How so?"

"You're not as clever as you think you are." She stopped her inspection for a moment and flashed me a coy smile. "It's just that Eddie and I are the only ones brave enough to call you out on all your antics."

"And yet"—I stood straighter—"that in and of itself *proves* how clever I actually am, because I have people running away in fear."

She shook her head. "Most people wouldn't be proud of that."

"Eh. To each their own."

She did a quick turn around the room again, and then slapped her hands against her hips in frustration. "Okay, just spill," she said. "What were you messing with?"

I took a step toward her. "First, I want the name of that self-cleaner deal in your toilet. That thing is like gold. Second," I pointed over to the chair with the career outfit on it, "are you going back to work?"

She looked over and lifted her hands up for a moment, almost in abandon. "Yeah. Might as well, right? I was watching one of those shark shows on Discovery or Animal Planet, whatever, and they said a shark dies if it stops swimming, if it stops moving. And lawyers are called sharks, so it resonated."

"That's quite profound."

"I thought you'd like that."

We stayed there for a moment, both looking at the outfit and, I think, both knowing a page in her recovery was turning.

It made me think about asking her about the pregnancy again.

"Jen?" I asked, my voice sounding like a million miles away from the jovial tone we had just shared.

"No," she answered.

"No what?"

"I don't want to talk about it," she said.

"Just think about it then."

X

I went to watch that one, the one who got away, ran away, and I found the cop lady walking out. I only came to see if the cops were still around this place, see what they're going to do. I sometimes think I don't need to kill either of them, that I don't want to. There has always been the heat of the moment and that's when I go all the way. Then things cool and I do my work and quietly plan and watch just in case I want another one and can't control myself.

If she knew who I was, she would've said something by now, they would've come by now. But maybe they're getting closer and that's why the cop was there. It got me worked up all over again but it was daytime and there were many people around.

I drove away quickly, and kept driving until I found myself back at the place where my father likes to hang out with his friends. I wanted to go in even though it wasn't a scheduled day for me to be there. I was going to pretend to fix something but then found out that something was broken anyway. Those idiot old people, always breaking stuff.

I went snooping in his wallet after I did my repair. He was playing something out there on the courts and left his gym locker open. Probably playing lawn bowling or something the rest of them play. He was so old. I've done the math. He would've had to be fifty when he got my mom. Wouldn't think an old man could do it, but once when she had been drinking she told me two of them were there that night. One held her down, a younger one, and this one, the old man, the full-named father that got screamed at me over and over in my ears, he was the one who really got her.

Maybe that's why he liked to be friendly to young, strong guys like me. So we can hold them down for him. I laughed and my laughter bounced off the empty walls and ceilings. There was hardly anyone around that day. A handful of old ladies playing cards inside, and then old farts rolling balls outside.

He probably couldn't do anything even if I held them down for him. I laughed again at his impotence and then shoved a picture into his billfold. It was a picture I printed from my phone.

A picture of what I did to Layla.

If he figures out it was me that put it there and then asks me who did it to Layla, I might admit it. And then I might try to convince him that I'm his son and if they find anything on Layla and track it back to me, I might say that he taught me how to do it.

EIGHTEEN

Ricochet

I got out of my car and strolled up the Milhelms' front walk for the second day in a row, pausing a few feet from the door to listen. It was as quiet as anyone would expect suburbia to be at about ten in the morning. I knocked on the front door and waited. Nothing. I really should have called first but if they weren't home as I was now starting to suspect, then it would be a phone call one way or another. I reached around and pulled out a torn piece of paper I had stuffed into my back pocket. I had written all of the Milhelms' numbers on it: their home, his cell, and her cell.

I knocked again. Still nothing. I moved to a front window on my right and casually looked in. I proceeded in a way that was a stretch short of total peeping for fear someone would come around the corner and I'd scare them. No lights were on, but that seemed typical for the time of day. There was a television set to the far right in the living room, but that was off too.

Pulling out my cell, I called their house number first. I could hear it ringing inside but it was left unanswered. I moved next to Mr. Milhelm's cell number.

"Hello," he said.

"Hi, Mr. Milhelm. This is Evelyn Barrett. I'm with the San Diego Police Department. I came by yesterday to talk to you about Krissy."

"Yes, sure, I remember. How can I help you?"

"Is everything better today?" I asked.

"It is and it isn't. Beth has managed to sift through the anger. I still feel horrible about it. She asked if she could have the morning to herself to work things out inside of her, so I'm golfing today. You said yesterday you had a question to ask?"

"Yes. Did Krissy run outdoors?"

"Hmm. You know, I don't recall. She tried to exercise when she could, but she worked long hours at the bank. I'm not sure she ever had the chance to take up running, but I wouldn't know for sure. My wife would know. She's at the house if you want to ask her. Although, I can't promise she'll even open the door."

I looked again through the window, back at the living room with no one inside. "I'm actually at your house right now," I said. "No one is answering either the door or the phone."

"Oh, well she must've stepped out. Let me give you her cell number."

"That's all right. I have it right here."

"Very good, then. Give her a call. Beth would know. And um, Ms. . . . ."

"Barrett," I answered.

"Ms. Barrett, I feel obligated to apologize in advance if my wife doesn't manage a coherent or even a nonconfrontational conversation if you're going to be bringing up Krissy. Still, she's the one who would know your answer."

"I understand."

He sighed. It sounded like he was temporarily in a wind tunnel with the force of his exhale. "With all due respect, Ms. Barrett," he said, "unless you've lost a child, you couldn't possibly understand."

I had no need to tell him. It wouldn't help where he was at and it wouldn't have helped where I had finally managed to get.

"I'm sure," I answered. "Thanks for your time," I said, and ended the call.

I tapped in Mrs. Milhelm's cell number. That also could be heard ringing inside. Maybe she had heard me knocking and decided not to come to the door as her husband had predicted. My call went to voice mail and I hung up.

"Huh." I hit redial. Same ringing from inside and this one went to voice mail as well. Maybe she was in the back yard. I could try to go back there, but that made me more worried about catching her by surprise. I called her cell one last time, following the sound of the ringing as best I could from outside. I was maneuvering through a garden bed to get to another of the front windows. This one was on my left, on the other side of the front door.

Up against the inside of the large, tall window was a small buffet table with a golden bowl on top, cradling a set of keys, the ringing cell phone, and a fistful of loose change. As I looked through the window, I left a message.

"Good morning, Mrs. Milhelm. My name is Evelyn—" I froze, cutting off my own message, when I saw what was farther inside, having looked past the buffet table and into their central hallway, an open area with a tile floor and big staircase.

I dropped the phone. My hand had gone numb, paralyzed for a moment and unable to move.

"No!" I screamed. All I could see was dangling bare feet. I tilted my head to get a better look and saw blue-and-red-splotched legs, a flannel nightgown, and then her pale, dead face slumped to the side as she hung from the top of the stairwell.

Stomping and demolishing the flowers and greens, I went back to the front door, my eyes pouring over every inch of the porch. I was looking for anything solid and big enough to break through one of the windows.

I found a flowerpot tucked in a corner. As I picked it up, I could make out the words "Mommy's Garden" on it with several little handprints acting as sprouting flowers. The paint was chipped and faded, something from a while back. Likely, the prints belonged to little Krissy, from a time when the hope of tomorrow seemed certain.

I had to get inside. I had to try to help.

A tear skipped down my cheek as I chucked the "Mommy's Garden" pot through the right-side front window. While I did it, I couldn't help but picture a tidy and folded pile of a young woman's laundry sitting over in some dark corner, the inanimate mastermind of that slouched, dead face hanging off the stairwell. The pop of glass echoed through my ears. As I watched the hand-printed pot move in what seemed like a skidded portrayal of slow motion on the other side of the glass, I wondered if Mrs. Milhelm—even when she was trying to choke out her last breath— could've really understood that it was never really about a load of laundry to begin with.

I flinched at the sound of the pot crashing against a glass floor vase. No, it wasn't about laundry. It was a ricochet of her daughter's murder. It had started with one filthy, raping, murdering man; a man playing one of the many cards in Evil's hand. He was the one who had pulled the trigger on Krissy Milhelm but the bullet kept going, bouncing, clinking, clanking, and reverberating until it found its final resting place in the part of Mrs. Milhelm's brain that decided none of it was worth it anymore.

I looked at the window. There was no shattering, no gazillion little pieces of glass tinkling to the ground. The only damage done was a self-contained hole, a little bigger than the flowerpot itself.

When the pot finally made its final hit, I studied it, upside down with dirt and crumpled flowers splattered all about. And there, on the bottom of the pot, was a bronze key taped in place. Presumably, a key that would have opened the front door for me.

"Perfect!" I screamed. "Really, just perfect!"

A voice suddenly boomed from behind me. "Stop! I'm calling the police!"

I turned and saw an overweight, elderly man with an unmerciful black dye job and snowy white eyebrows. He stood on the sidewalk in his bathrobe, holding it closed at his crotch.

"Do it!" I yelled back. "Mrs. Milhelm hanged herself and I'm trying to get in to help her!"

The man paled, his mouth starting to flap open but only managing to stutter a bit, and then he took a few steps backward, nearly tottering over when he hit the edge of the curb. Suddenly, I didn't feel so inept. Bathrobe guy was clearly more useless than I was and at least I was trying to move forward, whereas he was retreating.

My eyes scanned the porch again and its surroundings. I was looking for something else to throw. Spotting an empty, dried out hummingbird feeder toward the edge of the house, I ran to get it. I yanked it out from its solitary spike in the ground and ran back to the window. I took fervent hacks at the glass until most of it fell down.

Before I climbed through the broken window, I turned back to the man in the bathrobe. He had made a few more steps in retreat but he remained without any real target or purpose. A car was surely going to plow him down at his current rate of progress and I wasn't up for another dead body this early in the morning.

"Are you going to call the police or what?" I shrieked at him. I would've made the call, but my phone was in the *somewhere* vicinity of the far garden bed. I didn't want to stop to go look for it yet.

There wasn't any furniture under the window I had bashed in, so I went in leg first. Adrenaline was coursing through me at such a rate that I doubted I would've felt broken shards of glass slashing into my jeans if I had missed any.

Once inside, I ran to the foyer. She was too high to lift from the bottom so I ran up the stairs and tugged on the rope she had used. I couldn't make myself look directly at her, at the top of her head. I could only pull and pull and try not to fling myself over while I looked at the floor below. That's when I saw a crumpled blush something. A small blanket? A towel? I looked harder and saw the end of a cuff. A shirt. I winced, my fingers losing their grip, losing their nerve.

I didn't want to think about it . . . I didn't ever want to know whether that was one of the items of clothing Mr. Milhelm had disastrously washed and whether Mrs. Milhelm could've been holding it in her hand when she went over. Only dropping it when she gave in to the suffering. Mr. Milhelm wouldn't want to know about that either, but someone was bound to tell him. Telling grieving people things they don't want to hear was simply part of the onslaught of those first few steps over the edge. "Oh yeah, while you're falling, here's some more pain that will make you plummet into the abyss faster. Catch!"

But maybe he didn't have to know. I wasn't going to be able to pull Mrs. Milhelm up anyway, and if I could, to what avail? But I could hide that shirt. I could tuck it into the waistband of my pants and run away with it, burning it at my first opportunity. No, not burn it. No, I couldn't do that. Not now, not after all this. I'd put it in a shoebox and bury it. Better yet, I could hang it up in Krissy's closet.

He wouldn't have to know about the accursed blouse.

I tried a final time to get Ms. Milhelm up to the landing because it dawned on me, in every which way of foolishness, that perhaps I could put her back too, just like the shirt. I could drag her to her room and put her on her bed, like she was taking a nap but then lo and behold, she keeled over and died.

"She didn't give in to the despair, Mr. Milhelm, nope, she had a bad ticker. She had a bad ticker and the sun will be darker for you for a bit, but not as dark for you as, let's say, if she had hung herself and you were left to claw your way out of that dank and forgotten well."

Still, my efforts amounted to nothing more than swaying her lifeless body in sickening little circles, emphasizing to me that I was doing more harm than good. She probably had about forty pounds on me, not to mention that part where dead weight was no joke. I was useless.

I let out an exasperated breath. It was the fullness of realizing there was nothing I could do except leave her hanging, dead.

All I could do was plant the shirt back in the closet, not really caring that I was tampering with evidence—especially when it would be more evidence for Mr. Milhelm to blame himself—and then leave through the front door, where I fell into a sitting position on the front lawn, my arms wrapped around my pulled-up knees. The neighbor in the bathrobe was nowhere in sight. Since there wasn't a bloody mess of squashed flesh in the middle of the street, I figured he must've made it back to his house without a car using him as a speed bump. Hopefully, he had done the right thing and called the police.

I supposed I should have been the one to make a call to Thatcher but he'd find out eventually. I also should not have even remotely considered fleeing before the first cop arrived, but that's what I did for a moment or two. But no, I needed to stay. I was responsible for smashing the front window, trying to get Mrs. Milhelm's dead, choked body out of the foyer, and leaving the front door ajar on my way out. Oh, and the shirt. I had messed with the shirt, but that wasn't on my "to be disclosed" list.

Yet, those tidbits of rationality were nothing compared to the panicked, sunken feeling growing in my chest, reaching up and trying to squeeze itself into my mind. The sucker-punch of it all, probably the reason I felt overly distraught at Mrs. Milhelm's death, was that I realized this could've been me. I could've been the dead momma who couldn't deal with the blow of having a child murdered.

I remembered wanting to do something like this after I had buried Corinne. Not something as open and blatant as a hanging, but one too many of the pills I had loved back then would have done the trick. If not for the compulsion I felt in finding Corinne's killer, I probably would have. And now, there was Owen. But not for Mrs. Milhelm. Poor Mrs. Milhelm. Pity really was the only thing left in this one. What would words do? What would action do? She'd still be dead and pale and hanging.

Sirens sounded from a few streets over. I guessed bathrobe guy had managed to call the police after all. It was too late to escape, so I gave the first cop on the scene my version of events and told him to relay the event to Detective Brian Thatcher down at Central.

I went back to the flowerbed under the other window and searched for my phone. When I found it, I gave a moment's thought to calling Mr. Milhelm, but no, I couldn't. I wasn't sure if it was more of not wanting to or not being able to, but it sat better with my conscience if I told myself it wasn't my place. I had to return to Owen, to feed him. It's what I needed to do—in every sense of the word—but more so, I wanted to.

Owen.

Simply thinking about him made me realize how much I both hated and needed to do this job. On the one hand, I loathed being away from him, even if only for an hour or two at a time. That morning alone, I could've spent the whole day rolling the gazillion socks we seemed to have for him in tightly packed balls, fresh from the laundry. No bigger than small apricots, those were, and yet they meant everything to me. They did that morning, they did last week when I had done the task, and they always would.

What was it about folding a child's laundry? How there's always a few pieces where it's very plucking from the dryer or basket brings to a mother's consciousness a backstory that includes a trip, a memory, a smile, a soft tussle of hair, or even the little peek-a-boo of belly button that comes and goes.

Oh . . .

I got it, about that silk shirt. I mean, I understood about it before, but yeah, I really got it at that point.

And that's the flip side of thinking about Owen when I was doing what I was doing; he made me realize that I needed to do the job, no matter how much it hurt. Owen reminded me that in a world of undone, not everything had been unraveled, tainted, spat upon. Not yet, anyway. I had to protect that for my son. I had to.

NINETEEN

A Warning That Slithers

I had Owen laid out on my lap. I was slowly, and I mean *slowly*, getting him into one of his little outfits. In my mind, it was simply nostalgic. Or, contemplative. Commemorative, even. His skin was soft, unmarred, a testament that life hadn't yet gotten to him. The knocks of life, as they say, not just the marks made by the sun or a fall from his bike.

It was hard to deny at this point in my life that even if someone is spared from the bad stuff, and by that I mean the gristle-and-spit-you-out variety of bad, they are still left with marks. Even the luckiest of us, those who only waddle in the shallow end of grief, have a patchwork of scratches and etchings when it's all said and done.

Everyone. It's like that shrub outside a bedroom window. It doesn't do much but sit there and look pleasant, except in a storm. Then it can be heard scratching up against the glass and the side of the house, screeching and rattling its branches. And that thing, although small and beneficent, doesn't seem like it'd do too much, even in a storm, but the windowpane begs to differ. Its grooves and lash marks will disagree with you.

So yeah, I took my time running my hand over Owen's chest, his belly, and even his shoulders, because one day he was going to be a man. And when that day came, he'd have the markings of life to prove it. Even in his best-case scenario, only attacked by a little shrub in a storm here and there, he'd still have the lashes of pain.

And for that, I felt sorry for him and for his perfection. Weepy almost, because I was already aware that I can't stop bad things from happening to the loves of my life, just as Mrs. Milhelm couldn't stop her daughter from being a victim. But I could try to shape the way Owen reacted when it was more than a shrub lashing against him.

I chuckled a little, but only in the back of my throat as a bit of truth rattled within me. If anyone could teach him to keep going after the worst, it was definitely Eddie and me. Well, more Eddie because even I acknowledge I went a bit off the deep end.

Owen's dressing got a little quicker after that. Not because I had wanted it to be over, but because I sort of, almost, realized that change—even the marring kind—is inevitable, but so is the evolution of strength. If you have a mind for it, that is.

What I didn't know at the time, however, was that I needed my own resolve to adapt, to grow stronger, for what lay ahead.

I heard a soft knock on my front door. I figured it was the postman leaving me something, so I didn't bother getting up to answer it. I just kept caressing Owen and taking him all in, holding tight to those small, gentle hands. The knock came again, soft as before, but now in a succession of six raps.

I rose and put Owen in his swing, near the front window, and then looked through the peephole. I saw the old lady from next door. I had already forgotten her name but remembered she liked gardening, had tried to pick on me with Eddie's help, her late husband used to work as a homicide detective, and that his career choice still seemed to scare her to this day. I also remembered that she was trying to scare me too, in her own subtle way. At least, that's the way I'd interpreted it. But her name . . . nope, that was gone, not in the memory bank.

By the time I opened the door, she had her back to me and her fist up in the air, shaking it. Her glance followed a small car zipping down the street. "Slow down, you speed demon," she barked out, a clash against her soft knocking from only a moment earlier.

Leaning against the doorframe, I said, "I don't think they heard you."

She spun back around. "Oh, Evelyn," she said, pulling her gardening hat off and revealing her gray hair. "I didn't hear you open the door. I'm sorry, what did you say?"

"I said, I don't think they heard you. One has to assume with all that speeding, they likely have the radio cranking too. Don't you think?"

She scoffed, waving at me. "Yes, the two often go hand in hand. But sometimes"—she suddenly looked sheepish, as if she were about to tell me a dirty little secret—"it just feels good to yell."

I stood back, letting her in, "You ain't just whistling Dixie," I said. "Come on in."

She smiled up at me and raised her small hand to pat my cheek. If it had been anyone else, I would've fantasized about pinning the hand behind her back and shoving her face into the wall. But not her. She meant well. Besides, I think I liked her. There was something both fascinating and familiar about her.

"What's up?" I asked, closing the door and watching her make her way into the living room.

"Oh, you know . . ." she said, trailing off and looking around.

I didn't know, which is why I asked, but thought it wise to keep my mouth shut until she got around to finishing her sentence.

"Where's the baby?" she asked.

I guessed she wouldn't finish that first sentence after all.

"Right over here." I walked over to the living room window.

The neighbor drifted over to him and let her mouth fall open in awe and wonder, looking at him as if he were a magnificent jewel. "May I hold him?" she asked.

"Of course," I said, bending over and unlatching him from the swing.

She took him to the couch and sat down, laying him in her lap, and stared at him in wide-eyed glee. A great many weird and fantastical noises came out of her mouth, but Owen loved it. He smiled up at her, a skill he had only picked up the other day.

Taking his little fists into her hand, she spoke to him. "Okay, I fess up. I came over here to see *you*. And I'm so glad I did. You're so handsome. You smell so good. Oh, I love little babies, I do!"

I couldn't help but smile at her fervor. She took a slow, relaxed breath in and then let it all back out again. She looked up at me, the baby goo-goo face suddenly replaced by the no-nonsense woman I'd seen during some of our previous visits. "This is 'what is up,' young Evelyn."

"So I can see," I replied. "Can I get you something to drink?"

"Oh no thank you," she said. "I was just outside in my yard when I heard your husband clanking around with his toys out back."

"That metal detector," I grumbled, bearing my teeth.

"Oh, but men need their hobbies, don't they?"

"Sure," I said. "A hobby, let's say, that doesn't involve bringing trash and rusted metal into my house."

She smiled and looked back down at Owen. "Yes, well as it is, I'd say you need to learn the fine art of 'accidentally' throwing your husband's things away."

I took a seat next to her on the couch. "Keep talking."

She laughed. "In due time, my dear, but not today. Yes," she said, looking down at Owen, but I assumed still talking to me because Owen couldn't comprehend words and whatnot, "I heard your daddy out back, playing with all his metal toys and I knew it was the perfect time to come and see you and your mommy."

"Why's that?" I asked, curious to know what she meant.

"Because Daddy might freak out a bit with what Ms. Marguerite is concerned about."

That was her name. Bingo! Marguerite. But she liked to be called Mag.

"Wait, what? Something's bothering you? About Eddie? Has he done something to you?"

She pursed her lips. The map of wrinkles around her mouth looked like she had sucked on a whopper of a lemon. "Good heavens," she said, "it's nothing about Eddie, dear. I just figured I'd bring something up with you first. And if you want to share it with him afterward, then by all means, please do so."

"Okay," I said, "but does what you wanted to talk about start with those tips on 'accidentally' throwing stuff away? I was wondering if I backed over the metal detector like ten or twelve times, could that still be interpreted as an accident?"

She gave Owen's nose the sweetest little tap and then looked at me, shaking her head. "You are one lucky lady to have that man out there love you as much as he does. Also, remind me never to anger you."

"Consider this your reminder," I said, giving her a wink.

"Fair enough," she said, her smile slowly dropping as I watched her expression turn somber. "Evelyn, dear," she started. "How versed are you in the . . . um . . . strange and unusual?"

I wanted to say, *"Hold on to your flipping hard hat while I tell you,"* but instead said, "I'm pretty versed, you could say."

"That's good," she said, balling Owen's tiny hands within her own again and rocking him back and forth upon her upper legs. "Do you believe then that God gives people, let's say, certain abilities which, if used properly, give them a glimpse into the darker things of this world?"

A little shiver went up my spine. Who was this lady?

I simply nodded in response.

"So then, do you believe that God equips regular people with what some would consider unusual gifts?"

"*Dateline*, right?" I blurted. "You've seen the episode?"

"I don't watch too much television, no. Which episode are you talking about?"

"You don't know my story? My past?"

"Only what your husband has told me over the fence, which isn't a lot. But this is about me and some dreams that I've had."

I leaned back into the couch, staring at her. "I'm sorry," I said. "Go on."

She scooted back, too, now laying Owen in the crack that formed where her cushion met mine. His legs kicked rapidly, his little bootied feet pounding against the couch. He was so happy. Must've been the outfit I put him in. It was awfully soft. Or Mag. She did have a calming presence even if she was getting a bit freaky on me.

"I've had these dreams all my life that feel like warnings, you see. My husband, Frank, would sometimes call them prophecy, but I don't know about that. Anyway, do you remember me telling you that he worked as a homicide detective?"

I nodded.

"Doing things that are similar to what Edward has told me you're doing these days."

I nodded again.

"It's a dark profession. I'm sure you're aware of this."

I didn't have any more nods to give. I could only stay there, pressing myself into the couch and letting Owen wrap his little fist around my finger as my line of sight lingered out the window, somehow knowing that Mag was about to take me somewhere I didn't want to go. I picked up Owen and pressed him against my chest, his head perched above my shoulder and looking around behind me.

"Sometimes all you see is the bad in the world and then it becomes like normal living," she said as she smoothed the length of her peach polyester pants. "Mayhem and mangled lives seem to turn into something as dry and simple as a bowl of cornflakes. When that happens, I believe people—good men and women in those types of environments—need to be reminded of where they're really at."

She paused. The length of the pause caused me to look at her again. That's when I realized she'd been staring at me the entire time, knowing I was letting my mind slip into pretty-la-la land rather than grasping at what she was trying to tell me.

But I had been listening. Sort of.

"Where is that?" I asked her.

"In someone else's mess," she replied. "I remember Frank said early on in his career that when you play in someone else's mess, their wrecked playground if you will, it starts to seem not so messy and broken-down after a while. He said he was afraid that would happen to him and many of the men in his precinct. He said most forget to stay vigilant and guarded, forget what they're up against, and how what they're up against never really rests. That's why I think I started having the dreams.

"It would start out innocent enough, but then the dream would take a turn for the worse." She put her index finger up to her chin and gave it a tap. Her glance fell to the floor and she gave herself another tap as if recollecting something. "There was this one dream in particular that comes to mind. It was about a dozen years ago, I believe. I had a dream that Frank was bowling with his friends. His friends were all policemen, mind you. Not to mention that Frank doesn't even like bowling, but there you have it. I dreamt all his policemen friends were bowling and having a good old time when all of a sudden, a black snake slithered out and went for their pant legs," she said, pointing down and flaring out her own pant leg for emphasis.

She had my full attention when she'd said *snake*. Not the courteous part of me that knew I should listen, but *all* of me, even the goose bumps rising on my arms.

"And that snake, he started biting them one after another. I remember feeling distressed, even in my sleep. I tried to wake myself, but when that snake went over to Frank, it started climbing up his body until it bit him right in the chest. That's when I woke up in a cold sweat. I shook Frank awake and begged him to wear that darn bulletproof vest the next day at work because I was afraid he'd get shot in the chest. He hated wearing that thing for an entire day at a time, but he pacified me."

"Did he go to a bowling alley that day?" I asked as my brows pinched together in suspense and anticipation.

"No. Several detectives gave him a hard time about his wearing the vest just because his wife had a feeling. But, two other detectives heeded my feeling and put their vests on that day, and you know what happened?"

No! For the love of Pete, no! That's why you need to tell me! I screamed inside my head.

"Those two detectives were doing a routine Q&A with a bowling alley proprietor about some vandalism on the outside of the building when a gunman came in, trying to rob the place in broad daylight. When he saw the detectives, he opened fire."

My eyes widened. I think I gasped.

"Those vests," she continued, pointing at me, "saved the detectives' lives. They had silver hole markings on them to prove where the bullets would've gone. The proprietor died that day, though. So sad."

I was looking out the window again, mesmerized by what Mag was telling me. Mesmerized by the cops who survived and how Mag's dream started it all. The old me would've said it was a fantastical coincidence, but I think Mag was right on one account: God equips.

"You came here to tell me something." I looked at her in panic.

She nodded.

"You've had another dream, haven't you?"

She nodded again, her eyes watering. Of all the neighbors, of all the neighborhoods . . .

The back door opened. Mag quickly stood from the couch and gave a warm smile to Eddie who had just made his way into the living room.

"Hello, young Edward," she said, her voice steady and soothing.

"Hello back to you, Mag," he said. "What are you up to today?"

She looked down to me on the couch and gave me a gentle nod, then looked back at Eddie. "Oh, your wife and I were doing nothing more than engaging in girl talk."

Eddie moved closer to us, smiling. "What sort of girl talk?" he asked.

"Periods," I barked out.

"Evelyn!" Mag exclaimed, looking like she wasn't sure whether to laugh or chastise me.

"She's a nonstop ball of fun, this one," Eddie said, bending down to kiss the top of my head.

Mag laughed a little at Eddie's comment and then said, "Well, no, we weren't talking about periods. I am, after all, past my prime in that regard."

My eyes shot to Eddie. I knew he wouldn't have been upset about what I had said, but Mag was pushing seventy and talking about a dried up baby baker but, alas, Eddie was handling it like a pro.

Mag moved toward the front door. "Evelyn, dear, walk me out front."

She got to the middle of my front lawn and faced the house, pointing to a small brick planter that Eddie and I had running alongside the very window Owen was swinging near when Mag came in.

"Right there," she said. "My young friend, right there is where I dreamt the snake was. He stretched up to the window and I could've sworn he was looking in."

I wanted to let my mouth drop open in fear and puzzlement, but instead, I kissed Owen on the cheek. Then again on his forehead. His swing would be moved. Immediately.

TWENTY

What a Tin Box Can Do

My phone rang. Jen's cell number popped up on the caller ID, and a small smile crept up on me. Things were definitely looking better if she was making a call. But then I heard her panicked breathing, crying almost, before she realized I had said hello.

"Evy?" she shrieked. "Evy, are you there?"

"Yes. Jen, what's wrong? Where are you?"

She let out a cry and in response, my free hand splayed on my kitchen counter, rigid in fear. "Evy, you have to come quick. Bring the police. I found . . . I found—," she said right before she cut herself off, crying again.

"Jen! What's wrong? What's happened? Are you okay?"

She made quick little huffs, letting out dry sobs. "Yes, yes, I'm okay, but I found a dead body. You need to come quick. With the police."

"You found a body? Where?"

"I was . . ." She stopped, taking in a deep breath. Then another. "I was going to go back to work today, but I was so scared. So I decided to face my demons. I came back here and I started digging—"

"Whoa, whoa, whoa," I interrupted. "Tell me where you are. Let's start there."

"At the . . . at the place where he raped me. At the place where the guard found me."

"The Senior Center?"

"Yes, hurry!"

I still wanted to know *why* she was there, but I knew that information would come later.

"I'm on my way. Stay put. Wait, no. Go inside. Are there people in the center?"

"I guess," she whimpered.

"Okay, go inside and be safe. Then call 911."

"That's why I'm calling you!"

"Fine, all right, I'll call. Stay put. I'm on my way."

By the time I got to the parking lot, a few crime-scene vans were already there, as well as a growing crowd of silver-haired patrons. It was about 10:30 a.m. and I was late because I had to feed Owen and then wait for Eddie to come home.

Judging by the number of elderly around, there must've been another event at the Senior Center. Before I could wonder too long if any of them knew what was going on in the far corner of their parking lot, I noticed that pervy old man trying to catch up to me, with one of his little buddies in tow.

He waved at me and I returned it quickly, with no intention of stopping my forward march to where I wanted to go. I could see Jen in the distance, standing next to Thatcher.

"Just a minute, young lady," the old man called out to me. I only slowed a little and craned my neck to look back at them, still keeping a safe distance.

"Now come on," he called out after me. "You're worth chasing down but where the mind is willing, the arthritic bones are weak."

Oh, fine. I looked once more to Thatcher and Jen but didn't think they had noticed me yet. Jen was talking and Thatcher was writing something down. Her hand kept going up to her face, touching her forehead, and then dropping back down in frustration.

Past them, in the same wooded area Jen had used to escape, there were a small influx of men and women in blue jumpsuits with gloves, booties, and eye gear. When one walked out from the crime-scene area, another walked in.

Twenty seconds. That's all I'd give the old man and his even older sidekick.

"I don't mean to run off on you gentlemen," I said, "but I'm needed over there." I pointed.

"Is it true they found a girl's body?" the pervy one asked.

They stopped me to gossip? Some social ills never die. "I'm sorry. What was your name again? I've forgotten it."

"It's Kirk," he said. "And this here is my buddy Bob."

Bob was looking over my shoulder to where the police and crime-scene investigators stood. When his friend mentioned his name, Bob gave the slightest eye contact, paired with a tight smile.

"You remember Bob, don't you?" Kirk asked. "He was that Navy boy I was telling you about. The one that left you and your boyfriend detective at reception because he didn't have the gutsos to let you just walk around."

Bob's smile, though constricted and miniscule, dropped as he glared at his friend. He then started waving his hands around. "You can't let cops walk around willy-nilly wherever they want to go," he said. "They're cops. All they want is to tell you what to do and where to go and own your every move."

I scoffed. "Well, I have no interest in owning you. Now, if you two will excuse me, I have no information to give since I myself just arrived, and even if I did have any news . . . well, you two are smart, you can figure out why I can't share it with you."

Bob turned first, only reaching back for his friend. "Come on, Kirk," he said, his free hand rubbing up and down near the side pocket of his gray slacks.

"Why? We still got twenty-some-odd minutes before lunch," Kirk said, his eyes getting excited as he turned to me. "It's Taste of the World Buffet Day. *Whooee.* Once a month and that's today. There's this one dark kid in the kitchen that makes up a mean dish of Indian curry. It'll give you the craps for the rest of tomorrow, but it's well worth it."

I closed my eyes, taking a slow, pained breath through my nose, and then let it back out again.

"How can you think about food or your bowels right now?" Bob asked. "There's a body out there."

They turned and walked away but I could still hear Bob. "You know what? Never mind. I'm going home. This place gives me the creeps. I don't like it here anymore."

Off they went and I headed back in Jen's direction. When she saw me, I could tell she had to fight back the urge to cry. She looked around to see if anyone noticed.

Somewhere inside my head, I wanted to commend her for being a champ, but truthfully, I needed to burn those distinctions that had bounced around up there for eons. Maybe if we all cried more, we could flood this place. We could wipe the scum away. It was hopeful, but these little tidbits of hope helped me get through the days and arrive back home donning a smile for Eddie and Owen. I often liked to picture those two blissfully oblivious, even about Mag's snake at the window.

"Have you told Thatcher everything?" I could see Thatcher out of the corner of my eye, nodding. "What happened?" I asked.

Thatcher looked at Jen. "Do you want me to tell her so you don't have to go over it again?"

"That's fine," Jen said in a hushed voice.

I noticed she was wearing the outfit I had seen on her bedroom chair the other morning. My eyes lingered on her blouse. Such a blouse was to that morning's business as a fresh rose petal was to a dump. It didn't belong.

"Ms. Ness decided to come back to the scene of her attack to find some closure," he said, his right hand making abbreviated, tense circles.

I knew that meant he was itching to do or say something. My guess was that he wanted to go look at the body rather than talk to Jen and me.

"She decided to go back to the rock formation where she had hid that night—"

"I wanted to give thanks that I'm still alive," Jen interrupted. She turned toward me and as soon as Thatcher was out of her line of sight, he walked off, turning into the wooded area. He really needed to work on his people-presence skills. His were simply woeful. Luckily, Jen didn't seem to care.

"So I put my thanks in a note and then put the note in a tin box," she said. "I was going to bury the box as a reminder that I'm alive. That I made it." She let her tears fall now. "I decided to come by here today because I was nervous about going back to work. I went to the rocks, working off memory and trying to fight off the fear. I mean, he could've been here, right?"

I nodded.

"But there were lots of those senior citizens around, so I figured I would be safe. Anyway, I got to the area where I had lain that night. I only had the lid and the box itself to dig with, and found that the ground in between the rocks was too hard. So, I went around to the other side of the rocks and could tell just by walking on it that the ground was much softer, like it had been tilled recently."

She grimaced, seemingly reliving a gruesome scene.

"I don't know why I did it," she said. "I mean, look at me." She ran her hands down her career outfit, now streaked with bits of dirt and leaves. "Why would anyone get down in the dirt and start digging wearing this? But then I told myself that my first day back at work didn't have to be this day, it could be tomorrow, but today I needed to start with my closure. So, I got down and dug."

Her voice trembled and her hand went back up to her forehead.

"I was just digging and digging with the tin . . ." She paused, closing her eyes. "That's when the weird smell hit me." She looked at me again. "All of a sudden, I just knew. And I've never smelled a decomposing body before, but it's like I innately knew something was terribly, terribly wrong.

"And then my stupid curiosity." Her hand went back to her head, as if she wanted to take it all back. "I did another two scoops and that's when I found her hair." She let her head fall back as she looked at the sky, sighing.

"I'm actually glad that's all I saw," she said. "Just some hair scattered around the dirt. That's when I jumped up and called you. I didn't need to confirm anything else."

"How long have Thatcher and the rest of them been here?"

She shrugged. "I don't know, maybe ten or fifteen minutes before you. What took you so long?"

"I had to feed Owen and then go out and find Eddie so he could watch him. Eddie was on a morning j—," I cut myself off, literally biting my own tongue and wincing at my stupidity.

Her arms crossed over her chest, and she shook her head. "It's okay, Evy. I get it. It's a double standard. It's an injustice. Whatever. The perils of being a woman."

I stretched my hand out to her elbow and squeezed it. "You didn't do anything wrong. You know that, right?"

"But I did. Didn't I? Men can go out and jog and it's no big deal, but I go out to jog and I get raped and pregnant and when I come back here to *try* to heal, I unearth a dead body. But you know what? Fine. It's just fine." Her face fell to an immediate flush and I could see the first drops of perspiration around her hairline.

"I've told your partner everything, I think," she said. "I even left the box back there. They can bag it or tag it or whatever they do to it, but I think I'm going to go back home now."

"Don't be mad, Jen, please."

"I'm not mad!" she yelled, making my eyes widen. "I'm . . . I'm . . . I'm frustrated! That's all. I had a good life before all this. I had a decent life. And now it's like this stuff, this horror, is following me wherever I go."

She covered her eyes with her hands. "I just want to go home, Evy. I'm sorry. I just want to go home."

"Do you want me to follow behind you? Or how about you come back to my house? I'll make you lunch or I'll take you out to lunch. You want to do that?"

She looked at me, biting her lower lip and her eyes welling up with a new ramble of tears. Suddenly, she reached out and hugged me, squeezing me tight. We stayed like that for a few moments, my arms trying to reach up from under hers to return the sentiment.

"Evelyn," she finally said in my ear. "We shouldn't be here. We don't belong here. This isn't our place and we can't dirty ourselves like this. Why are you doing this to yourself? How can you stand to see this and be a part of this after what they've done to your family, after they took your daughter?"

She was pinning my arms down, hers over mine, otherwise I would've been able to wipe the single tear that dropped from my check onto the shoulder of her pretty blouse. Her words hit my core because I had often said the same things: *We shouldn't be here; we don't belong here; this isn't our world . . .* But not in the way she was saying it. Not even by a stretch.

I wriggled free of her hold and then lifted my arms so I could hold her at arm's length. "Jen, if you only knew how right you are, but how severely you're misapplying it because you're stuck in the middle of unbearable pain. And maybe one day, when things start to look a little clearer for you, you'll realize why I feel I have no choice but to expose myself to this. As long as each day carries with it the hope that one less person, a person like you, or Eddie, or even my little Owen, doesn't have to see this Evil in the flesh. I'm so, so sorry you've had to see it, though. I can only offer you the comfort I try to find in it: I will never be able to dismiss the dire need to take a knee before God and beg for help, because I intimately know the true thirst of Evil within the world."

She nodded slowly.

"Evy, I'm going to go home," she said. "Thank you for your offer, but I want to rest and think about some things."

"Call me whenever, Jen. I'm always around. And look, just for kicks and giggles, how about I try to sneak past your doorman tomorrow night and bring a pizza?"

She gave me a little smile and then lowered her head, shuffling one of her patent-leather pumps in the dirt and looking like she was thinking something over. When she looked back at me, she said, "Sure, but can you sneak past him with Eddie and Owen in tow?"

"Of course!"

"I'd like to meet your baby, Evy. I really would," she said, drying her eyes.

After I watched her get into her car, one of the crime-scene guys nearly clipped my foot with an empty gurney as he hurried down the little path beyond me.

I guess it was time to retrieve the body.

TWENTY-ONE

The Special Place

I turned away, bending over quickly to put my hands on my knees and trying not to retch. Big breath in, and then several little breaths out. If it was supposed to work for that baby birthing business, then it should work here. But no, I still wanted to puke. Television, movies, real-life pictures, and even the fact I had once blown a guy away didn't quite prepare me with enough gruesome resolve. It wasn't on account of the brief look I got of her as two kneeling crime-scene guys were digging the last parts of her out; it was the sheer vulgarity behind seeing an innocent in this fashion.

All that pretty, flowing hair did me in. Though roughly three feet of dirt had covered her, and even if she had had her visitors of bugs, slugs, and maggots in that shallow grave, there was no denying that hair had once bounced and shined in the land of the living.

Deep breath in, deep breath out. It still smelled like rotting corpse even though I overhead one of the crime-scene guys say it was faint by now, her body having already done a good portion of decomposition.

"Are you all right?" a man's voice asked, coming from my right.

My hands were still on my knees, arms rigid and head down. I knew he was speaking to me, but I didn't bother straightening out to look back at him. I could see his shoes though. A pair of black Converse. They were the old-school high-top version, and he had them partially covered up with those little blue sanitary booties everyone but Thatcher and me seemed to be wearing.

"Nice shoes," I said to my inquirer, slowly standing up to meet his eyes. He had curly blond hair, severe looking black-rimmed glasses, and an impossibly young face. He also had a five-thousand-dollar camera right below his chin. I knew this because I had been shopping around online for a new one so I could take a bazillion perfect pictures of Owen.

"Thanks," he said. "You okay? Is this your first crime scene? Don't worry. It gets easier."

I gave him a small smirk. "How would you know?" I asked, trying to estimate his age. "What are you, twenty? How long can you have possibly been doing this?"

"I'm twenty-four, actually." He smiled as he answered. His tone almost matched the frivolity of his sneakers. "And I've been doing it for nine months."

"Nine *whole* months?" I asked.

"Yup, and I'd say it got better around the eighth month."

I chuckled.

"Is that funny?"

"Yes and no," I answered, shaking my head. "I like you. And your shoes. You're refreshingly young and hopeful."

"Um, thanks, I guess," he said. "I like you too. I've heard some stuff about you."

I was staring at his camera. "That's great," I mumbled. Then I pointed to his camera. "That's a nice camera. You take pictures of anything other than dead people?"

He nodded. "Of course. I also shoot pictures of all the evidence around dead people."

"Fascinating," I said.

"It is," he said. "But like I said, it takes some getting used to."

"What's the matter with you, then?"

An air of offense quickly encompassed him. "What do you mean? There's nothing wrong with me?"

"Let me rephrase. Why aren't you out in happy-smiley land, taking pictures of bun-side-up newborns and freshly coifed brides?"

He gave me an understanding nod, the curls hanging in his forehead bouncing slightly like miniature pogo sticks. "I like photography," he said, "but I don't like the fake universe it has become. These days it's ten percent the shot in the camera and ninety percent in photo-editing software. The photographers who have the busiest studios make their clients look the least like themselves. I'm not into that."

"So, that rationale just screams out photographing dead people then?" I asked. "Because it would be bad form to Photoshop bullet wounds and arterial spray?"

He smiled. "I'm actually a part of the investigative team, analyzing evidence and running down leads, so I'm not just a photographer who takes pictures of dead people and bullet wounds."

"Don't forget the arterial spray," I added.

"This job is the best of both worlds for me, if you want to know. I get to apply both my science and photo background."

"And wear Converses to work." I pointed down to his shoes. Then I looked past him and saw Thatcher putting on some of the blue booties. I hoped that didn't mean I was next.

"I'm Tyler," the photographer said to me.

I looked at Tyler again, extending my hand. "Hi, Tyler. I'm Evelyn." He put his hand out to me, but as soon as I saw the purple glove he wore, I pulled mine back. "Um, have you been touching . . . well, dead stuff?" I asked.

He laughed and lifted his camera toward me. "No. I'm taking the pictures, remember?"

"Why do you have the gloves on, then?"

"Standard procedure."

I looked over at Thatcher. Sure enough, the gloves were on. That's when I noticed another detective standing near Thatcher, hovering over the crime-scene investigators that were down on their knees and working to get the body out.

"Who's that guy?" I asked, pointing to the other detective.

"I think he's part of the local precinct, but this is a Central case. Ours."

"Ours?" I asked. "You work at Central?"

He nodded. "That's why I said I'd heard about you."

"I'll see you around, then," I said, proceeding past him to get to Thatcher.

Before I moved another ten feet, the detective standing near Thatcher said, "Stop right there." He held up his hand to me. "Who are you and why are you coming back here without any gloves on?" His voice was terse and desperately reaching for superiority.

"I'm Detective Thatcher's pet and I don't plan on touching anything." I looked anywhere but at the man addressing me. "So, crisis averted. You can calm down now."

Thatcher laughed.

The detective turned his scowl to Thatcher. "Why is that funny?"

Thatcher threw up his hands and shrugged, walking away from the group and coming to me. I figured there had to be something I didn't know about those two because I've hardly ever seen Thatcher back down when someone talked to him like that.

Before Thatcher got too far, he turned back to the other detective and said, "And she's right, Burke. She won't come much farther than she is."

Burke replied by looking over at me and saying, "Ah, don't have the stomach for it, do you? And if you don't have the stomach for it, what good are you? What can you do?"

I wanted to say, "I can breastfeed. Can you do that? No. So, shut up." But I didn't. I simply crinkled my nose at his remark until I could think of a better response, one that could be said aloud.

Thatcher spun me around and led me away. "Who's the meanie?" I asked as we cleared the area and found ourselves back in the parking lot.

"A detective from the local precinct," Thatcher said. "They're just giving some assistance."

"What's your problem with him?"

"My problem?" he asked, his face twisting in confusion, but his eyes were calm and knowing. Thatcher knew exactly what I was talking about but didn't want to spill it. "I don't have a problem with him. I barely know the guy," he said.

"Well, I barely know him and I already have a problem with him. Maybe I can say something on your behalf. You know, like metaphorically turning a dagger in his gut. I'm good at that stuff. Hurry, tell me his weaknesses."

"No. Geesh! No daggers in the gut, and no, I'm not telling you any of his weaknesses."

"Fine," I said. "I'll just put on a pair of those ugly purple gloves and walk back in there to ask him what your weaknesses are and we'll start that way."

He smiled. "Be my guest." He pulled out a spare pair of the gloves from his left pocket and handed them to me.

Thatcher had called my bluff. When he realized it, he put the gloves back in his pocket and said, "He was in the running for my job, but clearly I won."

"Clearly," I said.

"He used to work at Central, but then transferred out when I got the job. He's been itching to interfere and undermine me since your friend first turned up in this parking lot back when she did. I kept him at bay then, but as you can see he's managed to show up and try to meddle anyway."

"Can't you tell him to go away? If this is your crime scene, then tell him to beat it."

He hoisted his hands to his hips and looked back to where everyone was still huddled, the body now on the gurney. She looked like a large child, as miniscule as she was with hardly any flesh or muscle. Then again, she looked like a hollowed-out person. My stomach fluttered and I felt a bit dizzy, but I couldn't turn away. If this is how we end up when it's all said and done, why do we fight for our sovereignty as fiercely as we do? Truly, we are fragile and weak. Truly, the only thing that makes our species wonderful isn't something that gets buried in the ground and oozes out as the months pass. There was something more.

Thatcher replied to my query about giving Burke the boot. "We don't really know if it's our case yet, or I should say related to our case. And if it isn't, then this is a homicide in his area and he gets it. If so, he wants to make sure nothing gets messed up."

"Like me, having the nerve to walk around without booties and gloves?" My eyes went down to Thatcher's feet. "You look ridiculous by the way."

"Thank you. Where's your friend?" he asked.

"She left."

"What? Why?"

"She had a wee bit of a breakdown."

"What did you say to her?"

I quickly squared my frame off with his and furrowed my brows. "Why does it have to be something *I* said? Can't she have a breakdown for the sake of having a breakdown, on account of, oh, I don't know, uncovering a dead body in a shallow grave?"

Thatcher blinked once, then kept an unwavering gaze on me.

"Well," I said, "it really was the body that freaked her out, but I guess I sort of pushed her over the edge by commenting that Eddie was out by himself this morning on a jog."

"What's wrong with that?" Thatcher asked. "Of course a man can go out and jog by himself. You women can't because it's not safe. Learn these things."

"See? Why do I even tell you this stuff? You prove the point in every wrong way. But whatever. Do you need her again?" I asked, speaking of Jen.

He shook his head. "No, but Burke might."

"Oh, poor Burke might not get what he wants," I said, finding Burke's soured face in the small crowd of crime-scene techs. "When will you find out if that body is related?" I asked Thatcher. "And why is there hardly anything left of her?"

"One of the investigators said she's probably been out here for three months."

I counted the months backward on my fingers. "That would be right before Charlene's murder."

He nodded.

"Do you think this might be his first victim?" I asked.

"Maybe."

"So, why bury her?"

Thatcher shook his head. "I don't know."

"Thatcher?" I asked, half-looking at Tyler, the photo kid, who was packing up his camera in a stiff, black bag. "If that body is related to our case and he buried her here, and then brought Jen here to rape and murder her, then something else is here. This place means something to him. It's special in a very sick way."

"Agreed."

"Want some lunch?" I asked. "It's apparently Taste of the World Buffet Day. I've heard the curry will give you the runs. Care to try it?"

XI

The service call came through that I had to go back to the Senior Center because one of the machines was broken again. I could tell someone had been messing with it because a smaller sized screwdriver was tossed over in the corner and the marks to the cables were a close match. I picked up the screwdriver and put it in my bag just as he walked in and closed the door on the two of us. He had a look on his face that he was mad and he was going to do something about it.

I was only scared for a minute but then I realized I was better than him, my father, because I took it all the way. I purged the world and he could be next for all he knew. He had questions for me. Who was I? What did I want? Why did I put the picture in his wallet? Didn't I know how much trouble I could get him in?

I asked him, "What picture?" and then he spit on my shoe.

HE SPIT ON ME! I knew then that he'd die. I'd have to kill him. He was nothing because the strength I was building up inside now was everything. All the reassurance a man could need, telling me that I make my own destiny and my own rules.

"I saw you do it, that's how," he said. "I was coming back in early from my game because I had to take a leak and I saw you. I stood on the other side of that door and watched you." He pointed to the door that led from the men's locker room to the men's toilets. The top half of it was glass.

"I didn't say nothing because I thought you were trying to rob me and I ain't got nothing, but I was going to let you finish so you'd get fired. But once you left and I went to check my wallet . . ." He shook his head in disbelief, his lips starting to form up like he was going to spit again and I balled up my right hand, ready to punch him in his veiny nose.

"You think you're playing some sort of game with me?" he asked. "Do you know what could've happened if anyone saw that girl's picture in my wallet after they dug that body up? What kind of sick freak are you? What do you want from me? I know we've had our shared moments, but I don't do that." He sighed and looked at me funny again. "What sort of worthless, weak man goes that far? I just liked to smack them around a little and show 'em who's boss, but this?"

The fury pulsed so loud in my ears that I couldn't think of anything else other than wrapping my hands around his old neck. I felt my arms tremble and white flashed over my eyes like it did right before I killed them all, like it was nothing, like it was all nothing but a matter of me following through with what I had to do.

But the door opened and the white flash faded and I saw someone else standing there.

He had a smile on his face but he called my dad a faker and said that he always left to take a whiz whenever the other one was winning the hand. He was a weird noise that kept squawking when all I wanted was the white to come back and to squeeze my father's neck.

He had more to say, my father, after he told the other old guy to go away and then there was no way around it. I needed another one.

TWENTY-TWO

The Sky Is Blue . . . Somewhere

Thatcher rapped on my front door at five thirty in the morning. I knew he was coming but the sound of his arrival still made me jump. As quiet as the earth and all that was within her was at that moment, Thatcher coming to gather me for a body found in Torrey Pines felt like an intrusion of epic proportions.

He probably thought I'd open the door forthwith but I paused, thinking of Eddie and Owen lying in bed. Owen was back in dreamland and Eddie—last I checked—was giving me those sad eyes of his. I thought he was only feeling lonely, but when I quickly snuck back into the bedroom to do a last-minute shoe-choice swap, I heard him praying.

It was just a small whisper, really. "God, please protect her. Bring her back to me. Always."

A painful little ball of emotion seemed to have wedged itself in my throat, trying to suffocate me with the reality of knowing Eddie wasn't as oblivious to the dangers as I figured him to be.

He and I had discussed it over and over again: I didn't *have* to work with Thatcher. Yet, Eddie seemed resolved in the situation and up until that point, I had thought it was because he was enjoying his free time, totally unaware of the risks I sometimes felt exposed to.

Thatcher knocked on the door again, louder this time. I couldn't put it past him to kick the darn thing in next time if I made him wait any longer. I wanted to lie back down with Eddie and slip away into the little cocoon that felt snug, warm, and safe, but I owed Thatcher the fulfillment of my word. I had already agreed to christen the start of this day with a gruesome death.

"It's a dark day," Thatcher said to me as he drove us to Black's Beach.

Thatcher wasn't talking about the homicide, or even the case dragging behind like a plastic grocery bag stuck on a bumper. He was talking about the thick, dark clouds, a layer of cover that likely wasn't going to budge as the day progressed. The clouds seemed to have a purpose in sitting there, squat and heavy. I supposed they were also trying to scare the natives, threatening rain that would result in a ten-car pileup somewhere in the county. Rain was quite a freak of nature in these parts.

"It's a dark day, indeed." I wasn't talking about the weather at all.

I sighed, wanting to change the subject. "You realize what Black's Beach is, right?" I asked him.

He turned his head to me for a moment. I could tell he was tired. Or worn down. Probably both.

As the weeks and months progressed, and as the body count escalated, it seemed harder and harder to prevent any sort of contamination of this lifestyle onto my loved ones. It was boogeyman caliber thinking to be sure, but I felt convinced that the gunky, oppressive presence at those crime scenes tried to cling to me, like refuse, stink, and pain as old as sin itself. Yet if that were the case, wouldn't it be true that my loved ones contaminated me with their love and goodness too?

Thatcher was staring at the road ahead of us, letting his headlights do most of the work as he navigated along the dark, twisty road, leading us down to the coast. "Black's Beach is a beach, right?" he asked, having given my question some thought.

"Way to nail the obvious, Thatcher," I said. "But do you know what type of beach it is?"

"I'm guessing a black one. With black sand?"

"It's a nude beach, Thatcher."

"Really?" His interest piqued perhaps more than it should have.

"You didn't know?" I asked.

"Why would I know?"

"You're of the male species. I would think you'd know the GPS coordinates of all the nude beaches in the area."

"Well, how do *you* know?" he asked.

"Everyone who lives or has lived down here knows," I said. "I thought you learned your lesson over the map deal. Haven't you been studying?"

"I'm not studying nude beaches."

I looked out the window. The sky looked like a bunch of sooty lint balls pressing down. So many slumbering houses with only one eye open, a porch light left on. On a different day, one without the cloud cover, the sky would be red or pink by this hour, maybe a bit of purple to make people think the sky stretched as far as the hand of God. Rightfully, it did. The sky was beautiful somewhere though, right? Strike that. The sky was beautiful here. I just couldn't see it yet; maybe tomorrow. Maybe after we catch this demon.

"You want to know how I found out about Black's Beach?" I asked Thatcher.

"Does it start with, 'Back in my wild and crazy days when I had a clothing-optional philosophy'?" he asked, smiling.

"Yeah right." I continued watching darkened home after darkened home zip past as we drove to the sea. "It was this ex-boyfriend of mine—some idiot I was dating during law school. I thought he was being romantic, taking me up to the bluffs at Torrey Pines and saying we were going to see the sunset. He said he even knew of a special place for us to sit and watch it. When we got there, I tried to form some sort of emotional attachment to the setting sun so he'd think I was sentimental and whatnot. I couldn't muster it, though."

Thatcher chuckled.

"Anyway, I noticed people down below at the beach. It was late so it was hard to tell at first, but then I realized that the beachgoers didn't have any swimsuits on. We were far enough up on the cliff that you couldn't really make out, you know, contours, but I could still tell they were naked. I asked my him about it, and all he said was, 'Yeah, you wanna go down and join them?'"

Thatcher laughed. "Did you?" he asked.

"Of course I didn't."

"Did you dump the guy because he made the suggestion?" Thatcher asked.

"Specifically no, but it did add to my general presumption that he was a fool, and it was that general presumption that ultimately made me get rid of him."

Thatcher pulled into a dirt parking lot just off Torrey Pines Road. I sighed with both exasperation and fatigue, and that was before my feet hit the dirt outside the car.

The ocean and bluffs looked like they were still resting at that hour, quiet and soft, yet I could almost sense the horror both felt from the senseless death that occurred earlier, right on their borders. At least when the ocean or these crumbly cliffs took a life, they did so indiscriminately. No hard feelings.

Thatcher gently elbowed me as I stood next to him. "Well?" he asked.

"Well what?"

"How far down is it to the beach?"

"About 7,562 feet."

"Really?" he asked.

"No," I said and laughed. "I have no idea how far it is. Why would you think I'd know that?"

"I thought you said you were familiar with the beach."

"I said I'd only been up here on the bluffs, and even that was too close for me. It troubles me that you'd think those sorts of trail specifics are within my knowledge base. I told you on the way over here how I find this particular beach repulsive."

My eyes found the trailhead along with a weathered wooden sign with white lettering. I pointed to it. "Why don't you go see if that trailhead sign says how far down it is?" I asked.

"Because if I go all the way over there," he said, using a whiny voice, "I might as well just head all the way down."

"Sounds like you've developed a solid game plan, Thatcher. Good for you."

He huffed, tucking his hands into his pockets. "Are you coming down with me, yes or no?"

I looked back at the trailhead and then noticed a rickety, wooden fence that bordered the ocean side of the trail. There was also a yellow, diamond-shaped sign, its black and painted image synonymous with the warning of falling rocks. I especially liked the two-dimensional, androgynous stick figure it portrayed who had not only been bashed in the head by a falling rock, but was now plummeting to his/her death because the rickety fence was a good-for-*nothing* rickety fence.

"Let's go with no," I told Thatcher.

"What are you going to do if I leave you up here?" he asked.

"This, that, and some other stuff too."

"Of course," he answered. "Hold on, though." He walked over to the nearest crime-scene-unit vehicle and began a bit of small talk with one of the men standing by the opened van door. Thatcher grabbed a few items. Most notably, an extra set of those purple gloves. He waved them at me the entire time it took to walk back to me.

I grabbed the gloves and put a few of the fingertips into my mouth, suspending them while I zipped up my jacket, the cold now biting at me.

"What are you doing?" Thatcher asked, yanking the gloves from my mouth. I felt the glove material snap against my lower lip. "If we don't want your fingerprints all over everything," he said, "we definitely don't want your saliva everywhere." He turned to go back to the crime-scene vehicle, grabbed another pair of gloves, and marched back to me.

"Here," he said, giving me a curt look. "Don't put them in your mouth, or anywhere else. Just put them on."

"What if I don't touch anything?" I asked. "You didn't seem to mind at the last crime scene."

"Because I could watch you at the last one. Here, I think we've already established that I'll be down there, and you, the scaredy-cat, will be up here."

I stretched one of the gloves over my hand and more than halfway up my forearm, letting it snap back into position.

He pointed behind me and said, "See those guys over there?"

I turned and looked. "Yeah."

"They look like witnesses. Confirm that with the uniformed officer over there and then do whatever it is you do to enrage people into telling you what you want to know."

I gave him a stiff grin. "You get me, Thatcher. You really, really get me."

"Of course," he said. "And be careful because the last thing I need is you falling off this cliff."

"Fear not," I replied. "I have no interest in going off the cliff. That's why I'm not going down the trail." I also wanted to add that I didn't want to go down there on account of the dead body, but didn't feel it was pertinent to highlight such to Thatcher. Especially since he had already called me a scaredy-cat.

Thatcher turned and went down the trail.

On my way to the uniformed officer, I spotted the same photographer from the last crime scene. I changed directions and headed over to him. "And a good, unholy morning to you," I said. "How are you doing?"

He was squatting, one of his knees only millimeters above the packed dirt of the bluff, taking a picture. There was a small, white placard in front of him with the number twelve on it. After a final flash of his camera, he stood. "Hi there, consultant lady," he said, pushing his dark-rimmed glasses back to the top of his nose.

I crossed my arms over my chest, trying to sink into my thin coat as the wind raced up the sides of the bluffs from the ocean. "What's with these markers up here?" I asked. "I thought the crime scene was down at the beach."

He squatted again. He didn't do it to take a picture, but to point something out to me. He was showing me a wet spot. I put my hands on my knees and bent down, leaning forward and trying to see why the particular spot held his interest. It could've been motor oil or even urine. I shot him a confused look and then he pushed a button on his camera, letting the flash illuminate the area and revealing the spot's dark and congealed nature.

Blood.

My eyes darted to him. "He killed her here?" I asked him.

"I don't know," he said. "We don't even know if it's her blood or not. I did hear, though, that she's got bruising around her neck, just like the others, and then a gash on her temple. Guys think it's from this rock, but postmortem."

"If she was already dead when he brought her here, but she was dropped on this rock, would it still leave the blood?"

"Don't see why not," he said.

He stood, pointing behind me where one crime-scene investigator was doing a tire imprint. At least that's what it looked like.

"We found tire tracks coming in, nearly right on top of the ones going out, so he probably backed in and then drove out."

He pointed to another marker. "And we've only found one set of muddled footprints leading up to this bloody rock, then a scuffle here"—his hand circled the area I was practically on top of—"suggesting, as you noticed, he dropped her and then picked her back up. And then more muddled footprints all the way to the cliff. He threw her off there," he said, pointing west.

"Muddled?" I asked.

"Yeah, like he was dragging his feet on his way back to cover his tracks."

"How do you know it's only one set?" I asked.

He used his flashbulb to illuminate the ground once more. "He tried covering up his footprints by dragging his shoe in wide sweeping movements. You can tell the cover-up was done by one person, with one pair of shoes, from the start point of each sweep. Each point has the same rim and press pattern. But the sweeping movements didn't get everything, and from what's left, you can still see it's from the same pair of shoes. Hey, by the way," he added, "if you were going to puke seeing that other body, wait until you get a look at this one."

TWENTY-THREE

Built

I left Tyler to walk over to the officer and witnesses. On the way, Thatcher was ringing through on my cell.

"Yeah?"

"Are you sure you don't want to come down?" he asked.

"Yup, why?"

"There're already bystanders down here. You can come talk to them."

And see the dead body. I still wasn't interested in that. Especially one I assumed was naked, like the other ones had been, and had taken a nasty free fall off a sheer-faced cliff. She was probably mangled. Tyler's warning seemed to indicate such. My steel-cut tongue didn't have a partner in my lily-livered nerves when it came to seeing that sort of thing. I kept thinking it would change but I was sure of it now: I didn't want it to change.

"Nope," I told Thatcher. "I don't want to talk to them unless you send them back up here."

"Fine, but I'm keeping tabs on how much you're backing out on me," he said.

"Noted."

"Stay up there and I'll talk to the people down here. Have you talked to those other witnesses yet?"

"I was on my way when you called."

The three witnesses were sitting on what I could only liken to a hitching post, a wooden barrier at the end of the dirt parking lot. Out on the road, just beyond the lot, a few more cars had lined up since Thatcher and I had first arrived. Either lookey-loos or surfers wanting to ride the early morning swells. Maybe even a nudist or two, waiting to pull into the parking lot and let it all hang out. This was Black's Beach after all.

A patrol car blocked their access but it didn't stop them from getting out of their cars, some even standing on the hoods to get a better look.

The three witnesses whom the officer had detained were all men, two of them looking as if they were friends because they sat close to one another on the wooden rail. They were young—sixteen or seventeen tops—still in high school and seemingly in no hurry to get there on a Monday morning. This crime scene made an interesting excuse for their tardiness.

The third witness sat about four feet to their left. He was long and muscular with a look of impending doom and perpetual frustration etched on his face. Unlike the other two, he appeared to have somewhere to go and had to be there long before he seemed to think the cop would let him leave. Not to mention his destination likely wasn't a place where a note from Mommy would get him out of trouble for being late.

There was a side conversation ensuing between the two young ones as I walked over, but it came to a stop when I got within fifteen feet.

"You three saw something?" I asked.

One of the friends said, "Yeah. They told us to wait here. We're the ones who found the body."

"Together?" I asked. "You all saw it at the same time?"

The older one answered, the guy who had somewhere to be. "No. I was here first, and these two," he pointed to the boys, "pulled in right after me. They were still getting into their wet suits when I headed down. I saw her first from the trail. They started coming down, but I shouted for them to go back and get help while I went down to see if she was still alive. They had already made the 911 call and were waiting for the police when I got back up."

"What did you do to the body once you were down there?" I asked the older one.

"Nothing," he said. "She was pretty banged up. Once I was close enough, I could tell she was dead." His head dropped and he shook it in despair. Looking at the ground beneath him, he said, "People who look like that aren't alive. So, I came back up."

It made me that much more glad I hadn't gone down there.

One of the kids stood up, eager to speak, "And we're the ones who called 911."

"I already said that, you ding," the older guy said.

"Yeah, well, we're also the ones who Tweeted everyone saying dawn patrol was canceled today because of a dead chick on the beach."

It occurred to me that the two younger ones didn't have much else to add. If they had, they would've led off with something more riveting than repeating their feat of the day: calling 911.

The big guy let out a huff.

I looked at him and something occurred to me. Muscles, his muscles.

My index finger went up to let them all know I wanted a moment of their silence and when I had it, I pulled my cell back out and placed a quick call to Thatcher.

"Everything all right?" he said when he answered.

"How much do you think the victim down there weighs?" I asked.

"Um, I don't know. Hold on," he relayed the question to someone else. Probably the medical examiner who was better versed in eyeing such things.

A muffled voice replied, "Between one-thirty-five and one-forty."

"A buck forty," Thatcher said. "But she's really thin, so I'm not sure about that."

"She's tall. I'm right," the muffled voice added.

"Yeah, but skinny women don't weigh—" Thatcher began, but I interrupted.

"Don't even finish that sentence, Thatcher. Skinny girls aren't all in the one-tens, so be quiet." I hung up the phone. I weighed one-thirty-five and that was on the low end of the range for someone my height.

I looked over at the oldest surfer again. Even sitting on the wood beam with his wet suit looking like a thick, black coating over his form, his girth and strength were obvious.

"What's your name?" I asked him.

"Jet."

My nostrils flared. "Seriously?"

He folded his arms across his chest, straightened his legs out underneath, and then cocked his chin up at me. "Yes. Jett. Two *T*s."

"Okay," I said. "Jett." I turned to the kid who had called 911. "And what's your name?"

"Matt. Also two *T*s."

I smiled. "Matt, do you think you could pick me up?"

"As in try to hit on you?"

I brought my hand up to my forehead and let my face sink. "For the love of . . . Let me be clearer," I amended. "Matt with two *T*s, do you think you are able to lift me up from the ground and carry me?"

His eyes said no, but his ego made him puff his chest out and say, "Of course I can." He stood.

"Okay, Matt," I said, shoving my cell phone back into my pocket and holding my arms up so he could pick me up and cradle me. "Just do that typical damsel in distress hold. One arm around the back of my knees, and the other in the middle of my back."

He looked nervous but still carried that hint of good old machismo. I put my arm around the back of his neck, wanting to help him a little as he bent down to lift my legs. It was against the point of my experiment but then again, I really didn't see the benefit in him dropping me on my rear because he was too prideful to admit he couldn't bear my weight.

The muscles in his neck strained and I was pretty sure he was holding his breath. I jumped out of his arms. He would've surely let me fall otherwise. He was an average-sized teen for his age and about my height, five-eight. He had a slim, but not string-bean, physique, with enough muscles to sustain his surfing habit, and maybe even lift a few ladies if they were in the five-four, five-five range with only a hundred or so pounds on them. But not that poor lady on the beach, and not me.

The other victims were shorter, smaller. Jennifer was about my dimensions, but he hadn't carried Jennifer to a cliff and tossed her off.

"You, Muscles."

"It's Jett," he answered me.

"I know. I just can't bring myself to say it."

"You're a real tart, you know?"

"Right on the money, but let's go."

"What if I don't want to?" he asked.

"You do. Show up the pip-squeak, come on."

"Hey!" Matt interjected. "You were heavy," he said.

"For you. It's okay. Just date shorter women." I turned back to Muscles, Jett, whatever. "Come on," I said to him. "Don't make me tell you this is police business and force you to do it."

He gave me a blank stare.

I turned my head away from him for a moment, trying to think of something else that would make him comply, when I was whisked off my feet and held tightly against his solid chest. He started to walk, quickly, to the edge of the cliff, cutting in through a break in the fenced-off "Danger Zone."

He swung me back, as if he were winding up to toss me over, and I screamed, thinking I was but moments away from being chucked to my death.

"Put her down!" a voice yelled from behind. It was the uniformed officer.

I craned my neck to see him and noticed he had his weapon drawn, pointing it at us.

"She asked me to do it!" Jett shouted back. He then dropped me to my feet, only hanging onto the sleeve of my coat so that I wouldn't topple off the cliff—a minor courtesy.

He pulled me back with him a few steps before fully letting me go. I looked into his eyes and realized he didn't intend to hurt me. The officer had already holstered his gun.

"I wasn't going to throw you, but you got a smart mouth. I'm sure you've made many people think about it," Jett said.

"Eh, so I've been told." I straightened out my shirt and coat. "Listen, though," I said before he walked off. "Was I heavy for you?"

"No."

"You don't need to lie through your testosterone. This is for a homicide investigation and no one else can hear us right now. Be honest. Hard, medium, or easy?"

"Medium. I wasn't straining if that's what you're thinking. I wouldn't carry you a mile, but I could carry you a bit without putting you down."

"What about chucking me off the cliff?"

"I thought I wasn't allowed to do that."

I shook my head at him, curling my lip. "No, I'm not asking you to do it. I'm asking if you could."

He nodded. "I throw hundred-and-fifty-pound tires with my bud at the back of our gym."

"Mercy," I muttered. "Why? Just why?"

He opened his mouth to answer, but I put my hands out to stop him. "No, no. It was rhetorical. I don't need to know. Anyway, I take it you do weight lifting."

He shrugged.

"No, seriously. I need to know."

"Yeah, I do a lot of weight lifting."

"Hold on," I said, reaching for my phone and calling Thatcher again.

"Thatcher? Did the victim make contact with the face of the cliff, or did she just land on the beach?"

He passed the question to that other someone else on the beach and they had another dialogue I couldn't hear. Thatcher must've been holding his phone against his shirt.

Thatcher answered, "Landed on the beach according to the ME. She was actually in the tide at one point, pretty waterlogged, but it never took her all the way out. ME said his guess is that she was thrown out at a distance to avoid the face of the cliff, rather than rolled off, which would have done much more damage to the body than is present."

"So, he has to be a strong guy," I said, "like my new friend Jett."

"Who's Jett?"

"I'll tell you later. Bye."

Speaking to Jett, I asked, "How much do you work out in a week?"

His face lit up, a manner of pride and accomplishment. "Seven days a week. A few hours a day."

"You have a job?" I asked.

"Yes."

I shook my head at him, wondering if I had to spell everything out. "*What* is your job?"

"Why?"

"Because it will help me find a killer."

"I bartend."

I leaned forward as I waited for the rest of his answer to spring forth. His mouth had stopped moving, but his eyes seemed to be going over the rest of the details like the tail end of the credits rolling in an empty theater.

Yet he didn't give anything else up. "You're lying."

He didn't seem as offended as I expected. I pointed at him, trying to figure out what he wasn't saying and then it came to me. "It's a lie, but only *half* a lie," I said. "Jett! Of course, I should have known it the second you told me your name. Okay, so you bartend, but you do something else after you pour the drinks, don't you?"

He sighed and then answered in a lowered voice, "I do bartend for about an hour each shift. The other four hours of my shift . . ." He looked at the ground and rubbed the sides of his mouth with his hand, looking like he was either trying to find a way to say it or he was second-guessing saying anything at all.

"You strip," I said, having figured it out.

His eyes darted back to mine while his mouth hung slightly agape. "Yes, fine. Can I go now?" he asked. "I'm late."

"What for? It's the crack of dawn on a Monday morning. Isn't this a recovery day for you?"

"What's that supposed to mean?" he asked.

"Whatever it needs to."

"I have somewhere I need to be, all right? It's nothing related to my job, but I don't really feel like telling you anything else because you're already having a field day at my expense."

"Oh, fine," I said. "Tell me your real name and I'll leave the stripping deal alone."

"Hank."

"So, Jett it is. Noted."

He turned and started to walk away from me.

"Wait, wait, wait," I said. "Just a few more questions and then I'll call my partner back up here. He's the one who can let you leave."

He put up his hands in frustration but then nodded, letting me continue.

"Okay, so with your job, you typically have several free hours during the day to do what you want, which is surfing and a lot of body building, right?"

"Yeah."

"Because if you didn't have a job that gave you that much free time, you wouldn't be as built as you are, right?"

"I guess."

"And, from the amount of hours you put in, do you think a guy with a normal nine-to-five job could get biceps like yours?"

He scoffed. "No. Please. Guys in offices and desk jobs are mushy." He looked at the officer. "Even that guy is mushy and he's on his feet a lot. But because he's at work all day, he's got no time to spend at the gym."

I yelled over to the officer. "Do you have time to go to the gym?" I asked.

He nodded. "At the precinct weight room, sure."

I looked at his left hand, spotting a gold band on his ring finger. "How much time do you get to put in before the wife starts to complain?" I asked.

He chuckled once. "I can probably squeeze in thirty minutes a few times a week."

I looked back at Jett.

"Nowhere near enough time to build this up," he said, spreading his arms out.

About thirty minutes later, I heard a grinding and cranking noise. The coroner and a few of the investigators were pushing and pulling a gurney up the steep slope, a dark-blue body bag strapped on top. The morning was still a monochromatic pallet full of gray, offset by the strained faces of the four men pushing up the gurney. I'd still take the darkened, gray morning over what I imagined was a fury of black and purple on the body inside that bag.

Thatcher made his way over to me. "Are you done here?"

I nodded. "That officer is waiting for you to release the witnesses."

"Fine," he said. "Then we're going to follow the coroner's van back."

TWENTY-FOUR

Notepads

Outside the station, I saw Burn. I told Thatcher to go inside without me and then I walked over to the concrete planter Burn was sitting on. It was still early in the morning, with hardly anyone up and on their way to wherever they needed to go. Burn wasn't the only homeless person around at that moment, as he usually was when I saw him, likely because they were free to move around without public hassle at this time of the day. I also figured they'd all been up about the same time I had risen that morning thanks to the biting cold.

I didn't truly know anything about it one way or another, though. The more I thought about Burn and others like him, the more I wondered if there was something meaningful I could do to help. That line of thinking often made my insides feel like a bucket with a big, fat hole in the bottom—what good would it do if I gave everything and that still wasn't enough? Then again, by the way Burn sprung up from where he was sitting, looking eager to talk to me, something seemed to be working, even with the little I tried to do.

He strolled over to me, the rattle and bang of his cart echoing through the concrete expanse known as Police Plaza, between the street and the front door. As he got closer, I patted down my pockets looking for an offering. Not only was I devoid of the pens and notepads that I'd been swiping from Thatcher to give to Burn, I had no money either. He seemed to appear more on Tuesdays and Thursdays, and on those days I was prepared. But it was a Monday. He was a day early and I was twenty dollars short.

"How ya doing, Baby Eater?" he said.

"I have no money on me today, my friend. I'm sorry."

"I don't want your money," he said, chomping on his lower lip as soon as he completed the sentence.

"Why not?" I asked.

"I want it but that's not what I want right now," he said, keeping a tight grip on his cart behind him. He was wearing a new hat and jacket, and I looked at both for a moment. They weren't only new for him, but were *new* new, as in someone had recently ripped the price tags off. Both items were in the military-gear category. The desert-camouflage hat was wide-brimmed and floppy with a pull string hanging beneath his chin. His jacket looked standard Army green.

"I have no pens or paper either," I said, assuming that would be the next thing he'd ask for.

He turned to his cart and lifted up a torn off piece of cardboard that he used as a covering. "You want some?" he asked, pointing down. "I got plenty."

I looked. "Huh. You do have plenty. Are those all from me?"

He shook his head, chomping again. The strap from his hat swung back and forth and I could tell he liked it, probably liked to hear it *swoosh* against the crisp material of his jacket. "No, wasn't you. I bought these."

"Why buy them when I give them to you for free? The only reason I keep giving you new ones is because you say people steal them from you when you're asleep. Over and over I've heard that, but by the looks of it," I said, bending my head over his cart again for another peek, "you haven't lost any of these pens. You're hoarding them."

He slammed the cardboard piece back in its place, his pupils dilating. "What's it to you, Baby Eater?"

"Calm down. It means nothing to me. Keep them all. I don't care. Where are the notepads, though? Do you still have those?"

"Yeah, yeah. Those aren't up for sale."

"Wait, so you're selling the pens? How enterprising of you."

He nodded, tapping his hand down on the cardboard covering his stash. "I got a business plan," he said. "Pens are a nice commodity on the streets, you know. Especially with the young ones. They wanna write letters because they're scared and wanna go home. They try saying sorry and ask for amends to a parent or sibling or grandmomma, even a neighbor up their old street because sooner or later the young ones wanna eat crow if it means theys got a bed and a meal."

"That's quite a truth, Burn," I said.

He waved his hand at something in front of his face and then took a quick peek over his shoulder before he went on. "'Cept, then there's the ones out here because theys folks are the ones who tossed 'em out. Those young ones still wanna write those letters of amends, 'cept they're not the ones who have to eat crow. You know what I mean?" he asked.

"I do." My mind suddenly flooded with thoughts about young people on the street. The fears, anxiety, and pain they must confront on a daily basis. And thinking that way made me remember this rotted old specimen of an attorney at my old law firm, one of the partners. When I had first told him I was pregnant with Corinne all those years ago, he only had one thing to say, and it was a great bit of stupid if I say so myself. He said that once I started having babies, the opening of my womb would make me soft, the likes of no man's shame. That I'd suddenly turn into a bleeding heart, cry at commercials, and have the gall to ask for time off to see kids in plays and soccer games.

Oh, I was going to show him, wasn't I? That's why I kept working insane hours after Corinne was born. That's how Corinne got her nanny. That's how Corinne slipped through my fingers forevermore.

Yeah, go ahead, womb. Consume me. I'd rather choke up at commercials and lose jobs than pretend I'm not a woman who cares about children.

"Burn?" I asked, thinking about those minors on the street. "How many teens are out here?"

Like Burn had said, sometimes it was the teen's fault, and other times it was the parents', but they were all still kids. To me, there was no greater allegory of mankind's fall from grace than a teen living on the street, subjecting themselves to who knows what because of a love lost, forgotten, even scorned.

"Theys come and go," Burn said. "There's always a bunch. But listen to the rest of my plan. I have the pens to sell and I can sell thems a piece or two of paper, but if I could get my hands on some envelopes and stamps, I'd be in business right quick!"

"Yes, and you could call yourself PostCart," I said, pointing to his cart.

"Are you making fun of me?"

"No. Sorry. Sort of. It's not funny. Is that why you wanted to talk to me?" I asked. "To get stamps and envelopes?"

His brow furrowed. "No, but do you have 'em? Could you get 'em for ol' Burn?"

A thought occurred to me. "I think so," I said, figuring I'd be buying the supplies this time instead of swiping them from Thatcher and his division. It was fun for a while—the thrill of building up Thatcher's frustration—but the idea that came to me about Burn's PostCart would be better served if it weren't steeped in petty theft.

"And, I'll give that stuff to you on one condition," I said.

"You ain't gonna get freaky on me are you?" he asked. "'Cause one thing I've never gotten into all these years out here is that sex-for-hire business."

I groaned, my eyes wincing in disgust.

Burn added, "I'm just sayin' 'cause it's a pretty common request out here. I can't tell you how many times—"

"Burn!" I exclaimed. "Please, no. Stop, no, this has nothing to do with sex-for-hire. I was only going to ask if you'd let me come along with you when you give—I mean sell—the materials to the teens to write their letters."

He started shaking his head before I had even finished the request, also giving me a horrified and hollow look. Somehow, I think he would have been less offended if I had, in fact, solicited him for some pants-dropping.

"Why not?" I asked him.

"You shouldn't, that's why. You shouldn't see what we have to do."

"Says who? You? Come on, I just want to help."

"Theys mean business out there and it's those teens that do most of theirs commands."

"Wait," I said, "What are you talking about? The teens are bad?"

"Some are but I'm talking about the same ones who told me to burn it down."

Oh, *them*. And *that*. When Burn had brought this stuff up before, I had figured it the ravings of a man whose mind was the consistency of a smashed cracker. That he had mentioned it either for shock value or to establish a sense of power in my eyes. But the delusion, if it were only that, persisted. Was it real? Did he really burn something down? If so, who else knew about this?

"Who exactly are they, Burn? Real people?" I hated asking it, but had to.

"Theys real enough, sure are."

Even if actual people weren't involved, they might either be figments of Burn's imagination or real manifestations of the worst kind. Society might turn their noses up at the homeless, but the Devil and his minions never turn away an open vessel—no matter where they find one, no matter how they find one. They only want the vacancy.

"Are they the ones who gave you your new hat and jacket?" I asked.

He pawed at both, giving me a look of panic, as if he was worried I was going to punch him in the gut and rip them off him. He started to turn from me.

Sure enough, I thought. He wouldn't have been so protective of his new gear if it weren't such a high commodity to him. I imagined high commodities on the streets came in one form alone: gifts. And in order to give a gift, one had to have real fingers with warm blood running to them. That didn't stop them from being of the monstrous demon sort, though.

"Come on," I said to Burn. "I'm harmless. And besides, if I'm good enough to get the supplies from, aren't I good enough to pass them out? I mean sell them."

"No, no," he said, shaking his head again. He put both hands on his cart and turned it around to face me, looking like he was about to shove past.

"Okay, but you looked like you had something to tell me earlier, when you first saw me. Do you need something?"

He clamped his teeth and scrunched his face. Then he said, "Oh yeah. I came to tell you I liked you."

I couldn't help but smile. My words of gratitude and reciprocation were on their way out when he spoke again. "So don't die."

My eyes blinked a few times. Part shock, part horror. "I'm sorry, what?"

Then he turned abruptly and started to trot away.

I wanted to grab at him and make him explain, but I knew better than to make sudden movements around Burn, especially if it meant restricting his movement. Left only with the solution to repeat myself and hope he answered, I called, "What do you mean, Burn? Anything specific you're talking about?"

He turned his face to his shoulder to address me, but kept on walking. "You don't notice the black car?" he asked, shouting back at me. "Don't get in it, that's what Burn's saying!"

I looked around, nearly spinning myself to the ground as the street and neighborhood seemed to blur and focus in rapid measure. Then I breathed deliberately, pressed my hand to my forehead to slow my thoughts, and took a paced, careful look at all the cars in the vicinity. Of course there were several black cars parked on the street. But not one of them was occupied.

I let my hand drop down and rest at my side, taking another deep breath. That was Burn for me, I told myself. I couldn't really trust anything he said. At least, that's what I told myself to slow my pulse.

TWENTY-FIVE

Choice

The rest of the day had nothing else going for it except for heavy doses of sulking. The early morning homicide and Burn's particular brand of crazy bothered me a bit too much. Perhaps it was time to tell Thatcher about Burn, but odds were Thatcher would label Burn a lunatic, send him packing, and demand I stop giving him the notepads. But I believed this was the hand dealt to me—for my eyes only. I didn't want to lay my cards on the table just yet, so I was keeping them close.

Then there was that sinking feeling that even if we caught this rapist and murderer, wouldn't there be more after him? Facts, circumstances, methods, and faces would change, but at the end of it all, I finally understood what thousands and thousands of police knew: there is no peace and there's always a new mess.

It gave me a whole new respect for cops. Still, I was pretty sure I wasn't cut out to be a part of their fold in the way Thatcher had hoped. The overpowering feeling that goes along with spinning your wheels was maddening. Being a lawyer in the old days, I was versed in spinning my wheels because, if I'm being honest, that's what attorneys are paid to do. But this police work—and having innocents involved—was like having a gas-station toilet as your one and only commode. Get used to the heebie-jeebies because the surface never gets cleaned. Not really, anyway.

I didn't know how much more of it I could take.

"I'm not sure I should give you this right now," Eddie said, standing over me while I pretended to sleep the bad feelings away on the couch. "But I think it'll be worse if I don't show you and then you find out I was withholding it from you."

I looked up at him with one eye, leaving the other closed. He was holding a sheet of paper in one hand while cradling Owen against his chest in the other arm. "Is it bad news?" I asked.

"It's not bad as much as it is frustrating."

"Are you speaking from your point of view or mine?"

"Mine."

"What about from mine?"

He backed away, carefully laying the sheet on an end table we had near the front door. "Owen wants to go for a walk. He told me so. I'm leaving this here for you to read, you know, whenever."

I jumped up from the couch. He unbolted the lock on the front door and opened it. "Just, please, try not to break anything after you read it," he said as he crossed the threshold and closed the door behind them.

I grabbed the sheet. It was a printed out email from the assistant district attorney up in Fresno, the one who was responsible for prosecuting my daughter's killer, Gordon Racobs.

There was another delay in bringing that demon to trial.

That piece of junk pedophile was still having heart problems. Cry me a flipping river! Couldn't we just get this over with and have someone give him one giant scare, or force-feed him a cartload of bananas? Dose up on that potassium, child murderer. Your degenerate ticker will love it. Trust me.

This was not the first setback in Racobs's prosecution, but it was the first since I had moved away, when I was now unable to barge into the Fresno DA's office at will to scream and shake my fists at their tightly wound, complacent little faces. Each assistant DA's expression seemed to calculate how I was number 432 in their grand scheme of whom they'll try to fry in the calendar year. So there. Get back in line. You got your ticket number from the little red dispenser, right? Good. Shut up.

The last delay occurred on the first—the original first—day of trial. Eddie and I were dressed in what I lovingly called "lynching attire" and sat in the courtroom, almost salivating for the gavel to drop. Right between Gordon Racobs's eyes, if anybody had asked or bothered to poll for preferences.

But then, that wee little toothpick of a woman, Racobs's defense attorney, Lisa Posey, started doing her song and dance about Racobs's "surprise" heart issues. I thought I had only been squeezing the ever-loving juice out of Eddie's hand, but based on the judge's threats to me, I guess I had actually acted out what was playing inside my head: standing up and panting, mumbling something to the effect of wanting to break Racobs and anyone associated with him.

Eddie pulled me back down into my seat and reminded me that I'm not allowed to break people. Noted. As far as courtroom etiquette goes, that was.

When Posey started spouting off portions of the Eighth Amendment, how making Racobs endure a stressful trial for his life in his current condition could be interpreted as cruel and unusual punishment, I jumped up again, highlighting her version of so-called cruel and unusual punishment with what Racobs did to my child's body.

Some sparsely applauded my outburst—I think it was another mother—and then the judge threw me out. This was another one of those televised moments of my life. Local only, though, so I considered it a win.

Now, after reading the email Eddie had left by the front door, I walked to the corner window in the living room and opened the shutters to see if Eddie was still milling around nearby. He wasn't. He was probably already down on the sand. I started calculating how much time I had alone so I could put in yell-ridden phone calls to both the ADA and that stinking defense lawyer before Eddie came back and told me to simmer down.

Instead, I stuffed it. I was already feeling worn down and exasperated. People like Eddie—calm, cool, and collected people—would've said it was the right thing to do. But what Eddie didn't understand is when I stuffed it down, it reared up elsewhere.

That elsewhere was in a nightmare later that night.

I dreamt someone shoved me in a car, an old black sedan. Two thugs flanked me on the back seat. Uncharacteristic of me, I was scared silent by their presence. The thugs, somehow cognizant of my fear, started mocking me for my weakness. Their faces painted with both wicked smiles and malevolent sneers, they said nothing. They didn't have to. Their abhorrence of me was second only to the fact that they wanted to crush me into submission.

I was waiting for one of them to start cracking his knuckles, or to fling a bit of spittle at me with a, "You're going to pay."

There was a simple shadow up in the driver's seat and a lanky, slippery looking fellow beside him. That guy, the slippery one, was unbuckled and now faced me as he crouched back on his knees, ready to pounce like a cat. No, not a cat. Something more sinister. Something that eats away at living, wriggly flesh. He was half the size of the two thugs beside me and based on that, it occurred to me that he was the venom and they were the bite.

"You want to scream," he said to me. It wasn't a question. He knew it was true.

"Go ahead," he teased. "I'll even open the windows."

The windows opened. The day was bright, high noon, and the street crowded with other cars and pedestrians.

"Help yourself," he said, smiling.

I looked at him as if he were all sorts of stupid. Of course I'd scream. Of course someone would help. There were so many people around and all it would take was one person to notice or hear me.

I screamed. I screamed for help, I screamed for my life. I even screamed that there were no-neck imbeciles who smelled of wet dog hair and smudged newspaper ink holding me hostage. I did this even as the sedan came to a stop, idling at a red light. People passed by on foot, only an arm's length away from the windows, but none seemed to hear or care.

Nothing. No one did anything. No one even turned their head to stick out their tongue and gloat about their indifference.

Venom laughed but I was too stupefied to care. I screamed again. I did it until my voice went hoarse. More laughing from that slimy looking jerk up front.

I didn't understand. How could it be? How could no one hear?

To answer my confusion, Venom said, "Look again. Tell me what you see. Because what I see is that your God may have the world, but I have its souls."

I looked. It was too preposterous of a statement not to.

All the men, the women, and even the children, had a black creature on their bodies. The creatures' haunches rested on the backs of the hosts' shoulders, their black, sinewy forms of shadow and neglect curled over host heads, claws digging into each and every forehead.

"What are they?" I asked, my voice feeling choked and steeped in panic.

"You know what they are," he said, almost hissing. *"May their eyes be darkened so they cannot see, and their backs be bent forever."*

The slimeball was quoting Scripture to me.

I turned away in disgust. I told myself to wake up. I told myself it wasn't true. Game over. Evy wasn't having fun any longer. Wake up, wake up, WAKE UP!

Venom pounced on me, grabbing me by my hair and forcing me to look at him, his eyes glinting from red to black to something eerily human and familiar, and then he forced me to look back out the car window to all those hunched demons and oblivious humans.

He held my hair tighter. I worried he was going to rip whole chunks out and then felt a wisp of steam hit the side of my cheek as his fiery breath came at me. He leaned closer to me, speaking only in my ear.

"Listen," he said, "I pull the triggers, I thrust the knives, I rape the women, and . . ." he paused, inching even closer still, the feeling of a forked tongue slid out and lapped once at my earlobe. An eerie foaming of disgust made me shiver. My body felt like it was melting into a sloppy puddle of toxic waste.

The hiss was now unmistakable. "I push the pillows down on the little girls who cry out for Mommy while I'm doing it."

"Corinne!" I shouted.

My eyes burst open.

It was dark. So dark. It was the middle of the night and I was in my bed. Eddie lay next to me, asleep, but I could still hear it . . . that voice. He had one more thing to say as his sound drifted back into the shadows. "I hate you. All of you."

My body did an involuntary convulsion, a shake or two to make it all go away. My pillow was wet. I had been crying. I had been terrified.

I stood and walked to the bedroom window, careful not to wake Eddie. I pulled back the drapes and saw that the moon was full and bright. The clouds must've burned off from earlier in the day. I crept into Owen's room and couldn't help crying some more.

Tears streamed down my cheeks, falling onto his baby-blue comforter set with little red propeller planes scattered about.

"I'll tell you this again when you're older," I whispered to my sleeping Owen, "but I'm going to say it now anyway, even if you can't understand me or hear me. Sometimes, it won't seem as if there's a choice to make in life between God and the Devil. Other times, even when there appears to be one, it won't seem like it's a pressing matter. And then there'll still be times when the choice seems stupid, archaic, maybe even imaginary. You may be called mindless and weak if you make the unpopular choice but, baby, the default position is with the one who hates you. I assure you he exists. You must choose love. You must choose God"

I bent over his crib and kissed his forehead. I said again, "Choose life."

When I got back to bed, Eddie seemed unnaturally quiet for being the sleeping bear that he typically was. I thought he was awake at first, but he didn't stir. I laid back down, curled up in a ball, my back to him, careful not to put my face on the damp spot my tears had made on the pillow. When I got in a comfortable position, Eddie rolled over and put his arm across me, letting it rest on my side.

"You've been crying," he whispered.

"No, I haven't. Shut up." I regretted saying it the moment it came out.

His arm pulled back until it was just his hand upon my waist. He squeezed. Nothing hard, only to let me know he was there and wasn't going to go anywhere, even if I was being a pill.

"Why are you *not* crying, then?" he asked.

"I'm tired. I don't want to talk about it."

"A bad dream?" he asked.

I scooted out from under his grasp but that made my face land right into that damp spot.

"Can I give you my pillow?" he asked.

"What for?"

"So you can have a dry one."

He'd been awake longer than I realized. When I didn't reply, he started tugging my pillow from underneath me.

"Stop it." I turned to him and tried to throw off his hands.

He relented. "Then come on my side," he suggested.

"No, I'm fine."

"Well, I'm not," he said.

I stopped thrashing about and lay still. "What's wrong with you?" I asked, letting my face turn toward the ceiling. I had left the drapes open on our bedroom window and saw an elongated wisp of moonlight making its way across the top of our room.

Eddie raised himself so he could perch above me, looking down. "I just want to get inside of your anxiety," he said, "and make it go away for you."

It was hard to make out his expression in the dark, especially since the small amount of light that was coming in was behind him and casting his features into a shadowy pool.

"I don't know what that means," I said. "Getting into my anxiety. That sounds uncomfortable."

He shook his head at me. "When you used to do your lawyer stuff," he said, "I understood why you shut down. What was there to tell me, anyway? How would I even know what you're talking about? *Ad limine* this, summary adjudication something."

"It's *in limine*," I said.

"But now? I think I might be able to follow along with some of the details. You could let stuff out with me and I can help. Is this about Racobs's trial getting postponed again?"

"No, but that did get me riled up."

"What is it then?"

"You wouldn't understand," I said, turning my face away and pressing the side of it into the pillow. I felt the dampness again.

"And why not?" he asked.

"Because."

"That's not your typically precise answer."

"So?"

"So?" he repeated. "So, it means I want more."

I tried to look at him again. "You don't get more, so deal with it."

"Why not?"

I went all the way over onto my side, even though he was still hovering over me. He'd get tired. He had some magnificently strong arms, but they'd give out sooner or later and I told him as much.

"Nope," he replied. "Come to think of it, I'm not all that tired right now. I had a nice, long nap with Owen today."

"So I witnessed. I was cleaning the toilets and doing the dishes. It was awesome."

"Yes, and because I've already slept some, it means I'll be able to stay awake longer and pester you."

"Sounds like fun for you. Fortunately, I did not take a nap today, I only pretended to. I'll pass out here real soon. And you know me, I'll fall asleep in the middle of anything. Even your pestering."

He lowered himself on top of me and immediately went for the side of my neck, kissing it. I tried to push him off. "What are you doing? Stop it," I said.

He rolled me on my back and took hold of my hands, pinning them above my head. "I'm doing the one thing I know you can't sleep through."

He started kissing me again, this time down toward my chest. I wriggled to get free.

"Just tell me what's been bothering you and I'll let you have your beauty sleep," he said, playing with me. "You and I both know that another minute of this and you'll be putty in my hands. All mine."

"Stupid," I muttered.

"Yes, yes I am, and you love me for it."

I managed to wiggle out from under him, and I quickly sat up. "I don't want to tell you any of it!"

"Why?"

"Because."

"Because why?"

The room had suddenly become much brighter, but I think it was out of fear.

"Because I don't want to taint you!" I yelled. "There's so much . . ." I hesitated, balling my fists. I could feel my nails digging into my palms. It hurt, so I punched the bed, letting out the angst before I opened my mouth further. "There's so much crap out there. The death, the rape, the mayhem, the feasting after feasting on the innocent until there's nothing left but wallowing anguish and defeat. And then mankind walks around like the hollow, empty shells the world has left us as.

"I haven't even begun to share with you the gory details of this case, and how I can't shake the feeling of all this death, even the ricochets of the deaths and rapes and abuse that stem from one man's selfish and apathetic hate. And one question I can't seem to answer is why even kill? I get selfishness and apathy, even hate, but why not just be the jerk who tries to clip your bumper so he gets the parking spot before you? Why not just be the idiot who sneers and pushes and whines that life isn't fair?

"How does anyone get to that supreme feeling of entitlement to actually take away someone else's life? And this guy, this murderer, he's the base of the iceberg that we can't see because he hides everything about himself. What about the bits of iceberg we do see but do nothing about, all those other people out there who have it out for us but we think, we hope, we'll just sail around it like it's no big deal? The sulking teens, the sexually destructive women, the men who dream of gore and gunfire like it's a gumdrop?

"Do you want to hear about the homeless guy? He talked to me once about how 'theys' told him to burn something down."

"A homeless guy told you this?" Eddie asked, skepticism tap-dancing on his tone.

I groaned.

"Sorry, sorry," he said. "But listen, this is good to get out. You need to get this out."

"No, no I don't." I stood up and walked around to the foot of the bed. "And I certainly don't want to talk about those things here."

"Why not?"

"Because they'll stay! They'll set up camp and they'll stay!"

"That's not how it works."

"The heck it doesn't! It's like filth, like a poison. You can pretend all you want that it's not there but it is. It's like a disease . . ." I paused, thinking of my nightmare. "It's like a parasite that wants its dominion, that wants to consume us."

He walked to me. He put both hands on me, one on each side of my waist. "Listen to me, Evy," he said, holding me tight and bringing me close to him. "It's *not* the way it works. Not for us. It can't set up camp unless we're open and willing to receive that sort of evil, and we're not. Do you understand me?"

I laid my head against his chest, biting down on my lower lip. A moment later, he put his fingers under my chin and lifted my face. I panicked at first because it reminded me of Venom in my dream trying to dictate what I saw. But there was no malice or hate in Eddie's features or tone. He was pure love.

He kissed me. Then again. He moved me to the bed and laid me down, hungry for me. "Evy?"

Choices. Always there, always present.

And for all the disgust and calamity I saw in the world, even the portions that I worried would taint my life forever, Eddie reminded me that slivers of heaven and its love existed right here on earth.

"Yes," I whispered to him.

TWENTY-SIX

Treasure in the Trash

There had been this internal gnawing within me. It was as if I knew something but couldn't exactly recall it, an important detail that lay tucked nice and tight for the rest of winter, hibernating within the folds of my brain. I begged it to wake up. I pleaded with it. I hated having it so close but still so far away, becoming like a foe to me. If I smacked it around a bit, poked it, prodded it, maybe even called it a name or two, it would inevitably muster up the nerve and give me a nice, hard slap across the face for all its trouble. Because then, even with a stinging cheek, I'd remember.

It had been two weeks since Jen found that body at her attack site. The body was still a Jane Doe, the police having ruled out all open missing-persons files for her age and other specifications. Whoever she was, either no one seemed to know she was gone or no one cared. Either way, it made me feel bad for her. Billions of people in the world and yet some still trod around without any claim.

Some forensics guy gave up an evening otherwise devoted to playing World of Warcraft and recreated what the victim might have looked like. Thatcher put the picture into the Missing Persons Database, but still nothing.

Techs didn't pull much off the body, but what they did get was similar trace evidence of that bleach and antibacterial wash that matched the others. But no DNA to match with what was left on Jen, and she never got her bleach wash so we still couldn't link Jen to the others.

I didn't think it prudent to tell Jen this was the status. As a fellow lawyer, she'd be able to follow the logic that it was quite possible, maybe even probable, that if we got someone on the rapes and murders of the others, it might not include her because there was nothing concrete that tied her to the rest of them. I could even imagine the way a defense lawyer would put it: Ms. Ness is alive, isn't she? If my client was in the habit of raping, murdering, and then dousing his victims with bleach, explain how Ms. Ness is alive and nonbleached.

Unfortunately, countering with something along the lines of "Ms. Ness lucked out" isn't really admissible. It's conjecture. And objectionable. And still good news, considering.

Sure, the culprit would be locked up anyway—wasn't he up to five bodies now, six if you counted the woman in the grave?—but that would be of little relief to Jen, still carrying his baby but without her portion of the final nail in the man's coffin.

There had to be something else to tie Jen to the others. Even if circumstantial. There had to be.

That's what was bugging me. My mind was in such a state of disrepair, I wasn't quite sure if the connection, the answer, was truly up there or whether I had wanted it so bad that I tricked myself into thinking something existed.

Either way, something was tick, tick, ticking along in my brain, wanting to click and settle.

I stood in my bathroom, opening a new facial wash. When I tossed the empty box into the trash, it bounced off the tall pile and came to rest in the farthest corner behind the toilet.

"Eddie!" I called out.

"What?" he answered from the living room.

"It's Wednesday, right?"

"Yeah."

"Then why haven't you taken the trash out?"

He didn't answer at first. Then I heard his steps coming toward me. He leaned against the bathroom doorframe.

"Because the trash guy has been coming late on Thursdays," he said.

"But the trash is full now."

"Don't worry. It'll be empty tomorrow. I figure why bother putting it out tonight if it's just going to sit on the curb until three in the afternoon."

"But what if tomorrow is the day he comes early again?"

"Doubt it," he said.

"Famous last words," I said, returning to the task of washing my face. When I finished, I went out to the living room, taking a seat beside Eddie on the couch.

"When you take out the trash tomorrow, don't forget to get the box that fell behind the toilet," I said to him. "It toppled off the top because the can was too full."

"Why didn't you pick it up?" he asked.

I reached for a magazine to my right. It was actually an entire stack of catalogs. They would inevitably have to go in the trash too.

"You have to get it. It's your job. I read it in the manual."

"What manual?"

"The manual of our marital roles."

"Oh, that manual," he said, nodding his head in exaggeration and donning an unconvinced look on his face. "You should know that I don't follow that manual."

"Why not?" I asked.

"I find it biased."

"How so?"

"Because you're the one who wrote it."

"Well, someone had to. You should thank me for taking the initiative. That's on page twelve, by the way. Of the manual."

The television he had been watching flipped off. "So, not only do I have to pick up a piece of trash you left behind the toilet, but I have to thank you for making me do it?" he asked.

I shrugged. "We all have our crosses to bear."

"I'm so going to get you tonight," he said, smirking.

"I certainly hope so."

The unmistakable grinding and whirring of the garbage truck woke me at 6:03 a.m., only thirty minutes after I had put Owen back to bed. I tried to drown it out at first but as soon as my eyes closed, I remembered that little box wedged behind the toilet.

I shot up in a sitting position, my hand simultaneously slapping down on Eddie's sleeping chest. "Eddie! The garbage truck!" I said, panicked.

"Ow," he said, rubbing where my hand hit him. But when he heard the clunk of a neighbor's trash can dropping back down on the ground, he bolted upright too.

"Sorry!" he pled, jumping out of bed.

From the sound of the last clanking trash can, I knew we had about a half a block before they rolled on by us, with or without our weekly offering. Eddie would need help if he was going to pull this off, so I got up too. "I'll get the kitchen, you start with the bathroom," I said. When I got to the pantry, I pulled at the drawstrings of the white trash bag. The overstuffed bulk wouldn't budge from the can. I shouldn't have offered to do the kitchen. I felt a small twist, like a bit of barbed wire rolling within my chest, and I knew it was my pride that sent him to the bathroom instead of the kitchen. To pick up that little green box behind the toilet, of course. I told him he had to get it and by goodness, he was going to get it.

I kicked out the bottom of the kitchen trash can, letting the whole thing tilt nearly parallel to the floor while I hoisted a foot on the rim and gave the bag another yank. I heard the clank and clunk of another trash can thrown down on the sidewalk by our garbage collector. The truck was one house closer.

"Come on!" I gritted through my teeth, trying to pull that stinking bag of trash into submission.

Eddie came around from the back of the house, holding two small trash bags from the bathroom and our bedroom. "I'll get it, just hold these," he said, shoving the two sacks toward me.

But no, I wanted to finish what I started. I gave the kitchen trash bag one more strained and forceful yank, my nails digging into the stretched plastic at the top. With my foot still on the rim and most of my weight on my back leg, the top of the bag severed and I fell backward onto my left hip, taking the torn portion of the trash bag with me.

Eddie only took a cursory, cautionary glance to see if I was hurt and then turned to where the can was. His eyes widened and fixated on the spilled trashed. Of course, the nastiest, stinkiest stuff had been near the top of the bag, right under all those catalogs I'd been thumbing through the night prior, and now the mess was all over the floor.

"Forget it," he muttered. "I'll just give him what I have."

Off he went, out the front door.

Everything was covered in coffee grounds and cantaloupe guts, and I decided to use one of the catalogs to scoop some of the other stuff up.

With the catalog in my hand, I took the obligatory look at the front cover and it provoked a great and sudden harmonization, one that I likened to a choir of triumphant angels.

It was because I saw her, the model on the front of the catalog.

It was what had been gnawing at me, that internal pestering that taunted me because I had missed something of the capital H-U-G-E variety.

Eddie came back inside and found me still on the ground, holding a dirty Lana Braun catalog and biting my lip.

"What's wrong?" he asked. "Are you hurt?"

"No," I said, grabbing onto his outstretched hand and letting him hoist me to my feet. "I think I know where the rapist is finding his victims."

TWENTY-SEVEN

Scattered Pieces

Thatcher and I stood in front of the Lana Braun store at the University Town Center mall. After the epiphany that morning with the dirty catalog in my hand, I spent most of the day hunting down and asking friends and family members of victims one, two, and now five, if the women had happened to shop at Lana Braun. All confirmed they had. If anyone could figure out who the woman in the grave was, I would've asked her family and friends too.

I knew Jennifer shopped there because the very blouse I saw on the cover of the Lana Braun catalog was the same blush-colored blouse I saw lying on her bedroom chair, the one she was wearing when she hugged me after she accidentally unearthed a corpse. It was the same blouse that I had hung back in victim number three's closet after her mother had killed herself.

That was the piece of information that had rattled around in the darkened recesses of my mind. The blouses were identical. Those sorts of coincidences are hardly ever coincidences at all. I should've been able to pair it sooner.

A part of me rationalized the slip up. On the one hand, seeing the blouse at Jen's meant a new start, getting back up and giving it another go. The same blouse at the Milhelm house meant endings, death, and hope snuffed out.

One beginning, one end, and still, why hadn't I been paying close enough attention to know they were winding up or down around the same item? It took the spilled trash on my kitchen floor to put it together for me. The catalog was from the previous spring and packed in one of our boxes when we moved from Fresno. There was hardly a time when I found it appropriate to thank Eddie for his pack rat propensities, but this had definitely been one of those moments.

Since Thatcher and I had established that all the victims had either lived or worked near La Jolla—the most recent victim was walking alone at night across the college campus in the area—the Lana Braun store at University Town Center seemed the best bet.

"You don't really think our perp works in the store, do you?" Thatcher asked me.

"*If* a man worked in Lana Braun, I don't think he'd be of the raping variety, no."

"Then why are we here?" He ran his hand through his loosely disheveled hair, then took a seat on a nearby bench. He tapped his foot, looking like he had several other places to be, none of which included sitting in front of a women's clothing store. At the rate his discomfort and frustration were rising, maybe he was worried I was about to go into the store to try on pants, asking him if they made me look fat.

I pointed at him. "See what you're doing right now? That's why we're here."

"You've lost me," he said.

I looked around, taking in the people walking by, and then turned back to him and said, "It's your angst, Thatcher. You, like most red-blooded males, don't want to be hanging out around a Lana Braun store. You don't want to go in, and no way are you working there."

"Yeah, so?"

"So," I said, looking around again, this time taking stock of the stores in the vicinity. "It's not the Lana Braun store, but rather what's *around* the Lana Braun store that we need to be interested in." I reached down to pull him up by his elbow, bringing him to a standing position. "Look at the other stores," I said, methodically pointing them out. "A sandwich shop, a Williams-Sonoma, and Nordstrom." I had hoped by saying them aloud, something would jump out at me, but nothing resonated.

From the corner of my eye, I noticed a person pop into view from a ledge right above us. It was a teenager. He was looking down at me. Then another person looked over. She was twenty or so years older than the kid, likely his mother. Prior to those two sticking their heads over and looking down, I wouldn't have thought there was a walkway at that particular spot.

"Hold on," I said to Thatcher. "Stay here. I'll be right back."

"Whoa, whoa," he said, grabbing my forearm. "When you say right back, do you mean that in the normal sense, or should I check first to see if I have enough money to get a cab ride home?"

"You drove, Thatcher."

"Yeah, but that doesn't bring me as much comfort as you might think"—he shoved his hands into his pockets and rocked back on his heels—"because I never know what you're going to do or how you're going to do it."

"Join the club. Even I barely know what I'm doing, but I'm willing to extend a little faith in myself."

"That's rich," he said.

"Isn't it? Stay here."

I took off to my left, toward the sandwich shop, because I had seen some stairs climbing to the next level in the mall. At the top, I found a mounted map of the mall as well as individual map pamphlets in a plastic holder. I grabbed one of the pamphlets and continued up to the next level, the uppermost in the three-floored mall. I hoped I'd find the angle to peer down at the Lana Braun store like the mother and her son had done a moment earlier. When I got there, I found Astroturf covering the area, forming a small-scale putting green. Miniature white flags delineated the holes and one child with a putter was taking a few sloppy shots at a ball. Toward the wall, where the two onlookers had been a few minutes earlier, were three benches. A couple was sitting on one of them.

I walked to the chest-high wall and leaned over the edge. Thatcher was sitting again, still out front of the Lana Braun store, holding his phone. Looked like he was checking his emails. Talk about a bird's-eye view. From where I stood, I could see everyone and everything down below, including the front door and the front half of the Lana Braun store. I saw a bleached-blonde near the front window looking at some crocheted sweaters. I could see down her blouse from where I stood and quickly looked away.

If she looked up, she wouldn't see me. She'd only see the ceiling within the store. It was a perfect perch for an ever-watchful monster.

A man in a black shirt sat down on the bench affixed to the wall, his lunch in his hands. He bore a nametag on the left side of his chest and a cell-phone-store logo on the right. I remembered seeing the same logo on one of the walkway kiosks, one near Nordstrom. The employee hadn't ventured far from his work to enjoy his break.

"Do you eat here every day?" I asked him.

He pretended not to hear me and took a bite of his sandwich. I watched a piece of lettuce fall from his bottom lip onto his black shirt, wondering if I should ask the question again. Before I could, he answered, "Yes."

His mouth had been full when he spoke, and he shoved his sandwich back in its bag and stood. He swallowed and said, "It's usually the quietest place in the mall." He turned and left. The man had that certain anti-social, I-hate-everybody flair to him, but he was soft and almost droopy. He was no weight lifter, like I figured our guy to be.

If the rapist worked in the mall, he might also eat his lunch or take breaks here. I looked around again at the surrounding retail stores. Nothing screamed out at me as a place where a sociopath could blend in. I thought again about what that surfer had said, about needing lots of spare time to lift weights for that muscular build.

Behind me, I saw an antique furnishings place. Pass. Then, just beyond the antique store, I noticed a large concrete wall. It had no commercial markings on it but the sheer size of the structure indicated it was a big place, a department store even, but it didn't look like there was a way inside from where I stood. Wondering why it wouldn't have access from this level, I opened up the map and looked to see what was on the other side of that wall.

I smiled.

Leaning over the ledge and looking down at Thatcher, I said, "Hey! Come up here! We're going to get a gym membership."

Thatcher and I walked almost the entire length of the mall to get our-selves to the outside lower level, where the one and only door to the gym was located. It wasn't as if the gym took up that much space but rather the mall builders had decided to make you walk past as many stores as possi-ble before you could make it back out to the parking lot. The farther we walked toward our destination, the more discouraged I became, knowing we were backtracking. If that perch above Lana Braun was something the guy had used to select and spy on his victims, and he also had a connec-tion to this gym, the walk should be shorter. Unless I was wrong. About lots of it.

Up to that point, the day had come at me with sort of an excitable fer-vor that we could finally end this. Things were starting to come together, like nearing the end of a marathon. When we'd cross the finish line, we'd see the image of the killer's face. But if I had been wrong about this part, this last leg of the day's journey, then I might as well just scrap it all.

Maybe even forget I had even seen the Lana Braun catalog, as if it were just a silly coincidence that I was putting too much stock in.

We were no more than a few feet from the gym's front door when I saw the edge of the building. "Hold on." I walked over and turned the corner, finding a stairway. I made a quick jog up and sure enough, there was the Astroturf putting green. Hope sprang anew. There was a shortcut between the gym and the perch. Too bad we didn't see it at first.

"Figures," I said aloud and then walked back to Thatcher. He had taken off his suit jacket and was letting it hang over one arm. He was now rolling up one of his sleeves until it rested right below his elbow.

"There's a stairway right over there." I pointed behind me. "I even saw the first part of the Nordstrom sign. We could've walked down that stairwell instead of going all the way around."

He started on the other sleeve. "You thinking he'd come out of the gym and go up those stairs to look at the store?"

I was mesmerized by his movements, trying to figure out what he was up to with his sleeves.

"Why are you doing that?" I asked.

"Doing what?"

"The sleeves. Why are they going up?"

He made some quick movements with his arms, a mock sort of bench press. "We're going into a gym. I might as well knock out some reps. Why not, right? We're already here."

I shook my head at him.

He flexed his muscles for me and I had to look away so I wouldn't laugh, turning my face toward an adjacent parking lot. I spotted something that hit me as if I had seen a shiny new toy, and every ounce of me wanted to touch, touch, touch it.

"Thatcher, look . . ." was all I could get out before I started crossing through the parking lot, darting to the edge of it. I never turned around to confirm Thatcher was coming with me, but I heard the sounds of his footsteps, trying to catch up to me.

"What's going on?" Thatcher asked once he got to my side.

"Come on," I said. "Look." I was pointing to a vehicle. "That van, Thatcher."

"What, that?" he asked as we closed the gap to our destination.

"It's a delivery truck," he said, correcting me.

We stood side by side, a foot away from it. "It *is* a delivery truck," I said, quiet and subdued. "But then again, it's not." My brain was going a million miles a minute, putting pieces together. I put something here, dropped another bit there. "That would make everything fit better," I said to Thatcher as if he'd been participating with the back and forth going on in my head.

"Jennifer said a van because it sort of is. And—" I froze, my hands held out in front of me as I let the realization course through my body. "That freak, that meth freak. Do you remember what he said, Thatcher?" I clasped my hands together in excitement as I smiled.

It was as if I had been staring down at an unfinished puzzle, pieces piled in a heap on my dining room table; a task I had begun with fanciful thoughts of completing within the hour, if it took even that long. And yet, it remained. Sitting incomplete, a sloppy reminder of what I hadn't done.

But now I was nearing the end and I loved it. My body, my very soul, hummed with determination because I could see it all coming together. Take that, you merciless puzzle, you ratfink conundrum.

"Remember?" I asked Thatcher again. "We asked the meth guy if he saw a van parked at the end of the alley or across the street. And what did he say?"

Thatcher's face twisted. He was noodling it, trying to remember the detail.

"He said he couldn't really see anything, not even a van, because a white delivery truck was blocking the alley." Thatcher looked at the truck. "This thing?"

"Something like it, yes." I gazed from Thatcher's face back to the truck. "And that teen said it was a truck too. Then add Jen's van description . . . I've never seen a vehicle that looks quite like this. Have you?"

He shrugged. "I guess. I think I've seen something like this on the freeway before."

"This could be something like what he's using and that's why two witnesses called it a truck but our main witness called it a van. We don't have witnesses with two different accounts, we have a new breed of vehicle and an issue of semantics."

First things first, it wasn't white. It was a hybrid of sorts. Half van, half truck, but also, arguably, a big van or small truck. Wanting to play it safe, I settled on calling it a hybrid. It had the front and grille of a truck, with big, truck-type side view mirrors. It had a high roof, like a delivery truck would, too, but—

I walked to the back of the vehicle. It had doubled doors that would swing out like a delivery van, whereas a truck would have a roll-up door. Walking around to the passenger side, I found another door, a sliding one like you'd find on a minivan. There were no windows on the side, only the ones in the cab.

"What made you notice this?" Thatcher asked.

I was looking down at the tires—small enough to match the van-type treads forensics gave us the other day—but upon hearing Thatcher's question I raised my right hand and tapped my fingers on the side of the van to give him his answer.

"Oh . . . ," he said, trailing off.

My hand was near an image of an animated weight lifter. He was done in all red, holding a barbell over his head and sweating profusely. He looked as if he were either going to break in half or mess himself. The red figure, the red barbell, the red sweat droplets falling to the ground, and then the red lettering: Optimal Training Performance and Weight Machinery.

My eyes lingered on a detail I found on the sliding door. There was a misaligned edge on the seam, jutting out between the body of the vehicle and where the door would open. I stuck my finger in the seam, lifting up at the misalignment. It pulled with relative ease like peeling the label off a water bottle. The whole thing, the company logo, was like a static cling window decal, and it covered the entire body of the vehicle. I kept lifting, exposing a solid white van underneath.

Thatcher slapped at my hand.

"Are you crazy?" he asked. "You can't ruin people's decals like that. Leave it alone."

I raised my hand and slapped his in return. "Like I care at this point," I said. "This van is white, Thatcher. It's white underneath. What if he takes the decal off when he's doing his deed and then has it put back on? This could be the vehicle we're looking for."

"Or, it could be some business's delivery truck and you're ruining it."

"Look at it, Thatcher!" I pointed to the decal. "It's only a different color right now because it has some sort of custom . . ." I struggled with what to call it, and all I could think of was *wallpaper*.

"I think it's called a vehicle wrap. It's used to advertise on cars and trucks."

I nodded. That sounded much better than wallpaper. "Vehicle wrap,"

I repeated. "That would allow him to escape scrutiny if we were looking for a white van." I looked back at the front door of the gym. "You think it belongs to the gym?" I asked.

He shrugged. "I don't see why not," he said, looking back at the red decal on top of the black wrap. "Training plus weights plus machines equals gym."

I darted back to the gym to finish our initial pursuit. Thatcher pulled me back right before I rushed through the front door.

"We have to play nice in here, all right? Even if it is the same van, he could be using it without their knowledge and it'd be much easier to get their permission for us to search it, than mess around and have them throw up their walls and demand a warrant."

I nodded, only half-meaning it.

TWENTY-EIGHT

When the Dog Bites

We walked into the gym and a young woman greeted us from behind the reception desk.

"Hi, welcome to All-Time Fitness. How can I help you today? Are you new to our club?"

"Yes," I said, smiling at her. She was maybe all of five feet tall and had an orangish complexion. I figured she'd taken too much liberty with her onsite spray tanning privileges.

"Would you like me to get you a membership counselor so he can give you a tour of the facility?" she asked.

"Um, no. Not yet," I said, walking right up to her counter and resting my arms on top. I made a point of not looking her directly in the eyes. For what I had in mind, I figured it'd be better if I looked distracted. I was contemplating the word "training" I had seen on the van. "I was wondering if you could help me with something first."

I turned to find Thatcher. A moment earlier, he had been standing right behind me but now he was to my left, peering into a tall, glass display case. His breath fogged up a portion of the glass as he read the labels on the supplement bottles, which I assumed contained a bunch of protein and endurance products. Most of the bottles were bigger than his head, but that seemed to be part of the draw.

"Sure, I can try. How can I help you?" the young woman said.

"I have this friend," I began, "well, not really a friend but more of an acquaintance. She told me she's been getting some amazing results with a personal trainer here. But she's such a hog, she won't give me his name because, well, she doesn't want to share him, if you know what I mean."

The young lady smiled, although I thought it disingenuous.

"I was hoping you could direct me to your trainers so I could figure out which one she uses and then hire him."

"So, you'd like to interview some trainers?"

"Yes, please."

She half-turned, pointing, and said, "If you walk against that side wall over there, you'll find several glass offices. That first one belongs to the gentleman who does the body-fat percentages for our members and prospective members. He's also our head trainer and can help you find the right trainer."

I smiled at her and then turned to wave at Thatcher, wanting him to follow.

"Oh, but since you're visitors," she said, jutting a pen and a clipboard toward me, "you have to sign in."

I contrived the names Matilda the Magnificent for myself, and Hercules the Lesser for Thatcher because I couldn't get the image of him rolling up those shirtsleeves out of my mind, his man-glee shining on his face like someone had just buffed him with testosterone.

I looked over my shoulder to see if Thatcher was watching me write the names down. He wasn't. The script was messy enough that the receptionist wouldn't bother to make it out, but still legible if one tried.

As I went to set the clipboard down on the counter, Thatcher snuck up on me and took hold of the board, looking down at what I had signed.

"Really?" he asked, shaking his head at me.

He held an expectant hand out to me, motioning for the pen, but I set it down as far from him as possible. He got a new one. I peeked at what he had written down after he scratched my contribution out.

He wrote: Detective Brian Thatcher, SDPD, and guest.

I scoffed, then leaned toward his ear to whisper. "You're just going to slow us down with that."

The young woman took the clipboard back and said, "Oh. I see. Hold on then. Let me get the manager."

As soon as she turned to go, I said, "Seriously, Thatcher. Now we're going to have someone following us and saying no, like a big, old squawking bird."

He shrugged. I think he knew I was right, but he was playing it off. "Well, I think I want to start roping you in a bit," he said. "For every ten times you want to do something inappropriate, I hold your reins a bit tighter on at least two of those so you don't get me into trouble."

"Better have a strong grip," I mumbled. When I turned away from him, I caught sight of those glass offices the young woman was talking about. Sure enough, there was a guy sitting in the first one, staring at a computer.

I pointed behind Thatcher. "Here comes the manager."

When Thatcher turned, I walked away. I was just a guest, after all. No manager escort needed for me.

The head trainer's name was Rafael and although he was beefy enough to be able to throw that victim off the cliff, he wasn't our guy. His lack of culpability was due in large part to his skin color. Thanks to Jen surviving, we knew our guy was white—from the little she saw of her attacker—and Rafael was black.

Rafael quickly agreed to parade me in front of all the trainers on the premises at that time, although that only equated to two, three if I included him.

On the way out of his office, we passed by the front desk and I tried to hide my frame behind Rafael's girth. Thatcher appeared to be stuck in a myriad of explanations with a middle-aged man wearing a polo shirt and khaki pants that looked like they'd rip at the seam if Mr. Manager took a seat too quickly. The manager was fit, but apparently liked to buy his clothes extra snug.

Good one, Thatcher. What if the manager was our guy? And there was Thatcher, spilling peripheral details, nothing too important, but enough to trigger a wall of cover-up if he were the rapist. No one who worked here, or even exercised here, was exempt from suspicion.

I sighed. If everyone with bulging biceps was a suspect, this could take awhile.

Thatcher noticed me as Rafael and I walked by, but he quickly looked away. At least he gave me that. If Tight-Pants didn't know Thatcher and I were together, I had more freedom to roam on my own, even if I was chained to Rafael for a bit.

Rafael had already explained that most of the trainers didn't come in until later in the evening or earlier in the mornings, but that he'd introduce me to those who had already checked in with him for the day.

The first was too skinny. I shrank at the prospect of wasting precious time chitchatting my farce up with him. I unequivocally knew this pint-sized male was unable to throw a one-hundred-forty-pound female off a cliff. I could even tell which of his gym short pockets he had stashed his car keys in—he was leaning to his left. He was an Asian guy with spiked hair and black socks pulled up to his knees. I understood the spikey hair; the socks were a conundrum. Was that in now? And if so, why?

My aim was to be polite to him—especially with Rafael around—but that didn't really pan out. It must've been the combination of not wanting to waste time paired with my ever-growing frustration at trying to progress the case. Whatever it was, I lashed out at the little guy.

"Who do you train?" I asked. "The anorexics?"

I was the only one who thought this was funny.

"Who's this?" he asked Rafael, pointing at me.

Rafael looked dumbfounded. "Um, she's looking for a trainer," he said.

"Not me, I guess," Skinny Guy answered. He shifted his gaze from Rafael to me. "I train a lot of other Asians, if you want to know. Many of us can't really bulk up the way other ethnicities can, so I have a specialized clientele, thank you very much."

"Why are you thanking me?" I asked, giving him a smirk. "I didn't do anything but insult you."

"Okay," Rafael said, ushering me away. "I'm not sure what your angle is, but I'm already regretting this."

"Sorry," I said. At some level, I really was. "You said there's one more trainer on right now. I'd like to meet him. I was just thrown by the skinny guy. I could break him, you know?"

Rafael laughed. "I'm sure you could, but he's cool. And he's a friend," he added.

"Sorry," I repeated, and then turned my eyes toward our next target. The trainers were easy enough to spot because they wore bright red shirts with the word TRAINER written on the front and back in big, black letters.

We ascended a metal staircase to the second level, entering the women-only section, to find the next trainer. Right away, I felt a flutter in my stomach. This guy was viable. He was the right size, Caucasian, enough muscles not only to pick me up, but to twirl me above his head too. He also looked unaffected and detached from what was happening around him. That seemed quite a feat considering there was a plump, whimpering, sweating female trying to do crunches at his Zeus-like feet.

Rafael and I walked closer to the pair and, on our way, passed a bald guy—a kid really, at least to me. He was kneeling on the ground, fidgeting with a weight machine. He drew my attention because I felt it an affront to have a male daring to exercise over here in the female-only section. I aimed to give him a dirty look, but quickly turned away in shame, realizing that he wasn't fidgeting with the machine to use it, but rather to work on it.

My eyes hit the trainer again. He wasn't even pretending to cheer his client on when she said she was about to puke. "Ten more," was all he said in a placid, distant voice. He didn't even look at her. He sat on a weight-lifting bench, near her head, and his attention was fully on his cell phone. I couldn't understand why this woman would hand over her hard-earned cash to pay for a trainer who was giving two percent, max.

That's when I noticed the stars in her eyes. They were obvious whenever she looked up at him, right before she crashed down on the mat after each rep. She had splotches of red on her cheeks and her sweat bled through like a burst dam wherever it could find a swatch of clothing to offend. Oh, but she was buying it all right. Everything the guy didn't have to offer and then some.

I moved toward the trainer, Rafael by my side, explaining the dynamics of the women-only section. As if the humongo sign on the wall when we rounded the corner wasn't self-explanatory enough. But I let him talk. It helped me size up the trainer. When we stood only a few feet away from the pair, the trainer looked up. He gave a nod of recognition at Rafael and then he went back to his phone.

Some of the details seemed like they'd fit. He had constant access to weight lifting and the ability to set his own schedule. But the truth of it was that if a man could get through a training session for hire like this—with the sweating, convulsing heap of female in front of him—I just couldn't see him losing his cool getting all rapey and murdery in his downtime.

It didn't quite pair.

A woman's voice echoed over the loud speakers, calling Rafael up to the front. That was my cue. I told Rafael I'd seen enough anyway—that this other trainer wasn't right for me either—and wanted to get a better look at one of the exercise machines nearby. When I said I'd join him back in his office if I had any questions, he smiled and left.

It was both good news and bad news. The good news was that I was losing my chaperone. The bad news was that I figured it had been the manager calling Rafael away, expecting him to bring me back in tow. The manager might be onto the fact that he had a cop-like creature roaming around his gym.

I didn't know how much free time I had, but I wanted to see what was on that trainer's phone. What he was looking at when he thought no one else could see would either confirm or rule him out as a suspect. Truth of it was, though, I just wanted to know what was so blasted important that he felt he had wide girth to be so inattentive to the woman in front of him.

I walked slowly behind him, pretending to size up the dumbbells but also peeking over his shoulder to see what he was viewing.

Mountain bikes. Nope. I just couldn't imagine a raping murderer having any sort of extracurricular activity, save for, of course, the raping and murdering part of his day.

I couldn't dismiss him wholly, though. I thought I still had a few minutes left before someone summoned me downstairs, and I wanted to use those to poke at the trainer. See what he did when he was angry.

"Let me ask you something," I said to him, standing now to his side so he could see me properly.

He turned his phone so that the screen was now facing the ground and looked up at me. The woman on the floor looked up at me too, and that was good because she was the one I really wanted to address.

"How much an hour do you take from this woman so you can look at your phone while she sweats and you could care less?"

The woman's mouth dropped, and that was in addition to how low it already was from all her panting.

"I— I . . ." she started.

I turned to her. "I mean, because look, I'll charge you half of whatever he's asking, and then I can be the one to tell you ten more this or ten more that. But with me, you can expect—and will get—eye contact."

The trainer stood and let his phone drop into the right pocket of his gym shorts. His chest inflated and his eyes narrowed at me.

Thatta boy. Get mad.

"We're in the middle of a session here," he said, propping his hands on his waist and jutting his chin out at me.

"No, you're not," I replied. "*She's* in the middle of a workout and you're just having some free time over here, checking out pictures of mountain bikes on your cell. All the while, she's paying you to care about her physique, except I very much doubt you give a crap. For her, that is. Mountain bikes, well, you do seem to care about those."

He put his hands up to me in slight surrender, but his face was set on defending himself. "I don't need to prove myself to you. If you don't like the way I do things, you're not obligated to use my services. But I think my results speak for themselves."

I looked at her.

She scrambled up to her feet and now looked as disturbed as her trainer was. Seeing her expression made me see that she was as responsible for this sham as he was. She didn't have to agree to let him and his cell phone slight her, but it was probably the highlight of her day. Her eyes still had a hint of that puppy-love-at-moonlight euphoria to them. Oh, self-confidence, where art thou?

Then again, it wasn't really about the workout for her. That seemed clear now. Maybe she was too confident in herself. Why else would she attempt to beguile a trainer within these confines? The nitty-gritty of the surroundings and actions reminded me of childbirth. Couldn't really see how any of these positions, not to mention the facial expressions, were sexy.

Two things occurred to me: One, I shouldn't have opened my ridic-ulous mouth about their wasteful training session, and two, he couldn't be the guy I was looking for. He had none of that cavernous, hidden rage I would expect from a man who brutalized women. People can pretend all they want that their character is lollipops and Skip-to-my-Lou, but if you're evil, then baby, you're rotten.

And the cover-up, the hiding of the fangs, that part only fools the inex-perienced, and I was not inexperienced. I had lived this. Because of the mayhem and evil that had come to my life, kicking me in the chin and laughing as I doubled over in blinding pain and confusion, I was a firm believer that the hole in a monster is something that's always there, calling out for victims or playmates. It'll take whoever answers first. It's not picky. It just wants the company. And when it gets it, it'll put a notch in its belt. The belly crawler just waiting for people to wake up when few ever do.

A person with a hole inside them was like a sleepy but ill-tempered pit bull waiting for the right person to stick their plushy little hand through the chain link fence. But with real dogs, people are instinctual about keeping their distance, knowing when to heed the hair rising on the back of their necks and keep to the other side of the street, to spare their flesh from the chompers.

We should be the same with the vacancy of a man's soul. We should mind the hair rising. We should mind the bad senses.

I stared at the trainer. No. He was just a self-absorbed tadpole who needed a good long lesson in work ethic.

"Well then, I'll just leave you two at it."

A loud *clang* sounded through the area. It was the sound of a stack of weights crashing down to their starting position on one of the machines. I thought someone had lost their grip on the machine's handlebar, but it wasn't. It was the bald guy, the one fixing the very machine that made the crash.

The sound was so alarming and jarring that I expected him to stand or wave or do something in recognition of the faux pas, but he didn't. He remained kneeling, looking down at the ground, seemingly trying to hide, as if that were even possible. I could see his back rise and fall slightly from taking a breath, but the tempo was too fast for a normal heart rate. For a miniscule moment, I imagined him as a squirrel who had stolen someone's nuts and didn't want to be caught trying to stuff them in his own tree.

I wondered about his squirreliness.

I walked closer and his head remained lowered. His muscles became taut, as if he were now holding his breath altogether. That's when I noticed that his scalp had what looked like pepper dots all over, indicating that he otherwise had a full head of hair that was trying to break through and regrow. He wasn't bald because of hair loss. He was bald by choice. His arms were shaved too. Then I saw his smooth, muscular legs.

It came out before I even thought through the implications. "Is that your van outside?"

That snarling dog . . . that vacuous hole . . . that feeling . . . my hair rising. . . *GET TO THE OTHER SIDE OF THE STREET!*

But it was too late.

He sprang up and charged me, his hands in front of him. They rammed into me with a force that in and of itself would have winded me, but he'd angled his hands up so that when he made contact with me, he sent me airborne for a slight second before I landed across a few running beds in a line of treadmills.

It was him. It had to be. I had to get him but I was now on my back, unable to breathe and writhing in pain. I heard his footsteps pounding the metal staircase. The stairs would take him down to reception and out the door. Past Thatcher.

"Thatcher!" I cried out, unsure whether he could hear me. "Thatcher!" I screamed out again.

It was only when I recognized Thatcher's gait coming up the stairs that I realized what I had done. By calling Thatcher's name, he was coming to my aid and leaving the front desk. He was leaving the door open for the guy to escape.

TWENTY-NINE

The Legal Eagle of Them All

Thatcher tried to pick me up but I swatted him away. "That bald kid, running out of here. Go!"

Off he went. I got up as fast as I could, which really wasn't fast at all. The trainer I had been messing with earlier, as well as his overweight companion, didn't seem to want to lend a helping hand. Either they were dumbfounded or unsympathetic.

I almost stumbled down the stairs, even holding onto the banister. There was a shooting pain running down my left leg but I had felt worse, so I kept going until I pushed through the front door of the gym and saw Thatcher in the middle of the mall parking lot road, squinting at the backside of that van, the delivery truck, speeding away.

He started mumbling numbers and letters and then grunted. He balled his fists and then grunted in exasperation.

"Guess that answers that," I said.

"Answers what?" he asked.

"About the van. Not only was it the right sort of vehicle, it was the actual van."

"What happened up there? How did you make contact with him?" Thatcher asked.

Instead of answering, I asked, "Did you get the license plate?"

"No, I saw an *R* and a *Q* and thought I could see numbers, but then it was too far. What happened?" he asked again.

I leaned up against a nearby tree in the lot, taking the weight off my left leg. "It was him," I said. "I guess he felt cornered and, for lack of a better explanation, he charged me."

"How did you know it was him?"

I gave it a moment's thought, wondering whether I should tell him about rabid dogs, but I didn't quite feel like going into metaphor and meaning with him at the moment. "I didn't know it was him at first. It was a hunch. Now I know, but I'm still not a hundred percent sure. Does that suffice?"

"Give me more specifics on him."

"He's muscular, almost totally shaved, which would explain the lack of hair evidence, and one has to wonder why he felt it necessary to charge and toss me onto a treadmill unless he's guiltier than original sin. Jen was right about that refrigerator-box face. I want to say brown eyes, but he was squinting. Thin lips, high cheekbones. A solid, straight nose." I said the last with a sneer. He clearly enjoyed being quite the pugilist when it came to a woman's face, but his own nose had never been broken. He wasn't receiving blows back. "He was young," I added as a final note. "Are they usually that young?"

Thatcher was still staring off past the parking lot, even though the van was long gone. It took a second for him to process what I'd asked. "Hmm?" he mumbled. "Young?" He looked back where the van had driven off. "Um, yeah. The angry, impulsive ones are."

"But methodical too," I said. "Totally shaven is methodical in escaping detection." I kept rubbing my back, wishing time to bend or warp or whatever it needed to do so that we had made sufficient effort to secure that vehicle. To even just get the plate because the less we had now the harder it'd be to get him. And then something occurred to me. "Methodical plus angry plus impulsive means—"

"Crazy," Thatcher finished. He turned to look at me again. "So, what did you say to him to make him toss you?"

"There you go again," I said, trying to straighten up. "I didn't say anything to him." But then I replayed the event in my head. "Oh, wait, I did ask him if he had a van outside, but"—I waved my hand, displaying the disappearance of said van in the parking lot—"asked and answered, I suppose."

Thatcher sighed, his fingers pushing into his left temple. I thought he was trying to either erase or imprint something. "I should've been able to get that plate!" he exclaimed, balling his fists once again. *Yeah, you should have,* I had wanted to say, but that was only me deflecting my own incompetence. Instead, I offered what I hoped would make him feel better.

"Thatcher, I have much better vision than you do and there's no way I would've been able to see that plate from where it was parked."

"I should've gotten it before. When we were standing right next to it."

"Yeah, but you didn't know it was his. How could you?"

He turned to face me. "Because you said it might be, that's how I could. Would it have been so hard to write it down while we were standing right there?"

"Don't beat yourself up," I said, thinking about that weight machine from the second story of the gym.

"And why not?" he said, practically screaming.

"Because if you call your crime-scene nerds, I'll show you where they can find his prints."

"David Lopez," Thatcher said to me over the phone.

It was the name associated with the thumbprint pulled off the weight machine.

A name, a name, a glorious name. It was glorious for Thatcher and me, but I doubted Jen or any of the remaining family members of his other victims would find the effects of the hallelujah chorus happening over the utterance of such a thing. Names don't raise daughters from the grave.

The print match came through the California Department of Motor Vehicles. In order to receive a driver's license, you had to give them a thumbprint. Otherwise, Lopez had no prior record. He didn't have an up-to-date address either. No employment records—save for the gym manager later vouching for him as one of the many independent contractors that come and go through the gym—and no record of him ever paying taxes either. Still, my mind reeled with the conclusion of the chase. It had taken awhile to isolate and identify Lopez's prints from the plethora that were on that machine, and I assumed we were but moments away from getting our hands on him.

"He doesn't have any utilities in his name, no loans with any banks, no credit cards," Thatcher said. "The only thing we have on him is he graduated from La Jolla High, did one year at Cal State San Diego, and his last known address was with his mother."

A mother, I thought to myself. Let me at her.

"La Jolla, huh?" I asked. "Does that mean Mommy Dearest still lives in La Jolla?"

"I don't know, but I got something else on the mom that might interest you a bit," he said.

"Lay it on me."

"She's a practicing attorney right down here in San Diego."

I felt a jolt. It bounced and ricocheted through me and then landed with a dull thud in my gut. "You're kidding," I finally muttered.

"Do you want to hear something even worse?" he asked. "Or even better?"

"Spill."

"She's one of the partners in your friend Jennifer's firm. She's her boss."

I didn't mean to do it, but my surprise took the form of shutting off the phone, as if some dirty, oozing secret was leaking out and I had to stop it, quick.

I gasped, not sure if it was the ongoing slap of Thatcher's comment, or because I shocked myself when I impulsively hung up on him. I started dialing his number back. By the time I got to the fifth digit, something was already tinkering in my head. It was a thought that started spreading around like a thick, encompassing fog. It soon covered my eyes and all I could see was that Thatcher sometimes had a way of slowing me down when all I really wanted to do was charge.

I put the phone down, hoping he wouldn't call back. A few seconds later, it rang. It was Thatcher all right. But I didn't want to hear what he had to say because he'd probably say "not yet" when I desperately wanted to meet the woman who raised a raping murderer.

I hit the elevator button for Jen's office floor, twenty-one, but it opened on sixteen. I saw a polished brunette sitting behind a receptionist desk, almost ready to spare a smile if I had managed to get myself off the elevator. I figured my arrival on that floor had been a mistake so I waited for the elevator doors to close again, hitting the button for twenty-one a second time.

The arrival bell chimed immediately. The doors reopened. The same brunette appeared. This time she smiled, knowing before I had that yes, this is where I wanted to go.

"Are you trying to get to twenty-one? My indicator says you pushed that button. If so, you need to start here," she said, waving at me to walk into her gold-and-wood paneled cave. "The administrative office for that floor is here on sixteen. We clear your admittance and then send you up."

This was quite the holdup. I had envisioned more of a sneak attack, not someone heralding my presence.

Maybe I could get up to twenty and take the stairs the rest of the way up. I had to shake the brunette first.

"No habla," I said to her, letting the elevator doors close on me again, now hitting the button for twenty.

The doors closed. Chime, doors opened. Brunette, gold, wood, blah blah blah.

"Dang it," I muttered.

She chuckled once. "You habla," she said. "All the remaining floors above are accessed by permission only, and, again, you'll have to start here. How can I help you?"

I stepped out of the elevator, biting down on my lower lip as I tried to mask my frustration. Outdone by a stinking elevator.

Jennifer's law firm clearly had a Fort-Knox-security flavor to it. One had to surmise that the security precautions meant either the attorneys had a presidential complex, or the public really, truly hated this particular bunch of lawyers. It was probably the latter. With bigger firms, such as the one I used to work for in Fresno, there was always that conglomerate of attorneys who not only lit bridges afire, but also napalmed them and danced on the ashes. Retaliatory threats, shouting matches, and the occasional Molotov cocktail on a Tuesday morning could thus be avoided by keeping their reception area several floors below their actual offices.

Yet, I'd be lying if I said I wasn't somewhat excited to elude yet another gatekeeper. Perhaps this time, there wouldn't be any blood. Everyone wins.

"The law firm takes up seven floors?" I asked the receptionist.

"No, this is the access area for five different companies, but because my computer let me know you first pushed the button to twenty-one, I take it you'd like to visit the firm. Who are you here to see and whom may I say is calling?"

Sometimes, going for broke and telling the truth works, even when you're trying to be terribly wily.

"I'm here to surprise someone, actually."

"Surprises are fun," she said like the good little employee who couldn't care less. "I still need to announce your visit."

"That would ruin the surprise," I said.

"You know what else ruins a surprise?" Her flat tone drifted to pragmatic. "When someone says they have an appointment but is really wielding a semiautomatic weapon to blow everyone away up there."

"Hmm," I said, nodding. "Pity for you in that scenario, though."

"Why's that?"

"Because if someone wants to start blowing people away, aren't you the first to catch expended fire? You know, because you're the first person they see."

"People don't seem to have a problem with me," she said, shrugging her shoulders.

"*Most* people," I emphasized.

She nurtured the smallest of smiles yet there was a masked sense of power and dominion behind it. "I'm sorry," she said, "are you threatening me?"

"My personal philosophy is: Prewarned is prearmed."

She mulled that over for a moment, her brow furrowing.

"That means no," I said. "Besides, I'm not a fan of semiautomatic weapons, or armed violence in general. Anyway," I said, "I'm here to see Mrs. Lopez up in that law firm on twenty-one."

"Is she an attorney or a member of the support staff?" Her voice made a clear change in the direction of icy.

"An attorney," I replied.

"Do you have a first name for her?"

"No, sorry."

"And what's your name?" she asked.

I was tempted to give another name, but thought better of it. To Lopez, my real name would be as foreign as a contrived one. Not to mention we were getting closer to nabbing her son with every step. It was best not to muddy the waters. Especially not now. "Evelyn Barrett," I said.

"Just a second." Her eyes pulled away from me and went to the computer screen in front of her. Without looking back up at me, she said, "I'm sorry, I don't see an attorney Lopez at that firm. Are you sure you have the right law office?"

"Yes. Are you sure there isn't anyone by that name?"

"Well, a couple of the staff members, but regardless, this firm has a strict policy against personal visits to their staff. Even if one of the staff members was the Mrs. Lopez you wanted to see, you'd have to make other arrangements for your visit. Potential and current clients, as well as other lawyers and their clients, are the only visitors allowed unless otherwise cleared," she said.

"Sounds like a lively place to work."

Why couldn't this be as easy as the time I snuck past Jennifer's doorman?

Jennifer! Yes, Jennifer! She would give me permission to come up, and I could just bypass her office to find the woman I was really there to see. I could only surmise that this mother's surname wasn't the same as her son's, but that wasn't unusual.

"Hold on," I said to the receptionist. "I just remembered her first name. It's Jennifer. And I'm certain she's an attorney."

"Yes, but I already looked and there were no Lopezes under the attorney names," she said to me. She was getting curt again.

The elevator doors chimed, letting out a fresh face to challenge entrance. A young man, the quiet and obliging type, stood behind me. His certain obedience would make me look bad. Or worse. He was holding a long blue canister in his hand, looking like it housed blueprints.

"Can you just look up under Jennifer Ness?" I asked the receptionist. "And now that I think of it, Lopez was her maiden name, so that would explain why it could be under a different name."

"Don't you have an appointment?" she asked again, letting out a sigh.

"Well, I told you it was a surprise, so no. But even if I did have an appointment, don't you think I would've led off with that rather than engaging in this back and forth with you?"

Her fingers banged against her keyboard, showing me her increased frustration. Then her shoulders relaxed and her face lightened. "Yes, I have a Jennifer Ness here."

"That's the one."

She gave me a 'yeah right' look, but it was also clear she was anxious to get rid of me. "Hold on," she said, picking up her phone and dialing.

She started talking to someone on the other end that I assumed was Jennifer. The receptionist hung up and looked at me. "She'll be waiting for you in the upper lobby, right as you exit the elevator on twenty-one."

"Another lobby?" I asked.

"Yes. I'll give you floor access, but hold on." She rolled her chair over to my left to see who was standing behind me, the gentleman who had just exited the elevator. "What floor were you trying to get to, sir?"

He said he had a delivery for the architectural firm on eighteen.

She did the same inquiries for him but it didn't take nearly as long as mine did. Probably because he didn't have the burden of making it all up as he went. She gave us both the green light and we rode up together.

Of course, I jumped off with him when the elevator landed on the eighteenth floor.

I had to keep some of the high cards in my stack, didn't I?

THIRTY

Sending a Message

Jennifer sent me a text.

```
Jen: Where are you? I'm waiting by elevator. What's up?
Me: Sorry. Had to go to bathroom. Can I meet you in your office?
Jen: Sure. Make a right after the lobby, then 5th office on right.
```

Thank goodness she didn't ask where I planned on finding a bathroom.

Already in the stairwell at the twentieth floor, I slid my phone back in my pocket and finished climbing the last flight of stairs to my destination. As I started winding myself through the back hallways, making my way through Jen's floor, the first few offices held little interest to me, but as I got near those coveted corner offices, I knew the odds of finding a partner's nameplate were going up.

One male, two males, and then a third as I passed three consecutive open doors. At the fourth door I froze. I guess I had arrived at the right place.

"Oh, hey, there she is," Thatcher said, standing and pulling out the guest chair next to his. Obviously, he wanted me close enough so that my choke chain was within easy grasp.

"I was just telling Ms. Maloney, Erena Maloney, that I was waiting on you," he said. "Close the door on your way in, if you don't mind. Ms. Maloney wants us to talk in private."

I left her office door slightly open.

I looked at the woman behind the desk. Not Lopez. Erena Maloney. She was incredibly well preserved for her age, not the sort who looked like she could have a twentysomething-year-old, raping murderer or not. The roots of her hair had a slight gray, but the rest was a warm brown. Her suit was crisp, clean, and a cream color to boot. Not many women dared to pull out that color in winter, but paired with a bright red blouse, it seemed evident she wanted to be noticed wherever she went.

"Nice suit," I said. "Lana Braun, by chance?"

She looked down at her lap for a second and then lifted her gaze back to me, donning the slightest look of appreciation.

"It is," she answered. "Good eye. You like Lana Braun too?"

"You can afford better," I said, walking to her desk. "I mean, it's not like Lana Braun is on par with Kmart, but"—I picked up the Montblanc pen she had laying across one of her yellow legal pads, eyeing it carefully—"you like to show off a bit, so I'm thinking you'd be the type to stick to higher-end suits. Yet," I said, dropping her $400 pen back onto her pad, "you don't."

I looked over at Thatcher. I saw a vein bulge in the middle of his forehead.

Oh well.

I turned back to Erena. She was now sporting a hint of satisfaction on her face. That's when I knew the dynamics between Thatcher and myself were airing themselves like dirty laundry. I felt a little naked. She was likely as good at sizing things up as I was, making me realize she'd be a harder conquer than I first imagined. I supposed it went with the territory. No one quite knew when a stunt was being pulled like the ringleaders of all stunts: attorneys.

"If you must know," Erena said, reaching forward and picking up the Montblanc pen and holding it tightly as she leaned back in her chair, "I *can* afford better than Lana Braun, but I like the way the cut falls on me. You should know," she said, motioning her hand in my general vicinity, "being older does a number on your body, so anything helps."

"Detective Thatcher," I said, looking at him, "what have you two pals been talking about? I'm sorry I was late. I forgot how much closer you are to Horton Plaza than I am. I should have considered that," I added, just under my breath.

He recapped that he'd told Maloney we were here to follow up on a tip, but as he spoke, he was writing something down on one of his ubiquitous notepads that he'd pulled from inside the breast pocket of his jacket. Before I could mention to Maloney the specifics of why we thought she had bred a murderer, Thatcher handed me the pad under the ridge of

Maloney's desk. It read: *I'm here because I had a bad feeling about the two of you together. Deal with it.*

I thought about dropping the pad on the floor, but decided against it. Mainly because Maloney might see it. Instead I opted to get back to the point with Maloney.

"So, what I'm hearing is that you two have yet to arrive at step one?" I asked, letting my gaze go from Thatcher to Maloney. "You know step one, where we ask you where your murdering, rapist son is hiding these days?"

Her eyes flinched but it was the tiniest of movements. Otherwise, she kept her composure.

"No, Evelyn," Thatcher said. He was trying to modulate the tone of his voice to mask his frustration. "We hadn't gotten to that part."

"Evelyn," Maloney said. Not to get my attention, but simply to utter it. "That's a lovely name. It's almost regal sounding."

I couldn't help but laugh.

"What's humorous?" she asked.

I scooted to the edge of my seat, shifting the right side of my body in her direction and placing my arm on the edge of her desk. Evy's lesson number three in conquer: When you want to let someone know you can take them, you better be touching their stuff while you're sending the message.

I lifted up her nameplate, set it back down, and scooted it a few inches to the left. I made sure it was crooked.

"Oh," I said, letting another chuckle escape, "it's just that I accused you of having a rapist and murderer for a son, and the first thing out of your mouth is your opinion of the regality of my name."

Thatcher leaned back into his chair. I wasn't sure if it was a defense mechanism because claws and staples were about to fly, or whether he was finally relaxing and letting me rope and drag my saucy little calf back to the barn. I assumed it was the latter. I hoped so.

"And that's amusing?" she asked.

"It's hilarious."

"Why's that?"

"Because you're making our job so much easier."

"And your job is finding an alleged murderer, I presume? One whom you also believe to be my son?" When she finished speaking, she sat straight and stretched forward to fix her nameplate.

"Do you have a son by the name of David Lopez?" Thatcher asked.

Ms. Maloney didn't take her eyes off me while she answered. "Yes, but I can assure you he's no rapist, let alone a murderer." She leaned forward, propping an arm upon her desk. She looked at me as if she felt sorry for me, but it was a plastic, contrived pity. I knew whatever was about to spill from her mouth wasn't going to be pretty.

"I'm not trying to deflect the seriousness of your task because I made a remark about your name," she said to me. "I merely wanted you to feel there was something valuable about yourself before I shot you down by telling you you're a raving lunatic for making such a statement about my son."

"Hmm, that's quite thoughtful of you." I put my index finger back on the side of her nameplate. Tap, tap, *tap*. I sent it several inches to the right this time.

She immediately grabbed it and dropped it into one of her top drawers. "I'm genuinely surprised the SDPD allows such children to become police officers," she said to Thatcher with a coy smile.

Thatcher opened his mouth to say something, probably to defend me, but I interjected. "I'm not a police officer or a detective. In fact, I'm an attorney. Well," I tilted my head so that my ear neared my shoulder, "retired attorney who now consults with the police." The truth would've been more along the lines of disbarment but . . .

She shook her head. "I couldn't possibly see the benefit of using someone with your social skills. Whatever are you supposed to do? Enrage people?"

That comment amused Thatcher, but I knew he wasn't laughing at me.

"Whatever your use is," Erena said, "I have nothing to say regarding the accusation you've just made about my son. Yes, I do have a son by the name of David Lopez, but no, he is not a criminal. And, correct me if I'm wrong, but your other question was along the lines of do I know where he is, and the answer to that is also no. We, uh . . . ." It was the one and only time I saw her look down. She smoothed her tidy skirt. "We don't speak or see each other very often. He was a very willful child and I had to teach him some tough love. It apparently didn't take." She looked back up at me and forced a tight smile. "He's been on his own since he was sixteen."

I shook my head at her, wondering what version of tough love she had employed. Yet, I sensed something else was at play.

Maloney watched me with a familiar intensity, one that seemed aimed at breaking me down.

"Can you give me a brief explanation of the difference in surnames between you and your son?" Thatcher asked.

"Lopez is my maiden name. I wasn't married when David was born and I've since changed my last name for personal reasons."

I sighed, feigning total disinterest by flippantly tossing my hand by my shoulder. "I don't want to hear those boring parts, Detective Thatcher," I said. "I want to hear about the crazy stuff she did to him." I looked up and to my right, contemplating something. "Well, not just crazy," I amended, "I think she should start with her certain cruelty."

She ushered a small chuckle, but there was nothing humorous about it. It sounded plain mean. I didn't think she'd actually comment.

"Cruelty?" she asked.

I looked at Thatcher again. He seemed to be getting nervous. I gave him a quick tap on the knee, under Maloney's desk and out of her sight, to let him know I felt in control of the situation.

She mocked me again by laughing. "I am not a cruel person, or even an inconsiderate person," Erena said. "If you knew even an ounce of what I had to suffer in raising—" She cut herself off, leaning back in her chair and curling her lips inward to stop herself from saying more.

Thatcher and I both leaned forward. We were both thinking the same thing: Finish it, finish it, finish it!

When she looked at us, we must've appeared like eager schoolchildren wanting their treasure-box treats. She stood. "Never mind that. It's irrelevant. However, if you'll excuse me, I don't care to have any more of this conversation unless you find a reason to do something more formal, with my lawyer present. You remember that part, right, Evelyn?" she said, grinning and crinkling her nose at me.

"You can call me Ms. Barrett, Ms. Maloney."

She looked up at the ceiling for a second. "Evelyn Barrett . . . now why does that sound so familiar?"

"Google it later, talk now," I said.

"I don't think so. About the talking, that is. I *will* do the Google search."

Thatcher stood too. "Do you have any idea where your son is?" he asked.

"Also," I interjected quickly, "did you know that each of your son's victims also shops at Lana Braun? He must like the way the cut falls on them too. I think he picked up his fashion sense from you in that regard.

There's got to be some sick tie to that, don't you think? Like, for example, your son wants to kill you but instead takes it out on innocents."

She blinked once. "I believe I've communicated all I need to."

"We will be making this more formal if need be. And then we'll be asking our questions down in an interrogation room at the station," Thatcher said.

"Of course," she said, her voice trying to drip honey. "I wouldn't expect any less of the diligent efforts of our men in blue. Do it right, and I'm yours."

I raised my index finger in the air, as a wondrous, biting remark occurred to me. But Thatcher must've realized I was about to open my mouth with an inappropriate comment.

"Oh no, no," Thatcher mumbled while taking hold of my elbow and ushering me to the door.

When the door was open, he turned around to Ms. Maloney and said, "We'll be back with your formalities."

On the other side of the door stood Jennifer, bearing both an ashen complexion and a raging fire in her eyes. She must've been eavesdropping, which wouldn't have been hard since I hadn't shut Maloney's door all the way. I broke free from Thatcher's hold and took a step closer to her, shaking my head, trying to silently indicate "no."

Her jaw was set, her lips drained of blood.

"Jennifer," I said, dodging my head so that she couldn't see past me and into her boss's office. "No, Jennifer. It's not worth it," I said in a forced whisper.

Her eyes locked on mine. "You know who he is?" she said through her teeth, tears pooling on her lower lids. "And he's still walking around?" She was trembling. "And it's Erena's son?"

I held her upper arms, trying to settle her down and hold her back. I looked to Thatcher for help. He sidestepped me and went to stand behind Jennifer.

I looked back at my friend.

"Jennifer, don't. It's not worth it" is all I could repeat. "Later," I added. "We don't know for sure."

But I did. Saying I didn't know was stale and meaningless. I also didn't want Jennifer to lose her job over this. She saw right through me, though. She knew I knew and glared at me.

"Move," she said. The sound the word made as it came out of her mouth was decidedly more effective than the content. Even for Thatcher. He reached around her to get ahold of my arm and gently pulled me out of the way.

"Let it play out a minute," he whispered in my ear. "What you started unraveling in Maloney, she may finish."

I could see Erena positioning herself behind her desk, dead center, and already looking down at any number of papers. She was playing it cool again, especially in front of underlings.

Before Jennifer could open her mouth again, Maloney said, "Ms. Ness, I surely do not care what you have to say, considering you were, as it would appear, eavesdropping on my conversation with these visitors. I can only surmise that you've done such so you and your co-workers can have something to chitchat about at the water cooler. I'm already seriously considering firing you for your complete lack of decorum at this moment." Maloney looked up at Jennifer. "And that's before you even open your mouth and vocalize anything that would undoubtedly get you fired anyway. I suggest you move along without another word."

"Chitchat? Water cooler?" Jennifer spat out.

"I assume that's why you're playing hurt and shocked right now. So that you could go back and beef up the ridiculous lies that have been brought to my attention. And again I'll state, lies you have deceitfully overhead."

I heard the shuffle of feet behind me. When I looked, a few more people emerged from their offices. When Maloney saw them, she rushed to her door and slammed it shut.

"Mouth-breathing fools!" I could hear her say from behind the door.

Jennifer popped the door back open.

Oh no, I thought.

"Which lies would that be, Erena?" Jennifer shouted. "The fact that your son raped me?"

"Weeeelll," I said, "we don't really—"

"Shut it, Evy!" Jennifer yelled. "You know it's him. That's why you're here."

Jennifer turned her fury back to her boss.

"And even if they don't have the proof yet, they'll get all the proof they need soon enough," she said, slowly putting a hand to her belly.

No, no, no! I screamed inside my head.

XII

In the gym she looked right at me, even spoke to me. Her being there so close, speaking to me, I saw a flash of white again and it was that rage. The world narrowed and all I could see was her at the end of the tunnel and everything in me wanted to come out and hurt her right then and there. I started another anabolic injection cycle last week to take the edge off the old formula, to take the edge off the bursts on the old stuff, and I wasn't going to let this new stuff make me another stereotype. Not today. Not for that. Definitely not in public. I only meant to run before I did something else, but when I looked back, real quick, I saw her laid out on some of the machines. It must've been me and most of me hopes that it was.

It's true that when I close my eyes, I can see that I did it and it makes me glad. That is why I know this is me. Not the steroids, not my mother, not my father. And for that, since it's me, I should've popped her one. I should have ripped her limb from limb because before I felt the fury, I saw something in her face. Like she wanted the end of me.

I was feeling more confident every day, understanding on my own what I was doing and why it had to be done. Do my work at the gym, do my reps for hours after, and plan, plan, plan. I could do it forever. It made me complete. I barely thought about my old life. None of that mattered anymore. I'd grown. I'd become my own man and no one could touch me.

But she looked me in the eyes and spoke to me. She wanted something. To make me pay, I thought. And for that, she had to die. Not for that other stuff anymore because none of that matters when I'm untouchable. I can't be taken down now. Especially not by her.

THIRTY-ONE

And Then . . .

We have to track this guy down right now," I said to Thatcher. "That Maloney woman can say all she wants that she doesn't know where her son is, or that they don't speak, but she's shrewd. You don't get where she is in that sort of law firm without an overabundant portion of self-adoration and preservation. Even if she had absolutely no love for her son, she'd want to protect herself, as well as her position in that firm." I opened the Lopez file on the corner of Thatcher's desk, thumbing through the first five or six pages and hoping it'd give me something about his location that I didn't glean the first thousand times I had looked through it. Thatcher took my pause as permission to look away, so I moved closer to him.

"That means knowing exactly where all her old and ugly bones are hanging in various backroom closets," I continued. "If Jennifer's baby can prove that David Lopez is our murderer, then it can also prove that Erena Maloney is the mother of a murderer, and I assure you, that woman will protect that from gaining more momentum. We need to move before anything bad happens."

Thatcher was opening and shutting the top drawers in his desk. He slammed the last one. "I'm sick of losing all my pens. I know it's you. And the notepads too. Where are they and when are you going to replace them?"

I stared at him blankly. We were going to go over this *now*?

"Just get new ones from supply," I said. "Did you even hear what I said to you about moving on this right now? I think Jennifer might be in danger. If Maloney contacts Lopez, he'll finish what he started. There's even more incentive now because of the baby."

Thatcher stood, leaving his chair. He faced me with his mouth set tight and his arms folded across his chest.

Great, I thought. Yes. We were going to do the ancillary squabble now. He's going to harp on the pens when all I want to do is make sure my friend wasn't gutted that night.

I groaned over the fact that Thatcher wasn't as interested in Jen's safety as I was. Holding up one of my hands to him before he opened his mouth, I said, "Put a pause on that thought, Officer Petty." I turned my back to him and pulled out my cell phone. I texted Jennifer. "Go to your mom's. Go somewhere. Just leave now."

When I finished the text, I turned back to Thatcher.

"Fine. I took your pens and I'll replace them. The notepads too. It wasn't because I was trying to be tricky. It was merely an easy access type of transaction. No big deal. But right now, I need to know how you can protect Jennifer."

He uncrossed his arms and put one hand down on the desk, leaning into it. "Great. Replace the pens and pads. We have enough budget problems as is," he said. "But," he stood, his hand still on the desk, "the only reason I was even looking for a pen, was to write down the names and cell numbers of the two plainclothes I put outside her building. That way, when you want an up-to-the-minute account, you can hear it straight from the horse's mouth. So, I'm sorry about harping on the pens and pads at this exact moment, but I feel confident we have Jennifer's situation under control."

He walked over to someone else's desk, a momentarily unoccupied one, and took a pen. He pulled a receipt out of his pocket and was about to write down the numbers when his phone rang.

"Are you sure?" he asked the caller. "Have you called the number I gave you? Fine, I'm on my way. Stay there."

When he hung up the phone, his eyes met mine and his look managed to seize every nerve in my body.

Oh, crap! I screamed inside my head.

"Evelyn," he said, but then looked away. He went right for his top drawer and grabbed his car keys. Without looking back up at me, he continued. "My instinct is to tell you to go home, but you probably won't."

"What are you talking about? What's going on?"

He slid his keys into his right pants pocket and then sighed. "Before I say anything, I want to ask you to give an honest evaluation on whether you can be away from your baby for the next few hours. From what I've witnessed with you, it's about time to go back home and"—his eyes closed and his mouth twisted with discomfort—"you know, that thing you do to feed your baby dinner."

"It's okay to say *nurse*, Thatcher."

"You get what I'm saying. But evaluate that right now and then I'll tell you what's happening."

My heart started beating quicker, stronger, landing in dull, echoing thuds I was sure Thatcher could hear. Even my eyes felt like they were throbbing and thumping in anticipation of what had to be bad news. I appreciated Thatcher's ploy and knew he meant well, but asking me how long I could be away from Owen, how long I could go without breastfeeding him, confirmed that something horrible was at play.

"Just tell me what it is!" I begged, unable to attempt any sort of rationalization or weighing of competing interests until I knew what was on the other side of the scale.

"Your friend Jennifer never made it out of her parking garage at work," he said.

My heart stopped its thumping. It had sunk somewhere deep and worthless, somewhere where its beating wasn't necessary.

"Those officers I was telling you about, the ones I assigned to trail her, had been waiting for her to leave for the day. When most of the garage had emptied and her vehicle was still there, they went inside the law firm to talk to her and found she had left hours earlier."

She could just be in hiding. She could be. I pulled my cell out again to see if she had responded to my text, but she hadn't. Feeling dizzy, my hands numbly felt around for a nearby chair. I eased myself into it, realizing that the world was starting to spin because I had forgotten to keep a steady breath. We did this, I thought. No wait, *I* started this today.

I had been so anxious to confront Lopez's mother and so anxious to bypass the firm's visitor policy, that I had set this all in motion. I had spilled the gunpowder trail, and I had made the spark. If I hadn't told the receptionist I was there to see Jennifer, Jennifer wouldn't have been on alert trying to figure out what I was up to and probably wouldn't have been able to hear the Maloney conversation.

And then . . . and then . . . and then.

I swallowed the ball of nerves rising in my throat. "She could've walked out, or maybe she got a ride home with someone," I said to Thatcher, hoping that by saying it, it would take on verity, even though the truth was screaming out at me, just as Jennifer may be screaming at this very moment.

Thatcher's eyes waxed cold. "Yeah," he said, low and scared, almost in a whisper. "That part about getting a ride with someone is what's concerning me. Could've been the absolute worst someone and I'm worried it wasn't voluntary on her part."

I wanted to shout at him, *Shut your mouth! Don't say those things!*

But who was I kidding? If it walks like a duck, if it talks like a duck, if she's carrying her rapist's baby and is suddenly gone . . .

"What's the plan?" I asked, feeling my eyes pool with tears, an indication of raw panic. It was one thing to be scared for Jen, which I was, but it was another thing to have been the one who brought about the situation that generated the fear.

"Patrol already called into La Jolla and they're checking her apartment, but I think we, or just I, should check it out too."

"She's not there," I said, sounding robotic. It had the emotive response of what was left in me.

"That's what I'm betting too, but I don't know where else to start and I have to rule it out."

I stood. "The Senior Center. Let's go there."

"Why?"

"Because there's something there. Something or someone. There's just too much of a circle of circumstance around that place."

"He won't go back there," Thatcher said. "Even without a police presence, he'd be too nervous to try anything because the neighborhood is now aware of the things that have happened."

I squeezed my cell phone, ready to call Eddie. "I'm not suggesting we go back because I think we'll find him," I told Thatcher. "I want to go back and figure what it is about that place that draws him there to begin with. If we find that, we may find him."

"How's that going to help us get to Jen in time?" he asked.

My heart started thumping again. A new panic was setting in because I had to call Eddie. I dialed the first few digits of my house phone.

Thatcher looked at his watch. "The Senior Center is probably shut down for the night, don't you think? Don't those places close down around three or four?"

I shot him a disturbed look just as Eddie answered. "Eddie," I said, the gravity of the moment making those pooled tears jump ship. I was about to lie to him, lie about something of catastrophic importance, but if I didn't, he'd put his foot down and then Thatcher would be alone for the night and he'd never find Jen alive. "You know those cans of formula the doctor gave us for Owen?" I asked.

"Yeah."

"Owen will need to be fed here in the next hour or so, so do you think you can whip him up some of that stuff? I need to stay for a bit longer, we're getting close." Instinctively, I wanted to raise a hand to my breasts because they had started to tingle, knowing that they were about to miss a feeding. Maybe more. Maybe all. I couldn't quite explain the force of determination that pushed me to pursue something potentially dangerous when I had an infant at home. I think it had something to do with the over encompassing will of humanity wanting to be of some measly use, wanting to step up even if it meant stepping off forever. That, and the guilt I felt for throwing Jen back to the wolves.

"Is everything all right?" he asked.

Tears, lies, I turned away from Thatcher, rinse and repeat. "Yeah, we just have to follow through with some stuff and I'll be home later."

The silence on Eddie's side of the line was brutal. I figured he knew, but not really. Not entirely. Yet, if he did know, then his quiet acceptance of my lies was even more condemning.

"I can give him the formula," he finally said, the hesitation and resignation ringing in my ears like church bells. "But, Evy," he added, "be careful."

I wiped at my eyes. "I will. I'll have my cell on me."

"Evelyn?"

"Gotta go, hon. I love you."

I hung up the phone.

"I think you should go home," Thatcher said. "You're making him nervous, it sounds. As much as I want to say it's not true, I don't think we're going to find anything tonight. Sorry, but there's no need to put him through this."

"Oh no, I *will* find something tonight." I felt a surge saying it, like God Himself was letting me know that it was time to charge and the end of the line was there, finally visible on this night.

"I'm ready to finish it now. You and I both know that if we don't make contact tonight, we'll find Jen's body dumped somewhere and I can't stop moving *now*, knowing that that's what tomorrow will bring. Now come on, let's go to the Senior Center."

"No. I'm going to run by her apartment first," he said.

"There's nothing at the apartment."

"Well, the Senior Center is probably closed, and even if not, hardly anyone will be around."

"I don't care. I was planning on kicking down the front door and committing a bit of B&E if I have to."

His hand went up to his forehead. "Are you kidding me?" he whined.

"You know what? I don't have time for this. Number one, *no*, you are not going to do a 'bit of B&E' and number two, I will not be taking you to the Senior Center only to watch you pretend you weren't going to kick in the door until you actually do. I'm going to her apartment. You can either come or you can go home to Eddie."

"Or, I can do what I know is the better plan and go to the Senior Center. If we hurry, I bet we can find someone still there. In fact, I'm sure someone's there. It's still daylight."

He reached for his cell in his top drawer and tucked it into his pocket opposite of where he had earlier stuffed his keys. "I'll just call Eddie on my way out, let him know you've gone out somewhere solo. Maybe he can talk some sense into you." He started to walk away but I grabbed his arm.

"Thatcher," I said. "Please." I said it in that soft sort of petitionary way that wasn't customary of me. But at that point, I was completely lost. Lost because even though any other day of the week I would've had no problem going on my own, something in my gut told me I shouldn't be alone tonight.

"Please." I pleaded. "She's not at her apartment. And I know she's not at the Senior Center either, but if you could just see how everything has played out in my head, you'd understand why I need to go back there right now. It's like an enigma to me, the last piece that I need to find a home for. Everything else has made sense, yet we still haven't found him. And now, he's got my friend again. I need to go back and figure out that last piece and if I do, I believe we'll have a better shot at finding him. At finding Jen. I can't really explain it but I'm telling you, everything inside of me right now is saying that Senior Center is the exact place we need to be."

He sighed, lowering his head and thinking about it for a moment. "Fine," he said. "We'll do a quick run by, and if the place is closed for the night, we're *not* going in."

THIRTY-TWO

Elder Abuse

Thatcher and I pulled up to the front door of the Senior Center at five thirty p.m. Only one other car was in the parking lot but a few lights were on inside, near the front door. Before Thatcher could put his car fully into park, I threw open the passenger door and jumped out, running to the entrance of the center and fearing that whoever was in there was a moment away from shutting everything else off and locking the door.

I gave the door a quick tug. Locked. *No!*

I banged on the door with an opened hand, my prints smudging up the otherwise clean glass. From around the corner a figure appeared. It was the pervert. I mean Kirk. When he first scuttled into view, he was wearing a grumpy look on his face, like he was in no hurry to see who was banging at the door.

When he saw it was me, the disturbed look made a quick ascent into one of frolic. He pretended to tap at his heart with glee as he walked up to the door. Once there he put his face to the little metal slot where the postman might drop the mail. "Hey there, Officer. What brings you back?"

"I need you to open the door, Kirk. I need to come in."

"Hold on, then," he said. "I have to find my lady friend. She's the one with the keys. Don't disappear on me now."

Thatcher came to the door just as Kirk walked away. When Kirk reappeared, he was holding a ring of keys but no lady friend was in tow. He opened the door and Thatcher and I walked inside.

"We were about to shut the place down for the night," Kirk said, "but then Bea and me decided to take advantage of some quiet time, having the place all to ourselves." He gave me a wink. "Bea is the manager of sorts of this place and I was hoping she'd *manage* me into a comfortable position," he said, letting most of his face turn up with a wide grin.

"Oh, please," I exclaimed, shutting my eyes. "Spare the details."

"No, no," Kirk said, "not like hanky-panky business. I only wish." He leaned closer in to me, holding a hand near the side of his mouth to whisper, "Truth of it is, I can't get my captain up, and the blue pills are too expensive. So, Bea and me only neck a little."

My hand went up to stop him as I took a step away. "Please, no. Seriously, no," I said, shaking my head. "We need your help." My head turned to the left as I said it.

Other than the light on above us in the foyer, a small light was on in a nook, just off the entry. It illuminated just enough to see through another glass door where I could make out a few weight machines hiding in the shadows of an otherwise darkened room.

I pointed to the door, walking over to the area, and said, "Kirk, you have exactly two seconds to tell me whether or not there's a bald guy who comes in here to fix these weight machines. If so, I'll give you an additional two seconds to tell me everything you know about him."

Kirk raised his hand and scratched at the top of his head with his ring finger. "Are you talking about that kooky kid who says he's Bob's son?"

I did an about-face, walking back to where Thatcher and Kirk stood. I got so close to Kirk that I thought I felt my own hot breath bounce back to me.

"Bob who?" I asked.

"Navy Bob. You remember. My buddy that was with me when we asked you about that dead girl. Hey . . ." he said, looking down at the ground. His hands dove for his pockets and I could tell he balled both up once they got in there.

I knew that look and that posturing. I'd seen it plenty of times with both jurors and witnesses. It was always the same thing: wondering whether it was worth it to spill their pretty little guts.

I could almost feel the seconds stretch by while Kirk contemplated the value of proceeding. Each click of his internal clock—figuring out how he'd proceed—was like chewing on sand or the dragging of metal on metal. It must've been a good bit of information he was holding back. A real humdinger. At one point, I even expected Kirk to be cliché and claim the Fifth.

I got tired of waiting for him to think it over. "Let me help you with your decision," I said to him, narrowing my eyes. "Yes, you *should* tell us what you were about to say, and no, I promise we won't give you any problems about it, even if it's questionably criminal."

I could see Thatcher's mouth open to protest, but he said nothing.

Kirk looked up at me, his head still lowered. He studied me. It seemed like another eternity passed.

"Listen up, Kirk," I said while rubbing my hand across the back of my neck, "my patience has already expired for today. It went bye-bye the moment I heard my friend was taken by a raping murderer. Again! That bald piece of crap that comes in here to fix those machines, Bob's son you said, he's the one who did it, and I want to know *everything* you know about him. And that includes blurting out whatever you're noodling right now."

He looked at Thatcher. I did too. Thatcher had that vein bulging again. If I could get inside his head at the moment, I'd likely find that he was either mad at me for saying we wouldn't pursue questionably criminal behavior, or that he wanted to know what Kirk was hiding as much as I did.

Kirk finally spoke. "I don't know anything about the kid except that Bob says he bothers him every now and then."

"How old is your friend Bob?" I asked.

"Seventy-four. And I'm seventy-three."

"What else do you know?" I asked. "Where does the bald guy work?"

"I don't know. He just comes in every now and then to check the equipment. More so than I think the equipment needs to be checked, but then again he talks to Bob every time he comes around. In fact, last time he came around was a day or two after you guys found that woman's body. I caught him and Bob yelling at one another." Kirk's eyes did that quick shift to the floor. He was toying again with the elements of disclosure.

"Old man, so help me, if you don't tell me that little nugget of information you got bopping around up there in your brain, I'm going to shake you until you fill your adult diaper."

"Hey now!" he said, gruff. "I don't wear none of those diapers. I'm fully functional in that regard."

From around the corner, a woman appeared. She must've been Kirk's lady friend. Her feet were bare except for the pair of tan stockings that she scuffled over the rough rec center carpet. Her face was set in a mix of white-hot fury and black contempt. She seemed frail but set on a malignant purpose. I would have been scared if her eyes weren't locked on Kirk, her shoes in one hand and something small in the other. It was a picture.

When she got to Kirk, she put the picture in the front breast pocket of his shirt and then cold slapped him across the face with her dainty and liver-spotted hand.

On a younger man, it would have been the wisp of a willow, but with Kirk, his saggy cheeks had just hit a cement barrier.

"You make me sick, you pervert!" she said to him.

I turned to Thatcher and mouthed, "Told you so."

"I found that picture folded and tucked into your cardigan pocket back there," she said, pointing at the picture. "And don't you dare accuse me of snooping, because I wasn't. I was getting cold and wanted to cover up while I waited for you to talk to these people, and that's what I found. You disgust me! Give me back my keys before I call the police on you right this instant."

Kirk had turned to a pluck of white cotton the moment she came barreling around the corner, but a little color rose in his cheeks as he dutifully fished through one of his pant pockets and then dropped a set of keys into her expectant hand.

"Ma'am, we are the police," Thatcher said.

"Well, hallelujah!" she exclaimed. "You ought to arrest this man immediately and then euthanize him for his sick and twisted—maybe even murderous—ways."

"I didn't do that to her, Bea, please. Let me explain," Kirk said.

"Save it," she said. "The police are here and I'll leave it to them." She turned to us. "I'm leaving and there's nothing you can do to stop me. I found a humanly despicable picture of a hurt woman in this man's cardigan. I won't answer any of your questions because I've already said the extent of what I know. Now I'm leaving."

As she walked to the door, Kirk said, "I'm telling you, Bea, that picture isn't even mine. It's Bob's!"

"I don't care."

"But, Bea! You're my ride home."

"I *surely* don't care." Out the door she went in her stockinged feet, shoes still in her hand.

Kirk quickly reached for his breast pocket and Thatcher jammed a finger toward his chest, saying, "If you touch that picture, and I mean even if the thought of your fingerprints grace its edges, I'll be the one who shakes you until you pee yourself."

THIRTY-THREE

Lying to Kirk

I only looked at the picture for a second before turning away. It was now in Thatcher's hand and last I saw, Thatcher was splitting his time between observing the picture and giving Kirk cold, hard glances. It was quite a gratuitous manner of luck. No, that makes it sound like I was happy to see the picture and that wasn't the case by any stretch. I'd have to call it providence, then. Whatever it was, it only served to confirm that we were destined to be at the Senior Center that night.

The picture was of a woman, laid out on her back. Her arms splayed to the side and her face listless. She was either unconscious or dead, with a busted lip and blood running down her chin and part of her cheek. There was more blood and swelling around her eyes, face, neck, and chest. All in all, she had the general appearance of being utterly finished.

With my back to Kirk and Thatcher, I said, "It's the girl from the grave."

"What?" they asked in unison.

"How do you know?" Thatcher asked.

"Her hair," I said, remembering seeing it from the unearthed grave. "And even though she's pretty messed up in that picture, the similarities are enough to compare it with the enhanced picture forensics made of the Jane Doe."

I heard movement from Thatcher's direction and turned back around. He had pulled out his phone and appeared to be flipping through screens. He stopped when he found what he was looking for. His eyes went back and forth between whatever was on his phone and the picture he took from Kirk.

"I think you're right," he finally said.

"I am," I responded. "It's the same hair."

I looked at Kirk. "I assume you have a perfectly justifiable reason for having this picture."

He nodded, his face lowered though, not so sure that he did. He was showing either shame or remorse, but I certainly didn't care which at that point.

Looking up, he said, "I told you that bald kid had a fight with Bob, and it started when Bob and I were in the middle of a game of gin rummy. The kid came in and Bob said he'd be right back. I was winning, you see, so after several minutes when Bob didn't come back, I figured the old cheat had ditched the hand because he knew he'd lost. It wouldn't have been the first time he'd faked some sort of illness—"

"Speed up to the part that will interest me," I demanded. "And keep the fluff to a minimum."

Kirk pointed his finger at me. "You're too young to pretend you're in a hurry and I'm just an old man who likes to talk. Can't you give me some respect?"

I pointed back at him. "No. Not when my friend is going to end up like that girl in your photo."

"I was getting to the good part anyway, if you would have just held your horses," Kirk added.

"Talk!" Thatcher shouted, waving the picture in front of his face.

"If you two arrest me for having that picture—"

"Is that what you're afraid of?" I asked, cutting him off. "Give me a break. I already told you we only want to know where and how you got it, now talk!"

"Fine, fine, it's Bob's. I have to go back to telling you about the gin rummy game. Can I? Or will I get kicked?"

"Go," I said.

"I went to look for Bob, thinking he ran out on our hand, and I found him in the exercise room with the kid. They had the door closed but it's glass so you can see." Kirk pointed to a room about fifty feet away from us. "I could see Bob was yelling at the kid for something and the kid was just taking it, his head down like a dog that's been beat and the hits keep coming. I've never seen Bob talk to someone like that and I guess there was a reason. I already knew that kid had been bugging Bob about information on Bob's family, and I figured this was Bob telling the kid for the last time that they weren't family, and he should buzz off.

"Bob went out the back way from the exercise room to the courtyard, and the kid immediately took off, shoving that picture," he pointed to it, still in Thatcher's hand, "deep into the trash can outside after he crumbled it."

"And you dug through the trash to find it?" Thatcher asked.

"Yeah," he said, without even moving his lips.

"Why?"

"I don't want to say."

This was clearly the part that Kirk was trying to keep under his hat. But it didn't matter. We had heard enough.

"Guess what, Kirk?" I asked. "Let's make a deal, shall we? We won't ask why you wanted that picture so badly, nor why you kept it without reporting it to the police, if you do us one quick favor."

"What's that?" he asked.

"Take us to Bob."

We drove quietly over to a retirement home in La Mesa where many of the seniors who socialize at the rec center live. Kirk was sitting in the back, behind Thatcher, and I felt his eyes on the side of my face almost the entire time.

"How can I be sure the police won't give me grief about that picture?" Kirk asked.

I turned my head to look back at him for a moment, and then glanced back to the front, looking out the windshield. It was dark by now and the sensation to feed Owen was growing painful. It still didn't compare to the sinking feeling I was experiencing about Jen, knowing that each moment that passed us was one less tick of possibility that we'd find her in any sort of savable state.

"You can't be sure," I said to Kirk. "In fact, I'd even argue you'd have to be stupid to think you'll be left alone. You were holding on to a picture of a dead, beaten woman. I'd put my money on you paying for that one."

He lunged forward, grabbing the side of my seat closest to him. "You said you wouldn't—"

I didn't let him finish. He had no right to.

"I don't care what I said." I looked back at him and pulled his curled and wrinkled hand from its grasp on my seat. "Let me give you a little dose of the reality behind the world of women. Number one, I think you're pervy. I've thought so from the beginning when you made a comment about my 'bosom.' The fact you had that picture with you and failed to notify authorities of any possible wrongdoing, *especially* considering you saw the actual person who threw the photo away and could give a description of him, only serves to prove you're not only a pervert, but also a sadistic pervert. Number two, women reserve the right to lie to perverts. I think the rationale behind that one is pretty self-explanatory.

"And number three, women stick up for other women. Even if I don't rat you out, your 'lady friend' from earlier tonight will. In fact, you're lucky we decided to take you with us right now because I bet she's already called the police and they're at the Senior Center looking for you."

I let my words sink in for a moment, measuring his silence. "What's the matter, Kirk? *Now* you have nothing to say?"

"I was only thinking, that's all," he said. "Thinking that I shouldn't have told you where Bob lives until I had something in writing about not investigating me."

"Oh, Kirk, silly Kirk. Why do you think I pushed you for the address before we even let you in the car? Besides, I used to be a lawyer in my former life. I would've made sure anything in writing would've been full of loopholes."

Thatcher smirked.

We arrived at Bob's retirement complex a few minutes later. We figured Kirk also lived here because once Thatcher let him out of the back he hurried off, pulling out a coiled, green plastic key-chain bracelet with one key on it.

He also flipped us the bird before he got too far. We would've laughed, Thatcher especially, but this wasn't the time for such things.

"Should we follow him?" I asked.

"Nah," Thatcher replied. "I mean, we're going to follow him a bit," he said, looking down at his phone. "The address he gave us for this Bob person is over in those bungalows too. Same direction Kirk's walking."

"Over there?" I pointed in the distance, to our left.

Thatcher nodded. He had parked his car near the main entrance, where from the look of the dilapidated building, the lower income residents resided. But not Kirk. Not pervy old men who had free rein to terrorize a senior center with a picture of a beaten, raped, and murdered woman.

"Move the car, then," I suggested. "That way, if you have to drag geriatric Bob kicking and screaming, you don't have to drag him very far."

"I can handle him," Thatcher said. "But yeah, I'll move the car."

"What's the unit number?" I asked. "I'll walk and meet you over there."

"One-fourteen," he said and then got in his car. "Wait a minute." He searched the length of the parking lot with his eyes. "How do I drive over there? I don't see a road that leads back there."

I looked too. Kirk had cut across a lawn and I had planned to do the same thing. The only paved portion of road was the horseshoe driveway we came in on.

"I guess go back on Dryer." I pointed back to the main road just west of us. "Make the first right turn you see. That should land you in the right area of the bungalows. Maybe they have a separate entrance between the assisted and the independent tenants."

"Okay, I'll meet you right out front of one-fourteen."

I nodded and cut across the grass.

THIRTY-FOUR

Man Down

When I passed by unit one-eleven, I noticed an open door a few bungalows down. The row of small homes was quaint, quiet, and dark except for the occasional blue glow of a television set seeping through the front windows. The one door left ajar looked like a drooping mouth, dazed and scorned next to every other little place snuggled up in a row of tightly shut units. I continued my approach, hearing a small dog bark in the distance, yipping its little life away.

Where was Thatcher? I had already expected his headlights to flood the small parking lot I had managed to find on foot, lining the front of the bungalows.

I stopped and counted the number of units ahead until the open door, rattling the progression of numbers in my head. If I was standing in front of one-eleven, then, one-twelve, thirteen, fourteen . . .

That had to have been Bob's door open. My heart sank. Everything sank. It felt like it was always the same thing, a constant proliferation of bad news, bad luck. Bob's door left open couldn't be good. Call this match for the killer. Just give it to him. I could almost see the Devil in the details of it all, constantly throwing down that wild card of his. This was his game and he wanted us all damned.

I had to keep going. I tried to convince myself that maybe the door was open because that yipper-dog barking in the distance was Bob's and had free rein to come back whenever he was good and ready. I took another step and felt my first tingle of fright, thinking I should go back and find Thatcher instead of waiting for him.

What could be taking him so long?

My discomfort grew. The yipper had stopped barking or was too far out for me to hear. I pulled out my cell to call Thatcher.

"Yeah?" he asked.

"Where are you?"

"All I'm finding is closed gates at every other entrance into this place. It seems to me that the only open gate was the first one we went in. I'm going to go around once more just to make sure."

"You need to hurry," I said. "Bob's unit has its front door open and it's making me nervous."

"Did you check inside?"

"No. Why would I do that?"

"To make sure everything is all right."

"That sounds fun and all, but what if everything *isn't* all right. I have no gun, I have no super punch 'em in the pancreas skills like you do. I have nothing."

"Right, I forgot about that," he said, sounding distracted. "No open gates," he muttered. I could hear him straining, his voice sounding farther off from the microphone.

"Have you pulled up into one?" I asked. "Maybe they automatically open when you pull up to them."

"This is ridiculous!" he shouted and I heard a thump, figuring he smacked the steering wheel. "Okay, listen, Evy, go to Bob's unit, but stay on the phone with me. Take a quick look inside without actually stepping in. Do you understand?" he asked me.

"Yeah."

"Do *not* go in," he repeated emphatically.

"I heard you the first time."

"Fine. I'm just going to park where we started, and I'll cut across the field like you did. Are we clear about the part where you're only to look into the open door and not go through it?"

"No, I'm utterly confused. Am I to go inside running screaming, or shall I just back my thing up, going *beep, beep, beep*, like a dump truck?"

"Don't go in."

"I think I want to now. You're making it sound almost fun."

"Don't go in!"

"Settle down. Geez. I heard you straight the first time. Okay, I'm at the door," I said.

"What do you see?"

"Nothing."

"Nothing at all?"

"Well, some faded furniture from the nineties and all the lights look like they're on, but there's not much else to tell you."

"Is the television on?"

"No, but he's got one. Oh, wait, I see a little doggie bed."

"And?"

"And, no dog is coming up to either greet me or bite my ankles. A few minutes earlier, I had heard some yipping. Sounded like it came from a ferocious little warrior, but it's since stopped and I'm looking at an empty doggie bed . . ."

"Okay, look," Thatcher said, "I've just pulled into the front parking lot again. Make your way back to where I dropped you off and we'll walk back together."

"Why don't I just stay here? I'm already here."

"Because I haven't cleared the rest of that unit, that's why. I don't feel comfortable with you standing out front of a home with a door left open and half the house out of your view. Get yourself back here right now."

I hung up on him and did as he commanded, making my way back across the darkened field between the buildings.

When I got back to the first parking lot, I saw Thatcher's car, but didn't see Thatcher. There wasn't really anywhere for him to be, or hide, so my mind immediately thought the worst. My heart thumped, making me think this was the flavor of the night: terror, panic, and my bearings crashing down around me. I kept telling myself that if I put enough into this, things would come up butterflies and rainbows in the end. I'll find Jen alive and then she, Thatcher, and I can sing and dance and roll down a grassy hillside.

Then the waves came crashing upon my silly little notions. And they kept coming, humming their lullaby, *crash, crash, crash.* Suffer, suffer, and then, oh yeah, die.

Dread pressed against me as I stared at Thatcher's empty car. It was as if my butterfly-and-rainbow ending had succumbed to being a bleating lamb tied to a post, horror music playing in the background. Guess what, little lamb? You're some crazy monster's dinner. You're in the hands of darkness.

From the moment I'd heard that Jen had disappeared, no, even before that, when I heard Jen announce to Erena Maloney that her son had impregnated her, I could almost taste and feel that evil. I could feel it shift its greasy pawed pieces into play. It was as if there was some unseen, ethereal chess game where black moved Bishop and was smiling ear to ear.

He had the whole thing plotted, three, four, five moves in advance. There was no hope for a reversal of fortune but my, my, my . . . he still wanted to screw with you.

That's when I realized I had been standing too long, far off from Thatcher's car, frozen like a lump of stupid. And still, where was Thatcher?

I started into a jog, running until I got to Thatcher's car, tears already forming at the sides of my eyes. Maybe it was because of the air whipping at my face, but then again maybe it was that sinking feeling in my gut. With each step I progressed toward Thatcher's car, Queen moved to flank Bishop and that sadistic voice cackled: "You're all going to be picked off tonight, one way or another."

With my hand on Thatcher's driver side door, I looked inside the windows, confirming he wasn't there, not even slumped over in what I imagined could've been a pool of his blood. Then I heard scraping, gagging, and scratching sounds on the other side of the car. I ran around the back and found Thatcher squirming on the ground, crunching himself into a fetal position while writhing on his side. The scraping was coming from him trying to kick out his feet every now and then, to stand, or maybe it was only a matter of involuntary jerks. His hands were covering the front of his neck as he struggled for breath.

I flew to him and got down on my knees, hunched over him. When he turned his face to me, I saw his left eye cracked open above the brow, blood dripping down and his lid starting to swell shut.

"Thatcher, Thatcher," I cried. "What happened?"

Only the one good eye was widening at me but it seemed to be signaling panic. The light in the parking lot was dim at best but I could tell his complexion was turning a darker shade as he continued to clasp his throat. I grabbed at his hand and lifted a few of his fingers, seeing a bright red spot forming just atop his Adam's apple.

My tears spilled. "Was it him?" I begged, wondering if David Lopez had tried to crush Thatcher's larynx.

The one eye rolled back, but it looked like Thatcher did it more out of frustration than anything else. One of his arms took a swat at me, hitting me in the stomach. I figured this, too, was one of those involuntary jerks as he tried to breathe. He was breathing some, but not enough to sustain his gasping efforts for too much longer. I reached for his throat. It was instinctual almost. I squeezed in from the sides, hoping that would open his airway if it had been pushed in from the front.

He let out a raspy cry of pain and I couldn't tell if I helped or hurt him more. He immediately took another swat at me, his one good eye widening even more.

I hunched over farther, leaning in, still squeezing his neck in the opposite direction, thinking it would help him breathe. "Please, Thatcher, hold on," I said. I grabbed his cell phone from his side pocket and pushed his emergency call button. I set it down next to us, hoping they'd simply know to come instead of wanting to pester me with inane questions. It was an officer's phone, after all. They'd come. *God, please!* I prayed. *Have them come!*

To ensure we'd have as much help as we could, I opened my mouth to scream for help, but I felt a baseball mitt of fingers grab my hair and lift me away from Thatcher.

It was my turn to hurt. This I knew. "Help!" I yelled anyway. I was spun around and then Lopez clocked me in the face.

My eyes burst forth into white pops of light and a flood of tears. My legs slushed and I started to crumble. Any woman would've been glad when strong arms caught her before she hit the ground, but not if the strong arms belonged to a flesh-eating demon who'd eventually use those arms to hold her down and rape her. I would've rather hit the pavement. I would've rather fallen into a pit of broken glass.

The battle was over. "Victory for us!" the darkness seemed to shout. Lopez's checkmate was imminent. My conqueror reached for my cell phone in my back pocket, pulled it out, and threw it against the parking lot. I heard it splinter into pieces of plastic, technology, and my last thread of safety.

I thrashed in his grasp but he reached up to my face and tweaked at my nose. A *whoosh*, then a brief illumination of many twinkling lights. In my fleeting consciousness I imagined a gaggle of masochistic fireflies coming out to dance upon my broken face. My eyes sprung forth more tears and my head felt like it had snapped backward. I was certain my nose kissed my face good-bye. The pain seared. My jaw fell and something was ringing in my ears. It might have been fear, it might have even been everything in my life—the memories, the moments, and all the ever-loving hope—racing and clamoring away, knowing there wasn't any more use for those things after this animal had his way with me.

This was happening.

I blacked out.

XIII

She hadn't called in years. If she wanted to talk, she'd show up at my place to yell at me and blame me. But she called and said they're on their way for me and that she hopes I burn in hell for it. She also said that no amount of my own burning could justify letting either the child in that woman or the woman herself live. Because then it will come back as proof that if that baby belongs to me then she's the mother of a rapist. Then she'll have no way to muddy the waters of my guilt, especially she said in the hopeful event I'm dead and can't talk to convince people of the opposite.

She said a lot more than that too. A lot of screaming.

I didn't know I had a kid out there and it confused me. I took an extra injection to calm myself because Mom was right and I hated her for that. And even if she wasn't right, she asked it of me and I hated myself for wanting to provide it to her.

The last thing she said to me was that if I was making it a habit to kill people, why had it never occurred to me to go after my own father since I knew who he was?

"Who says it hasn't?" I screamed back at her and hung up. I didn't get a chance to hear it, but I knew it. It was the first time I had the potential to make her glad.

I went to Bob's and told him bits and pieces and even brought her, the one pregnant with my child, laid out in my van in case he wanted to help me finish her off. A gesture of good faith that I only wanted to be like-minded, nothing else.

It was his one and only shot and he blew it. I could've lived with the fact he had insulted me and neglected me, as long as we could move forward. But he'd have none of that. He laughed at me and the story I had about being his son and I never even got a chance to show him what I had in my van. I broke a few parts on him and his stupid dog barked and barked. I opened the front door and threw that mutt outside so far, like he was a football, and went back into Bob's room to find him trying to slip off the bed and escape. That's when I heard her voice. I knew it was her, the cop. I pressed my hand so tight over Bob's mouth so he couldn't squeal and the dog was barking farther and farther away because I gave him a good kick, hopefully running for good.

She kept talking, but not to me, not to Bob, but to someone about finding an open gate. I could tell her voice wasn't getting any closer. She hadn't come in, but she might. Bob had a slider out his bedroom and that's the way I'd go, so I looked down at Bob again but his eyes were dull. Gone. I had been covering both his mouth and nose. I didn't realize I had them both pressed until it was too late. I wasn't sure if I felt sorry.

There's nothing I could do about Bob and they'll have no problem tying me to it. It was going to end soon, the panic kept telling me this and there was no reassurance to be found. Only sweat and fear and anger and it had to end tonight.

THIRTY-FIVE

Not Ready to Die

I was in a van. *The* van. It had to be. It wasn't moving, so Lopez had likely parked it somewhere. A place far away, where people couldn't hear my screams and cries as he beat me to death, amongst other things he'd do to me that I dared not think. My panic made me feel like I was running laps within the pits of hell, but I knew my body was in no condition for such a thing, neither literal nor metaphoric. After the first, immediate surge of fear, the pain in my punched face crippled me. And this was all before I tried to move.

Once my hands started to reach out, my first thought was that Lopez had already raped me. My hands dove to my hips. I felt my jeans, the zipper and button still intact. I sighed in relief. I touched a bit lower, just to make sure. Everything seemed normal. I felt around myself to gauge the situation, touch being the only one of my senses I could rely on in the blackness surrounding me. I felt a plastic tarp spread out upon a metal floorboard beneath me.

He had prepped it so that this was the sort of van where no one leaves alive. If they did, it was because they accidentally had a few more breaths in them to numbly, futilely watch their monster finish them off. I already knew this about the van, though. If I hadn't, it became real the moment Lopez pulled me away from Thatcher.

Oh, Thatcher. I clenched my fists, my nails digging into my palm as I thought about Thatcher. I thought about my own prospects too.

How had I let this happen? I was smarter than this, yet here I was, about to lose it all. My face throbbed again with a fiery, crushing pain. I was certain Lopez had busted my nose. For all of that, one would have thought the agony of my fate, the pilfering of my body and soul at the hands of a ravenous beast, would have caused my greatest anguish, but that wasn't what tipped me over the edge into gut-wrenching despair. It was my breasts. They were what did me in.

They ached. They were painfully hot and tight, with a fullness I had never known. They were crying out to me, shrieking really, letting me know they had wanted to feed Owen hours and hours ago. That's when my panic did its crescendo. Who would nurse Owen when I was dead? Oh no . . . who would be his *mother*? Of all the terror and despair I'd seen in this world, nothing cut me closer than the thought of my child wandering around in the world without a mom. All else I could handle because the operative word there was the big fat "I."

I acted like tough stuff and it's what I proffered to the rest of the world. Tough stuff is what I had slapped across the faces of those who had dared cross me all these years gone by.

I had somehow managed to survive the loss of my first child, hadn't I? I was finally able to walk upright in the aftermath, even on rainy, gray-pressed days when the memory of her was so real, I could've sworn she was singing softly somewhere in the house, out of my sight but not truly out of my life. Thus, "tough" was a label I knew I could wear.

I could take my blows, but why should Owen have to?

I knew I could suffer shedding razor blades as tears and swallowing despair like it was a lump of thumbtacks, but he shouldn't have to do that. Sure, he'd still have Eddie to take care of him and I knew they'd carry on, but I had birthed that little boy and he was my second chance. There was no way I was going to let this piece of filth rapist and murderer, this demon incarnate end my life before I got a chance to show my son how perilously awesome his mother is.

I swung my arm farther this time to get more bearings, but it thudded on flesh.

My hand recoiled as if it had touched a piece of seething filth. But no, not filth. A person. And if this person was here with me in the darkness, lying on the same tarp, a sheath of industrial plastic that would be our final adornment wherever Lopez dragged our limp, profaned, and dead bodies, then no, the body next to me was not filth. Rather, it was a scorched daisy, a butterfly with its wings plucked off, a boot stomping on a birthday cake. That's what the body was. It was discarded but it was not filth.

It was Jen. It had to be.

"No!" I shrieked, paying no mind to the searing pain the expression caused my face.

My hand went back to the body. I grabbed her hand. "Jennifer?" She wasn't moving, but was she dead? I strained to see her in the blinding dark. My hand went higher, aiming for her shoulder so I could shake her a bit. When I found it, I gave her a quick poke. Her hand grabbed mine and shoved it away. "Evy, stop" she whispered, a faint whimper chasing her request.

I thought she was trying to cry because the noises she made sounded deep and muffled, even choked-off attempts to moan.

"Jen? How bad are you hurt?"

She kept trying to moan. I couldn't be sure, but it sounded like she turned away from me. I went to reach for her again, this time to comfort her, and felt her shoulder in the same spot. She must've just turned her head away. Her breathing tempered, I could barely hear it anymore. I begged for her to keep breathing.

That's when I caught my first glimmer of hope making its round back to me. It wasn't as I had originally figured it, that my desire for hope had shot off like some rogue misfire the moment Lopez got his hands on me. Rather, the slivers of hope on this evening were more like a boomerang. I hoped they'd make their way back to me. Eventually.

Yet, I've never been the naïve sort. David Lopez was going to kill Jen and me unless we did something about it. I wanted out. Out of this van. Out with Jennifer, out to Owen, or to die trying.

"Jen?" I said again. She didn't answer but I could hear her shallow breathing, panting harder. "Jen!" This time louder. "I need to know how you're doing. I need to know how badly you've been hurt."

A thump echoed from the exterior of the van, sounding like it came from where our heads lay. "Shut up!" a voice blasted through.

Lopez. It had to be.

Why was he telling us to shut up, banging on the van, no less? Why speak at all? It was so human, less devilish. This was good for me. I was used to humans. Less scared of them too.

I moved my head closer to where Jen's voice had been, my face feeling hot and achy with something rattling around in my skull. It could have been that small bone in my nose. It could've even been my brain, for all I knew. I whispered down to her, "Did he hurt you again?"

I could hear her choking something back, like she was trying to be silent. "Evy . . . I . . . be quiet. Okay? I just want to end this in quiet."

Was she so resolved in her fate that a few extra minutes of lying in a van was worth not putting up a fight? I mean, I guess I figured we were going to die as much as she did, but I wasn't going to be a good little girl for the occasion so I could get a few more minutes of peace before he bashed our heads in.

I felt alone. Not only was our attacker working against us, but Jennifer had no more fight in her and she was the one who had more knowledge about our attacker. All I knew of this guy was that he was strong and sadistic. She knew plenty more, tragically so. I wanted to ask her for details, but then figured she was in no mood to talk.

An idea buzzed around my head. Fight like hell. That's all I had left. It's what Jen had done the first time. And even if it was the teens that created the diversion that saved her life, I still thought the two of us together could beat this guy into our freedom.

I had a baby to nurse. Until I was either home with Owen or taking my last breath under Lopez's hands, my game plan was to fight.

"Jennifer, listen," I said. "I need you and you need me. We need each other to stay strong and get out."

"Oh, Evelyn, you're such an idiot," she said, her voice sounding like bits and pieces of her were dropping off for good. I could've sworn, though, that I heard a tiny cackle in it, but it might have just been another suppressed moan. "It's over. Don't you see that?"

Demon incarnate pounded on the side of the van again. "Shut up, sluts!"

"Shh, shh. I know you're tired, but we have to go on."

She choked through a gruff laugh again. "You don't get it. He's going to finish us, Evy." I heard her roll her face away again, but she reached for my hand in the dark. When she found it, she pulled it over and dabbed it slightly on her belly.

She hissed in pain and I felt something sticky, gooey, and hot on top of her shirt.

I pulled my hand away and shot upright, crouching on my knees, even though the quick movement sent my head spinning. "Jen!" I tried to shriek, but it came out softer than the impact within my mind. "What happened?"

She made that wiry, almost gargling chuckle again. "He started telling me about forgiveness and starting over on account of the baby. Forgiveness for me. I'm the bad one. He said that first we had to get his old man's permission and maybe some extra cash to start somewhere new where we wouldn't be bothered by the police investigation. I scoffed at him and even spat at his face. I told him I'd rather be dead. I told him I should've aborted the baby when I had the chance."

There was a faint whimpering in her tone. I know she wouldn't have. I just knew it.

"Before I even finished my sentence, he drove a screwdriver into my belly." Her voice quavered at the recollection. "He pulled it right back out. The pain was unbearable. Then he turned off the lights and left. Next thing I know, you're here. Way to be stupid, by the way, and get caught by him."

"Ditto," I said to her, my hands and voice trembling because I hated that I had said it. Hated that we were both so tragically right.

"How long have you been like this, Jen?"

"I don't know."

"I hate to state the obvious here, but you're still alive. Somehow, you're doing it, so can you keep doing whatever you're doing? Thatcher will find . . ." I trailed off, my mind pressing with another dashed hope. Thatcher might be dead too. I had hit his emergency call button, but did he hang on long enough? Did Lopez finish him off?

I heard banging again outside the van.

"He's frustrated," I said aloud, meaning for it to be a thought.

"Who?" her voice scratched.

"Lopez."

"So?"

"Frustration and hesitation sometimes go hand in hand."

"I'm sure he'll kill us anyway. It might even hurt more if he's frustrated, so I hope he manages to soothe himself."

I huffed. "Why are you so resolved to just lie here and let him kill us?" I asked.

Through the cloak of silence, her hand grabbed at my wrist again. It made me twitch in fear because even though it could have only been her, I still wasn't entirely sure. The darkness was messing with my mind.

"The baby," she said. It was like the last stone of the fortress came tumbling down. Defeat. Conquer. Death to us all, especially the little one in Jennifer's belly who probably went first. I truly didn't want to think about the mechanics of her getting stabbed in the belly while pregnant. Her womb was still small, but . . .

It made sense now. Her lack of resolve seemed more justifiable. Not because she had likely lost the baby, but because she was more injured than she was telling me. Perhaps she was merely waiting on nature to take over as her blood and amniotic fluid continued to spill on the floor of this van. With the tarp. With me. If the last piece fell in Lopez's favor, he'd be dragging this tarp out of the van, wrapping us up in it, puttinig a little death bow on top, and disposing of us forever.

Still, I had to try. Stab wound or not, I'd have a better chance with Jennifer's help. Even if she was bad off, she was still able to communicate, though I could hear the strain and hurt in her voice.

"Jennifer, I can't tell without any lights, but how bad is your stomach?"

A sardonic bit of air wisped from her mouth.

"Keep holding on," I urged her. "Even if the most I'll get out of you is some sarcastic huffs. Just keep holding on."

I stood up. My hands were above my head to make sure it didn't bang into the van's ceiling. It felt like an entire jug of water sloshed to the forward part of my brain. My mental bearings were down, way down, but my body seemed to be begging me to go into fight-or-flight. I looked forward, then to my left, my right, and behind me. Nothing but darkness. I don't know why I expected anything different. I had no idea which direction I should move, but I resolved to go forward, hoping I'd find a driver's seat. When I got to a solid wall, I went backward. Another solid wall.

"It's a box, Evy," Jennifer said. "We're locked in a box. Can't see him when he drives, can't see the outside, and the only time the light goes on is when he turns it on."

"How does he come in?" I asked.

"I could swear there is more than one door, so it could be from any side."

"How did he get you?"

"I never even got to my car after leaving work. I saw a van parked a few spots up from my car, but it was a different color and had some floral graphics on it. How could I be afraid of flowers?"

She did that sarcastic laugh again, and then howled in pain. After she stopped panting, she said, "I had to walk past the van to get in my driver's side, and then bam."

"We're in a florist's van?"

She didn't answer.

"Did he punch you again?" I asked, trying to blink my eyes. They felt crusted with what I guessed was blood, pus, and tears.

"Yes," she said. "I'd say I'm getting pretty sick of it, but what's the point?"

"Let's get ready," I said, holding my arms out so I didn't bang into anything as I braced myself.

"Ready for what?" She moaned.

"For our friggin' debutante ball!" I snapped, instantly regretting it. "We're in here and he's out there." I tried to bring calm back into the picture by lowering my voice. "If he's going to do something else to us, then he's got to open a door. That's when we have to fight. We don't have a choice except to put all our effort into it."

"I don't have any fight left, Evy. I just want to go to sleep. I'm okay with dying because then at least it will be over."

I went down to my knees and felt for her, leaning my body over hers, careful to avoid her abdomen. I squeezed her shoulders. "Jennifer, listen to me," I whispered in her ear, holding her down so she couldn't turn away, though I doubted she had the strength for such a thing.

"Please listen." I paused. "I'm not ready to die. I don't want you to die, either. And I sure as heck am not in the mood for this piece of crap to win! We are not alone right now. We have each other and despite the fact that you and I have suffered such disastrous ills at the hands of very sadistic men, we are still here. We are both still alive. The fact that we're still kicking—after me losing Corinne and you suffering through the repeated violence of this man—means we are gloriously experienced in reaching to touch rock bottom and still breaking the surface back to the light.

"Jennifer, please. Fight with me. I want to see Owen. I want to see Eddie. I even want to take you to Corinne's grave and reach way past the pit of my own misery so I can smile for you. I'd smile to show you that life has a way of licking its own wounds if you have the humility to reach out for the good stuff.

"I can't give up like this. I won't. But I can't do this alone. I will if I have to, but if we do it together we have a greater shot. If we perish, we perish. But I'm not ready to go without a fight. If he ends up killing me, it won't be without me getting a few blows in first."

I felt her nod slightly beneath me.

"Help me sit up," she said.

"Will it hurt? Will you bleed more?"

"Does it matter?" she asked.

It did, but it didn't, and it made me feel like a villain for wanting this from her. The slightest movement to get her in a sitting position caused her to shriek and go rigid, forcing me to lay her back down.

Let her be, I thought. The movement to sit was too much for her. Great. I had only hastened her death and not even thirty seconds had elapsed. How typical of me.

I let quietness linger a moment, tying to contemplate a backup plan if Jennifer didn't make it. *My God*, I begged. *Help her make it.*

"Jennifer?" I asked.

"Just give me a minute," she said.

I listened to her breathe. So haggard. Each inhale and each exhale sounded deeper, more strained, and just . . . just *slower.*

"Are you asleep?" I asked.

She grunted.

"I need you," I said, wearing a look of earnest on my face that I realized she couldn't see. I felt selfish, felt wicked, felt scared, alone, and undone.

"I know. I'm sorry," she whispered.

I was sick of the accursed darkness in this van! I couldn't see her; she couldn't see me. We were just two bodies in the back of a blackened box waiting for the door to open and our lives to end.

But for me, I was done waiting. I wanted to race back. I was sick of being a victim. I was tired of waiting for a murderer to call my shots.

I stood again, telling my jellylike legs and my throbbing face that they were needed and they had better deliver. Or else.

Placing myself back where I had first risen, I surmised I was pretty much in the center of the hellbox. If the driver's area was likely where our heads had been, then the back door was where our feet were facing, where I now faced. I walked one, two, three steps with my hands out in front of me until I felt another solid wall. The back door. I hoped.

I banged on it. "Come on, Devil! Open the door!" I banged and banged and banged. Then I froze, waiting for it to open. I took a few steps backward in case I was banging on the wrong end and he'd be coming at me from another direction. I hunched over a bit, leaning on the balls of my feet, hands up and ready to fake it or make it at hand-to-hand combat with a powerhouse male that possessed hands the size of skillets.

But nothing. The silence consumed my nerves. It felt like several minutes had passed but the blackness was deceiving. Jennifer had either fallen asleep, passed out, died, or was being the bad guy's good girl by remaining silent and still. I went for the back wall again and banged some more.

"Open it!" I shouted several times, my voice reverberating through our little coffin, ultimately coming back void.

Nothing.

I had almost given up on my catlike pouncing stance when I heard something rustle against the metal. My gut was such a little quitter suddenly, but my mind told it to shape up. This was it. The door was about to open.

And it did.

THIRTY-SIX

The Unusual and the Unfair

The air from outside the van came at me with a rush of cold, but the night provided less of a darkened shroud than the confines of the van. Now, I could see my enemy.

"I'm done with you!" he shouted at me.

The low growl of his voice enhanced my fight-or-flight sense, making it beat and tick like it was going to implode inside my chest if I didn't make up my mind about which I was going to do.

"Get down!" he barked at me.

He wanted to fight, that much was clear. And he wanted to do so right there, outside the van. We were parked in some sort of field. I couldn't see much from my angle, but knew we were far away from civilization because of the lack of light and sound. Lopez was standing about ten feet from the van's bumper and I could make out the steam of his breath rising and sailing away from his square head, as if he were panting like a pestered bull. I would've had better luck with a bull, though. A bull would likely go gentler on that goring business than I expected Lopez to. He had his fists tightly balled, standing with his legs shoulder-width apart, and I hated him. I hated him for everything he was and meant and had done.

And what he would do. To me. My head spun and there was a quick tingle that ran itself into numbness, all the way down to my fingers. The panic was taking over but then I remembered: *Oh yes. I hate you!*

The fury breathed anew and if it were at all possible, I wanted to crush him with my contempt alone. To face the hand of the Devil knowing you're only human is a nasty place to be.

We don't want to be dead. At least not by you, Devil.

"Don't," I heard Jen mumble behind me. I didn't turn around to see whether or not she could see Lopez standing there. Yet, I was sure she had been alerted to him because of the cold air around us, stung and infected with his malice. I had been feeling it pricking at me since I first heard the latch turn to open the back door.

"Don't leave me," Jen whispered.

But I had to. Even if I was scared to.

When my feet hit the ground, I turned my body to the left and willed my legs to do what they were made for and ran. Perhaps he figured I'd stand and fight him. That was my original plan, but in the battle of my nerves, that fight-or-flight, my body decided to overrule my brain and booked it. Why be brave with someone who'd just pummel me? No. Running it was.

I hoped the momentary shock of my fleeing would slow him down long enough to get some ground on him. The sound of the air whipped in my ears as I ran, deafening me, so I didn't know whether he had given chase. Yet, it altogether seemed self-explanatory that he had.

It wasn't as if I had a plan of navigation. The goal was to move. Just move. Besides, frustrating the ease of his victory seemed a decent enough thing to give myself as a departing gift. If I perished, even if he ripped me limb from limb, I was going to be that jagged bone in a bite of fish, catching in his throat and making him gag.

Suddenly, my head jerked back. Lopez had grabbed hold of my hair and the abrupt stop pulled half my body in one direction while my legs kept moving forward, ending with me crashing down on my back. In one fluid movement, he was on top of me, pinning my hands over my head with his left hand. My face instinctually turned up to see my hands, to see if I could slither them free. I never saw his right fist sailing into my jaw.

Burst, pop! A conglomerate of twinkling lights.

My eyes felt like they were smashed far, far back into my brain. There was a ringing in my ears, a *ho-hum, you're hurting now, aren't you* sort of thing. Then again, maybe that was only me, screaming for what I thought were the last few moments of my life.

I was trying to gurgle something. "NO!" I think it was, but I'm not sure it ever vocalized. I felt him rip the shirt off my body.

My fingers clawed at his one hand holding mine down, and I started thrashing underneath him. He crashed down on top of me and drove his boulder-sized fist into my side. It felt like my last gasp of breath forced itself up and out of my windpipe.

Now I understood.

Now I knew why Jen wanted to curl up and die. Just please . . . please God, no more of this. I don't want to be a part of this any longer. Still lying on top of me, he reached between our two sandwiched bodies and ripped at the button closure of my jeans. My legs started to kick. A part of me wanted to tell them to stop so they wouldn't get me in trouble but it was too late. Lopez raised himself a little and rolled me over, landing a blow in my lower back that made my legs radiate with cold shivers. He unfastened my bra and ripped it out from under me, rolling me back over and exposing my breasts.

When the cold air hit my overly full breasts—breasts that had wanted to nurse Owen hours earlier—they erupted. Milk squirted straight out and right into Lopez's eyes. It was disgusting. *Oh, Gertrude, we've entered the wrong, wrong, wrong picture show!* Then again, it was wonderful, glorious, amazing. It was the most beautiful freak show I'd ever seen.

Lopez didn't seem to understand what was happening at first. He tried blinking the liquid out of his eyes and then raised his hands to them. I took my own freed hands and wrapped one around each breast, squeezing them like the ever-loving udders they were. Lopez shrank away, as if I were dousing him with acid.

He went to strike me again in the face, to make me stop, but a new surge of milk came bursting through as I squeezed through the pain of my swollen ducts. His fist missed. He overshot my face by a good six inches and his new, stunned position gave me leverage to move. I scooted out from under him, taking my hands off my breasts to push off.

There was only a flash of thought that I didn't have the strength or wherewithal to get up and move, but then I had another flash. The "I can't" thinking is what does you in. I was still breathing, wasn't I? Hadn't I said the same thing to Jen? I'd rather they find my stiff, dead body with my fingers stretched in anticipation of escape rather than curled up in defeat.

I did one blink, one split hesitation at the thought of pushing forward, but I knew I had to. Something deep inside of me begged for endurance. It was the part of me that said I hadn't come this far in life, hadn't suffered through what I had only to die now. Especially not now. I had a son to feed and love and raise.

I realized I wouldn't get far without giving Lopez some sort of wound first. The breast milk in his eyes wouldn't last much longer. Breast milk was mostly water, after all. I was sitting on my rear, leaning back on my hands after having scooted out from under him, and he reached forward. He tried grabbing at my calves, but he was still trying to clear his vision too. I took my leg, curled it up, and then kicked him in the face, heel first.

His head went down to the ground, his face cradled in both hands. I rolled over and prayed my body would work for another run. And it did. After what seemed the hardest movement of my life, I saw the van just ahead.

"Move!" I heard Jen's voice come at me. She sounded desperate and strained. I could barely make out her shadow outside the back of the van, about fifteen feet from me.

For the first time since I had escaped Lopez pinning me down, I turned around to see him. He was a big, black block of anger and filth barreling down behind me. It wasn't going to work. I couldn't outrun him. I couldn't outfight him. He'd win. He'd win. He'd win!

My knees, my muscles, everything wanted to buckle.

I wasn't sure if Jen's command meant for me to keep moving or to get out of her way but I didn't care. Either way, I had nothing left so I dropped to the ground in a kneeling position, still facing Lopez. If he was going to finish me off by bashing my head in, I wanted to see it coming. At least I could be brave in that.

He closed in. Ten feet, five feet, three feet, then *whoosh*. He dropped to his knees, too, holding what looked like a high-heeled shoe up to his face.

I turned to Jen. She was bent over, picking something off the ground and howling in pain from the movement.

Lopez screamed and I wanted to shrink away, far away from this world of pain and writhing because when he bellowed, everything seemed to shake and I feared I was about to be cracked in two. Lopez still had the high heel up to his face, his mouth gaping in some sort of exaggerated agony.

"Did I get him?" I heard Jen ask from behind me, speaking in a nearly snuffed out voice.

I dared not take my eyes off him even though I was trying to convince my stupid, quitter legs to get up and run again. He let out one last deep howl and threw the shoe to the ground. Darkness erupted from the corner of his left eye. Both hands quickly went up to cover it.

"Oh my gosh," I muttered under my breath, trying to swallow the gag rising in my throat.

"Did I, Evy?" Jen asked again.

Lopez stood and I did the only thing that seemed to make sense at the moment since he still had both hands over his eye: I sprang up and kicked him in the crotch. Thanks for coming back to the party, feet. You done did good.

Down Lopez went again. I turned to Jen.

"Get back in the van!" I shouted, praying and hoping that Lopez had left the keys in the ignition. Running to the front, I assumed Jen was following. But she wasn't. Out of the corner of my eye, as I was opening the driver's side door, I saw her walking to him. *To* him!

Like the hulk that he was, he collected himself and let the path of blood coming from his eye flow freely as he put both hands around Jen's neck and lifted her off the ground, choking and shaking her.

I went to her just as her thin, white arm rose above his neck. Her fist jammed into the side of it and his choking started immediately. When her arm dropped back to her side, something was sticking out the side of Lopez's neck, near his jugular. He took one hand off her neck and plowed it into her belly. She went limp and he collapsed down with her, one hand still around her neck.

When I got to them, I shoved Lopez off Jen and started dragging her away by her wrists. I felt like an enemy for doing such a thing since she was so injured, but the options were limited.

The back of the van was closer to put her in, but as tears trickled down my cheeks, mashing together with my blood, hurt, and fear, I saw Jen's head bobbing along in a pitiful, grotesque way. This was it for her. This was the end.

No, I couldn't put her in the back, even if it was closer to shove her in. I didn't want her to die in the coffin where her nightmare had begun.

I shoved, lifted, and flopped her into the passenger side of the cab. The keys were still in the ignition. Thank you, God. A small favor that meant an awful lot as my brain calculated this horrendous, gut-wrenching loss.

Jen was nearly dead, if not there already. Thatcher might've been dead, too, and even if Lopez was, I still didn't understand a lick of it. In the scheme of things, of things that are good and evil, and how the latter is in constant pursuit to rear up and devour the former, it didn't really matter if I knew all the ins and outs of why someone chooses to do bad things. By the time the world knows that demons exist and are amongst us, many dominoes have already fallen and we are all but in the way. Just like Jen. Not to mention all the other poor girls too. The lot of us humans are nothing more than collateral damage in a master plan that seeks to crush all.

The logical question would be, "Who pushed the first domino down?" By all accounts, I should've known that one. I had traveled the path to hell and there's only one who keeps pushing those starter dominoes down, one after one after six billion. All it takes is that one question: Will I live for me and me alone?

If you say yes . . . then *clack*, baby. The serpent just tipped your first domino.

I thought about driving back to San Diego, but truth of it was I didn't know where we were. With the first turn out of the abandoned field, Jen slumped toward the center of our two pilot seats, stopping short of completely falling off, thanks to the seat belt I put on her. Her arms hung limp, her head doing the same. As the van progressed, bumping and rolling, her hair brushed against my forearm and it was a cold, hateful thing. There wasn't anyone or anything on the road. Only me, limp Jen, the hellbox, and the demon's key chain swinging back and forth. It made a metallic, *whoosh*ing sound in the stillness, swinging with the momentum of the van. As my mind tried to grasp what had happened, wondering how the world could possibly spin tomorrow, the chant of the *whoosh*ing key chain seemed to sing out in the moment, *Vssh-vssh*. And then again, *Vssh-vssh*, until it manifested to a finer point of audibility: *Not fair, not fair.*

I cried and didn't care that it obstructed the little I could see in front of me. More of Jen's hair cascaded against my arm and it seemed to want to touch me. Touch me everywhere so that I'd never forget what was behind me. Death touched you. It knows your name. Its hair is shiny and pretty but altogether empty.

It reminded me of that hair from the grave, of that Jane Doe. "That's where Jen is going, isn't she?" I asked the night around me. She was going into a grave. Lopez had managed to kill each of the women he had raped, including Jen. Including her baby. I couldn't help but wonder if that extra effort she made to stop Lopez from getting me was the thing that did her in, that punch in the gut. What if she could've held on a bit longer?

But to save me . . . to let me get on by.

I took one of my hands off the steering wheel and buried it into her hair, bending over for a split second to kiss the top of her head, reaching out to embrace the moment, even if I'd be haunted by it for the rest of my days. It made me despise every single moment of life that is wasted on this constant tug-of-war of good and evil, of what we can and cannot control, of what the world blames as God's shortcomings, but of what I knew was the Devil's crown jewel of attribution.

I pulled away from Jen to study the road, to figure out how to go on. Meaning it in every way possible.

Wiping at my eyes was futile because it was too dark and too foreign to know where I was going anyway. I suddenly didn't care about Lopez anymore. If I ran out of gas or drove to Arizona, it wouldn't have mattered at that point because I figured I'd already made it to tomorrow and tomorrow brought new tears and one less friend in my world.

Of all the things that surfaced in me during that long, lonely drive, the most catastrophic was this overwhelming and pressing despair at the lack of control in our lives.

Any one of us, at any time, for any reason.

Yet, the core problem remains: the Devil's lust for our demise. I remembered that dream I had had about Venom. "Go ahead and scream," he had said. "No one will hear you."

But if we were a little less selfish and a little less apt to live by our own rules, then maybe, just maybe, there might be a little less bloodshed in the world.

After about twenty minutes through winding roads spotted with trees and other fields, I found a house and gave that poor old woman the scare of her life.

But at least she had a phone.

THIRTY-SEVEN

The Snake Watches

I spent those first few days after surviving Lopez staring out the front window of my living room. Sometimes for hours at a stretch. I could muster holding a cup of coffee in my hands, but that was only during the times I wasn't shaking and angry at the world. Eddie let me be for the most part, telling me that it was all right and that I needed to heal. The innards-type of healing was what he was worried about.

There was so much loss surrounding the life and times of David Lopez that I felt something needed to count as a win. Something in addition to knowing both Thatcher and I had made it out all right, and thanks be to God for that. Still, that elusive "something more" is what I wanted and was what I was waiting for, staring out the window.

It seemed certain that when my neighbor, Mag, told me about her dream of the black snake peeking in my window, she had meant David Lopez. That meant he had probably been staring into this very window, the one I had been standing in front of for days, like a lonely girl waiting to be not so lonely anymore.

I, too, wanted to know if my suffering would end.

I stared and stared and waited until it hurt. I was looking to see if the slithering snake was going to pop up again. If he didn't, then I won, and that would be a win I could hang my hopes on.

But was he really gone? Could he be? Ever?

No, not really. Not ever completely if I recycled what I had already discovered when I lost my daughter, about old sins on new days, not to mention the pursuit of old demons to fill new vessels. As for Lopez, yes, his body was gone. But his lust and hate, and the proliferation of both . . . doubtful they were no longer roaming and wafting over the earth like the stench of farm manure looking for freshly washed linens.

Lopez had driven us out to the fringes of the small mountain community of Julian, about an hour east of San Diego. By the time the police figured out which field we had been in, Lopez was nothing more than a frigid corpse in an open field. They found him a day later by following the crows having a heyday on that injured eye, amongst other fleshy parts. The crows had also picked around the small screwdriver jutting out of Lopez's neck. Blood samples confirmed it was the same screwdriver he had used on Jen, to kill both her and the baby.

If there was any sweet justice to it, I really did hope that a little of the baby's blood was on it as it jammed into Lopez. I don't know why that would be justice, but it resonated in me all the same.

My soul ached for Jennifer. I would never be the same and I was sick of changing in painful ways with the wrong sorts of inducements.

Thatcher's larynx was nearly smashed and my nose got bent in the scuffle. Small grievances, really. It was worth repeating: we were still alive.

Maybe that was another reason I was staring out the window. Because I could. I could see things and I could process things and I could feel things. I was, am, and will be for as long as God keeps me here.

It was somewhere along that fuzz of meaning and nostalgia that I realized I had been staring at the same black car for days. I was only cognizant of it at the moment because a tow truck was now backing up to it.

"Eddie!" I shouted, even though it still hurt my face to do so.

He approached and stood by my side.

"See that black car?" I asked.

"The one being hitched up to that tow truck?"

I nodded.

"It's been here awhile," I said. "I think I first noticed it when I got back from the hospital, and even then it had a yellow notice of tow on it."

Eddie was silent and I knew what that meant. "So what?" He just didn't have the constitution to frustrate me at the moment.

"I wonder . . ." I started, but trailed off, thinking of what Burn had told me all those weeks ago, about the small black car at the station, and then paired it with Mag's dream about the black snake who can slither up and spy in my windows.

I went out the front door, not bothering with shoes, simply letting the loose pebbles and sticks on the street hit and press into my feet without complaint. When I got beside the tow truck, the front of the small, black coupe was already hitched and rising.

"Can I take a quick peek inside the car?" I asked the driver. He was a big man with an even bigger gut, reeking of lunch meat and discontent.

He gave me an angry look. "This your car?" he asked.

"No, but—"

"Then it doesn't concern you, so back off."

"I just want to take a look inside. I think it may be the vehicle associated with serious crimes," I said, realizing that it only made sense that Lopez would have a second, lower profile car. I mean, even a psycho can see the rationale in leaving the hellbox at home to bleach it silly while he ran to the store for milk and potato chips in a little sedan. Couldn't he?

"You a cop?" the driver asked.

Say yes, I thought. "Yes," I answered.

"Then show me some identification."

Busted.

I shook my head.

"Get out of here," he reiterated.

Instead, I pressed my face against the passenger-side window. I saw a gym bag and a red file folder.

That's when I could've sworn the folder called out to me. "Look in here. Come see what I've got hidden in here."

I thought about smashing the window with a rock, but I didn't. It was more because there wasn't a viable rock around than for fear of how the tow-truck driver would respond. I called the station and after some shouting contest down at impound, we got inside the car.

Why he kept the maps, we'll never know. They were single-sheet printouts of directions from the Internet, including the directions to my house. We matched the locations to other victims as well. Even if on some strange occurrence where the DNA results didn't help, it would hopefully be enough to show he kept a record and the directions to where the victims worked or lived, and the DA could connect the killings that way. It wouldn't be justice only for Jen, but for all of them.

It was Lopez's trophy tell-all, if I had to give it a name. I had already put much of his raping and murdering spree together beforehand, at least by inference and good guessing, but the one thing we never had was a first name for that Jane Doe in the grave. At least he gave us that. Layla. Layla something, but it was still a Layla. At least, that was the thought. The maps were titled "Layla II," "Layla III," "Layla IV," and so on and so forth. The directions to my house had me as "Layla VI." I shuddered.

It still made me feel tainted all over again. It still made me feel watched, like a shadow that creeps in and scouts the place out in silence before you realize it has a knife to your throat and Grandmommy's jewelry dripping from its back pockets.

I don't know why he left the car there. I can only guess. Maybe it was to let me know he saw me. All of me, and all of those I loved.

As the weeks passed, I became the subject of a few novelty headlines, mainly about being the woman who escaped a rape by squirting breast milk into her attacker's eyes. At first, it was portrayed as a noble thing. Even the La Leche League tried to make me a poster child of sorts. At least for a bit. Then came the Internet memes.

Didn't like the current political candidate? Draw a meme with a bare-chested woman squirting breast milk in his eyes. The same for bad shows, a passerby who can't seem to get their trash into the bins, and some of the whacky outfits people wear to Walmart. All there and squirted with breast milk for their violations. Before I knew it, it was just a silly joke and Jen was still dead; Thatcher didn't seem so sure about his work any longer, and I had almost been raped. Not to mention I persistently stared out my front window wondering where that blasted serpent was hiding and when he'd pop back up.

I tried to put some people back on point about the gravity of it all, but people don't want to listen. I think I've already established that. Everyone goes on with living and making jokes and pretending that whatever motivated David Lopez isn't breathing down their necks next, slithering around their ankles, and sinking fangs in deep. Deep down to the bone.

There was a lot of talk about steroid use during those days, and that not-so-fancy term of "roid rage" caused a nationwide debate. The suits on Capitol Hill called for more laws and more regulations when the real problem is that we're more and more detached from the things that make us whole. Like each other, and love, and contentment, and the acknowl-edgment of our Maker.

"Are Steroids the Real Killer?" the headlines asked, and I simply shook my head. Whatever brewed in David Lopez was a perfect storm of rotten things that infected others in the most unnatural way. Only steroids? No. There was something else. Something*s* else, plural. I was sure that the

Maloney woman was a mimic of a devil in a Lana Braun suit, but last I checked, she skipped out and is likely hiding in a wide-brimmed hat somewhere in Baja.

Man, I hope the drug cartels sift her. I shouldn't say that. Forgive me.

Then, there was that other thing. The *other* other.

I can't help but wonder why they don't hear the serpent laughing right beside them. Don't they hear him whispering and enticing and saying, "Hey, Big Boy, you don't need anyone but yourself. Make your own rules, be your own king, and I'll put the world in your hands. Take what's yours, it's yours after all."

Liar.

Don't they see it?

Don't they?

What storm will brew next? It's never only this and only that. It's a collection of broken pieces that someone is trying to jam together and say, "Presto! I've made the whole picture." But, no. There's only one whole picture and it's never been broken and never been shattered, so it has no need to be fixed.

It's almost laughable that we've come to proclaim the so-called right way is to fix things once they explode in our faces.

No.

No, thank you.

I'm not interested in fixing the smashed vase once I've gashed my feet over the shards. I just want to be careful in not letting the vase teeter on the edge in the first place.

If I can.

I know it'll take help because I can't do it alone. When we're alone, that's when the vase teeters the most.

Years ago now, if I had held onto my pride and held onto my rights, I would've been alone. I would've pushed Eddie away for good, pushed our marriage into the gutter, and then Owen would've never existed. And then I wouldn't have had today.

A day where I had just finished giving Owen a bath. It was three-something in the afternoon and the sun was coming in his room, bursting through the slats of his wood blinds. I put a diaper on him, but then that's as far as I went, watching him squirm on his changing table and reaching for the sunlight as if it was something tangible. I kept my hand on his belly but took a step back so that he could have a real shot at it without me holding him back, even if the reality of the attempt existed only in his mind. Eddie must've been watching because he came in and put his hand on my shoulder, gently pushing me back toward Owen. He said, "Pick him up and help him get it."

For some reason, that was even cornier than my belief that I could let him grab the sunshine on his own. Perhaps because instead of one nutty Barrett trying to hold the sun, it would be three Barretts involved in the charade and at least one of us knew better.

Eddie urged me again, even grabbing my hands as we picked up Owen together and held him toward the window. Once, twice, then the third swat to get the light and then his eyebrows bunched until he found my face, then Eddie's, and then he smiled. A crazy, goofy, toothless wonder.

He put one hand on my cheek, the other on Eddie's chin, and I know he was only being a baby about the baby things of life, but I'd like to think it meant more than that. I'd like to believe that in all his glorious innocence, he had willingly given up trying to grab at what we had no right to harness, and instead, held on to what was right in front of him.

ACKNOWLEDGMENTS

Always, thank you to God.

Thank you to my husband and sons. They are endless in their cheer for me. It's splendid. I love you three so much.

Love to the rest of my family, my folks, my siblings, and all of the other dear ones in my expanded family tree. Your support always pulls me through.

I'm fortunate to have friends who not only care, but pray for me too. What a treasure you are.

To my editors. An author is nothing without the support and guidance of a good editor. (Especially ones who show no fear of my whining.) Thank you to Dawn Anderson and Natalie Hanemann.

To anyone who takes the time to read what I say, thank you. You make my little world a lot more fun.

And finally, thank you to the many Christian music artists who provide the soundtrack to my thoughts: Thousand Foot Krutch, Lacrae, Beckah Shae, The City Harmonic, Colton Dixon, and TobyMac.

Histories and
Mysteries:
Charm and Chills

Reviews on books from author Linda K. Richison

Lost and Found

"It was magical, mysterious, romantic, heart wrenching, funny and lighthearted! How adorable. It captured my attention and I couldn't put it down. These books are a fun way to escape."

Heather G. from Keizer OR

Heart and Souls

"This story pulls at your heartstrings, titillates your imagination and is full of mystery; it had me drawn in after reading the first two pages. I'm looking forward to reading the rest of the series."

Shawn H. from Salem, OR

"I love how well this author describes the characters in the stories, especially, Serena and Cliff and their romance. Mystery and romance held my interest and I was anxious to know what was coming next; very creative stores."

Patricia M. from Spanish Springs, NV

"I want to thank Linda K Richison for pulling me into a love mystery book! When I began reading her first book; *Heart and Souls*, it brought me exactly where the characters were, and made me feel what they felt."

Brenda A. from Woodburn, OR

"Linda has an amazing way of writing, taking the reader into the story as if being in the moment with the characters. Love, laughter, fear wonder and discovery! These books are such a pleasure to read. I highly recommend them."

C. E. from Dallas, OR

Histories and Mysteries: Charm and Chills

Linda K. Richison

ISBN: 1548224537
ISBN-13: 978-1548224530

Printed in the United States of America

DEDICATIONS

I just want to say "Wow!" I can't believe this is my fourth book. I was so excited and blessed, beyond words, when I published Heart and Souls, my first book. You can't imagine the overwhelming gratitude I have in my heart with the release of Charm and Chills.

I could never have done it on my own, nor would I have wanted to. The making of a successful book takes a team with dedication and determination to see the book through to publication. I am fortunate to be part of such an amazing team walking this journey with me. Since most of these members, who I refer to as my friends, have been with me almost from the start I find it an honor to recognize them as key players to the makings of this book.

Annette Truckee – Consultant

Rick Southerland – Graphic Designer, Business Manager

Doug and Suzie Cross – Editing team

Darcie LaFountaine – Photographer

I am also happy to welcome a new player to the team; Teresa (Missy) Smith. She has signed on to be my Promotional Agent. I look forward to working with her and see where the future takes me in his arena.

Of course, I have to give a shout out to everyone who volunteered to read the preliminary transcripts, sharing their opinions and offering constructive criticism. Thank you for helping me to see outside the box. I am also grateful for my friend and attorney; Jennifer Hunking, for volunteering her knowledge and expertise, in helping me to understand the details surrounding a deed. She has not only been a valuable resource but will also be making an appearance in the story as an attorney. Keep an eye out for her character.

There are so many people: friends and family, who have been with me, offering their support and encouragement as I travel down this path as a writer. If it weren't for you choosing my book, sharing my stories, and giving honest reviews, I probably would've stopped walking this journey, years ago. The love and kindness you have shown to me have been very rewarding, and I am blessed to have you all in my life.

TO MY READERS

I want to thank you for choosing my books and for your ongoing support and encouragement. Also for taking the time to leave an honest review, it was well appreciated.

Well, I have closed the doors to The Spirit of Love series and opened the doors into a new world; where romantic fiction and Oregon's history collide. The new series, Histories and Mysteries, will still keep the same writing style, and the stories will take place in Oregon cities, but I will add more depth by sprinkling in some historical facts throughout the books. You will meet fun loving characters, sure to touch your heart and rally your emotions. They will take you on a journey that explores the imagination and keeps you turning the pages. You will follow them into a ghost town that comes alive, and mingle with the townspeople, as the past and present come together to solve an age-old mystery. You will also be invited as a guest, to explore a haunted house where a stubborn spirit unwilling to give up his secrets, brings a new meaning to the words chaos and mayhem. So please sit back, relax, and enjoy my first book in this series; Charm and Chills. I hope you enjoy it as much as I did writing it.

Also please, if you haven't already, check out The Spirit of Love series, listed below. You will meet Serena, a quirky redhead and her friends and family, who are sure to make their way into your hearts as they come alive in your minds and take you on a journey filled with romance, mystery, fantasy and a touch of magic.

The Spirit of Love series available on Amazon.com

Heart and Souls

Lost and Found

Spice and Sassy

CONTENTS

"Let us always meet each other with a smile, for the smile is the beginning of love."

Mother Theresa

1) NINA

"Yes mother, I'm still planning to be there this weekend," Nina said reassuring her mom.

"Well I'm only making sure honey," Molly, her mom, replied.

"I'm leaving Friday morning and should be in town by noon. Then we'll have two days together," Nina said, as she leaned back in her office chair twirling the pen in her hand.

"I want to talk about that," Molly said with hesitation. "I need someone to take over the store while I'm recovering from my fall, and I hope you can do it."

Nina sat up straight as her mom's request caught her attention. The pen flew through the air. "I thought Aunt Becky had agreed to help out," Nina said, picking up the pen and returning to her chair.

"She did," Molly admitted, "but her flower shop is keeping her so busy, she can't manage my store as well."

Nina, frustrated, ran her hand through her shoulder-length blonde hair and moved it away from her deep-set brown eyes.

"Isn't there someone else who can do it?" Nina asked, crossing her fingers.

"Well, your sister Sara can't take Ava and Ariel, my precious granddaughters, out of school, and she can't leave them with their dad. Even though Joe is a good father, his job has him traveling a lot. However, Sara did say she'd like to fly up this summer and bring the girls for a week. Maybe you can arrange to come up while they're here," Molly paused for a moment, and then continued, "I'd ask your brother Scott, but he's just started a new job and can't get away."

"I know that leaves me; single and available," Nina sadly quoted.

"Can't you take a little time off?" Molly asked sweetly.

"Ah, how long were you thinking?" Nina asked.

"Well maybe a month or two," Molly answered.

"A month or two!" Nina shrieked. "I can't leave work for that long," she declared, walking to the window and stretching her 5'5" petite body frame, as she gazed down onto the street.

"Sweetie, we'll have to continue this discussion tomorrow when you get here. Right now I have to go, my friend, Mabel just arrived."

"But Mom," Nina said.

"Bye honey, love you," Molly said ending the call.

"Mom!" Nina yelled into the dead call.

"Aargh," Nina screamed.

"Mom trouble?" Rene, her friend and office assistant, asked.

Nina looked at the street below, as she thought about her mom's request.

"A month or more," Nina emphasized, turning around to face Rene. "That's how long she wants me to stay with her. Can you believe that?"

"What are you going to do?" Rene asked pulling her long, ginger-colored, hair into a ponytail and securing it with a hair tie.

"I'm going to go, and I'll find someone to run the store. It shouldn't be that difficult," Nina said convincing herself.

"Well," Rene said, "I hate to play devil's advocate, but what if you can't find anybody?"

"I don't know," Nina said as she paced, "I'm way too busy to be gone that long."

"What do your work-and-family-thoughts tell you?" Rene asked her friend with compassion.

Nina shot her a playful look, "You know me too well. At this moment they are in major conflict," Nina admitted.

"How did the thoughts-in-the-closet thing get started?" Rene asked, her face squinched up.

"It's the emotions-in-compartments," Nina corrected, giggling at her friend's definition. "It's something my dad taught me when I was thirteen." She felt a sting of sadness as she brought up a sacred memory of him. "I had a crush on this boy. Thinking back, he was a gangly kid moving into puberty. Anyway, he broke my teenage heart when he left me for a little redhead in his homeroom class. My world stopped. You know all the drama in the adolescent years," Nina stated, looking back at her younger years. "My dad helped me get through it by teaching me to put my emotions into compartments of my brain. We even devised comical names for them. At first, it was a game we played, but through the years they've been my saving grace. It's a tool I use to help me adapt and adjust in stressful and emotional times in my life. Sometimes I open the less painful ones for my entertainment."

"Sounds pretty cool," Rene expressed with a smile.

"You don't think it's odd?" Nina asked, her head tilted to the side.

"Not at all," Rene replied waving her arm dismissively. "It's what makes you unique and special," she answered with an endearing look.

"Well, if you want to know what I think; I really don't see a problem," Rene said getting up to stretch her long legs as she joined Nina by the window. "You're working on updating the corporate website; can't you do that at your mom's?"

"I guess so," Nina replied shrugging her shoulder, "but I just signed two new contracts. The owners of two separate coffee houses want us to handle their coffee supplies."

"I can do that!" Rene spoke up, her sea green eyes lighting up with excitement. "I've always wanted to work in the field," she said pulling her violet lip gloss from her jacket pocket and applying it to her dry lips.

"I'll keep that in mind," Nina said, smiling at her friend. "But, I don't even know if Mike will give me the time off," she mused.

"You know his motto, Family and health always come first," Rene said, quoting their boss.

"What am I going to do there for that long? It'll feel like an eternity!" Nina said, giving the poor-me salute. "Don't get me wrong. It's a cute, quiet little town, and the people are nice, but not enough stimuli for me. The highlights of the week are karaoke night at the local bar, Sunday church potlucks, and an occasional barn dance."

"I'm not cut out for the country life; the city is so deeply ingrained in me," emphasizing the dramatic effect.

Laughing, Rene raised her eyebrows, shrugged her shoulders and commented, "Maybe you'll meet a sexy cowboy."

"Yeah, that's exactly what I need," Nina sarcastically commented, remembering the last guy to whom she gave her heart. Shaking her head, she added; "It's not going to happen!"

"Not all guys are like that scumbag you were dating," Rene stated.

Just thinking about him caused Nina to shiver. "Meet nice and decent men on the internet, they said. Not!" Nina emphasized.

"Well, you have to admit he was nice," Rene said.

"Yes, he was, especially when he introduced me to his wife, who had been following us for weeks. The nerve of him," she sighed, anger flaring as she returned to her chair. "First and last time I'll try online dating."

"They're not all bad, just saying," Rene said, returning to her chair and turning her attention back to the interrupted task.

"Well, I'm not looking," Nina replied, putting her focus on her current project.

At 5:00 p.m., the girls said good-bye, locked-up the building and parted ways. Nina went to the train station and Rene to the bus terminal to catch their rides home. Nina's commute was usually thirty-five minutes to her stop and another two blocks to her condo. Today she'd forgotten her umbrella. She thought that since it was sunny when she'd left home that morning, she wouldn't need it. That was a bad decision on her part, as she was caught in a torrential downpour and was soaking wet by the time she reached her front door. As she entered her home, Nina turned to look outside, and to no surprise, the sun was back out. "That's Oregon for you," she chanted, closing the door.

Nina immediately removed her wet clothes and put on her favorite sweats. She turned on her oven to heat-up last night's leftovers and sat on her sofa with a glass of her favorite wine. With a glass in one hand and two signed contracts in the other, she smiled down at her bunny slippers. Then let out a sigh of contentment as she looked around her condo. She was a proud homeowner; thinking back on the day she signed what felt like a million documents, and then happily accepted the key. It had been a scary decision, but the best one she'd made in her life.

She still couldn't believe it was hers; that was until she looked around. Every inch of the 1600 square feet, gleamed with her personal touch; from the wheat colored wood floors to the textured painted walls. Nina kept her primary colors more towards Earth tones. The colorful throw pillows and lap quilts she had sprinkled around the house added a bold and cheery appeal. She splurged in the living room, spoiling herself with a tan leather sofa and chair, but mostly she kept to the traditional style. The walls held pictures of family and friends, and only a few choice pieces displayed on the shelves. She liked clean lines and little clutter. Two bedrooms and one bathroom took up most of the upstairs, while the main floor was the rest of the ordinary living space.

Taking a sip of wine, she laughed at Rene's earlier comment about finding a cowboy. "And give up all this?" she said aloud, looking around. More than likely he'd want the country life, in some farmhouse on some out-of-the-way dusty road. Well, he could have it. She liked her location; there were stores, restaurants, and bars within walking distance and a major mall down the highway. It was like a city within a city, and it worked fine for her, she thought, going to check on her dinner.

Later that night, as Nina was preparing for bed, she thought about her mom and wondered if she was selfish. It was obvious her mom needed her. Feeling bad, along with the help of the Guilt and Shame forum tossing thoughts in her head, Nina decided to discuss leave time with her boss first thing in the morning. It was going to be a long couple of months, she sighed. Then climbing into her four-poster bed, she turned off the light and called it a night.

The next day, Nina waited for her boss to get settled in his office, before discussing her request for leave time. Rene had been right; there hadn't been a problem convincing her boss for the time off. In fact, he was very much in agreement with her request to telecommute. She smiled as she left his office, remembering his exact words; "You know my motto: family and health come first." They also discussed a reasonable part-time work schedule. Afterward, Nina turned over some of her leg-work assignments to Rene and left instructions for her to call or email her anytime.

Friday morning Nina awoke from a bizarre dream. The main character happened to be a man in a business suit, wearing cowboy boots and a ridiculous looking hat. What an odd combination; my dream waves must have gotten crossed last night she thought. Deciding not to dwell on it, Nina prepared for her day. Dressed in her outlet store finds, jeans, T-shirt, tennis shoes, and hoodie, she finished packing, grabbed a muffin, loaded her car, and started on her road trip.

Nina focused on maneuvering through the rush-hour traffic. Living in Portland had taught her how to be a careful, yet aggressive driver. If not, she'd never get where she was going. This time, the flow was stop-and-go, but if there were no accidents, she figured on being out of the congestion soon and driving at a steady pace.

Before she left her house, Nina had made up her mind to try and enjoy this semi-vacation, although, Hawaii or the Bahamas would've been a more desirable choice. Usually, the drive to her mom's was pretty smooth, and according to the weatherman, she may experience a sun break or two.

Nina did like the scenery through the Columbia River Gorge; and of course, Multnomah Falls was a must-see. It would be the perfect place for her to grab a picture or two of the some of the majestic wonders in Oregon and to start her road trip album.

After her stop at the falls, she put on the cruise control, settled into her seat and turned on the radio to her favorite rock station. In a relaxed mood, she took in the picturesque view. The beauty of the Gorge never ceased to amaze her. Following the Columbia River, it was no mistake the scenic byway cloaked with fir, ferns, and rare plants had been named one of the seven wonders of Oregon. The crashing waterfalls were her favorite. And if the wind was right, she might get lucky and catch the windsurfers showing off on the ocean-like waves in the river. However, she thought, it might not happen today, there were only small gusts. She admitted the sport looked like a blast, but she wasn't daring enough to give it a try.

Finding a spot along the way, Nina pulled into a state park to stretch and use the restroom. She took a sandwich from her lunch bag, found a table next to a young family and enjoyed her lunch along the bank of the river. Nina was captivated by the beautiful nature surrounding her. She couldn't call herself a stranger to the woods; in fact, she'd spent some time in the wilderness. For her, it was a great place to escape, but when she had her fix with nature, she would return to the city. A girl could only take so much of the great outdoors; she thought laughing at herself.

Back on the road, she was happy to be on her last leg of the trip, even though she knew her magical byway would soon give way to desert and tumbleweeds. She smiled when she passed a sign noting thirty-nine miles until she reached the town of Maupin. That smile quickly turned upside down when a 'Work Ahead' detour sign came into view. "Great," Nina said in frustration as she was directed off the highway onto a side road, which led to who knows where.

After listening to the annoying GPS lady repeating 'recalculating route,' Nina unplugged the unit. She was so far off the beaten path even her GPS didn't know where she was. If that wasn't bad enough, the road was full of ruts and torn up pretty badly. After fifty minutes of being bumped around in the car, Nina was totally done with this detour and sighed with pleasure when she turned off the terrible road and found herself in familiar territory. "Whew, almost there," she said aloud.

Pulling into town, Nina stopped at a gas station to fill up. She also needed to find a restroom, especially after that bumpy ride. She was never so happy to be out of a vehicle and hurried to the room outside the station. Stepping out of the disgusting little room and trying to look inconspicuous, Nina rubbed her backside, which felt a little bruised. However, she hadn't noticed the man checking her out.

"Are you OK?" a deep male voice sounded from behind her.

Caught in an embarrassing moment, Nina composed herself and turned around, nearly falling over at the sight of a tall cowboy. And the crazy thing was, he happened to be the spitting image of the man in her dreams. The only difference was he wasn't wearing a suit. Smiling, she commented, "Ah, I'm fine thanks." Then headed for the car, hoping to give him a hint she wasn't interested in talking.

"You're not from around here, are you?" the man asked.

Nina made a disgruntled face and then turned around. Trying to be polite she replied, "Why do you say that?"

"Your clothes gave it away," he admitted with a shrug.

Nina wasn't sure if it was the road from hell or a headache coming on, but the cowboy's assumption irritated her, and something caused her to snap. "And what's wrong with the way I dress?" she asked, glaring at him, arms folded over her chest.

"Nothing," he answered, "you look great. It's just that the girls around her have a more relaxed style."

"Are you insinuating that my clothes reflect that I'm uptight?" she asked, forming an immediate dislike toward this man.

"Not at all," he said, trying to hide his smile, watching the pretty spirited woman.

"I'll have you know," she added, raising her voice, and making the z formation with her hand, "I am one of the most easygoing and kickback girls you'll ever meet," she said, raising her head, snubbing the man. "Now if you will excuse me, I've got to go."

"Be seeing you around," the man said, offering her a sexy smile and tipping his hat.

"Fat chance," Nina said aloud after she was inside her car. The man infuriated her, and she wanted to get away from him. He was probably some arrogant know-it-all, she thought. Before leaving the station, she set her GPS for her mom's house. It wasn't far from there, but she tended to get confused with all the country roads. They seemed to all look alike to her.

Within minutes she was turning down a gravel drive, and an ornate cedar privacy fence guided Nina to her mom's mini ranch, smiling when a quaint farmhouse came into view. At last, she celebrated, happy to be there.

Walking up to the house, she noticed the new flowers, bursting with color as they overflowed in the hanging baskets. Her mom had even added a new wicker table with two chairs and had recovered the pillow on the old porch swing. It does look cozy, Nina thought, opening the screen door to the house.

Greeting her at the door was an excited Cassie; her mom's loveable Australian Shepard. With tail wagging vigorously and dancing gracefully in place, Cassie waited impatiently for Nina to show her some attention. Nina bent down and hugged Cassie, ruffled her fur and said, "Where's mom?" Given a job, she led Nina down a carpeted hallway.

She found her mom in the living room, sitting in her favorite leather recliner, her leg propped up on a pillow, and garden magazine in her hand. It made Nina a little sad to see her mom incapacitated. She was usually so ambitious and going a million miles an hour. But even though she looked fragile at the moment, Nina could still see the fight and fire in her mom's emerald eyes. To her, Molly was still beautiful. It was easy to see time had been gentle, gracing her with only a few wrinkles and a smooth complexion. Her long, wavy, auburn hair was pulled back out of her face and showed only a light sprinkle of gray. Nina also could tell working on the farm had kept her runner's body lean and fit. She hoped Mother Nature would also bless her with the same gift in her older years. Letting her thoughts go she walked over to greet her mom. "Hi," she said, hugging her. "How are you doing?" Nina asked with concern.

Returning the hug, Molly commented, "Okay, but I think I overdid it today, my ankle is a little swollen. Hopefully, this icepack and rest will have it feeling better than it was."

13

"Can I get you anything?" Nina asked, willing to assist her.

"No I'm fine," Molly admitted. "Now sit down and tell me about the drive."

That's all it took. All Nina needed was a sympathetic shoulder, and after plopping herself down on the comfy upholstered sofa, she covered herself with a fleece blanket draped over the back of the rustic wood frame and vented about the detour. "I think I bruised my bottom," she said after rubbing her backside. "And I have a terrible headache," rubbing her head.

"Oh, I'm sorry dear," Molly said trying not to smile at her daughter's overly dramatic outburst.

"Mom, it's not funny," Nina said catching her mom's facial expression.

"I know dear," Molly replied trying to console her daughter. "Sorry you had to go through that, but you're here now. The spare room is all yours. I cleaned out a couple of drawers and made some room in the closet for your clothes. The bathroom has all your favorite toiletries. There should be some aspirin on the second shelf of the medicine cabinet and a heating pad in the bottom drawer."

"Thank you, I appreciate all you have done, but I thought you were supposed to be taking it easy," Nina said worried that her mom was doing too much.

"I am, sweetie," Molly said taking a sip of her iced tea from the frosted glass on the side table. "The people in this town have been very supportive. Someone is always stopping by to visit. They bring me food and attend to menial tasks. I am certainly blessed," she said, beaming. "I am especially grateful for Josh, Mabel's son. He has taken on many of the outside duties and tends to the daily feeding of the animals. He will also be helping out at the store part-time, mostly stocking the shelves and handling the heavy lifting. I've invited him over tonight for dinner, I think you'll like him," her mom said with a wink.

"Mom," Nina said frowning, "I hope this isn't a matchmaking attempt because if it is, call him right now and cancel. I'm not interested," Nina pronounced. "I came here to help you, not look for a relationship."

"Calm down. He's only coming for dinner. I thought since he's going to be helping around here and at the store, you'd like to meet him," Molly said, then smiling she changed the subject. "Why don't you get your things out of the car and get settled in your room?"

Nina wasn't convinced her mom was telling the complete truth. It wouldn't have been the first time she'd tried to set her up. Deciding to drop it, Nina went out to her car. She did need to plug in her laptop.

After lugging her suitcase upstairs, she walked into the spare room at the end of the hall. Setting her stuff in the corner, she sat on the daybed and ran her hand over the animal printed quilt. The room was exactly as she had remembered, Nina thought, leaning her back against the stack of contrasting throw pillows while checking out her surroundings. The room, like the rest of the house, still kept to the farmhouse appeal. Nina had to admit her mother had a gift for decorating and design.

She loved the Anton Chest of Drawers done with a white finish on the distressed wood and matching curved design three-panel mirror vanity. The setting looked as though it came out of a magazine.

Her thoughts were interrupted by her mom's voice. "Honey come down here, I'd like you to meet Josh Parker."

"Coming," Nina yelled back, pulling herself off the bed, and hustling downstairs. Reaching the bottom step, she froze. Then, staring at her mom's friend, she blurted out in a derogatory tone, "Oh, it's you." The man not only had the audacity to appear in her dreams but now he was stalking her during the day.

2) THE FARM

Molly, leaning on her medical foot chair, nudged her daughter and scolded, "Nina, where are your manners?" Then turning her attention to Josh, she continued, "Excuse my daughter, I think that bumpy detour not only bruised her butt; it must have also shaken up her brain. She's usually more polite," she said, frowning at Nina.

Nina, turning red with embarrassment, glared at her mom. She had not only revealed personal information to a perfect stranger, but she also reprimanded her as well. Nina wasn't happy with her. With how fast the gossip travels in a small town, everybody would know about her butt soon enough. Thinking that her inner child might be in control, Nina gave thought to her actions. Her behavior was probably due to her fatigue and the low-grade headache, which were both contributing factors. But, it could also be that this man made her uncomfortable. Whatever the reason, Nina decided to be polite and put on a front, he was her mom's friend, and he hadn't done anything wrong. So painting on a smile and trying to be sincere, Nina commented, "I'm sorry for my outburst just now, and earlier this afternoon, I don't know what came over me."

Josh returned the smile and replied, "Apology accepted, I might also have been partly to blame. What I said wasn't meant to be disrespectful. I'm sorry if I upset you. How about we call a truce and start over?" he said, offering his hand.

"Sure," Nina said, shaking his hand. Then feeling the electricity shoot through her, she quickly let go.

"I think I'll go feed the animals before we eat," Josh said, removing himself from an awkward moment. She wasn't the only one feeling the chemistry between them.

"Come on dear," Molly said, "let's go check on dinner and set the table."

Nina followed her mom, still feeling the effect of his touch.

"So what happened this afternoon?" Molly asked with curiosity.

"Nothing," Nina answered, dismissing the question. "Something sure smells good," changing the subject

"Nina, I think you're ignoring my question. It looked like something to me," she said. Her head tilted to the side, waiting for an explanation.

"It's not important," Nina replied getting agitated with her mom's persistence.

"I get the hint," Molly said changing the subject. "Will you get the good china and silver out of the hutch and set the table?"

"Sure," Nina said, glad for the distraction.

After she set the table, Nina pulled the roast from the oven and said, "It sure looks yummy, did you make it?"

"No, Mabel brought it over this morning. I haven't had to cook since my accident. Meals like this have arrived daily. There happen to be some good cooks in this little town," Molly admitted, separating the meat and veggies onto individual platters. "I have been very blessed. Someday I hope to pay back their generosity." Then taking the electric knife, she carved the savory meat, while Nina made the rolls. Within thirty minutes they were sitting down to eat.

Settled at the dining-room table, a soft glow from a lightly scented candle set a relaxing mood, as the trio quietly enjoyed the meal.

Josh finally broke the silence as he smiled at Nina, "Your mom tells me you work at a coffee distribution corporation. So how did you get the job and what do you do there?"

"Oh, you don't want to hear about that, it'll probably bore you," Nina replied, not at all interested in engaging in conversation with this man, no matter how good looking he was.

"Yes, I do, and let me be the judge of that," he said before taking a bite of his dinner.

"Fine," Nina said after taking a sip of water. "I was going to Oregon State University, working toward my Bachelor Degree in Business. While I was there, I met Serena, my dorm roommate. It turns out, she was taking some of the same classes, so over time we developed a close friendship," she said smiling as she thought of the crazy redhead. "Anyway, her dad happened to be CEO of a successful coffee company. He was the middle-man between the seller and distributor. He would get a good deal on the products so that he could offer an economical price to owners of the coffee-houses. During the summer we would go work at his office, and after graduation, they hired us full time." After taking a bite of her buttery roll, she licked her lips and continued, "It was only going to be temporary while I looked for a permanent position with a business firm, but I found it was a good fit." Then she added, "I started out as an office assistant, and was recently promoted to head of distribution and contracts."

"It sounds like an interesting job," Josh commented trying not to think about her glistening lips. "I'd love to hear more about it sometime. And see, you didn't put me to sleep," he laughed.

Nina smiled at his witty comment and replied politely, "What is it you do Mr. Parker?"

"Please call me Josh," he said with a smile.

She did not want to be on a first name basis with him. It would mean they were making a connection, and she had no desire to go there.

"Nothing quite as glamorous as yours," he said. "I own a ranch down the road from here which keeps me quite busy. When I'm not at home tending to chores, you can find me in town doing odd jobs for a friendly neighbor."

"Oh, so you're like the town handyman," Nina expressed.

"I'd like to think of it as one neighbor helping another," he said with compassion. "Speaking of projects," he said turning his attention to Molly, "I repaired the step you fell through and reinforced the other three. No more broken ankles for my sweet Molly," he added, with a wink.

"Thank you, Josh, what would I do without you?" she replied with appreciation.

Then as Josh and Molly fell into conversation about people she didn't know, Nina decided to take a quick glance at the man across from her, but what should have been a peek, turned into a lingering stare. Darn, she thought in her dream state, don't tell me he's sporting a five o'clock shadow. She was a sucker for a bristly face, sighing to herself. Nina hadn't realized she'd been gawking at their guest, until the sound of her mom's voice pulled her back to the conversation, "Nina," Molly called out.

Pretending to be in the present moment, Nina answered, "Sure, whatever." But by looking at her mother's confused expression, Nina was sure it was the wrong answer.

"Nina, I asked if you'd please serve the pie," Molly repeated.

"I know," Nina lied, picking up the dishes, ready to escape her embarrassing reaction.

"Wow, that was close," Nina whispered taking her frustration out on the pie, as she cut into the helpless baked item. How was she going to survive with this man hanging around her? There must be something she could do to keep their encounters brief; she thought partially catching their conversation in the dining room.

"Come here girl," Josh called to Cassie, "how's my girl?"

"She loves you," Molly said. "Why didn't you bring Whiski? Cassie misses playing with her sister."

"I came here directly after work, which reminds me, I should get home. Would you mind if I took my pie to go?"

"No, not all," Molly replied. "Nina dear, please make Josh's pie to go," Molly called to her daughter.

"No problem," Nina yelled back, already putting it in a container. Then, devising a plan, she pasted a friendly smile on her face and went to join them. After serving the pie, Nina commented, "Mom, you stay here and enjoy your dessert, I'll see Mr. Parker, I mean Josh, to the door."

Tipping his hat, Josh said goodbye to Molly and walked with Nina to the door. When they reached the entryway, Josh turned and almost ran into her. Looking down at her, he raised his eyebrows and said, "I guess I'll be seeing you tomorrow morning."

"Ah, about that," Nina said stepping back, putting a safe distance between them. "You don't need to come tomorrow."

"Who's going to feed the animals?" he asked with a confused look.

"I am," Nina said with confidence

"I'm not sure that's a good idea," Josh replied.

"Why," Nina said feeling a little agitated, then keeping her voice down, she added with a bit of anger in her tone, "don't you think a woman can handle it, Mr. Parker?"

Josh, knowing he had hit a sore spot, waved his hands in front of him and replied, "No I'm sure you're more than qualified for the job, it's just that the animals aren't used to you."

"Thanks for your concern, but I've got this," she said with confidence.

"Alright then," he replied. "I'll see you Tuesday at the store."

"I guess," she said conjuring up a fake smile.

As the door closed behind him, he thought to himself; she was one spirited woman. She reminded him of a filly running wild. If he were smart, he'd stay far away from her; only the girl presented a challenge. She definitely needed a taste of country life to tame that spirit; a sly smile appeared on his face as he headed to his truck.

Oh, that man, Nina said under her breath, and then taking a deep breath, she joined her mom in the dining room. Sitting next to her, she dug into the tasty pie.

"Thank you for seeing Josh out, he is such a nice guy," Molly expressed.

"He's okay," Nina replied, licking the sweet cherry filling from her lips.

"Nina," Molly said waving her fork at her daughter.

"Mom," Nina said making a face, which caused them to giggle, leading them on to another discussion.

"I'm glad you're here," Molly said, placing her hand on her daughter's.

Nina smiled, and lifted by her mother's gesture she replied, "What kind of daughter would I be if I wasn't here to help my mom?"

"You are a good girl, but I feel bad for taking you away from your work, especially after your recent promotion," Molly admitted with sincerity.

"Don't worry," Nina said endearingly, "that's all been worked out. Twenty hours a week I will apply to my job, whenever I can fit them in. Let's not focus on me, what's important here, is to concentrate on getting you well," Nina said, gathering the empty plates.

"I might say this too often, but I love you, sweetie."

"I love you too," she replied, kissing her mom's cheek. Then yawning, she added, "I'm going to turn in after I finish washing the dishes unless there's something you need me to do."

Molly smiled and answered, "thank you, sweetie, I have a regular nightly routine that I've developed, and it seems to work well for me. Go, finish the dishes. You've had a long day," playfully shooing her daughter away. "Oh one more thing, could you please drive me to church tomorrow? I've missed a couple of weeks and would like to attend the 10 AM morning service."

"Sure," Nina replied. She thought that should give her time to feed the animals and get ready.

Chores finished, and after making sure her mom was comfortable, Nina prepared for bed. Then taking her laptop, she settled into bed to check her e-mails before going to sleep.

Nina awoke early to an annoying screeching sound. Trying to focus through her sleep-filled eyes, she looked at her cell phone; "Six o'clock are you kidding me?" she said covering her head with a pillow. However, that only muffled the sound of Jerome, her mom's crazy rooster. The poor thing had never developed his crowing abilities.

Concluding he wasn't going to stop anytime soon, Nina got up and dressed in her scrounge clothes, and went downstairs. Following the scent of freshly brewed coffee, Nina found her mom in the parlor; drinking coffee and reading her Bible.

Molly smiled and greeted her daughter, "Morning, there's coffee in the kitchen, I also made some bacon and pancakes."

"Morning," Nina said returning her smile, "I thought it was my job to cook for you."

"What kind of mom would I be, if I didn't make my daughter her favorite meal?"

"Fair enough," Nina said laughing at her comment. "The least I can do is set the table and serve the food."

"I'll let you do that," Molly said, scooting into the kitchen. Then looking at the clock on the stove she commented, "That's funny."

"What?" Nina asked.

"It's after seven. Josh should have been here by now. I hope nothing bad has happened to him," she said with concern.

"Oh, I told him he didn't need to, that I could take care of the animals," Nina said nonchalantly, stealing a piece of bacon from the pan.

"Now why would you do a silly thing like that?" Molly asked, disturbed by her decision.

"Don't worry, I can handle it," Nina replied, assuring her mom

"Huh, huh," she expressed, knowing the outcome of this was not going to be pretty. "Well since you are determined and Josh is not here, at least let me give you a few tips while we eat," she said, scooting her chair to the table.

"Great," Nina commented, as she set the table and served the food.

Settled at the table, Molly began "I usually start at the chicken coop. There you need to be especially careful with Gertrude; she is overprotective of her eggs and will peck your hands. Try gently rubbing her neck to relax her before attempting to retrieve them," Molly said, showing the movement with her hand.

"Got it, massage chicken," Nina said, making a mental note.

"Next, I go to the barn to bottle feed the baby goats. Mary, the momma, barely produces enough milk for one kid, so I give them supplemental nutrition. Watch out for Mary, try to wait to feed them when she is distracted, she may feel threatened by you," Molly instructed.

"Bottle feed, baby goats, sounds easy enough," adding it to her list. "Wow, I never knew so much care went into raising your animals. I admire you," Nina said, wondering if volunteering had been a mistake.

"It does take time, but I enjoy it, and I love the animals. Oh, one more thing you need to know is the pigs get very excited when they see people and might run you down."

"No problem," Nina said matter-of-factually, thinking of the cute piglets.

After they were through with breakfast, Nina took her mother's advice and slipped on the mud boots, but decided to pass on the bulky overalls, besides it wasn't as if she was going to roll around in the mud. Standing on the porch, prepared for the adventure, Nina looked back at her mom.

"You certain you want to do this? We can still call Josh," Molly said, hoping her stubborn daughter would change her mind.

"Don't worry, I got this," Nina said with fake confidence heading to the coop, leaving her mother shaking her head.

Forty minutes later, Molly met Nina at the back door. Tears were running down her daughter's mud-streaked face as Nina cried, "I don't have this!"

Molly stared in amazement, her eyes wide open as she took in the sight of her daughter, all covered in mud and yuck, missing her left boot. "Nina, what happened?" Molly asked trying to cover a smile at the disheveled mess stamping her feet to get the mud off, with unsuccessful results.

"What are you running, an asylum for wayward farm animals?" Nina exclaimed.

"Why would you say that? They are such loving animals," Molly replied, covering her mouth and pretending to cough, to hide a grin. She didn't want to add fuel to the fire, learning long ago, it was better to let her daughter vent.

"Well that might be true for some, but not for Miss Psycho in the henhouse, or maniac Mary in the barn," Nina said, pouring out her feeling. "That Gerdy chick has some serious issues, look what she did to my hand. It looks like a human pin cushion," showing her mom the peck holes. "You should probably seek counseling for her. I told her she could keep her darn egg for all I cared because I had plenty already." Then she set the pan of eggs down, she thought for a moment, and added, "However, if someone was trying to steal my egg, I might react the same way. Oh no," she said, "I'm siding with a sick chicken. I've been here less than twenty-four hours, and I'm already entering into the black hole of Farmville," she screamed in distress, lifting her arms into the air.

Molly could no longer keep from laughing at her daughter's crazy outburst and had to comment, "Nina honey, you're acting ridiculous, come on in here, get out of those muddy clothes," Molly stressed.

"Good idea," Nina said following her mother's request, but I'm not done telling you about my experience down on the range."

"You can continue in the wash-room."

Inside the little room, Nina continued her saga, "So all the squawking had evidently been a call for help because as I turned to go out, there stood Jerome, feathers ruffled gawking at me with his devilish eyes." Nina said as she started discarding the disgusting clothes. "Not wanting a confrontation with the henhouse bouncer, I grabbed my pan of eggs and stepped to the side so that he could get to the psycho chick," Nina added, accepting a wet towel from her mom to wipe the mud from her face. "So as I was backing out slowly, I slipped in chicken poop, luckily I saved myself from the fall, and hence I can't say the same for the eggs," pointing to the pan of half-broken eggs. "I'm thinking quiche or scrambled tomorrow," she said, laughing hysterically. "You know, I wouldn't be surprised if it was Gerdy left the poop."

"After the fiasco in the coop, I went to the barn to feed the kids. Everything started out fine; Mary was busy eating and didn't notice me when I walked in. I quietly gathered the babies, and they must've been hungry because they were downing the bottles. Then from the corner of my eye, I saw Mary charging toward me at full speed. I tried to get away but wasn't successful with my attempt, and she rammed her horns into my side," she said, showing her mom the bruises. "Anyway that jolt caused me to drop the bottles, which started the kids balling. Mary wasn't about to let me get close to them again, but I'm sure they got enough to eat," she said, handing her mom the soiled clothes and wrapping herself in a towel.

"It still doesn't explain how you ended up looking like a mud monster," Molly laughed, putting her soiled clothes into the washing machine.

"I'm getting there," Nina said with a smile; finally starting to calm down. "Next I went to feed the piggies. You seem to have forgotten to mention, those little piglets had grown up to big pigs, and when I stepped into the pen, they came running toward me. Not wanting to get knocked down, I hurried to the gate, but stepped in a mud hole and lost my balance and your boot. I struggled to push the pigs away as I tried several times to get up; finally, I was able to crawl my way out."

"I tried to warn you, Missy," Molly said. "Now hurry up and shower, we need to leave soon. I'll call Josh and let him know to come tonight."

"No, you won't!" Nina said adamantly, "I'm not a quitter, so there were a few bumps. That was bound to happen the first time." She wasn't about to admit defeat.

When she returned downstairs, Nina found her mom in her recliner resting her leg. Smiling she asked, "feel better now?"

"Yes much," Nina said feeling refreshed.

"What's that smell," Molly said, making a sour face and rubbing her nose.

"I don't know," Nina said shrugging her shoulders.

"Come here," Molly politely called to Nina.

As Nina walked closer to her mom, Molly turned her head, "Whew, did you wash with soap?" she questioned her.

"Of course," Nina answered, "I used your little green bottle of G & S; gel and shampoo combo," she admitted.

"I don't know how to tell you this, but that was an organic solution called Gleam and Shine used for sanitizing the shower. It must have been left it in there after the last time I cleaned it. I'm sorry honey," Molly said trying to cover the grin on her face, catching sight of her daughter's pouting face. "The good news is it's all natural and shouldn't hurt you, but, it has a slight odor," she added hoping to help the situation.

"I washed with a cleaning solution? Nina screeched. "I'm going up and shower again," she added, turning to leave.

"Wait, Nina there's no time, we have to leave shortly," Molly stressed.

"Well, I can't go there smelling like this!" Nina exclaimed.

"I have a temporary solution," Molly said reaching for a can and dousing her with a spray.

Nina coughing and gagging tried to wave away the scent as she glared at her mom, "Gross, what is that disgusting stuff?"

"It's some natural air freshener," Molly replied.

"Well it stinks," Nina exclaimed, "now I have a lemony mint added to my already disgusting scent, I can't go into church smelling like this."

"We have to leave, turn the fan on high in the car; maybe it will blow away the stench. Come on," she encouraged.

"You're kidding right?" Nina asked a little surprised at her request, thinking that maybe the pain pills were making her delirious.

"I'm serious, come on sweetie we're going to be late, and I don't want to miss any of the service," she said going out the door.

Nina was at a loss for words as she helped her mom into the car, she was definitely not looking forward to this outing. As she pulled out of the driveway, Nina thought; at least the weather was playing in her favor. Fortunately, the mid-summer brought warm temperatures, so she was able to blast the air, down all the windows and open the sunroof. She hoped all the air would blow off the terrible smell after the five-mile commute or people at the church were in for an unpleasant surprise.

3) CHURCH SERVICE

Pulling into the church parking lot, Nina parked her car in a handicapped spot and hung her mother's temporary pass from the rear-view mirror. Closing all the windows, she went to help her mom from the car.

Walking to the church, Nina took in her surroundings. It was a small building, but it offered a welcoming appeal. She imagined it had been built in the early forties, but she noticed the freshly painted walls and lattice. It looked like it was well cared for. The stained-glass windows brought life to the old structure, giving it charm and warmth.

Stepping up to the front entrance, they took their spot in a short line and waited to be greeted by the man she supposed was the pastor. Nina guessed he was in his late forties. He was clean-cut, and the high and tight hairstyle and stocky build sent a hint that he might have retired from the military. Nina watched as he welcomed people into the church with his soft eyes and joyous smile.

When it was finally their turn, he took her mom's hand in his and spoke kindly. "Hi Molly, it's good to see you are doing better, and this must be your lovely daughter," he said smiling at Nina.

"Yes, this is Nina, she'll be staying with me for a while," Molly answered proudly, turning to her daughter, as she introduced her to the reverend.

"Nice to meet you," Nina said politely.

"We are happy you can visit our congregation." Then as he took her hand, he made a sour face and turned his head. "Wow, old man Grady's millpond is sure strong today, and it doesn't help that the wind is blowing it this way." Releasing her hand and rubbing his nose he said, "Sorry, guess that is one of the rewards of living in the country," he said with a laugh, moving to greet the next person in line.

Molly and Nina kept a smile pasted on their face as they hurried into the church.

"See, I told you they'd notice," Nina said through clenched teeth.

"Maybe it was the pond," Molly said, "Come on honey let's go find a place to sit down."

"Preferably in a corner, far away from human contact," Nina whispered following her mom into the chapel, trying to ignore the comments about the smell.

As they were making their way down the row to a seat, she stepped behind a pillar to hide from an unexpected familiar face. Great, Nina thought as Josh came up to them.

"Hi ladies, I didn't know you two were coming today," he commented.

"Yeah, I didn't know until last night," Nina said eager to find a seat.

Then making a face and rubbing his nose, Josh asked, "Do you smell that?"

Nina and Molly shook their heads, pretending not to notice.

"It smells like the inside of my barn with a hint of lemon mixed in. Some farmer probably forgot to clean his boots after trampling around the pasture, and thought he could hide the stink with some lemon scented deodorizer," he summarized. "Obviously it hadn't work very well," he added.

"Well, we'd love to stay and talk," Nina said. Liar, she thought, "but mom needs to prop up her foot."

Just when Nina thought she was free of the man, she heard her mom's sweet voice inviting him to join them. Nina was polite and commented, "Yes please do," but was screaming 'NO' inside her head. Why does her mom keep putting her in these awkward situations?

"I'd be honored to join you. Let's move on, hopefully far away from those smelly barnyard boots," Josh laughed.

Maybe she could work the disgusting scent to her advantage, and if she were fortunate, he wouldn't stay too long. But noooo, the stars were not aligned in her favor. He wasn't about to leave. To add to the fun, her mom had taken the seat close to the aisle, which forced Nina to sit next to him.

It's his fault she thought smiling inside, observing him search for the dirty culprit. But after minutes of watching as he tried to protect his nose from the smell, Nina's conscience screamed at her. Deciding to give up her dirty little secret, she cupped her mouth with her hand, and leaning in close, she whispered.

Josh burst out laughing, which wasn't the response she had wanted. His loud uproar drawing the attention their way caused Nina to slide down in her seat. Dozens of curious eyes seeking answers for the interruption had Nina wishing she had an invisibility cloak. She was extremely pissed off at the man next to her. A low boiling anger simmered inside. Giving him the evil eye, she whispered loudly, "Did you have to do that? Not at all appropriate Mr. Parker," she said turning away in a huff and abruptly folding her arms across her chest.

Josh hid a smile as he listened to the choir, thinking at least he was still maintaining the status of Mr. Parker. He might, however, want to get on her first name list, especially if they were going to be working together.

Why did he keep climbing on the bull, putting his body through hell, only to get bucked-off? Then battered, bruised, and possibly broken only to climb back up to repeat the insanity. It was the thrill of the ride and the excitement of the challenge that seemed to drive him, he told himself. Was he attracted to this woman because she posed a challenge, or was it because he was curious to see what she was hiding under her protective cloak? He would think about that later, returning his attention to the sermon already in progress.

After the service, Josh said a polite good-bye and went to join a group of friends, while Nina and her mom followed the people heading to the basement for brunch. Nina stopped after exiting the chapel and turned to face her mom.

Looking at her daughter with wonder, Molly commented, "Come on Nina," coaxing her to keep moving.

"I think I'll pass," Nina replied, declining the offer. "You can go, and I'll pick you up afterward. I'm going home and do a deep cleaning on my entire stinky body," touching her hair in disgust. "I'm afraid they'll eventually discover it's me and hose me down," she said, smiling trying to keep a positive attitude.

"Okay," Molly said with a laugh. "After you pick me up, I'll give you a tour of the store."

"Sounds good, see you soon," Nina said, placing a kiss on her cheek, and leaving her in the responsible hands of friends.

Nina left the church quickly and felt relieved when she reached her car. She couldn't wait to get the smell off her. It was starting to give her a headache. But when she was about to get into her car, she was startled by a tap on her shoulder. Turning around Nina came face to face with her bad penny, Josh. "Hello?" she said, questioning why he was there.

"Nina, I'm sorry about what happened inside. Is there some way I can make it up to you?" he asked, hoping to get on her good list. "It seems we got off on the wrong foot when we met, and I keep stepping on that same foot. There must be something I can do," he pleaded with a sweet smile.

"Mr. Parker, I appreciate your offer, but all is good with us," Nina lied, not wanting to talk. "Now if you will excuse me, I have to run. Catch you later," she added getting into her car.

Watching her drive away, Josh shook his head in frustration, wondering what it was going to take to break through her shell.

Nina, feeling refreshed after her shower, arrived back at the church just as brunch was getting over. She joined her mom standing with a group of women close to her age. After introductions, Nina waited while they finished their conversation, then they parted ways. Within ten minutes they were parked in the front of her mom's store. A large sign above the door gave notice to Molly's Country Market.

Entering the building, Nina let her eyes peruse the store. The place looked more like home than a store. The layout design was for a produce market. There were the usual coolers, refrigerators, and dry storage bins, all well stocked with goods ready to be sold. However, Nina could feel her mom's loving touch throughout the building, from the homemade ruffled curtains to the decorated display table where homemade jams and pies called out to her sweet tooth.

Nina did happen to notice something odd though; it was a portrait of a nice looking young man. The picture drew her in, and she became enamored by his striking blue eyes and charismatic smile. She bet he could charm the ladies back in his era. By his attire, she figured it was the early 1900s or late 1800s. "Who's the dude on the wall?" Nina asked her mom, pointing to the picture. "He wasn't there last time I was here," pulling her eyes away.

"Oh, I found that in your father's footlocker. I think it was his late uncle or something like that," she said, waving her hand dismissively.

Nina raised her eyebrows and commented, "You mean this dapperly dressed man is a relation? Nooo! You're kidding?"

"It's true. I believe his name was John Smyth. He was a miner in his time, and his picture seemed to fit the decor in here. I also see a resemblance to your father in him, it makes me happy," Molly said, with a loving smile.

"You don't find him a little creepy, his eyes always staring at you?" Nina asked, wrapping her arms around her, feeling a cool breeze.

"Oh Nina, you're being silly, it's only a picture," Molly replied making a point.

"I guess," Nina said turning back to view the picture. But what she saw caused her to freeze in place; the eyes were no longer looking straight ahead.

"Hey my daydreaming angel," Molly said calling to her daughter.

"What," Nina responded coming out of a trance. Then rubbing her eyes, she looked at the picture again and was relieved to see his eyes were back in place. Then, in the next second he winked at her, and after a few blinks of her eyes, she saw that his eyes were back to normal. Must be the light in here, Nina thought trying to convince herself, and then she turned away and went to stand by her mom.

"Honey, I'm sorry to rush you, but I need to get home and rest my leg," Molly said.

"We can do this tomorrow, you've already put many miles on your foot scooter today," Nina said with a smirk.

Smiling at her daughter's pun, she replied, "I think there's still a little tread left on these tires, besides it shouldn't take too long. I'll touch on the finer points today and fill in the details later."

"Sounds good," Nina agreed.

"Let's start here," Molly said referring to the cash register on the front counter. "It's pretty standard, and it's fairly easy to operate. You'll need to know the password," she said, logging on and giving Nina a brief tour.

"Moving right along," she continued, retrieving a three-ring binder from the drawer beneath the register. "In here you will find everything needed to run the store," Molly said, tapping on the cover, calling attention to the binder. Then opening it she thumbed through the sections, she gave Nina a high-level overview of where to find price lists, health regulations, policies, and procedures. She made sure to cover all the important information, especially the contact numbers of all regular business associates listed in the back, and also the local medical and fire department.

After answering all of Nina's questions, Molly put the book back and gave her a tour of the market. By the time they'd made it back to the counter, she was convinced and confident her store would be in responsible hands. "I think that about does it for now. You have enough to get started. You can always call me. I hope to be in the store when I feel a little better, twice a week for a couple of hours," Molly commented, and then cupping her chin, she searched in her mind for any more need-to-know points. Then hitting an ah-ha moment, she spoke. "Oh, I almost forgot about Josh. He'll be here on Tuesdays and Thursdays to handle deliveries and tend to the small greenhouse out back. He also informed me he'd be available by phone, and you could call him anytime," Molly expressed with a sly smile.

Happy, happy, joy, joy, Nina thought. Pasting on a fake smile, she replied, "That was nice of him, but I don't think that will be necessary, I can handle this." Nina said, with confidence. "Come on, let's get you home," she said, noticing Molly flinch when she moved her leg.

After Nina got her mom settled in her chair at home, put the thawed lasagna into the oven, and threw together a garden salad, she still had a few minutes left before preparing herself for the trip to farmland. Luckily this time she wouldn't have to disturb Miss grumpy Gerdy. Taking advantage of the extra time, she sat enjoying a cup of tea while going through her work e-mails.

An hour later Molly nearly ran into her daughter as she was letting Cassie outside. She was covered in mud again and not looking too happy. It was almost a repeat of that morning.

"Don't say a word," Nina strongly stated holding up her hand. "No, I don't want you to call Josh for tomorrow. I will get this," she said pulling the towel out of her mom's hand, and angrily storming past her as she headed for the bathroom.

Nina, after her third shower, dressed in jogging pants, went downstairs to serve dinner and apologize for her rude actions. Dinner done, they adjourned to the living room with coffee and dessert, for some mother and daughter bonding time.

Nina looked over at her mom and noticed how fragile she seemed. What happened to that vibrant lady with a zest for life? She wondered if it were because of the accident, or was it possible she was lonely. This revelation got Nina thinking, and she decided to bring up the subject, "Mom, have you ever thought of dating and finding companionship?"

What brought that up?" Molly said, with a puzzled look.

"Just curious, I guess," Nina replied. "It's been over five years since dad died and its fine with me if you want to get back out there in the dating scene."

"Thank you for your blessing," Molly said, smiling sweetly, "but we're doing just fine, aren't we Cassie?" she added, petting the loving dog at her feet. "Besides, I'm happy and content and very set in my ways. I have my farm and store to keep me busy, why would I want to complicate my life?"

"Don't you ever miss having a man around, someone to share your dreams and aspirations with, someone to hold you, take you on romantic walks and candlelight dinners?"

"Why do you have this sudden concern about my love life?" Molly said with a furrowed brow.

"I remember how happy you were when dad was alive, you deserve that happiness again," Nina said endearingly, picturing her parents together.

"Honey my life is good, and I'll never find another man like your dad," Molly admitted with sad eyes. "Stop worrying about me and start concentrating on your own love life. How come there isn't a special man in your life? You also deserve to be happy." Molly said, turning her focus to her daughter.

"I don't know," Nina said pondering the thought, looking up as if she expected the universe to give her the answer. "Probably for most of the same reasons you have. I keep searching for Mr. Right, but none of the men I've dated have measured-up to the man dad was," sadly coming to that revelation.

"Oh honey," Molly said compassionately, "he broke both of us. Guess we'll have to settle for second best," she said with a laugh.

"Guess so," Nina agreed and wondered if it was even possible. Then noticing her mom rubbing her tired eyes, Nina picked up the dishes, loaded the dishwasher, and placed a kiss on Molly's cheek before heading to bed.

The next morning, Nina awoke feeling refreshed and energized. She'd slept through the night and was ready to face the day. Normally she had a chronic affair with the snooze button, but not today, she was going to embrace life. Rolling out of bed and taking every precaution, she covered herself from head-to-toe and went to tackle the unruly chore of animal duty.

As she stepped out the door, the piercing bitter cold attacked her exposed face, causing her to suck in her breath. Wrapping the long scarf around her face to ward off the cold, she proceeded to the barn, with Gerome's squealing voice serenading her walk.

She wasn't going to let the weather ruin her mood; instead, she'd bask in the beauty greeting her over the ridge. It filled her heart with joy as she witnessed the glowing embers of the rising sun, giving birth to a new day. It radiated across the sky with powerful shades of red and splashed the clouds with endless colors of pink.

By the time she reached the gate, Nina felt empowered and was confident she had it this time, but when she stepped through the gate into the chicken yard, a loud noise inside the coop had her second-guessing her courageous notion. Thinking it might be a rogue animal threatening the helpless birds, she grabbed a two-by-four leaning up against the building, and with a tight grip on the board, she carefully opened the door.

What she found was not a threat at all, more like an annoyance to her. A sexy buff body in tight-fitting jeans type of annoyance, but never the less, she wasn't exactly happy he was there.

"Morning," Josh said, tipping his hat and offering her a smile.

"What are you doing here?" she asked with a perplexed look. Then answering her question, she replied, "Mom called you didn't she?" Nina added shaking her head in disappointment.

Noticing her becoming tense, Josh broke in, "Don't be upset with your mom, she means well. She thought a little coaching might make the task run a little more smoothly." He then paused as he noticed, what he surmised, was her version of a hazmat suit. What he found entertaining was that she had covered almost her entire body in clothing, and all the pieces were a different color. "You look like you are going to battle with the Smurfs," he commented with a laugh.

"Well if I'd known there was a dress code, I'd worn my mini skirt and stilettos," she replied sarcastically in a sharp tone, suddenly feeling silly in her choice of style.

"I'd like to see that," he replied raising his eyebrows.

"Humph," Nina replied, taking a stance ready to give him a piece of her mind. Then she thought what am I doing? His showing up might work in her favor, hiding a smile. Changing her attitude to more of her sweeter side, she commented, "You know, since you're here, you might as well take my place," Nina said turning to go.

"Oh no you don't," Josh said reaching for her hand, "I was told to help you adjust, and that's what I intend to do," he firmly stated, gloating as he pulled her further, into the coop.

"That's not necessary," Nina said giving him a kind look, trying to convince him to let her go.

Then with a playful laugh, he replied teasingly, "So are we adding a new chicken to the coop."

"Noooo! I'm not a chicken," she exclaimed, a little annoyed with his accusations.

"Well, that's not how it looks to me. Should we take a census and let them decide?" He laughed giving notice to all the hens nesting peacefully.

"Oh, you are too funny, Mr. Parker." Then holding her head high she added, "Fine you win! Gerdy is all yours! My hands still sting from all the peck marks she inflicted on me."

"That's why the gloves," he said lifting her hand and removing her right glove to inspect the wounds. "Ouch," he commented rubbing the sores. "What did you do to poor sweet Gertrude to make her attack you?" he asked letting go of her hand.

"Tried to get her stupid egg," Nina answered, trying to ignore her tingling hand where Josh had rubbed it. "And there's nothing sweet about her," she said glaring at the awful bird.

"Funny, she's never done that to me, always been a good bird, haven't you girl."

"Oh please!" Nina remarked.

"She must sense your fear. Animals are strange that way. Come here," he said coaching her to where Gertrude was nesting. "All you have to do is rub her gently under the neck like this," Josh said demonstrating the move to Nina.

She watched as the bird started to relax and almost fell into a comatose state. "Are you relaxing or seducing her?" Nina giggled. "Maybe I should get you both a cigarette," she added, bursting out laughing.

Josh cocked his head to the side and replied, "I see the girl has a sense of humor."

"Whatever," she said showing him a fake smile, "I'll get the rest of the eggs," dismissing his comment.

Once they finished in the coop, Nina walked with Josh to the barn and was surprised when the momma goat came up to him. After a rub on the head, she kicked up her feet and wandered off. It was as though she was permitting him to feed her kids. He definitely had a magic touch with the animals, Nina thought, intrigued on how comfortable they were around him. "What are you the animal whisperer?" she asked handing him one of the bottles of milk.

"No," he said, laughing as he took the bottle. "They can sense when you are tense or afraid, and it's a defense mechanism to rebel and act out. When they feel safe and know you are here because you want to be, you'll have them eating out of your hands."

"Maybe for you or someone else, but not me," she said, shrugging her shoulders.

"I bet you'd be surprised. Give me a week, and I'll make all the animals here your best friend, even Gertrude," he said with confidence, gently removing the empty bottle from the mouth of the satisfied baby.

"I don't know. Maybe this barnyard life isn't for me," Nina replied fighting her baby for the bottle.

"Well you'll never know until you try," Josh commented.

"I need a little time to think about it," she stated, nearly falling over as the baby let go of it abruptly.

Laughing at her near mishap, Josh commented. "I'll come over tonight, show you a few tips and you can decide then," he said, anticipating her answer and hoping she would agree.

"I guess it couldn't hurt," she said after a slight hesitation, wondering what she was getting herself into.

"Great. You can go up to the house. I'll feed the pigs and then head out."

"You are letting me go?" she teased, then for some crazy reason, she added, "you're welcome to come up. If I know my mom, she'll have a fresh pot of coffee brewing. There are also some homemade sticky rolls that one of your friendly neighbors dropped off yesterday."

"Yum," Josh replied, "I might've passed on the coffee, but it's the sticky rolls that sealed the deal."

"See you up there," She said with a slight giggle, exiting fast before he talked her into staying. As Nina left, she wondered why she had encouraged him to come up to the house. That darn Infatuation Committee in her head was trying to lead her astray. It was obvious she'd need to be more disciplined on her next self-talk gathering. It was also a known fact that befriending a cowboy wasn't indicated on her virtual vision board, and she didn't intend on adding it.

4) MEET MR. JOHN SMYTH

Back at the house, Nina looked at her mom through the screen door. Just as she suspected, Molly was sitting at the small table, enjoying her first cup of coffee, engrossed in a newspaper article. As long as she could remember, this had always been her parents' morning ritual, and it was always the physical paper copy, even after the digital version became available. Her mom always expressed that she'd felt more connected when she was holding the real thing.

Molly looked up and greeted her daughter, "Good morning honey." She did a double take when she noticed her rainbow outfit. "Did you have a battle with a box of Skittles and lose?" she teased, adding a giggle.

"Ha, ha," Nina replied stepping into the mudroom and slipping off her boots.

"So, how was your barnyard excursion?" Molly asked trying to stifle her laughter.

"Fine," Nina said giving her mom a callous smile. "I had a visitor appear in the hen house," raising her eyebrow as she climbed out of the overalls.

"Oh, who was that?" Molly asked turning away from her daughter, playing innocent.

"Mom, I am my mother's daughter. You didn't think I'd figure it out?"

"Guilty as charged," Molly admitted raising her right hand. "I thought Josh could walk you through the process, besides I couldn't bear seeing you covered in mud again," taking a sip of her coffee.

Giving her mom an endearing look, Nina replied, "it's okay, I do appreciate your thoughtfulness. By the way, I invited him up for coffee and one of those sinful sweet rolls."

Molly thought she saw a sparkle in her daughter's eyes but decided not to mention it. Instead, she commented, "That was kind of you. Why don't you fry up some bacon and eggs for that hungry man?"

"Yeah, that's a good idea," Nina happily agreed as she removed the hat and ran her hand through her hair for a quick five-finger style.

"Why all of a sudden are you having a change of heart?" Molly asked, curious as to what happened in the barnyard.

"I don't know," Nina answered shrugging her shoulders. "Maybe it's the fresh country air," she replied, humming while she washed her hands in the sink.

"Uh huh," Molly expressed under her breath.

"Mom!" Nina said sending her mom a displeased look.

"What?" she answered, "I plead the fifth," she added raising her arms.

"You are incorrigible. Quit assuming," Nina remarked shaking her head. "Just because I speak kindly of him doesn't mean I'm interested," she informed her mom, turning around to prepare breakfast.

The sound of footsteps at the door quieted the mother-daughter bantering. Dismissing the conversation, they turned their attention to their guest, who had arrived.

After Josh removed his boots, he joined the ladies in the kitchen. The savory smell of the bacon cooking reminded him he'd missed breakfast, and was looking forward to the meal and the company.

"Hi Josh," Molly said sweetly with a cheery smile.

"Hi Mol, you're looking as beautiful as ever," he replied hanging his hat on the hook by the coat rack and then hugged her.

"Oh you crazy kid," she said with a shy-like grin, "flattery will get you everywhere. Now go wash up. Breakfast will be ready soon," she said playfully waving him away.

"Yes Ma'am," he politely replied, accidentally brushing against Nina on his way to the sink. Then noticing her sexy tousled hair and flawless face, Josh raised his eyebrows and commented; "now you look like you belong here. The natural look suits you."

Nina felt a sudden rush of heat radiate through her and turned her head to hide her flushed cheeks. What just happened? Get a grip, Nina thought, trying the self-talk approach. The committee in her head was too busy doing inventory on him. Shaking off the heated moment, she took the food to the table.

Conversation freely flowed while they ate. Nina found herself relaxing as her mom and Josh shared harmless stories of people in the town. But no matter how hard she pretended, she couldn't deny the connection between her and Josh. It also didn't help feeling his eyes upon her.

After Josh left, Nina cleaned the kitchen before preparing for her day. After her shower, she dressed in blue jeans, turquoise sweater, and flat boots. Feeling a little girly today, she added a light touch of makeup. Completing the look, she brushed her lips with her favorite cherry lip gloss. A quick check in the mirror, and satisfied with the finished product, she went to help her mom get ready for her physical therapy appointment. However, Nina discovered she didn't need any help at all. She found her in the kitchen, already dressed and enjoying her second cup of coffee in the morning. Nina smiled when she noticed Molly had on her Lady V's jogging outfit and bright tennis shoes she bought her for Christmas last year. Before they left, Nina threw together a stew in the crockpot. It was another meal graciously donated by the town.

At 3:00 PM Nina chauffeured her mom to the therapy session. While waiting, she took advantage of the open time to work on her webpage. She did love this part of her work.

Before she knew it, the hour had passed. She made a note of her stopping point, as her mother came through the door into the waiting room. Nina could tell by the way she was walking and the expression on her face, the session had been rough on her. But her smile gave Nina a partial sense of relief. She collected her computer and papers then escorted her fragile mom to the car.

When they walked outside, the warmth from the sun greeted them. It was a "shades and sunroof" kind-of-day Nina thought. She put on her sunglasses as they left the building.

On the way home, Molly insisted they stop at the market for some fresh veggies and other staples she needed. Of course, Nina was nominated to go in. "It's only a picture," she said in a whisper as she stepped inside, avoiding eye contact with the creepy miner on the wall. But even though she didn't look at it, the presence of it being there still gave her goosebumps.

Nina tried to ignore it as she gathered the items and placed them in a shopping cart. While she was taking inventory of the items, a whistling sound startled her. It was probably the wind, Nina thought, fooling herself. However, it was hard to convince the Debate Team in her mind that it was the wind. Especially when the wind normally didn't carry a tune, and all the doors and windows are not open. Nina shivered as the sound became louder, which caused her to rush the process along. But something made her stop and evaluate the silliness of the situation. Of what did she have to be scared? It was a picture, and it couldn't hurt her, so facing her ridiculous fears, she decided to check it out.

It was a nice picture; she thought giving notice to the setting. The miner was standing alongside a creek next to a tattered old wooden bench. Tall grasses and mixed colored wildflowers made the scene complete. Nina studied the man. A light ray of sunlight cast shadows on his face, but she could still see some resemblance to her dad, especially in his deep-set blue eyes and chiseled jaw. Stepping up closer, she ran her hand along the frame, all the while unbeknownst to her; strange eyes were following her every move.

"A beautiful piece of art isn't it?" a strange voice sounded.

"Who said that?" Nina asked, looking around expecting to see Josh since he seemed to pop up everywhere.

"I did," the man in the picture answered, and then surprised her by sitting on the bench.

A shocked Nina stepped back as she witnessed the unbelievable. Shaking her head, she commented, "Pictures can't talk," she said aloud. "There has to be a logical explanation," she added moving her hands around the frame looking for wires, cameras or anything that would cause the interactive mode to come on.

"How does it work?" she asked to no one in particular.

"I've been trying to figure that out for years," the man answered. This time, Nina noticed his mouth open as he spoke.

"No, no, no," Nina exclaimed, backing away, waving her hands in front of her. "This is not real. This is not real," she chanted. Then a loud honking noise had her quickly gathering the groceries and heading for the door. After locking the door, Nina gave a big sigh, but her calm mood was disturbed by the fact she was going to have to work with the creepy picture on the wall at the shop.

"What took you so long," Molly asked as her daughter got inside the car.

"I was making sure the inventory was correct," she told her, starting the car.

"See, I knew you'd be perfect for the job," Molly said patting Nina on the leg.

When they returned home, Cassie excitedly greeted them at the door with a ball clenched tightly in her mouth. It was clear she wanted play time and wasn't taking no for an answer. "Okay girl, wait a minute," Nina said, getting her mom some medicine and helping her get settled in bed to rest.

Nina was outside tossing the ball for Cassie when Josh pulled into the driveway. He was surprised she didn't look his way. She either didn't hear him drive up or was ignoring him; either could be true. He decided to take the opportunity to study her for a couple of minutes.

"She doesn't seem like the same girl I met at the gas station," he said to his sidekick Whiski, who could care less what he was saying. She directed her attention to the game in the yard. "Just a minute girl, I know you want to join the fun," he said rubbing her head. "She claims to be a city girl, all glamour, and glitz, but she's more like wildflowers and long country roads than she realizes." This time Whiski barked in response to his comment, letting him know his time was up. "Okay girl, go get Cassie," he laughed opening the door to let her out.

Nina had been oblivious to Josh's arrival and wasn't aware of it until a dog that resembled Cassie came running up to her. "Oh you must be Whiski," she commented bending down to pet the excited pup. Then removing her headphones, she stood up to see Josh walking toward her.

"Hi," she said greeting him with a smile. "They sure do look alike, and she is such a sweet baby," she said tossing the ball and watching as both dogs playfully battled for the prize.

"Yep, she's a good girl," he replied, retrieving the ball from Cassie and repeating the process.

"So I see you arrived early, you weren't like, expecting dinner were you?" she teased.

"Maybe," he laughed.

"Table is ready," she said jokingly with a smile.

"Am I that predictable?" he asked tilting his head.

"Yes, Mr. Parker, when it comes to meals. I guess you are," she said picking up the ball and throwing it one last time before going inside. "Let's eat first, then we can feed the animals," she said opening the door.

"Fine with me," Josh agreed giving most of his attention to her sweet backside, as he followed behind.

After dinner, the two of them headed to the barn and this time Nina did feel more relaxed around the goats. The momma wasn't as friendly toward her as she was to Josh, but at least she hadn't tried to ram her either. The pigs were excited, as usual, and she had to be super careful around them to avoid another mud bath. Been there, done that, twice was enough.

After feeding time was over, Nina walked with Josh back to the house for dessert. Molly had also insisted he stay for a little while because she wanted cuddle time with Whiski. Nina could tell they had become quite close. Her mom had always been a sucker for animals. When they were growing up, Nina could remember always having a cat and a dog, and listening to her dad tease her mom that their house was home for wayward animals. Even though he tried to be tough, Nina could tell he was also a sucker for a cute face.

At 7:00 PM, Nina announced she needed to check in at work. There was no doubt unread emails were waiting for her response. Taking the hint, Josh called to his loving companion, said goodbye to Molly and walked with Nina to the door.

Before leaving, he looked down from his 6'1" height at the quirky little blond who rattled his emotions, tested his patience, and was slowly tugging on his heart. He couldn't understand the strong feelings, especially since they had just recently met. But he could tell something was pulling them together. Maybe it was fate, he thought. He could also tell by her sparkling eyes luring him closer, she was feeling it too. He wanted to seek out and capture her delectable glistening lips, which were calling to him. But as he was going in for a taste, Molly called out and broke the spell.

"Nina, remember your aunt is bringing dinner tomorrow, and of course Josh is invited."

"Okay mom," Nina replied, not sure if she was relieved or irritated by her untimely interruption. She'd almost kissed a mere stranger and a cowboy at that. Wouldn't Rene freak if she knew, Nina thought. The crazy thing was that part of her longed to be pulled into his arms and be devoured by his lips. However, it wasn't the place or time, no matter what the Committee on Intimate Relations was lecturing in her head.

The awkward moment left them both speechless and the sensual moment of bliss was long gone. Tipping his hat, Josh said good-bye and they parted ways, both wondering what would have happened in that window of euphoria.

On his way home, Josh gave thought to what almost happened. He wondered to himself if it was premature to be making a move on Nina. He liked her, that was a given. But, she was also the daughter of a good friend, and he wasn't sure what Molly's views were on this subject. Thinking more clearly, he decided to step back, give it some time, and see what happens. He only hoped he could follow through with his decision, especially when her presence drove him wild and caused his logical thinking to take off, like an untamed stallion set free.

The next morning, Nina was up early and wasted no time getting dressed. She tried to convince herself it was to feed the animals, but some of her excitement might have been linked to the handsome cowboy waiting for her. Today she had chosen her skinny jeans, tight sweater, and for fun, added gloss to her lips. After she slipped on her mom's boots and coat, she hurried to the hen house.

Just like yesterday, Josh was standing by Gerdy's nest. But today she noticed the man looking tall and sexy, like a cool drink of heaven. She tried not to stare while butterflies fluttered in her stomach. Shaking off the sensual moment, Nina smiled sweetly and said good morning.

Josh tipped his hat and politely greeted her. He then walked her quickly through the process, staying strictly on course. When they finished, he congratulated her on the progress she'd made, and told her she could probably handle it on her own now. He also said he'd see her at the store later and left.

Nina was furious, the nerve of him she thought, stomping her feet up to the house. He had not said one word about the kiss that almost happened, in fact, he didn't say much at all. Her temper soon led her to confusion. Nina wasn't ready for his cold shoulder attitude, which left an empty feeling inside her as she watched him drive away. After her quick pity party, she got it together and said aloud, "Well, if he can brush me away like a pestering fly, then I have no use for the man." Wrapping her arms around her to ward off the chill, Nina went inside to get ready for work.

At 9:00 AM, Nina sat on the back patio with her mom, enjoying the morning, listening as she went over again, some of the last minute need-to-know instructions.

"Mom," Nina said sweetly, "I've got this."

"Where have I heard that before," she said giving Nina a sly smile.

"Ha, ha," Nina expressed rolling her eyes at her comment. "I majored in business, not barnyard 101," she said kissing her on the cheek, and grabbing her lunch as she headed for the door.

"Call me if you need anything," Molly called out just as Nina closed the door.

When Nina arrived at the store, after unlocking the door, she immediately removed the picture of the miner from the wall and set it on the ground, picture side facing the wall.

"You might not be able to see me, but I bet you can still hear me," a muffled voice sounded from the portrait.

"You're not real, you're not real," she chanted aloud, trying to convince herself.

"But I am sort of. At least I feel like it," the voice commented, but this time it came from a picture of a beautiful woman in a sundress.

Nina froze in place as the woman came to life and navigated through the scene, happily watering her garden. "What is going on?" Nina screeched, freaked out at the scenario playing out before her. "Who are you people?" she asked looking around, making sure the other pictures were not animated.

"It's only me," the woman said. "It seems that I can slip in and out of pictures, and bring a character to life."

"How do you do that?" Nina asked inspecting the portrait.

"I don't know. It's been happening ever since you arrived. In the past I have attempted, multiple times to push my way out of the picture, always with unsuccessful results. But when I tried it yesterday, I was able to set my course and appear in this picture," he admitted. "I have been having fun testing out my new discovery. However I do feel a little prissy dressed in these clothes," he said with a laugh swooping the dress for fun.

"That's strange," Nina concluded. "In fact, the entire thing is strange," she added, shaking her head while sitting down.

"Tell me about it. Try being me."

"No offense, but no thank you," Nina answered, trying to wrap her brain around what was happening.

"None taken," the man answered. Before he could finish his sentence, Nina put the picture against the wall; along with the other two she found hanging on the wall, in case, he decided to take a stroll. She only hoped there were no other sources he could communicate through.

There was no way she wanted to deal with such a weird mess the first day of work. She needed to get busy to open on time. So after she turned on her mom's radio to a soft rock station, Nina went through the store performing the tasks on her list. First on the agenda was to set up the front porch; which entailed putting out the display signs and filling the sale bins with the more ripened fruit and vegetables. After she checked that job off her list, Nina went inside to continue the morning set-up. By 9:55 AM, she had money in the till, verified all the temperatures for the freezers and coolers were per regulation, and turned on the open sign in the window. Since everything was ready for business, and there were no customers yet, she decided to check in at work, handle her emails, and if time allowed, spend some time on her web page.

Nina was deep in thought when she heard the notification bell. Looking up with a cheerful smile, she was ready to greet her first customer. But the expression on her face was quickly altered when she realized it was Josh. She shouldn't have been surprised since he seemed to show up everywhere. Pretending not to be moved by his appearance, she said good morning, took a sip of her coffee and waited for his reply.

"Morning," Josh replied, wondering why she had suddenly become so distant towards him. Trying to lighten her mood, he added, "So how's business so far?"

"This is it," she answered, short and curt and then turned her attention back to the computer, pretending to be interested. After Josh's cold attitude that morning, she could also play it cool.

Deciding he was on the losing end, Josh replied, "Well I'm going out back, the delivery guy should be here soon, and the plants need watering."

"Sounds good," Nina replied, not bothering to look up.

Josh walked away, and as he stepped into the garden area, he mumbled, "Women!" and went to meet the delivery truck pulling into the driveway.

The nerve of him, he could have at least asked her what was wrong. It had to have been pretty obvious something was bothering her. "Men!" she said, closing her laptop, no longer able to concentrate.

First, her nerves were rattled by the pictures, and now she was stressed out over Mr. Cold Shoulder. She had no interest in him, especially with him being a cowboy. Now if she could get the Queen of Denial to agree, all would be well.

The sound of the notification bell again pulled Nina out of her thoughts. And for the next four hours, her mind was occupied assisting a steady flow of customers. She found the people to be very friendly and caring, as many offered their prayers and well wishes for her mom's recovery. By 6:00 PM Nina was ready to be done with the workday and looked forward to chilling and visiting with her aunt. Then panic struck when she remembered Mr. Parker was joining them. She was not looking forward to the night, so not to dwell on the inevitable; she focused on the closing tasks noted on her list. After she emptied the till and stocked the shelves and freezers, she put the pictures back on the wall.

"Are you just going to leave me here?" John said as she placed his portrait on the wall.

Nina laughing at the absurd question replied, "Well, I'm not taking you home with me."

"We'll see about that," he said with a sly smile, then froze in place.

Nina wondered what he meant by his last comment, but decided it wasn't important. She needed to get home she thought. She turned off the lights and locked the door.

5) THE KISS

When Nina arrived home, Cassie greeted her with a ball and requested immediate attention. After a friendly pat and a couple of ball tosses, the satisfied dog followed her into the kitchen, where Molly was busy preparing a salad.

Molly said with a smile, "I see my furry hostess captured your attention and heart with her persistence and cuteness," she chuckled.

"Yes, how could I resist those sweet loving doggie eyes?" Nina replied as she hugged her mom, and snatched up a mini roll, fresh from the oven. "Yum," she mumbled, taking a bite of the sweet bread.

"So, how was your first day at work?" Molly asked as she tossed the dinner salad.

"Fine," Nina answered shrugging her shoulders. "It was uneventful. I have no issues to report, and I met some interesting people. I'd say it was a good day. You seem to have many friends in this town. They all send their love, and wish you a speedy recovery." While she was savoring the last bite of her roll, a sudden movement on the wall caught her eye. The alarming sight nearly had her choking.

Molly panicked at the sight of her daughter's pale face. She wasted no time and scooted to her side. "What happened?" she asked, worry lines showing.

"Wrong pipe," Nina managed to speak, pointing to her throat. "Water," she said in a raspy voice, battling to get her coughing under control.

"Are you okay?" Molly asked filling a glass with water and handing it to her.

"I'll be fine. No 911 call needed," Nina expressed conjuring up a halfhearted smile, feeling relief as the cool liquid soothed her dry throat.

"Don't you ever do that again," Molly lovingly scolded. "You frightened me," she added while letting out a deep sigh.

Nina hugged her mom and said, "I'll try not to, it's something I don't want to repeat."

After convincing her mom everything was fine, Nina turned her attention back to the picture, hoping it was her imagination. But she wasn't that lucky as the Indian on the horse waved at her. She knew it was John bringing the rider to life and scowled at him. Nina let him know she wasn't pleased with his appearance. Trying not to alert her mom to any more surprises, Nina pulled her eyes away from the painting. She needed to find a way to talk to the pest alone. She certainly couldn't do it with her mom nearby. Nina laughed inside. First, she had a run-in with a cowboy, and now she had to deal with an Indian. How had her life turned into a western movie?

Nina turned to the lively woman, still hovering close by and said assertively, "Mom I'm okay, but I think you need to sit for a few minutes and rest your leg. I'll finish in here," escorting her to the living room without giving her time to respond.

"But I don't want to rest," Molly announced, as she put her foot on the ground for resistance, stopping the scooter.

"I came here to make sure you take care of yourself, and I assume that you've been busy today, trying to prepare for your guests. Please relax for a few minutes," Nina said giving her a sad puppy-dog look.

"Fine!" Molly said giving in. "But I don't need to," she admitted with a huff as she scooted away.

After making sure she was gone, Nina walked over to the Indian picture and whispered loudly, "What are you doing here? Isn't it bad enough you stalk me at the store and now you are here?" she said, glaring at the rider.

"Dear child, stalking is such a harsh word. I am merely studying you, a considerable difference. And I don't have an answer to how I got here. It seems I can come to life in pictures only when you are present," he said getting off the horse.

Nina shook her head in disbelief. "You're saying you can follow me around and interact through pictures? Anywhere?" she asked, wrapping her mind around the idea.

"I don't know about that. I've only experienced the freedom in the store and now this house," he answered.

Nina was getting frustrated with this man. Looking at him, she exclaimed, "Well that is not going to work for me. Go back to the store where you belong, and stand next to your bench," giving him a direct order.

"I'd rather not," he replied, "this is so much more fun. I've been trapped in that same picture for many years, and now I have a chance to explore," he said climbing back on the horse and freezing in place.

"Look at me now," he happily commented.

Nina moved her eyes to another picture, where John had now taken on a wolf's body trekking through the woods. "Stop that!" she yelled grabbing her head, not realizing she had raised her voice.

"What Nina?" Molly called out.

"Nothing, just talking to myself," Nina answered. Then, she brought her attention back to the wolf in the wilderness. "I don't have time to deal with this craziness now, so if you must stay, please be considerate and keep a low profile. Also, don't watch me, it's creepy," she said walking away.

When she finished in the kitchen, Nina went into the living room to make peace with her mom for being so pushy. Just as she sat down, Cassie let out one bark to notify them someone was approaching the driveway. Nina prayed that it was her aunt, as she went to greet their guest.

Nina smiled at her Aunt Becky and studied her as she opened the screen door. She was a couple of years older than her mom and a few pounds heavier, but her flowing skirts and oversized tops hid it well.

"There's my favorite niece," she said with beaming smile, setting down the bags she was carrying.

"You should have called me for help," Nina commented looking at the bags.

"Nonsense, there are only a few items," she said. Becky took off her hat and fluffed up her salon styled curly red hair, and then huggrd Nina. Then stepping back she added, "You are such a skinny little thing. It's a good thing I brought my homemade lasagna loaded with three types of cheese. Men like a woman with a little bit of meat on her bones," she quoted with a laugh.

Nina knew it was better not to argue with her aunt. Instead, she decided to change the subject. "Where's Uncle Hank?" she asked peering around her aunt, expecting to see the burly man walking up the path.

"His allergies have him held hostage inside. He sends his love and will visit later this week. Here, he wanted you to have this," she said, handing her a wrapped gift.

Graciously accepting the gift, she remarked, "He remembered." Her eyes watered as she opened the little package. "I love it," she said inspecting a little trinket. As long as Nina could remember, her uncle would surprise her with a charm. This time it was a silver coin with a carved relic of an old building. "It's beautiful. I'll call him later and thank him," Nina said, slipping the coin into her pocket before picking up the bags to carry them into the kitchen.

From the first bag, she removed the tray of lasagna which had a heavenly smell and placed it in the oven on low to keep it warm. Nina wasn't surprised to find in the second bag, two bottles of perfectly aged wine. She knew by the title they were from her aunt's friend, who owns a winery in Sonoma Valley California. After placing the bottles in the refrigerator to chill, Nina carried a tray containing a pitcher of iced tea, glasses, and freshly sliced lemons, and then joined the ladies on the patio.

"Honey, I'm so glad you could come and stay with your mom and help out at the store," she said patting Nina's leg. "I had every intention of assisting at the store, but I had orders to fill for several birthdays and a large wedding, all coming due next month," she said taking a sip of her tea.

"No worries, it's all working out. I can telecommute, handle the store, and be here with mom," Nina said compassionately. She lovingly looked over at her mom, hoping to make up for abruptly pushing her out of the kitchen earlier.

"Your mom was telling me about your barnyard adventures," Becky said with a laugh.

"Definitely not a fun time had by all," Nina expressed, shaking her head.

"I also heard you are getting cozy with a handsome cowboy," she added with a wink and a coy smile.

Nina shuddered at her comment, and wanted to clear up any rumors spread by momma bird; she replied, "Well you heard wrong."

"I wouldn't blame you if you did, he's such a fine catch," Becky admitted squeezing the slice of lemon into her tea.

Nina wanted to say, "Maybe if I were going fishing," but instead she smiled and looked away.

Becky, taking the hint, turned to her sister and engaged her in a conversation of flowers and floral arrangements. Nina sat half-listening to the ladies while her eyes perused the patio. She hadn't been in the backyard much since last year and noticed her mom had made considerable changes. The white wicker patio set was a new addition and brightened up the area. It looked perfect against the newly stained deck. She wondered if Josh had built it. Then her eyes wandered over to a circular bench surrounding a tall stone fire pit, and she thought, what a cozy spot with the right guy. Not going there, she silently told her mind's Romantic Department, which was already planning the interlude with Josh.

Drawing her eyes back to the patio, she marveled at the hanging flower baskets. They were filled with a variety of plants, bursting with color. Some proudly showed off their vines which hung over the side. Her moment of bliss dissolved as a movement on a Western magazine cover caught her attention. Are you kidding me? She thought to herself as the horse winked at her. Without giving thought to her surroundings, she blurted out. "Get out of here."

Both ladies turned in her direction; their expression questioned her outburst. Thinking fast, Nina remarked, "There was a nasty bug, a very, very big bug," she emphasized, more for John's purpose. "Wine anybody?" Nina asked, jumping up, looking for an excuse to escape into the house and find that pesky spirit.

"None for me, better not mix my medicine with alcohol," Molly replied.

"I'll take a glass," Becky said with a smile, "you know I'd never say no to a glass of the finest," she chuckled. "I think it is Helen's best batch," she added proudly.

Nina hurried into the house, ready to enforce the stay-out-of-sight rule to John, but was interrupted by a knock at the door. Oh great, she thought, letting out a sigh. That's all I need now. "How much more can a girl take in one day?" she said looking up for the answers, still knowing she was on her own with this one.

She went to the door, said a polite hello to Josh, accepted his six-pack minus the one he took for himself and sent him to the back patio. After putting his beer in the refrigerator, she went in search of John. After five minutes of checking each picture, she finally gave up. She thought John was either hiding or making himself at home in other parts of the house. If she were lucky, he had gone back to the store. Deciding it was a moot point, she poured two glasses of wine, downed half of one in a swallow, and then refilled it.

Feeling a little more relaxed; she went out back to join the group.

Another glass later, Nina was feeling no stress, even if Josh was acting like a jerk. He hadn't looked her way once. Not that she was keeping tabs. She told herself it didn't matter, but the Queen of Denial was forcefully pushing through her relaxed thoughts. So instead of dwelling on it, she fell into the conversations until it was time to serve dinner. It wasn't long until she and Becky excused themselves to tend to dinner. Molly and Josh stayed on the deck discussing plans for her new shed.

Waiting until after everyone sat, Becky led the group in a blessing for the food. Afterward, they filled their plates with pasta, salad, and rolls. Becky made sure their wine glasses never got below the halfway mark, as they ate and chatted about everything and anything. By the end of the meal, Nina was feeling a little light-headed, and she thought a tall glass of water would help her feel better. She excused herself, gathered an armful of dirty dishes and headed to the kitchen. It surprised her when Josh also stood and offered to help. This motion seemed odd since he had been avoiding her all evening. His presence behind her was making her uncomfortable and giving her cause to down the last half of her wine.

As she set the dishes on the counter, Nina turned around and nearly ran into him. Clearing her throat and stepping back, she said, "We should probably feed the animals after I wash the dishes. I imagine those little baby goats are getting hungry," she said in a childlike voice.

"You think you're up to it?" he asked, watching her sway a little at the sink.

His comment was enough to fuel the anger harboring inside her, placing her hands on her hips and with a scornful look, she replied, "Why would you ask that? Will the animals be offended by my intoxicated state?"

"No, quite the opposite, but first I want to make sure you're okay," Josh cautiously answered, trying not to rile Nina.

"I am perfectly fine," she said with confidence loading the dishwasher. She veered off balance and grabbed the counter to keep from falling.

Ten minutes later; dishes done, kitchen clean, and dressed for the occasion, Nina warmed up the goats' bottles, and they headed for the barn. Walking down the path, Nina tripped and ended up in Josh's arms. Looking down, she commented, "That rock must be new, I don't remember it being there this morning," she said with a straight face.

"Yep, new rocks grow around here all the time," he joked.

"Mr. Parker, are you making fun of me?" Nina asked looking up at him after finding her balance.

"Never, but maybe you should let me hold your arm in case anymore appear," he replied working hard not to laugh.

"Maybe you are right," she said letting him guide her, "one broken ankle in the family is already too many," Nina expressed.

When they reached the barn, Nina handed Josh one of the bottles and called to the baby goats. As they hurried over, it was easy to see they were excited for their evening feeding.

"What a lucky mom," Nina said, "I love these kids," she expressed rubbing the goat's head. "Have you ever thought about having children?" she asked, out of the blue.

Josh was caught off guard by her personal question. Up until now, she had kept their conversational topics strictly on the surface. After pausing a moment to intake and process her question, he replied, "I guess, maybe a time or two, but not until I find the right woman and settle down."

"I have," Nina confessed after a yawn. "I want a boy and a girl. The boy first, so he can be a big brother and protect his sister. My daughter will be named Nichole Sue, a family name, and my son will carry on his father's," she said looking up and picturing the scene in her mind.

Josh listened while Nina rambled on. He liked that she was opening up, even if it was the wine lending her the courage. He wasn't sure how to handle her tender side, and it scared him a little. But he quickly pushed the thought aside when he noticed Nina, done with the feeding, stand and almost fall. "Are you feeling well?" he asked with concern, removing the empty bottle from his goat.

Holding her head, Nina moaned, "I had two glasses of wine too many. My crazy aunt thinks it's a sin to let your wine glass get half full," not admitting she had to drink it all.

Noticing Nina wasn't looking too good; he walked over to her and took her hand. "Come on, you can rest while I feed the pigs, then I'll help you to the house," Josh offered, carefully leading her outside and over to a nearby bench.

When he had finished, Josh walked over to Nina, who was curled up and fast asleep. Bending down, he lifted her in his arms, a big smile showing on his face as she wrapped her arms around his neck and laid her head against his chest.

"You know Mr. Parker, you're not too bad for a cowboy," Nina confessed in a sleepy voice.

"And you're all right for a city girl, Miss Charm," he replied as she wiggled in his arms.

"Mmm, you smell good too," she said, burrowing her face into his neck before falling asleep.

Nina's soft body felt as though it belonged in his arms, and her warm breath against his skin set his soul on fire. He didn't want to let go of her. He'd never held an angel, but the rush he was experiencing led him to imagine Nina was close to the real thing. That was when she was asleep; he quietly chuckled at the thought. The last few days, her demeanor was far from being branded as angelic. But that didn't stop his heart from racing, calling to his primal instinct to take her directly to his truck. Luckily, his reasonable self fought off the urge, and instead, did the honorable thing and took her inside. Smiling, he carried her into the living room, where Becky and Molly were savoring some sister time.

As Molly spotted the two of them entering the room, she shook her head and glared at her sister, "This is all your fault. You know Nina can't handle that much wine. I had a feeling she'd end up like this."

Becky shrugged her shoulders and gritting her teeth; she answered, "I guess I forgot."

Molly brought her focus back to her passed-out daughter. Smiling at Josh, she commented, "Josh could you please be a dear and carry Nina upstairs to her bed; it's the first door on the right. There should be a cover at the foot of the bed to throw over her."

"No problem," Josh replied, already climbing the stairs. He flipped on the light before walking into the room, and the brightness caused Nina to stir. Disoriented in an alcohol-induced haze, she questioned Josh, "What's happening?"

"It's okay, you are safe and in your room," he answered softly, sitting her on the bed and removing her boots. Then he lowered her head to her pillow and draped the blanket over her. Before he left, something drew him closer, and out of impulse he brushed her hair from her eyes and lightly placed a kiss on her forehead. But as he was pulling away, Nina threw her arms around him and led his lips to hers.

The kiss caught him by surprise, and the angel was now leading him to heavenly bliss. And as her lips melded into his and her sweet tongue danced with perfect rhythm, he fell under her passionate spell. He savored each moment and never wanted it to end. That was until she tried to pull him closer alerting him to his surroundings. An uneasy feeling came over him, and he whispered to Nina, "I have to go now."

"Ahhh," she replied, feeling him slip out of her embrace she cuddled into the blanket and was out before he was gone.

Josh hurried out of the room and down the stairs. He would say his goodbyes, collect his dog and hope they don't see the word guilty plastered on his face. He was in luck. Molly and Becky were in a heated discussion which gave him a good excuse not to intrude, so he blew them a kiss as he scooted past them. With his faithful companion by his side, he left the scene of the crime.

As he was driving home, he thought about the encounter with Nina. Even though it was amazing, what he did was wrong; making out with his friend's daughter, in the room directly above her wasn't cool. What was he thinking? He wasn't raised that way. He would have to be more careful and see that it didn't happen again, no matter how much that city girl drove him crazy.

6) SHATTERING MOMENT

As Josh turned onto the road to his house, he could see the entrance sign. The brightly lit words, Parker Ranch, gave notice to the property handed down to him from his late grandfather. Josh had recently replaced the weathered sign with a modern one. High above his private gate hung a new steel plate. Its shiny appearance welcomed visitors to his estate. Using his remote, another updated feature, he opened the iron gate and drove through. Then, after hearing the sound of it closing, he proceeded down his tree-lined gravel driveway to his ranch house. There, at the end of his drive, was a glowing light from his wraparound porch, giving life to his recently remodeled home.

Stretching as he stepped out of his 4 by 4 Chevy truck, he could feel his tight muscles, the results of his long day of work. Tomorrow he'd take Whiski for a run and spend an hour in his indoor gym. As he walked across his porch to the door, his lazy cat Moses, jumped off the porch swing, yawned and nonchalantly sauntered over to him. "Hey boy," Josh said bending down to pet his oversize baby, happily purring and rubbing against his leg. "Come on, I'll get your dinner," he said as he opened the door. The cat was close behind until Whiski plowed her way in and pushed him aside. Josh, knew that Whiski put on a front, pretending to tolerate the cat, but when she thought he wasn't looking, she'd let Moses curl up next to her. Somehow Whiski had taken on the title of Queen of the House and always made it clear she was Josh's first priority. Right now she was letting him know it was time to eat.

Both animals faithfully followed him into the heart of his loft-style home, which he had just recently redesigned to be simple and spacious. As he walked into his living room, the large rock fireplace took center stage, and close by, a large sectional offered a comfortable place to sit. Next to it was a matching recliner, which he called a "nap trap." His fifty inch TV mounted on the wall, entertained him with sports and kept him updated on the news. His stereo sound system carried his favorite music throughout the house and outside.

While his furry children waited on the bear rug, Josh went to prepare their food. He walked into the kitchen which used to consist of a four-burner stove, a small refrigerator, and very limited counter and cupboard space. Looking around, he remembered how squished he'd felt inside the tiny room before the remodel. Now he had more than enough space and it was equipped with all the latest stainless steel appliances, including a side-by-side refrigerator. The focal point and favorite piece in the room was the inside barbeque encased in a large ceramic island.

Most of the house he had redesigned, but his mother and sister had helped with the kitchen and bathrooms. They informed him those rooms needed a woman's touch, in case he ever decided to settle down. At that thought, Nina popped into his head. For a brief moment, he let his mind wander. He pictured her at the sink, offering him a loving smile while her alluring eyes were begging for a kiss. The image instantly vanished as his furry pets nosily came to check on him. Putting his mind back on his task, he filled their dishes and fed his impatient audience. After they finished, Moses found a comfy spot on the sofa, while Josh and his trusty protector went outside to do their nightly rounds on his farm.

As usual, the chickens were safe in their house and nestled in for the night. His Arabian stud, Majestic, and his beautiful mate Starlet were bedded down in the small barn. Outside in the corral, his small herd of cattle, hearing him approach, walked over to greet him. There was also no escaping his two goats, Selma and Louise, as they ran over, kicking their feet, looking for a handout and a friendly pat on the head. After making sure all the gates were secure, he called to Whiski, who was also doing her part by checking the perimeter for unwanted predators. Seeing everything was in order, they walked back to the house.

After setting the security alarm, Josh called it a night, and he and his entourage headed upstairs to his room. Both animals settled into their respected beds, however, that sleeping arrangement was only temporary as they usually ended up in his. Fortunately, his super king size bed was plenty big enough for all three.

While the two of them slept, Josh went into his master bath which was still a total mess. This room was the last to be renovated and seemed to be taking the longest to finish. He was getting tired of climbing over the supplies and equipment to get to his small sink. He had everything to complete the project; a double porcelain sink, counter tiles, toilet, and medicine cabinet. Right now they all sat in boxes, waiting to be opened and installed, to complete the new room. Cursing as he bumped his knee on a box, he vowed to himself to set aside time next week to get it done.

When he went back into his room, he noticed his bed was no longer vacant, as Whiski and Moses had already claimed their spot. Laughing at the sight, he climbed onto his side and claimed his real-estate. As tired as he was, he couldn't seem to fall asleep. The memory of Nina in his arms was burning in his mind. He was experiencing emotions he hadn't felt in a long time and wasn't sure how to handle them. Funny, he wasn't afraid to ride that bucking bronco in the ring, but the thought of a relationship with that spirited girl scared the hell out of him. Maybe with the bronco, he'd always know the worst outcome; he surmised rolling over in hopes to find some sleep soon.

The next morning Nina had awakened with a slight headache and Jerome the rooster's off-key crowing wasn't helping. Sitting up, she touched her lips as she remembered fragments of the kiss the night before. Nina didn't know if the kiss was real or another dream. Knowing she couldn't stay in bed all day to figure it out, she gently pulled herself out of bed, threw on her clothes and went downstairs, dreading the thought of going to the barn.

The shock of the cold air quickly had Nina awake and alert. Within thirty minutes she had finished the morning chores and was back at the house. She wasn't surprised her mom was still asleep. She probably stayed up late gabbing with her sister, Nina thought as she prepared a pot of coffee.

"Good morning," a voice startled her. Frowning, she looked up at John, whom again took on the role of the Indian in the picture. Shaking her head in frustration, she commented, "I can't do this today," she admitted, going to the closet and returning with a pile of blankets.

Nina was on her laptop working on her website when her mom came sleepily strolling in. "Morning," she said with a yawn, then stretching and with a questionable look on her face she approached her daughter, "Nina, why are all my pictures on the wall covered with blankets?"

Nina had prepared herself for her mom's question; it wasn't like she could have missed it. Smiling at her mom, she said, "I am doing a spiritual, holistic cleansing" bringing her mom a cup of coffee.

"Okay," Molly said with a perplexed look, "that doesn't explain my pictures."

"I have to open all the purifying gates and let the energy flow and the pictures block the current," Nina said, hoping she sounded more believable to her mom than to herself.

"Hmm, I've never heard of that," Molly admitted with slight interest, "I'll have to research it," she added taking a sip of her coffee.

"NO!" Nina shouted, "I mean you won't find anything. My friend at college is conducting an experiment and asked if I would be a guinea pig. As far as I know, it's still in design mode," Nina lied.

"So how long are you planning to hold my wall art hostage?" Molly asked, a little suspicious of her daughter's request.

"Maybe a week," Nina said with a big smile, hoping she wasn't pushing her luck.

"A week!" Molly screeched, "Nina I can't have my house looking like this for a week," she said with a sweep of her hands, "maybe a couple of days," she informed her daughter.

"Good for you Molly," John said cheering through the blanket.

"But Mom," Nina whined, and trying to ignore the interfering menace, she replied, "two days isn't going to be long enough. I promised I'd do it for a week."

Molly shook her head as she looked at her daughter's begging face, "Four days but that's it," she stressed.

"I'll take it," Nina said excitedly, placing a kiss on her mom's cheek before preparing a light breakfast for them.

For the rest of the week, Nina kept to the same routine. She would go to work, take care of the animals, tend to her mom's needs, and the household chores. When time allowed, she would donate time to her website. She rarely saw Josh at the store and was usually busy helping a customer when he arrived. When they did have a brief encounter, not much was said, especially about a kiss. Nina figured it must have been a dream. She had developed a morning regime for feeding the animals, so she no longer needed his assistance. All the animals, but Gerdy had warmed up to her, Nina figured she was still keeping her guard up.

John tried every day to talk to her, but Nina did her best to ignore him. The only time she interacted with him was when she took him on and off the wall. Fortunately, her mom had given in and let her keep the pictures at home covered up for the week. She hoped it would buy her time to figure out what to do about John. Sadly though, her time was almost up, and no clues were leading to any answers.

On Friday, Josh stopped by the shop, claiming the plants needed watering. But he wanted to see Nina, admitting that he missed her. He wondered if she remembered the kiss. It was something he hadn't been able to clear from his mind. He recognized the fact that a city girl, all glamour, and glitz, didn't blend well with a country boy - dirty boots and campfires. That didn't stop him from wanting to be close to her.

He walked in just as she was hanging the pictures on the wall. He had secretly caught her doing the wall to floor shuffle a few times, and couldn't wait to hear the reason for this weird ritual. So with a perplexed look, he questioned her action, "What is it about those pictures you don't like?"

Startled by the sound of Josh's voice, Nina almost dropped the picture. She hadn't heard him come in and was surprised to see him. Turning around and putting on her innocent face, she replied, "I like them fine," then told him the same fib she had told her mom. Not wanting to get into a discussion surrounding that topic, she went about hanging the picture, but as she was adjusting the object in her arms, a piece of yellowed paper fell out of the back of the frame.

After placing John's photo back on the wall, Nina bent down and picked up the paper.

"What is it?" Josh asked walking up to Nina to get a better look.

"I don't know," Nina replied carefully opening the piece of crumpled paper. "It looks like some legal document," she surmised while studying the faded print.

"Where's aniko," Nina asked Josh inquisitively.

"I don't know," Josh said after giving thought to her question, "Could it be Shaniko."

"That might be it," Nina said squinting as she tried to make out the shaded letters. "Where is that?" she added, looking up at Josh with curious eyes.

"It is a few miles up the road," he answered pointing in that direction. "It was, at one time, the wool capital of the world. All that remains there now are some remnants of buildings making a ghostly presence."

"You think this might be a deed to a mine near Shankio?" Nina asked thinking of the possibility as she handed the paper to Josh.

"I don't know," he replied taking the paper and inspecting it himself. "It's hard to make out the writing, and what I can read doesn't make much sense," he admitted. "My sister Jennifer is an attorney in Bend. I could fax it to her. Maybe she'll be able to tell us more."

"Awesome," Nina excitedly commented, "maybe it's a deed to a gold mine," she said laughing at the thought.

After Josh left, Nina went back to picture of the miner and looking up at John, she commented, "So do you know what that piece of paper was?"

"Harrumph," he answered turning his back to her, "Now you speak to me, but only because you need something. Maybe I do, or maybe I don't."

She knew that he was waiting for an apology. Maybe she had been a little harsh with him. But who could blame her, it's not like she had pictures come to life before. Biting her lower lip, Nina said her piece, "Okay I'm sorry for being rude and trying to ignore you. You would probably do the same if you were in my place."

"Was that your way of apologizing?" John said slowly turning back around, "It didn't sound very sincere," he added folding his arms at his chest and looking away from her.

"Come on," Nina said whining a little, "are you going to help me or not?"

"Only if you are nice to me and let me come to your house," he said giving an ultimatum.

"All right, you win," Nina said giving in, "but you better be good."

"Always my dear, always," John replied with a boisterous laugh.

"So what can you tell me?" Nina asked kindly.

"That young man, your boyfriend I presume, was correct. The town noted on the form was Shaniko. I grew up around there." John said looking up as he tried to remember pieces of his past.

"He's not my boyfriend," Nina stated strongly.

"Well, you could have fooled me, sure was a strong current flowing in the room when he was here with you," he said with a sly smile.

"Whatever," she said with a sigh, "please, tell me about the paper," immediately changing the subject.

"I don't know too much about it. I do however remember your father putting it there."

"I thought you said you knew what it was. I feel I've been had," Nina expressed with frustration.

"That's all I know. My memory has several broken lines and many black holes," John said with a faraway look in his eyes.

"I'm sorry," Nina said with compassion and felt a pang of sadness for the man Molly claimed to be her uncle.

Forgetting about the document, for now, she proceeded to cheer him up. "So what should I call you, miner, John, or Uncle John?" she asked with a glowing smile.

The question brought John out of his temporary funk as he grinned and replied. "I like Uncle John."

"I will call you Uncle J then," Nina said.

"That will work. Are you ready to go home now? Your mom is probably wondering what happened to you."

"Oh wow, I didn't realize it was this late," she said checking the time on her cell phone. "I will call her and let her know we'll be home soon." Realizing her mistake, she laughed, thinking how strange her life was now, and had a feeling it was going to get a lot stranger.

When Josh arrived home, he devoted a few minutes to his furry kids. After feeding them, he threw a burger on the grill and fixed a salad using the vegetables from his garden. Adding a piece of toasted garlic bread and a cold beer, he was a happy cowboy.

Dinner finished, he relaxed in his recliner and called his sister as he held the yellowed document.

After the third ring, he was greeted by a cheerful voice, "Hi Josh, how's my favorite brother?" Jennifer asked.

"You only have one," he laughed playing along.

"I know, but if I had more, you'd still be my favorite," she teased.

"Love you too Sis," Josh replied with affection.

"So what's up?" Jennifer asked.

"Do you have a couple of minutes?" he replied, hoping he hadn't caught her at a bad time.

"Sure, I was just sitting here reviewing some court documents and preparing for a hearing. So what is it, girlfriend trouble again?" she said poking fun at him.

"Not friends exactly, more like acquaintances," he admitted, even that was stretching their connection.

"You care to elaborate on that?" Jennifer said, innocently prying.

"Her name is Nina. She's beautiful and the daughter of Molly Charm."

"You mean that sweet little lady who bought the Kroger ranch a few years ago?"

"Yes, that's her. Although her daughter isn't anything like her," Josh admitted. "She's a spoiled city brat, very independent and her stubborn streak is worse than an untamed mare."

"Sounds like you met your match," she laughed, "I like her already."

"Hardly," he said shaking his head at the thought, "her preconceived vision of a perfect man comes with a two-story house in the West Portland Hills, wears a business suit, and drives a BMW. Way out of my league," he admitted thinking briefly about the kiss.

"You mean you haven't won her over with your smooth talking charm? I've never known you to give up," Jennifer commented.

"It wouldn't do me any good to pursue her. I'm not her type. Besides, she's only here for a couple of months to take care of her mom who is recovering from a minor accident. How do you always do that?" Josh asked, realizing her sister had sneakily slipped into his private life.

"Do what?" Jennifer replied.

"Get me to talk about myself, especially my personal life."

"It's a gift," she laughed, "I guess I ask the right questions."

"I fall for it every time; you'd think I would learn. Enough about my life, let's get down to the real reason I called," Josh concluded, wanting to change the subject.

"Sure, what is it," Jennifer answered.

"Nina found what we think is a deed. It fell out of the back of a picture in her mom's store. I was wondering if I faxed it over, could you please examine it? The print is very faded; besides, we don't know how to read it."

"Yes, I would be happy to. Give me a few days to review it, and I will see what I can find out."

"Thanks. So putting that aside, how is everything with your life?" he asked. And with that, they spent the next thirty minutes talking about work, family, and made a date next month to get together. After he ended the call, Josh faxed the form, tended to his evening routine, and retired for the night.

When Nina arrived home, she was greeted with silence as she stepped inside. Her Aunt Becky had picked her mom up for a Bunko night at her house, and Cassie had gone along for the ride. Nina admitted the quietness was welcome. She loved being here with her mom, but she also missed the solitude of her house in Portland. Her blissful moment was short-lived. "Hi, long time no see," John said, positioning himself back in the Indian painting.

"You've got to be kidding me," Nina said under her breath.

"Now, now, remember to be nice."

"Fine," Nina said trying to comply. "I'm going to fix something to eat, and then put some time into work, so that doesn't leave much time for visiting," Nina said politely.

"I promise not to disturb you," he assured her.

"Thank you," Nina said, leaving John as she fixed her dinner.

After Nina was finished eating and made her rounds of the barnyard, she planted herself at the desk, ready to work. However, she first wanted to see how far Shaniko was from here. "Only less than an hour away," Nina commented aloud, as the results showed on the screen. Finding the current and historical picture intriguing, she got a crazy notion in her head and plotted out the route. Tomorrow was Saturday, and since the store closed early, she could easily make the trip and still be back before dark. Her mom would be with her aunt again, attending another function, so Nina didn't feel guilty being away. Excited for her road trip, Nina was not in the frame of mind to work yet, so instead, she awarded herself some play time on a social media page.

Nina smiled when her friend, Serena popped up on her page. She was celebrating her honeymoon and had posted pictures of their magical getaway. Smiling, Nina silently cheered her friend's happiness, and for a brief moment, she felt the envy bug tug on her emotions. But the feeling was quickly gone as she moved on to another post. After giving herself a few minutes of play time, she went through her emails then turned her focus to her web page until her eyes grew heavy. Then, she called it a night and went to bed.

The next day, Nina closed the store at two and started driving southeast from Maupin, following the Dalles-California Highway. She could feel the sun's warm rays as they kissed her shoulders through the open sunroof. The sky appeared laced with hues of infinite blues and translucent white. The rolling hills, silvery sagebrush, and a scattered oasis of greenery painted a desert-like landscape, which guided her along the vast and nearly deserted highway toward her destination of Shaniko.

Within the hour Nina had reached her destination. The name, Shaniko, painted on a barn, identified its historical presence. Josh had been right; there isn't much left of the town, she thought and stepped out of the car to take a look around. Some buildings still held their historic nature, while others were renovated.

Nina marveled at the partially standing boardwalk that had bordered the wide open road. Studying the ghost-like town, she wondered what life had been like when the town was alive and thriving. Nina was intrigued with the beautiful, serene setting and wished she had more time to explore. As the town seemed to draw her in, she decided on a quick look around. However, the moment she set foot on the town's main street, she felt lightheaded, and the earth rumbled underneath her. Luckily a post, within arm's reach, helped save her from a terrible fall, as she was whisked off her feet.

A disoriented Nina sat on the ground in dismay as she tried to comprehend what just happened. Then coming to the conclusion it had to have been an earthquake, she stood up, dusted herself off and rushed to the car. Panicked by the thought, Nina reached for her cell phone to check on her mom, but her anxiety only grew upon discovering there was no service. Wasting no time, she left the town on a quest to reach her mom, praying she was ok, vowing she'd be back another day. Nina knew this town and the painting were somehow tied together, and she could also feel something strong pulling her into it. It could be the emptiness calling out to her. Or was it? She asked herself on her way home.

As Nina drove the quiet highway, she looked in her mirror and happened to spot an old beat-up pickup trailing close behind her. It might have been the quiet road or her recent frightening experience, which caused her to get a feeling that it might be following her. As the truck lead-footed nearer, the feeling became a reality. It was freaking Nina out. Her heart raced as she hit the gas, going faster than she felt was safe, hoping to gain distance. Just as she thought she didn't want to end up a statistic on this vast highway, the truck turned onto a side road. Nina was shaking badly. She drove a few miles more until she was sure he wasn't behind her. She then pulled over to the side of the road and waited until her she could get it together before continuing her journey.

7) SHANIKO

"Honey there wasn't an earthquake reported yesterday," Molly said assuring her daughter as they sat having coffee on the patio.

"Well, it had to be something. Maybe it was too small, and it didn't register here," Nina said wanting an explanation.

"I guess that's possible," Molly replied sipping her coffee as she pondered the thought. "Tell me again why you went there."

Nina shrugged her shoulders and answered, "I wanted to go for a drive and explore the area, and Shaniko sparked my interest."

"Nina dear," Molly sighed, covering her daughter's hands with hers, "I'm sure there's no cause to be alarmed, but please do me a favor and bring someone with you next time you get a wild hair to sightsee," she said with concern. "There's no telling what might happen to you out there all alone."

Nina smiled and commented, "You are probably worrying too much." She did not mention her possible road stalker.

"I promise next time I won't go there by myself," she assured her, hoping to release her mom's worry lines.

"Good," Molly expressed with relief, patting Nina's hand before picking up her coffee cup. Then after savoring the taste of the rich liquid, she added, "I have a favor to ask of you."

"What is it?" Nina replied, a little suspicious of her mother's tone.

"You know I'm on the event planning committee for the town."

"Yes," Nina answered, her suspicion growing.

"Well, next Saturday, it's Mr. Crowley's turn to host the barn dance, and I was hoping you'd go with me."

Nina shuddered at the idea. Shaking her head and holding up two fingers she stated, "I can give you two very good reasons why this is a bad idea. One, I can't dance and two, I don't have a date. Sorry Mom," she said trying to sound sincere.

"Oh but dear, I have a solution to both problems," Molly said, grinning from ear to ear.

"Great!" Nina said with a fake smile holding in her sarcasm.

"I want you to meet my friends. I've told them so much about you," Molly said proudly.

"That's nice, but I don't want to embarrass you with my two left feet," Nina laughed.

"Nonsense," Molly said waving her hand to dismiss Nina's concern. "I happen to know your uncle is an excellent dancer, and I'm sure he'd love to give you a few lessons."

"It won't do any good, and remember I don't have a date," Nina said with confidence that she had won the debate.

"No problem. These dances are open to everybody, just come and have fun. You could ask Josh. I've heard he's pretty smooth on the dance floor."

"You said I don't need a date. Besides, you're not bringing one," she frowned. Her expression quickly changed when she saw the spark in her mom's eyes. "Or are you?" Nina asked with a sly smile.

Molly didn't reply as she looked away, not wanting to discuss this delicate issue.

"Your silence is speaking loud and clear, and your rosy cheeks are giving away your secret. Come on spill it. What's his name? Where and when did you meet him? I want to hear all the details," Nina said excitedly prying into her mom's life.

"Wow! Such a brutal grueling, I feel like dropping and giving you twenty push-ups," Molly said with a laugh.

"Mom!" Nina exclaimed, growing impatient.

"Alright, you are relentless," she said with a laugh. "His name is Dave. We met at the Bunko party Friday night. I'm almost certain it was a setup," she said with a smile. "Two men were playing, and one was your uncle. And I know he doesn't even like the game."

"So tell me everything. I want all the steamy details," Nina said rubbing her hands, showing interest.

"There's not much to tell. He's friendly, and like me, wary about getting into a relationship. He lost his wife to cancer seven years ago, and just started exploring the dating field."

"Hmm, I see," Nina commented gently nudging her mom.

"I barely know the man," Molly said with a frown. "For now we are just going to enjoy each other's company, and see if anything develops."

"Well I'm happy for you and look forward to meeting him," Nina said compassionately.

"You could come to the dance. Dave's planning on being there. I can introduce you," Molly's mouth curved into a smile.

"Are you trying to bribe me? Mom, I'd feel like a third wheel," Nina replied with a scrunched up face.

"Nina suck it up and ask Josh," Molly expressed with a smirk, and then patting her daughter's hand, she scooted into the house.

"I'll think about it," Nina heard herself yell back. She was sure the Intimate Relationship Committee in her mind was taking a vote.

It wasn't long after that, Nina went inside and prepared for her day. Dressed in laced-edged jean shorts, cold-shoulder summer top, and strappy sandals, she was ready. Even though she had work waiting for her, the thought of going to Shaniko plagued her mind. The problem was, she'd promised to take someone with her, but who could she get to go? It wasn't a safe place for her mom, the area was no place for her scooter chair, and she didn't want to impose on her aunt and uncle, which only left Josh.

As she sat contemplating calling Josh, Nina mentally noted the pros and cons. Finally giving in to her conscience, she pressed his number. After two rings, suddenly deciding it was a bad idea, Nina went for the end-call button, but before she could complete the action, Josh answered.

"Hello," he said surprised to see Nina's name in his display screen.

"Hi, so… what are you doing today?" Nina asked feeling silly for listening to her conscience.

"Just hanging around the house; tackling the fix-it list and maybe work on the bathroom remodel."

"Why?" he asked.

"Never mind. It sounds as though you're busy," Nina admitted feeling like a complete idiot for calling.

"Wait!" he said keeping her on the line, "what do you need?"

"It was nothing," Nina said.

"Let me be the judge of that," he sincerely replied.

"Well… I was going to ask if you wanted to take a ride to Shaniko today. Mom says I can't go alone," not admitting her fears.

"Your mom is a smart lady," Josh said in agreement with Molly's advice.

"I know, I know, she already gave me the lecture," Nina announced.

"When did you want to leave?" he asked, his heart pounding at the thought of spending the day with Nina.

"Around noon, I want to have enough time to explore the town. Maybe we can find a clue regarding the deed."

"I can do that. I'll jump in the shower, check on the animals, and be over in a bit," he said eager to get going.

"Okay, see you soon," Nina said ending the call, hoping she wasn't sending him the wrong signals. They were two friends going for a drive, nothing more. No big deal, she said convincing herself as she headed upstairs to get ready. After a makeup check, choosing her favorite silver hoops, lips glistening with cherry gloss and adding a spray of light musk, Nina waited nervously for Josh to arrive.

Hearing Josh's truck pull into the driveway, Nina walked to the window. Secretly she watched through a slit in the curtain, her heart skipping a beat as he stepped out of the truck, and stretched his taut muscles. She'd never dated a cowboy before. The country style had never impressed her. Give her a sharp dressed man in Armani, crisp white shirt, and a tie to complete the masterpiece, and her heart would be racing. However, she thought, the sight of the sexy man sporting the total western package, especially in tight fitting jeans, was making her pulse soar. Even the Fashion Police in her mind were holding up ten's and cheering. Checking herself one last time in the mirror, Nina grabbed her butterfly-filled stomach, scolded herself for acting like a schoolgirl with a crush, and headed downstairs.

"Hello, Josh, what brings you by?" Molly said answering the door.

"He's escorting me to Shaniko," Nina yelled running down the stairs. "You told me I couldn't go alone, so I asked Josh," she said standing next to him.

"Oh," Molly replied trying to figure out her daughter's fickle mind.

"We'll be back later. Bye Mom," Nina said kissing her on the cheek then rushing them out the door.

"Bye Molly," Josh called through the screen.

"Have fun," she answered as she closed the door. "Cassie I think my scheme is working," Molly said with a devilish smile. "Come on, I think there's a treat with your name on it," she said happily scooting into the kitchen, her precious fur baby following.

"Why are we hurrying?" Josh asked trying to keep up; following her to the truck and opening the door.

"I wanted to get away before we got asked twenty questions," Nina said with a laugh, securing her seat belt.

"She means well," Josh said in Molly's defense, strapping himself in.

"I know, and I love her dearly. She has such a loving and caring heart. How could you not?" Nina said reaching into her purse for her shades.

"That she does," he replied. Backing out of the driveway, he tried to keep his composure as the lace in her shorts played peek-a-boo with her thigh. Quickly pulling his eyes away and bringing his attention to the road, he commented with sadness in his voice, "I'll never forget the day I found her."

"What are you talking about," Nina said giving him a questionable look.

You don't know the story?" Josh asked.

"Evidently not," Nina expressed with wonder.

"I'm surprised your mom hasn't shared it with you," he began. Then dismissing the thought, he began, "I had stopped by her house to discuss plans for a new chicken house, and she had a fix-it list for me. Your mom is a strong and independent lady, and I see you carry those qualities. However, there are tasks which require heavy lifting or expertise in a particular field. That's where I come in. I offer my handyman services, and in return she graciously feeds me," he added with a chuckle.

"Anyway," he said back to a serious tone, "When I opened the door of the truck, Cassie was immediately by my side, and I knew by the sound of her frantic bark, something was wrong. Suddenly worried, I followed her to the back of the house, where she led me to Molly. She had fallen through the middle step leading to the deck, and couldn't get out," Josh said, pausing for a moment to take a sip of water. "I can still remember the glowing smile on her face when she saw me. I could also see her pained expression. So with caution, I carefully lifted her out of the hole. Noticing her ankle was swollen I prepared an ice bag. Then rushed her to the emergency room and stayed with her until your aunt arrived."

After Josh finished, Nina sat in silence for a moment, her emotions in overdrive. She swallowed to hold back her tears, before she commented, "Wow, I don't know what to say, except thank you, and she was so lucky you were there. We are grateful. Guess that makes you a hero," she said, giving him an endearing smile.

"Not really," he admitted showing a little shyness. "I was glad I was there, and your mom only suffered minor injuries."

"Well I appreciate your kindness anyway," Nina remarked.

"Just a friend helping out another," Josh said matter of factly.

Nina was gaining a new perspective on the cowboy next to her. Not only was he handsome, but Josh was also caring and above all humble. There had only been one other man who proudly carried those character traits, and that was her beloved father. She secretly wiped a grieving tear from her eye. She wasn't about to let her emotions rule; been there, done that, which only left her with a bruised heart. Needing to break away from the past and lighten the mood, she replied, "Whatever, you're a good man, Mr. Parker."

Josh laughed and replied, "What does a guy have to do here to get on a first name basis?"

Nina shrugged her shoulders, "You'll have to wait and see," she teased with a sly smile.

"Such a woman of mystery," Josh admitted. With that, the getting-to-know-you dance began. They talked nonstop about interests, passions, challenges, and dreams, which lasted until they reached their destination.

Turning off the main road into a parking lot next to the little town, Nina felt a déjà vu moment, recalling the weird experience the day before. But as she looked around at its lonely existence, Nina found there was no cause for alarm.

"Come on let's go check it out," Josh said opening her door and breaking her thoughts.

"It sure is dead around here," Josh commented walking with Nina as he gazed around.

"Yeah," Nina said, also taking in the view, "guess that's why they call it a ghost town."

"Maybe we'll see some spirits hanging around," Josh teased.

"I hope not," Nina said, shivering at the thought.

"There's supposed to be a secret museum of old abandoned cars somewhere around here," Josh stated and then looked up and down the street.

"That sounds fun. So where do you want to start?" Nina asked as she stepped into the town. But as the earth shook under her feet, Nina found herself in unfamiliar territory, and about to be run over by a stagecoach. Not having time to think about her predicament, she jumped out of its way; never hearing Josh's reply.

Not again she thought. She held onto a nearby pole for support and gazed around her. The town was now thriving and full of people as it took on its historical form. How was this possible? She thought. Five minutes ago she and Josh had been looking at the remnants of a town long gone. Then thinking about him, Nina turned and found he was no longer standing by her. That's odd, Nina thought as she looked around, they must have gotten separated, and he was probably looking for her.

Nina couldn't believe her eyes. It was as if she'd stepped into a page of history. Everything was so authentic, and it was uncanny how the layout of the buildings, lined up along the street, appeared in their original form. And the people dressed in pioneer clothes matched the pictures she'd seen.

Then it dawned on her, they must be making a movie, and she was on the set. But with that thought, more questions poked at her. Where were all the vans holding the filming equipment, the trailers accommodating temporary living quarters, and most important, how could the empty ghost-like town been transformed overnight. It didn't make sense. It could have been hiding behind a mural, Nina thought pondering the idea. There was also the question of what happened to Josh. Hopefully, they would meet up soon. But until then, Nina was going to look around. She'd never been on a movie set before. Then spotting an actor, Nina approached the man hoping to get the scoop on the movie.

"Excuse me, sir," Nina said politely, to the man dressed as the sheriff. However, the man did not respond and walked right past her. "Well, that was rude." Then spotting a sophisticated young woman, probably the teacher, standing by the red schoolhouse, she tried again, "Good afternoon," she kindly greeted the lady. But as it happened before, the woman ignored her. That is very strange Nina thought. It was as though they didn't acknowledge her existence. After three more unsuccessful attempts to get someone's attention, Nina grew frustrated. They must have been concentrating on their parts, or it was possible they didn't see her.

Just as she had decided to give up and find Josh, Nina noticed a woman dressed in gypsy-like clothing signaling her from across the street. Finally, someone to talk to, as she walked towards the old woman. But when she was half-way there, Nina heard Josh calling for her. Turning, she followed the direction of his voice, and within minutes, she was reunited with him in the same spot staring at the deserted little town.

"Nina where were you?" Josh asked with a perplexed look. "Better yet, where did you come from?" he added looking around.

Nina looked up at Josh, also a little baffled by the turn of events, "I was on the movie set looking for you."

"What movie set? There's nothing here but abandoned buildings, a couple of seasonal gift shops, and somewhere a car museum," Josh said.

"No, you're wrong," Nina said standing her ground. "Behind the mural, they are filming a movie. It was so cool how they recreated Shaniko as it looked when established. The set designers did an amazing job making it look authentic," she expressed trying to convince him.

"You didn't see it?" Nina asked with a deep sigh, looking at a confused Josh.

"Did you fall and bump your head?" he asked looking for any signs of head injury.

"No," Nina said shaking her head.

"Maybe you had heatstroke; it's getting warm out here, or maybe you saw a mirage, let's get you some water," he said with concern.

"It's not like we're out in the Mojave Desert," Nina replied her face scrunched up. "I'm perfectly fine Mr. Parker," getting annoyed with his interrogation. "You don't have to believe me. But what I saw was real, at least it seemed real," Nina admitted questioning her sanity.

"Nina," he said calmly, feeling helpless in the awkward situation, "I don't doubt you saw something, I'm not sure what it was. Look around," he motioned with his hand, "there's nothing here like you described. Besides the locals, we're the only ones here," Josh said running his hand through his wavy brown hair, trying to connect the dots.

"I don't understand. You think I could've stepped into the past?" Nina said, giving thought to that possibility. "You did say I disappeared, and then reappeared out of nowhere. Where did I go?"

"I don't know; maybe there is a trap door people step into; a prop to glamorize the ghost town," he suggested, not giving her suggestion a second thought.

"I guess that's possible. Maybe they're filming underground," Nina expressed.

"Don't know about that," he said. "So when you were looking around, did you see a place to buy a soda? I'm getting thirsty," he said changing the subject. Maybe she was dehydrated and not thinking logically.

"I remember a few places; like the country store, Silvertooth Saloon, and Gold Tooth restaurant, but they're not here now," Nina said feeling confused.

"Okay then… we can stop at a store on our way back. So are we done here?" Josh commented in a hurry to get Nina away from here.

"I have to go back," Nina commented heading toward the town.

"Wait, Nina," Josh said assertively gently reaching for her arm. "Why don't we go back and think about this before making any rash decisions," he stated feeling concerned about her condition.

"You're probably right, but I think the gypsy woman was trying to tell me something. I need to find her," Nina said as Josh helped her in the truck.

"We'll find her next time," Josh agreed to pacify her, not having a clue of what she meant, and wasn't about to ask.

"Can we come back tomorrow?" Nina asked, "I don't know how to explain it, but I feel some force is pulling me into the town," she added, her eyes glazed over.

"Let me check my schedule and get back with you," Josh answered, stalling as he contemplated another reenactment of today, also feeling spooked by Nina's stoic expression.

They stopped a few miles down the road for a soda and munchies. The rest of the ride back was silent, but their minds were actively reliving the strange events that had occurred.

8) MADAME LUCIA

Back at Molly's, Josh and Nina stepped onto the porch. They stood in a pool of uncertainty. The anticipation of the kiss created an awkward moment. Hearts racing and lost in each other's eyes, the couple tuned out the world, craving a piece of euphoria.

Nina shivered as Josh brushed a wisp of hair from her eyes, and her skin tingled as his hand glided along her cheek. She longed for him to kiss her. Licking her cherry glossed lips she gave him a subtle sign, but as he was leaning in, the front door opened causing them to step apart.

"Oh, I didn't hear you kids pull in," Molly said, her eyes open wide with surprise. "I'll let Cassie outside in the back," Molly said, feeling embarrassed, closing the door, while hiding her coy smile.

"Well I guess I should go in," Nina said, avoiding direct eye contact, and suddenly feeling uncomfortable.

"Yeah, I should head home too. Whiski is probably wondering where I am," Josh said turning to go.

"Hey Josh, I had a good time today," Nina said with a smile.

Josh, caught off guard, replied with a large grin, "You called me by my first name. I must have done something right."

"Maybe," Nina said teasing him. "See you tomorrow at noon?" she added with a wink.

"Ah sure," he replied, suddenly at a loss for words.

Noticing she had Josh flustered Nina laughed and opened the screen door. Catching his last comment, "Didn't your mom ever teach you it wasn't nice to tease?" She turned, and as she closed the door, she blew him a kiss and wondered what had provoked her flirtatious mood. But she already knew it might have something to do with a tall, smoking hot cowboy. Ah, Nina, you are a goner, she swooned, and then set off to find her mom.

"So how was your date?" Molly asked as Nina walked into the kitchen.

"It wasn't a date. It was only two friends going for a drive," Nina stated strongly.

"Okay, then how was your drive?" Molly asked with a touch of sarcasm in her voice, as she prepared a cup of tea.

"Fine," Nina replied, leaving out all the creepy details, "we are going back there tomorrow."

Molly looked at her daughter, her eyebrows raised in curiosity, "What's so fascinating about that little ghost town?"

"I guess I can tell you," Nina said pulling out the document from her purse and showing it to her.

"What is it?" Molly asked, staring at the yellowed paper.

"We think it's a deed to a mine that might be close to Shaniko. Josh's sister is an attorney and is researching the document. She is trying to find to whom it belongs, and whether or not it's valuable," Nina said also fixing a cup a tea and joining her mom at the table.

"Where did you find it?" Molly replied as she concentrated on reading the fine print.

"It was in the frame of the picture of the miner in your store. It fell out one day when I was examining it," Nina admitted.

"I wonder about you and your fixation with art. Are all my pictures covered up in the store too?" she asked glaring at her daughter.

Nina laughed, to make light of the conversation, "No. I was fascinated by the frame. When I took the picture off the wall to get a closer look, that's when the document fell out," Nina confessed, coming close to the truth.

"What do you expect to find there at Shaniko?" Molly asked raising her eyebrows.

"We're not sure yet, hopefully, the gift store will be open tomorrow and we can talk to someone that might know of any mines in the vicinity, or have some books that might lead us to a clue."

"It sounds like a fascinating mystery, you'll have to keep me up-to-date," Molly said, handing the paper back to Nina. "I am excited to hear what Josh's sister uncovers."

"Me too," Nina said getting up to start dinner.

After dinner, Nina cleaned the kitchen. She and her mom adjourned to the living room where they sat to enjoy their dessert and coffee. While they were relaxing, Molly looked at Nina. With her eyes lighting up, she commented, "I've asked Dave over for dinner tomorrow, and the invitation also extends to Josh, if you'd like."

"I wouldn't want to interrupt your evening," Nina said, noticing the sparkle in her mom's eyes.

"Honey, I've invited him over so you can meet him," Molly said reaching over touching her daughter's hand.

"Okay. If you're sure we're not intruding," Nina said smiling. She was happy her mom had found someone.

"So with that comment, I can assume Josh is coming."

"Yes," Nina said, already thinking of what to wear.

"I also spoke with your uncle, and he would be thrilled to teach you a couple of dance steps," Molly said, taking care not to overstep her daughter's fragile boundaries.

"Mom, what am I going to do with you?" Nina said with a sigh, sending her a scowling look.

"Just love me, dear," Molly said with a laugh. "We are invited to their house for dinner on Wednesday. You can thank me later," she added, scooting out of the room, away from her daughter's line of fire.

"I haven't even agreed to go to the dance!" Nina spouted, annoyed with her mom for meddling and for not staying for her scolding. "You are not playing fair," she yelled out.

"All's fair in love and war dear," Molly yelled back as the bathroom door closed.

"Err," Nina screamed, tossing a throw pillow across the room.

The next morning, Nina took extra time getting ready. After going through her closet and trying on a half dozen outfits, she couldn't come up with the look she had envisioned. If by chance she was taken back in time, she wanted to dress appropriately. All her clothes called attention to her being an outsider. But she didn't know why she cared. Nobody seemed to pay attention to her anyway. Maybe her mom had something that would work; she thought while going to hunt her down.

"This is what I have," Molly said, laying three western outfits on the bed. "I purposely bought them for 'Western Days,' an annual celebration we have in August."

"Hmm," Nina said carefully inspecting the clothing. She was intrigued by the lavish and yet cumbersome design, but after examining the articles of clothing, she concluded they weren't for her. There was way too much lace on the puffy-sleeved blouse, and the frill on the skirt looked like it would swallow her whole. She also wasn't crazy about the heavy wool-like material. "They are okay, but do you have something a little more modern?" she asked. "This isn't the look I was going for." Even the Fashion Police were siding with her.

"I have this one. I bought it last year, and haven't had a chance to wear it yet."

Nina slipped the dazzling blue colored dress off the hanger and draped it over the front of her. It was much simpler with lighter material and not too frilly. The skirt was still a tad fuller than she'd like, but it would have to do. She especially liked the low cut lace bodice and the mid-length flowing sleeves. The hem of the dress barely brushed the floor, but her mom's two-inch cowboy boots would lift it up. Add a hat, and she'd fit right in.

"Why are you dressing up?" Molly asked, her hand on her chin, watching her daughter.

"I thought it would be fun since we are going to a ghost-town. Might as well look the part, right?" Nina said gathering the clothes and going back to her room.

Dressed twenty minutes later, Nina looked in the mirror; she wondered if it were a bit too much.

Luckily a cold front had come in, and the temperature had dropped considerably since yesterday. She couldn't imagine wearing this outlandish outfit in yesterday's heat.

"You look so cute," Molly said as Nina came down the stairs. It's as if you stepped out of a western movie," smiling as she picked up her phone to get a picture.

"Good, that's what I was going for," Nina said, humoring her mom by posing for the shots.

"I can't wait to see what Josh is wearing. I'll get a picture of you together when he gets here." Molly said, excited Nina was enjoying her time with the young man.

"Oops," Nina said aloud, "I didn't tell him I was dressing up," she admitted showing a fake smile.

"Don't you think it might have been a good idea to fill him in on the plan?" Molly stressed frowning at her daughter's mishap.

"Maybe," Nina answered, giving the idea some thought. It hadn't occurred to her that he might be joining her in the past; if that truly was where she was yesterday. But what if he could? Shouldn't Josh prepare himself as well? Oh, this is too crazy. What had she been thinking? Could it be she was fantasizing about what it would be like to be part of history? Her thoughts were scattered. Nina wished she knew for sure what had happened. Maybe she wouldn't be able to go back. Putting away the "coulds and woulds," Nina decided to call Josh. There was still time left if he wanted to change.

Josh arrived right on time, and when Nina opened the door, her mouth dropped at the sight of the masterpiece standing in front of her. If her heart raced at his normal attire, it was pounding erratically as she practically drooled at the sight of him.

"Is everything okay?" Josh asked looking at Nina's strange expression and checking his clothes for anything unusual.

"Yes perfect," Nina said recovering from her dreamy trance.

"Well, you look positively exquisite Miss Charm," Josh said with a sexy smile, bringing Nina's hand up to his mouth and lightly brushing it against his lips.

"My, my Mr. Parker, you are going to embarrass lit'l ol me," she teased, trying her best at a southern drawl, and fanning herself with her hands, causing them to burst out in laughter.

"You kids are very cute," Molly said catching the act. "Now stand together so I can get a couple of pictures." She retrieved her cell phone from the basket attached to the roller chair.

After Molly was satisfied with the photography session, Nina and Josh headed to the truck. She turned toward him when she was settled in her seat but wasn't expecting him to be so close. Before she realized it, he'd put his arm around her and brought her lips to his. She shivered under his touch. Nina tasted mint on his tongue as it danced in her mouth, and a light scent of wood musk lingering on his neck enhanced the erotic moment. She never wanted the kiss to end, Nina thought. Her tongue was also taking pleasure in the rolling rhythm. But as she was falling deeper into the magical fantasy, Josh pulled away.

"Wow," he said coming out of the intimate haze. "I've wanted to do that again," Josh confessed, as he lightly trailed his finger down her arm.

"I'm glad you did," Nina admitted, touching her swollen lips and gazing into Josh's passion filled eyes. "I certainly wasn't expecting that. You sure are full of surprises Mr. Parker" Nina admitted, feeling vulnerable.

"You haven't seen anything yet, Miss Charm," Josh said stealing another kiss before heading out the driveway.

Nina was speechless. She hadn't imagined the kiss the other night. Her emotions were silently battling inside, each trying to rule. She was finding it hard to breathe, almost suffocating. She asked herself what is wrong. Maybe it was too early to go the next level. Nina stared out the window, her hands twisting together.

Josh wondered if he might have pushed himself a little too far. After the kiss, Nina had become silent and distant. She hadn't said a word in the last twenty minutes, and Josh decided to break through the eerie mood. "Did I do something wrong?" he asked with concern.

"No, everything is fine, just in deep thought," Nina replied trying to reassure him. "It's been awhile since I've been in a relationship and I'm terrified," she admitted.

"Nina," Josh said, reaching for her hand, "I didn't mean to scare you. I thought you were feeling the chemistry between us."

"Oh, I was... I am," Nina said clearing the air, "guess I'm not ready for the fall yet," she admitted. "Besides, surveys have shown that long-distance relationships don't work. I couldn't even make a close-distance relationship work. Of course, being married might have played a big part," Nina said, matter-of-factly. Then realizing that didn't sound right, she immediately cleaned up her verbal slip.

"It's not what you think. I didn't know he was married until a few months into our relationship," Nina said. She looked out the window, giving thought to that awkward and embarrassing time.

"You want to talk about it?" he asked noticing Nina's mood shift.

"Oh, you don't want to hear about my drama," she said waving her arm, dismissing the statement.

"Yes, I do. The way I see it, there are thirty minutes left until we arrive in Shaniko. So, fill me in," he said interested in the personal side of the sweet girl.

"All right, but you asked for it," Nina laughed. Then after a sigh she began, "I met Bryon online, and we hit it off like that," she said snapping her fingers. "We were the perfect couple. That's what I thought anyway." She opened a package of almonds and ate a handful. Then taking a drink of water to wash them down, she went on. "We spent every spare moment together. Friday nights we'd meet for a romantic dinner, club hopping on Saturdays, and Sundays we saved for movies, plays, or long lazy-day walks." Nina mused, thinking of those times. "I was worn out by the end of the weekend and early Monday mornings were always rough, but so worth it."

"So what happened?" Josh asked, involved in her story.

"I'm getting to that," she said snacking on more almonds. "One Sunday we were walking through the Portland Rose Garden. A beautiful place and a must-see in Oregon," she stressed. "He was acting very nervous and quiet. I got this crazy notion he was going to propose. We had been dating for a while, and we'd talked about taking it to the next level. My heart was racing, and I was scared beyond words," Nina expressed, feeling a pain in the pit of her stomach.

"We walked around in the colorful floral maze and stopped at the gazebo; it is popular as a wedding venue. Then he turned toward me and looked into my eyes. Suddenly, he squatted down behind me. I thought it was part of his plan, so I waited. Then this gorgeous woman with two young girls appeared, the children screaming daddy, and running into his arms. The woman stood there with an angry red face, eyes bulging and nervously tapping her foot."

"Oh, I think I know where this is going," Josh interrupted.

"Yes, it wasn't pretty," Nina said pausing as she finished off her almonds, "So my dear sweet Prince Charming morphed into a wolf in cheater's clothing," she snickered at her pun. "Then   standing,   a   daughter   on   each   hand,   my chickenhearted boyfriend spoke, Ah... Nina, I'd like you to meet my wife, Andrea and my girls Madison and Emily."

"Your what? I screamed, my voice echoing in the gardens. I was so mad I couldn't speak, my head was pounding, and my heart was breaking. My mind said move, but I froze in shock. Reaching deep inside, I found the courage. So looking at the broken family, and feeling mixed emotions, I ran as fast as my feet would go, until I reached the parking lot. There I grabbed a ride from a taxi service and cried the entire time to a sympathetic driver."

"What a jerk," Josh commented, after she'd completed her story, his hands tightly gripping the steering wheel going into protective mode.

"Yeah, he even had the nerve to call, said he was sorry and had asked his wife for a divorce. He then begged for a second chance. I said no way! We are through! After weeks of ignoring his calls and texts, refusing dozens of flower deliveries, nursing a bruised heart, and resisting the urge to kill him, I finally let go."

"Sorry, you had to go through that. He was a fool, and it's his loss and my gain," Josh said with a sexy grin.

"Thanks," Nina said blushing at his last comment. Then after stretching, she gave a devious grin and replied, "I heard it was his wife who had asked for a divorce, not him. Too bad too sad, he lost both of us." Then her facial expression turned sad, "I do feel bad for those two adorable girls. Divorce can't be easy," she sighed.

Then readjusting her body, she tucked her leg under to get comfortable and turned to Josh. "What skeletons do you have hiding in your closet?"

"Well, I assure you there are no wives stowed away in there, and as far as I know, no children either," he laughed.

"Ha, ha, now seriously Mr. Parker," she giggled.

"Okay, I've never been married, been engaged once and have done my share of dating," he admitted.

"What happened to the engagement?" Nina asked getting interested and not letting him get off that easy.

"Just like all my relationships seem to end up. She moved to a bigger city, claimed the country life was stifling and wasn't allowing her to grow. When I refused to go with her, she broke our engagement," he said thinking back on the past.

"I'm very sorry," Nina said compassionately and vowed not to be another on his list.

"Tell me," Josh said pulling Nina from her thoughts, "what is so special about big-city life?"

"Well...," she expressed with a large smile, "it's dining in one of the many five-star restaurants, catching a Broadway show, or favorite rock concert. There are museums, riverfront festivals, local parades, the bright lights showing off the city at night, and so much more."

"Wow, I wasn't aware there was so much to do."

"Yes, and of course I can't forget all the malls and galleries. You should visit some time," Nina remarked.

"Is that a personal invitation?" he said lifting a brow.

"Anytime, I'd love to show you around," Nina said pretending to ignore the underlying meaning of his comment.

"Now you tell me. Why did you chase the country life?" Nina asked settling in her seat.

"That's easy. There's no traffic or rude and obnoxious people in a hurry heading nowhere. There's very little crime here and a good environment in which to raise a child. I know most of my neighbors, and I can feel safe at night in my own home. We also have parades and festivals but on a smaller scale. I can go fishing every day, take a scenic hike, and on a clear night, you can see millions of stars. Do I go on?"

"No, I get the point. It does sound like an amazing place when you romanticize it," Nina agreed. "You know both areas have their pluses; I guess it depends on what you're looking for."

"I can agree with you on that," Josh said.

"I am enjoying my time here. It's a nice break, but that's all it is, a break," Nina emphasized. She felt a pang of sadness about leaving, knowing she had no choice. If only they had met in another time and place. They were from different lifestyles. Meeting in the middle was no option; he'd made that very clear.

"We can probably carry-on this debate of country versus city all day, but it's not going to get us anywhere. I vote we talk about what is going to happen when we get to Shaniko," Nina stated.

"Sounds good," Josh said, wondering if Nina did like it there, or was saying that to be nice. "What's your plan?"

"Hmm," she said, placing her hand under her chin thinking. "I don't have one. I figured we'd hold hands and step through the mural, black hole, or whatever. Maybe the connection will keep us together," she answered with doubt.

"You honestly believe we can go back into the past?" Josh asked, considering the idea, and questioning Nina's sanity.

"I don't know. But we'll be appropriately dressed if we do," Nina said laughing at the absurdity of the conversation.

Later, Josh stood on the outskirts of town, holding hands with Nina. He felt uncomfortable dressed like an outlaw. He worried someone might report seeing a suspicious looking couple loitering. What was he supposed to tell the officer? Probably they should have had a plan, he thought. Turning toward the little cowgirl, he waited for her cue.

"Let's count to three and take a step together," Nina said giving instructions. "Also, if you end up staying, would you please call me back in thirty minutes?"

Josh nodded and counted along with Nina. On the word three, they took a step forward.

Nina could feel her hand slip out of Josh's, and once again she was alone. Fortunately she didn't have to dodge an oncoming stagecoach; instead, she was nearly run over by a group of children running to the red schoolhouse. Stepping back, she moved out of their way, laughing at her reaction because they'd probably run right through her anyway. Concentrating on the reason she was there, Nina decided to search for the old woman. But where was she supposed to look? Given the lack of support she had last time visiting this scene, she was destined to do it alone. And with that thought, she set out to find her.

As she passed the store and saloon, Nina smiled wondering if Josh would like a soda, thinking they probably didn't have it back then. She'd need to check it out later; right now she was on a mission. "Now where would that old woman be?" Nina asked aloud, not sure in what direction to go first. Choosing to keep going forward, Nina walked along the boardwalk, having fun as people passed through her. Reaching the end of town, Nina came to the hotel. She enjoyed watching the women lounging on the balcony above and flirting with the young men below, luring them inside.

"Now which way do I go?" Nina raised her hands and asked the universe. Then, as if the universe answered, she spotted the woman near the livery stables pushing a small cart filled with various sized bottles. Nina wasted no time as she hurried over to her.

"It's about time you got here," Lucia exclaimed in a scolding tone.

"Were you expecting me?" Nina asked with a confused look.

"Yes, years ago," she replied with a deep sigh.

"Where am I, and who are you?" Nina asked the stranger.

"My dear you are in Shaniko. The date is 1897, and you can call me Madame Lucia," she said taking a drink from a small bottle.

"But how? Why?" Nina asked wanting the answers.

"I'm getting there," Lucia stated waving her arms, "Lordy me, give me some time and space girl."

Nina stepped back, giving the rude woman some room.

"You are here to help your Uncle John."

"I am?" Nina mumbled, keeping her voice low, not wanting to anger the woman.

"Speak up child. I promise I won't bite you," Lucia said, breaking out into a deep throaty laugh.

"Why am I in the past?" Nina asked.

"Silly child, you're not in the past. This is a dimensional image that captures a period in time," she said waving her arms, highlighting the image. "I'm an angel who is here to help you," she said taking another drink.

"That's funny. I've never pictured an angel to look quite like you," Nina said looking her over.

"Oh, honey," Lucia said, "This is not my original form. I had to choose a disguise that would help me blend in, but also be visible to you."

"I guess that makes sense. So, what are you suppose to help me do?" Nina asked in wonder.

"Find out what happened to your uncle," Lucia replied.

"How are we supposed to do that?" she asked with apprehension.

"Not we, that's something you have to find out on your own," the woman answered, rearranging the bottles in the cart.

"How do I do that? How about a hint here?" she asked growing frustrated and confused.

"Ask around. Get the town folk to help you," she replied, taking another big swig from her bottle.

Nina was beginning to wonder what was in those bottles; maybe it was homemade liquor. It would explain why the woman was talking in circles. "I've tried that, nobody can see me," she complained.

"You're not talking to the right people," Lucia stated blowing at a strand of hair hanging in her face.

"How do I find them?" Nina asked.

"That's easy, look for people with the green...." but the rest of the sentence was cut-off as Nina was pulled away by the sound of Josh's voice.

9) NINA GOES BACK

"A green what?" Nina called out, but Lucia was gone. Nina followed Josh's voice and instantly she was standing next to him.

"Where did you go?" a baffled Josh asked.

Excitedly, Nina explained everything to him at warp speed. After she was done sharing her experience and taking a deep breath, Nina commented, "I need to go back and find out what Lucia was talking about."

"I don't know if that's a good idea," Josh said shaking his head. "Maybe it's not safe," voicing his concern.

"It's fine. So far there's been no threat. How dangerous can a harmless old woman be as she clings to her bottle for life support? Besides, she claims to be an angel sent here to help me."

"I don't think you should go back alone," Josh replied fearing for Nina's safety.

"I wish you could go," Nina said affectionately touching his arm and smiling. "I'll ask Lucia about it. Please give me thirty more minutes," she said showing him her puppy dog eyes.

"What if something happens and I can't bring you back?" Josh asked feeling torn.

"Don't worry," Nina said stepping into the city like a woman on a mission, leaving Josh with his mouth wide open in surprise.

"Darn that girl," Josh said aloud as Nina disappeared. Not wanting to draw attention from the locals, he decided to act like a tourist and hunt out the car museum. As he was walking through the town, he felt a chill run down his spine, thinking he could be in the same place with Nina, but in a different time period. He was still having a difficult time wrapping his mind around the possibility. One thing he could admit was that Nina had disappeared. He just wasn't convinced she was in the past.

Nina was surprised to find that this time her entry was smooth. There was no stagecoach or running children anywhere. She wasted no time hurrying back to where she'd left Lucia, but the woman was no longer there. "Great," Nina said aloud, "why can't she stay in one place?" Nina asked the universe lifting her arms to the sky. "Now where do I look?" she expressed in frustration, searching the streets for Lucia's little wagon.

"Are you lost?" a man called out, tapping her on the shoulder.

After she recovered from the shock and had her erratic heart-rate brought back to normal, Nina turned to face the stranger. "You scared the beejeegees out of me," Nina expressed looking up at a very tall cowboy surrounded by a green aura. "Didn't your mom ever tell you never to sneak up behind someone?"

"I'm sorry ma'am," he said tipping his hat, "you looked distressed, and I thought you might need help."

"Thank you, but as you can see, I'm good," she smiled assuring him. Then something odd occurred to her, "you can see and hear me!" Nina shrieked.

The man stepped back, wary of Nina, "Are you sure you haven't taken ill? Maybe we should go see Doc," he said reaching for her arm.

"I'm not sick," Nina said swiftly moving from his touch. "If you could tell me where the gypsy woman went, I'll be on my way."

"Pardon," he said giving her a baffled look.

"You don't know her, do you?" Nina said shaking her head, checking out his expression. "Maybe I should go look for her. Nice meeting you Mr . . . , I don't know your name," Nina expressed.

"Oh, how rude of me, let me introduce myself," he said removing his hat, "my name is Thomas J Smyth."

"OMG!" Nina screamed, "Are you serious? This is awesome," she exclaimed bubbling over with excitement.

Thomas stepped back, a look of uncertainty on his face. It was obvious he wasn't accustomed to Nina's twenty-first-century slang, not to mention her open personality.

"Who are you?" he asked with a frown.

"Oh sorry. I'm Nina Charm," she said introducing herself. She grabbed his hand and started shaking it vigorously. "Are you by chance related to John W. Smyth?" Nina asked letting go of his hand.

Thomas put his hat back on and looked down at Nina, "Yes he is my brother. How do you know Jonathon?" he asked with a questionable look.

"John . . . ahh . . . Jonathon is my distant relative," she said.

"That would make us relatives then," he said raising his head pondering the thought.

"Yes it would," Nina answered. Then, thinking her allotted time was running out, she got to the point. "Do you know where I can find him?"

"Well he caught the fever and was gone," Thomas replied with a stern face.

"Oh, I'm sorry I didn't know," feeling her bubble burst. "What was it typhoid?" she asked with a sad look.

"Not ill, it was gold fever," Thomas confessed, roaring with laughter. "He and a friend took a stake in a mine. They picked up all their belongings, loaded up with supplies and food, and headed north," pointing in that direction. "I haven't seen them for months," he said shrugging his shoulders.

"Oh bummer," she sighed.

"What do you want with my brother anyway," he asked raising his eyebrows.

"I need to find him," Nina said, keeping it short, not wanting to dive into the circumstances. "Where is the mine? Do you have a map or something?"

Thomas took a firm stance and answered, "The mine is called Golden Vein, and it's about a day's ride, as the crow flies, and it's not a place for a fragile woman like you," he said with a stern face.

Fragile, Nina thought. If he only knew about how liberated women were in my era, she laughed inside. She had to remember that most women in his era were considered weak and frail.

"Oh, I'm not going alone," Nina said thinking fast. Hopefully, Josh can go with her next time. The only problem was she didn't have a clue how to make that happen. Then she caught sight of the gypsy woman's wagon turning the corner. "There she is!" Nina shrieked. "I should go." And without thinking, she reached into her purse and handed him her business card. "You can call my cell," she said hurrying off to find the woman. She left Thomas frozen in place, eyes locked on the card, mouthing the words; call and cell?

"Wait!," Nina yelled breathing hard as she raced to catch up with Lucia.

"What do you need child?" the woman said stopping her wagon. "Here," she said handing Nina a brown bottle filled with a milky-like substance.

"No thank you," Nina said turning her head, politely pushing the bottle away. There was no way she was drinking that disgusting smelly liquid.

"Okay, your loss," Lucia said taking a big swig from the bottle and letting out a loud holler, "my best batch yet!" she expressed wiping her mouth with a cloth. "So tell me how I can help," she said taking another pull from the bottle.

Nina tried not to cringe as a drop of the liquid leaked out the side of her mouth. Clearing her throat, she got to the point, "I have this friend that I want to bring here, but I don't know how or even if it's possible."

"Hmm," Lucia said tapping her crooked finger on her bottle, "that's easy. You need to connect with him, and he has to believe."

"What are you talking about?" Nina asked giving her a questionable look, but she never received the answer as Josh's voice called her back.

"I was starting to wonder what happened to you," a surprised Josh said when Nina appeared next to him. "I was getting worried," he expressed with a concerned look.

"Well I'm here now, and in one piece, at least I think," Nina replied touching her arms and laughing.

"Seriously, something terrible could've happened to you, and I wouldn't have known."

"Josh, I'm okay. But I find it sweet you were concerned," giving him an endearing smile.

"So what did you learn this time?" Josh asked, walking with her to the truck.

"I'll tell you while we eat. I'm hungry and thirsty. Let's get the picnic basket and find a place to sit. I'll fill you in on all the details."

Sitting at a nearby table, while they dined on Nina's homemade egg salad sandwiches and iced tea, she shared her experience. Done with her story, she looked over at Josh's straight face, waiting for his opinion. "Well?" she asked wondering what he thought.

"That's crazy. I really need to clean my hard-to-believe goggles," Josh expressed sarcastically.

"Yes, you'd better, or you'll blow any chance of going back there with me," Nina stressed.

"Say what?" Josh said with a confused look.

Nina gave a coy smile and said, "The gypsy, AKA Guardian Angel Lucia, told me that for you to go into the past dimension, you need to believe, and we have to be connected. I'm not sure what she meant about the last part," Nina said tilting her head.

Josh shrugged his shoulders and commented, "I do believe, at least I'm working on it. It's not easy for me to comprehend, or even fathom the possibility that you can go back in time. Give me a little time for the reality to settle in," Josh said. "So, how connected are we supposed to be?" he asked with a devilish grin, his eyebrows dancing as he started moving closer.

"Hold on Romeo," Nina said playfully pushing him away and giggling at his silly gesture.

"I was only practicing the more connected part," he said with a laugh.

"That we already know and we determined why it wasn't a good idea," Nina remarked. "I suggest you put your energy and focus into believing and you might have a chance," she said with a fake smile. Then finishing her sandwich, Nina disposed of her paper products in a nearby trash can.

Nina walked back to the table to gather the supplies and explained her idea. "This is how I see it will play out," she said eager to tell Josh. "We will hold hands like today, but we're going to add a friendly kiss and . . . What are you doing?" Nina said noticing Josh moved toward her and was surprised when he grabbed her hand, pulled her close, and gently brushed his lips against hers.

"I thought we might need a test run to get it right," Josh confessed pulling away. He knew he was playing with fire by pushing her buttons. It wasn't out of meanness. He was learning to appreciate all sides of Nina from her adorable quivering lips when she became flustered, to the serious furrowed brows at the bite of her anger.

"Ah, I think we can agree that our lips are in fine working order," Nina said floating in a dreamy state. Her lips tingling from the kiss and her face felt flushed. "Wow, would you look how late it's getting," Nina admitted, looking at her phone, creating a distraction. "We should get going. Mom has a doctor's appointment at 4:00 PM," Nina said collecting the picnic items and putting them in the basket.

"How is Molly doing?" Josh asked picking up the basket and walking back with Nina to the truck.

"Great, she's improving weekly. Today the doctor is going to discuss the possibility of her wearing a boot," Nina replied, relieved to be on a neutral subject.

"That is awesome," Josh expressed with excitement, "she is such an independent spirit, and I can tell that the last few weeks have been difficult for her," he said compassionately.

"Well don't let her fool you," Nina smirked. "I don't see how she does it, but my mom has an itinerary a mile long," she said with a laugh, spreading her arms wide. "She has discovered all the major social online groups, e-mails and texts, which allow her to participate in all her clubs and volunteer work. I think she's busier now than before," Nina admitted waiting as Josh opened the passenger door for her.

She definitely is a woman on the go," Josh remarked climbing into the truck and getting settled.

"Yes, always up to something," Nina expressed. "In fact, she's having dinner tonight, a-get-to-know Dave affair. By the way, you are invited."

"Sounds good. Let me know what time and Whiski and I will be there," Josh said looking forward to the gathering and another opportunity to be around Nina.

"I'll text you," Nina replied, and then she started laughing uncontrollably.

Josh glanced over at Nina, giving her a questionable look, "You want to fill me in on your joke?" he asked.

"It's nothing," Nina said trying to catch her breath. "I realized that when I left Thomas to find Lucia, I gave him my card and told him to call my cell," she said bursting into a giggle, causing Josh to join in.

When Nina was back in control, she took a drink of water and commented. "Speaking of dinner, you're also invited to my aunt and uncle's for dinner this Wednesday. My mom has convinced my uncle I need dance lessons. I'll let you know the time if you want to go," she added, trying not to elaborate on the topic.

"I think I've died and gone to heaven. Two home cooked meals and dates with you. I so love this!" he exclaimed flashing a smile.

"They're not dates, we are only having dinner," Nina stressed nervously. "I think my mom wants to make sure you are eating well," Nina said with a giggle breaking the tension.

"So why the dance lesson," Josh asked with curiosity, ignoring Nina's comment.

"She wants me to go to the dance this Saturday. She wants to show me off," Nina stated making double air quotes with her fingers, around the word off.

"I can teach you," Josh said.

"I appreciate that, but it would break my uncle's heart if I didn't let him," Nina said and happy to have a reason to decline. Dancing with Josh would only complicate her emotions. She was already having a hard time resisting him.

"Okay, but let me know if you change your mind. I have a few moves of my own," Josh said bragging with a smug look.

"I'll keep that in mind," Nina replied with a smile turning her head to hide her embarrassment. She thought I bet you do.

When they returned to Molly's, Josh opened the door for Nina, said he'd see her in a little while and drove off. He wanted to kiss her, but he didn't want to scare her away. She certainly was complicated he thought. He realized he might be wasting his time pursuing her, not to mention teasing his heart, but he couldn't help himself. He would have to work on self-control.

After Nina had returned home from her mom's appointment, she went upstairs to get ready for dinner. Deciding on a semi-dressy look, Nina put herself together. She chose a gray-blue maxi with a small slit on the side and mated it with a contrasting cold-shoulder sweater with a low neckline. She completed the look with a fresh appliqué of makeup and the pearls her dad had given her for graduation. Then, she slipped into her open toe black booties. She pinned up her hair on top of her head in a messy bun, leaving wispy curls around the face.

Looking in the mirror, she gave herself a look of approval, thinking it would do. Then she expressed aloud, "It's not a date, Josh is only coming over to have dinner, I'm just dressing extra nice to make a good impression on mom's friend," Nina thought, trying to convince herself. However, the Intimate Relations Committee was not buying it. And it was obvious the Department of Defense wasn't going to protect her. She was on her own with this one. She concluded the best she could do was to try and keep her distance. She headed down the stairs to indulge in a glass of wine and assist her mom with dinner.

When Nina walked into the dining room, Uncle John, disguised as the Indian again, greeted her with a smile and a wave. She figured he'd settled comfortably in that scene, since it had become his permanent residence while at the house.

Nonchalantly, Nina stepped close to the picture. Trying to look inconspicuous she looked up and whispered, "Hi

Uncle J, I have lots to tell you about our trip to Shaniko, but it's going to have to wait until tomorrow at work."

"Thank you. I will look forward to it dear," he replied politely.

"See you later," she said going to the kitchen.

"Wow Mom, don't you look nice," Nina said complimenting her on her royal blue mid-length dress. "Is it new?"

"Yes, I bought it last year."

"Well, it's your style. It goes especially well with your pearls and black boot," Nina teased.

"Ha ha," Molly said with a sigh, "I already feel frumpy enough."

"Ah mom, it's not that bad," Nina said trying to cheer her up. "Besides, Dave will be looking at your beaming smile. He won't even notice the boot," she giggled.

"Oh posh-ay," Molly said dismissing her daughter's comment.

"I could add a little bling to your boot, if you'd like," Nina offered, going to get the china from the hutch.

"That would only call attention to it, thank you, but I'll pass," Molly replied.

"How is it to walk on?" Nina asked following her mom to the dining-room table, noticing a slight limp as she stepped.

"It's an adjustment. I'm sure it will take time to get used to it," Molly said leaning against the table for support. "It definitely beats rolling around on the scooter, that's for sure."

"Well, I'm happy you're getting better and healing quickly. I know how much you hate to be confined and have to depend on people," Nina lovingly stated.

"It hasn't been all that bad. It brought you here," she said squeezing Nina's hand.

"Ahh mom, I love you too," Nina replied, giving thought to her living alone, and wondered if someday she'll find someone else to make her happy like dad.

"Hey, what are thinking about dear?" Molly asked, pulling Nina from her thoughts.

"How did you know dad was the one? Was it love at first sight?" Nina asked while setting the table.

"Heavens no!" Molly said laughing so hard; she sat to avoid falling. "He was the most annoying and obnoxious man I'd ever met."

"What!" Nina said, her mouth gaping. "Now you've tainted my vision of how I imagined it," Nina said frowning as she joined her mom at the table.

"Oh honey, it turned out fine," Molly commented convincing Nina.

"So tell me about it," Nina said, her curiosity aroused.

"Okay," Molly replied, happy to share the memory.

"Well, I was working part-time at a cafe while going to college. One day this young man came in. He reminded me of a young James Dean. The hostess set him in my section. I remember it was a Friday night and the place was quite busy. It was a popular hangout for the college students," Molly expressed thinking back on that cherished time. "My section was full, and I was racing around trying to accommodate everyone. Finally, after what seemed like forever, I made it to his table. After I took his order, he lightly touched my arm and said: You are very beautiful and someday you're going to be my wife." Molly smiled as she remembered his words, her head resting in her hands.

"He always was a man who knew what he wanted," Nina said practicing her origami skills as she attempted to fold a napkin into a bird. "What happened next?" Nina asked engrossed in the story.

Molly continued, "I was totally shocked. Laughing nervously, I politely excused myself to turn in his order, and to assist another table. This man was relentless, every night he'd come in for dinner, ask to be seated in my section, and beg me to go out with him. Finally, after two months, I agreed to a movie and dinner. I figured after our date he'd have me out of his system. But my plan backfired," Molly said with a sigh, "I had a fantastic time, he was so polite, easy-going, and made me laugh." Then shaking her head she cried out, "he said we'd be together forever. It wasn't supposed to end so soon."

"Oh mom," Nina said her eyes watering; "he didn't leave you on purpose."

"I know that honey," Molly said wiping a tear from her eye, "but sometimes I get so angry at the universe," she admitted.

The sound of the doorbell and the one bark from Cassie lifted the emotional feelings lingering in the room. Relieved by the interruption, Nina bounced up from the chair and said, "I'll get it. C'mon Cassie, race you to the door," she called out to the dog close on her heels.

"Hey you two, don't knock over grandma's vase," she yelled out laughing.

When Nina opened the door, she was almost run over by Whiski who had spotted Cassie and was making a beeline to her sister.

Nina smiled watching the reunion, "They sure do love each other," she said turning to face Josh.

"Yep, been that way ever since they could walk," he commented hanging his hat on the rack. Then with a sexy grin, he remarked, "You look very pretty, but you didn't have to dress up for me."

"I'll accept that as a compliment, but don't flatter yourself, Mr. Parker," she smirked. "I just wanted to make a good impression on my mom's friend."

"I'm sure he'll like you the way you are," Josh said with tenderness.

"Thanks," she replied blushing.

"I thought I heard a familiar voice," Molly commented walking with a cane trying to adapt to walking with the boot.

"Another beauty in the house," Josh said walking over to Molly, arms open for a hug.

"You are sweet Josh, but I feel very frumpy in this boot. Maybe I should have waited to have this dinner when I'm out of the boot," she said disappointment showing on her face.

Josh stepped back, and with a smile, he commented, "Nonsense, Dave's not going to care. He'll be too busy staring into your beautiful eyes. He won't even notice."

"You sound like Nina, such a flatterer and a fibber, Joshua," she said. "But you also have a kind heart. Someday you are going to make a special woman happy, right Nina?" she remarked glancing at her daughter.

"Yes," she agreed, suddenly feeling a bit of jealousy at the thought of him with someone else. Also, she sensed the Conflict Compartment was in turmoil over the intrusion of the new bug stirring. Shaking the emotions off as quickly as they surfaced, Nina commented, "Mom why don't you relax with Josh in the living room and I'll finish dinner."

"Sounds good. Dave should be arriving any moment," Molly replied making her way to the room. "Could you please bring in my iced tea, sweetheart, and I imagine Josh would like a beer."

"Yes ma'am, thank you," he said following Molly.

Nina was grateful for the distraction. She needed to pull herself together and stop pining for a man she couldn't have. He was never going to move to the big city, and Nina could never see herself settling down here in this tiny town. With that decision made, she served them their drinks, along with a meat and cheese tray, and bones for Whiski and Cassie. Just after she'd excused herself to finish dinner, the doorbell rang. This time there were two barks, one bark from each sister. Nina smiled at the furry sisters as they joined her to greet their guest.

Nina opened the door to find a tall man standing outside the screen door. She guessed he had a good two inches on Josh and a stockier body frame. His brown eyes had a softness to them as he gave a friendly smile and introduced himself.

"Hello, I'm Dave," he said politely, before opening the screen.

All of a sudden Nina was struck speechless, her mouth hung wide open. She realized she had seen this man before. It couldn't be possible; she thought studying him.

10) THE QUEST

"I'm Nina, glad to meet you," she said. Then noticing she had been staring, commented, "I'm sorry for my reaction, but you look familiar to me. You probably have a doppelganger somewhere," she laughed recovering from her embarrassing moment.

"The pleasure is all mine," Dave said tipping his hat. "You mean to tell me there's another one like me running around in the world?" he smirked removing his hat and exposing his short wavy brown hair, frosted with nature's gray.

Nina laughed at his comment. She thought he was quite handsome, friendly, and liked to joke. She sized up his major qualities and mentally gave her approval. Then remembering her manners, she replied, "There's a hook by the closet where you can hang your hat. Mom and Josh are in the living room. I'll show you the way," Nina said escorting him to the room. "Would you care for something to drink? We have wine or beer, and I think there may be some vodka or scotch in the liquor cabinet," she offered.

"Beer sounds great, thank you."

"Please make yourself at home. I'll get it," Nina said, leaving to play hostess and finish preparing dinner.

As they sat at the table, Dave led the group in a prayer before they ate. Moments of silence filled the room as they dined on Molly's special pot roast, homemade rolls, and fresh greens. Into the meal, conversation easily flowed as they went around the table sharing.

"So Nina, your mom tells me you have a fascination with our little ghost town," Dave said directing his attention to her.

"Yes, it's quaint in an eerie way," Nina expressed. "I imagine she's told you I found a deed, to what we believe, belongs to a mine near Shaniko."

"She did. I can see why the place interests you," he replied.

"It could be nothing, but it does make for a great adventure," Nina remarked. She shared the memory as she glanced over at Josh.

Josh catching the sign, nodded in agreement. "It sure has. Who would've thought the little city could hold so much mystery?"

"Josh sent a copy of the deed to his sister, and we are waiting to hear back, hopefully soon," Molly expressed.

"Oh yeah, I forgot to mention this, I received an e-mail from her, but haven't had a chance to read it yet," Josh confessed.

Nina excitedly replied, "Please let us know what she had to report. I'm dying to find out."

"I plan on it," Josh said smiling at her glowing expression.

"Maybe I can help as well," Dave suggested. "I have some books and old maps of Shaniko which were given to me. You're welcome to borrow them if you think they might help.'"

"Thank you," Nina said graciously, "I'd appreciate it."

"I could bring them over, or better yet, are you two kids going to the dance this coming Saturday?"

Nina glanced over at her mom. Getting THE look; she kindly responded, "Yes we'll be there," wanting to kick Josh under the table over his gloating smile.

"Great, I'll have them for you there."

Nina was eager to get the documents. Now there was no way she could miss the dance. She was still curious about a couple of things but didn't want to sound as if she were drilling him with her questions. Careful of how she approached the subject, "Have you lived here long?" she asked working her way into his past.

"Yes, all my life," he commented proudly.

"Do you know any secrets about Shaniko or any of the mines close by?" she cautiously asked.

Dave looked up and took a pull from his beer, as he gave Nina's questions some thought, He answered, "I'm sure there are lots of secrets, but I don't know any. I had a grandfather that lived there in the town's early years. If he were alive today, he'd probably talk your ear off with all the tales. And, I think, if the mines still exist, they are not close to the town; at least a day's hike on a battered trail," he admitted. "I know I'm not much help. Maybe the books will give you the answers you are searching for."

Nina smiled, remembering those same eyes from Shaniko. She had spoken to Dave's grandfather, Thomas J. Smyth, on her last visit. He identified himself as John's brother. Nina wondered, after meeting Dave, if their connection with Thomas will be different on her next visit to the town.

The rest of the conversation continued around the table as Molly talked about her volunteer work and the list of projects she had lined up for Josh. Dave gave a snapshot of his life. His past and present impressed Nina. Josh talked about his contracting jobs, odd jobs in the city, and entertained the group with comical stories of his experiences with the townspeople. Nina gave a quick overview of her web page, keeping it simple as not to bore anybody. She also expressed that she needed to make a short trip to Portland for a show-and-tell demonstration to her boss. Nina was planning on Sunday and Monday since the store closed on those days.

Molly expressed to Nina that it would be fine. With the boot, she felt more confident and didn't have to rely on someone being here twenty-four-seven. Dave graciously offered to come over and help, causing Molly to blush.

Nina, noticing Josh's gloom expression, heard herself say, "Josh would you like to come to the city with me in a couple of weeks? I could use the company on the drive, and we can play in the city."

Josh's eyes lit up like a Christmas tree, taking in Nina's proposal. "I guess I could rearrange my schedule. Molly can Whiski, stay with you for a couple of days?" he asked, mentally arranging his schedule and already packing.

"Of course, Cassie would love it," Molly smiled at the thought of Nina and Josh spending time together.

"And I can tend to your animals," Dave offered.

"It's settled then," Josh said looking over at Nina.

"All right then, we're going on a road trip," Nina said hiding her sarcasm and hoping this wasn't a big mistake. She didn't want to send Josh the wrong signals. Only at this moment all her wires were crossed, making it impossible to determine the right ones from the wrong ones.

After dinner, Josh and Nina cleaned up and served apple pie with coffee. They took their dessert to the porch swing, giving Molly and Dave time together in the living room.

"It sure is beautiful," Nina said, finishing her pie. Shivering a bit from the kiss of a light breeze, she wrapped her hands around the warm cup.

"Are you cold?" Josh asked, setting down his empty plate, removing his coat and coming to the rescue.

"Maybe a little," Nina said, taking comfort sitting next to him.

"Look at all the stars. I've never seen this many," she said looking up, enjoying the view. "So close, it's as if you can reach out and touch them," she said lifting her arm to the sky. "They look so much more vibrant and alive in the country. Why do you think that is?" Nina asked, her eyes fixated on the sparkling planets.

"Well my theory would be, we are at a higher altitude, and even though the lights of the city are nice, they rob the sky of the starlight," he surmised, also studying the sky.

"Speaking of the city," Josh remarked, "thanks for inviting me to go with you. It's been awhile since I've been to Portland and it is past time for my big-city fix," he laughed.

"You're welcome. I figured you should see the more glamorous side of life," Nina teased.

"What, you don't think the country holds any glamour?" Josh asked, playing along.

"I suppose if you leave out the stinky barnyard smells," she commented with a laugh.

"I'll give you that. But some of us locals find it very aromatic."

"Eww," Nina said pinching her nose in fun.

"It's not that bad," smiling at Nina's quirky expression. Then, before Nina could reply, he put his finger up to her lips and said, "Shh, there is so much more; listen," as they became quiet. "Can you hear the musical serenade of the crickets, the coyote baying in the distance, and the hoot of the owl lurking in the night? That's the song of the country."

"It's nice," Nina commented feeling melancholy, seeing the love of the country in his eyes.

"It's nature's concert, free and always open to the public. Tonight the tempo is calm. On stormy days, the rhythm intensifies with the howling of the wind through the trees, thunder pounding, and an electrifying light show in the sky."

"Wow, that's amazing. I never viewed it like that," Nina admitted, mesmerized by her new awareness of nature around her.

"Did you just give a compliment to country life?" Josh teased.

"I guess I did," Nina said a smile curling on her face, "not at all like the city," she added. She leaned back and stretched her legs. Then gazing up at the moonlit sky, she viewed her surroundings with a new pair of eyes.

"So, do you have any idea when we'll be going back to Shaniko?" Josh asked, enjoying the last gulp of coffee, and changing the subject. "I do have some concerns."

"I'm not sure, hopefully soon. My schedule is full this week. How about Sunday? What's on your mind?" Nina said tilting her head half-listening to the crickets sing.

"For starters, if I do go with you, who will call us back to the present?" Josh replied in a serious tone.

"Don't worry I have a plan. I am going to record your voice calling our names and set a timer for it to go off. "We'll keep the recorder plugged into the charger in your truck. We can test it on me first." Nina said proudly of her idea.

"I don't know. What if it doesn't work and we get stranded in the past?" Josh replied feeling apprehensive about her idea.

"We'll find Lucia, she'll have the answer," Nina said, trying to stay positive. "What else?" Nina asked with curiosity.

"How are we going to get to the gold mine? What if it does take a day to get there? That's a long way to walk. I can't be away from the farm that long, and what are you going to tell your mom?" Josh said.

"Those are all good questions. I guess my fantasy world was pulling me so far in; I didn't see the outside picture. I never thought about how long it would take," Nina said, her mind searching for answers. "We could always catch a ride on the stagecoach, doesn't that sound fun?" she expressed, with a fake smile, also trying to convince herself.

"And what about your mom, and my farm?" Josh reiterated.

"We could tell her we're going to stay in a hotel overnight, and I bet Dave would feed your animals," Nina said sharing her solutions.

"Hmm, let's chew on that awhile. Now about the transportation; I do have an alternative to the stagecoach, which could shorten the journey. We can rent a couple of horses and make the trip on our own. Sounds more adventurous and we won't have to make all the stops," Josh said, offering Nina another option.

"Ride horses," Nina said in a high-pitched tone, eyes alert. "I've never been on a horse. I don't want to sit on a hairy animal for a long period of time," Nina stressed, shaking her head at the thought.

"Oh Nina, don't tell me you are scared of such a sweet animal. There's nothing to worry about, I'll teach you how to ride," he said looking at Nina.

"Wouldn't you rather sit inside a nice secluded cab and leave the driving to the coachman?" Nina said her faced squinched up, hoping to lure Josh to her way of thinking.

"Nina, the trip would be much shorter, who knows how many stops the stagecoach makes. Come over after work on Friday, and I'll introduce you to Majestic and Starlet. They are both fine horses, but I'll put you on Majestic. He's gentle and will give you an easy ride. Starlet is a good horse too. But, she tends to be stubborn at times. She likes a little more excitement," Josh said waiting for Nina's response.

"Hmm," Nina sighed. "You are probably right about renting horses. But maybe you could pull me in a cart," Nina said, happy with her new idea.

Laughing at her comment, he remarked, "Come over and check out the horses. If you decide you can't do it, we'll figure out another way," he said offering Nina a choice and not wanting to pressure her.

"Thank you," Nina said with relief as she returned her focus to the stars. "Look a falling star," Nina said pointing at the sky. "Let's make a wish. Remember, you can't tell anybody," she said, neither of them aware that their wishes were the same; never wanting the night to end. But their time together did come to an end as the night grew on. Nina walked into the house with Josh as he said his good-byes and called for Whiski, who was snuggling with Cassie. Walking out on the porch, Josh turned to Nina, his eyes full of passion he moved her hair to the side, and whispered, "I so want to kiss you."

Nina quivered at his touch. With her eyes locked on his, she answered softly, "I want you to kiss me too," parting her lips in anticipation.

That's all it took. Josh put his hand behind Nina's neck, and pulling her toward him, he gently kissed her, sneaking a little taste before pulling away.

Nina wanted the kiss to go on, as she fell into a dreamy state.

"See you tomorrow," Josh said leaving for his truck.

"Yeah, tomorrow," Nina repeated floating on air as she waved goodbye and went inside.

Minutes later, Molly said goodbye to Dave, and Nina smiled as she glanced out the window and found her mom in his arms. Wasn't life wonderful? She thought, quickly moving away from the curtain as she heard her come in.

Molly raised her eyebrows as she caught sight of Nina, "Were you spying on me, Missy?"

"Not I" Nina fibbed. "Why would you think that?" she giggled quickly exiting the room. "I like him," Nina yelled, as she headed upstairs eager to send Josh a text before bed. "Night mom, love you."

"Glad I have your approval, love you too," she answered with a laugh. Then after calling for Cassie, she headed for bed, her fingers touching her swollen lips and smiling.

As the lights went out, John smiled. Taking in the romantic scenes which played out tonight, he thought; Love was happening at the Charms.

The next morning, Nina hit the snooze button on her alarm. She wanted to stay nestled under the covers, relive the kiss from last night, and bask in Josh's scent still lingering on her skin. Part of her knew that their involvement could lead to hurt feelings or a bruised heart, but a strong desire was telling her to take a chance. Deciding to live in the moment and enjoy being happy, Nina stretched, climbed out of bed; ready to start her day.

Arriving at the store, Nina felt a cold breeze as she stepped from the car, feeling thankful she'd dressed appropriately in her leggings and a long sweater. The crisp ground crunched under her boots with each step, as he made her way to the porch. The weather-man had predicted they'd reach eighty-five degrees, but not till midday. Nina walked into the store and immediately cranked up the heat enough to ward off the chill. She had to be careful to keep the temperature balanced for the produce.

After completing her usual morning routine, Nina chatted with her uncle. She told him of their adventure in Shaniko, her encounter with Lucia, and meeting his brother.

"That's quite a day my dear," John commented. "How is my brother doing?"

"Fine . . . ," Nina answered with a questionable look, "You do realize that Thomas isn't alive, right?"

"Oh sure . . . I got caught up in the past. I haven't seen Thomas or heard his brotherly voice for so long. It brought up feelings, especially with you bringing up his memory," he admitted sadly.

"Clearing his throat he commented, "I wish I could go back with you if only to see him for a moment, but I know that's impossible. You can't very well carry this big picture with you," he said with disappointment.

"Wait a minute!" Nina exclaimed, "There might be a way. It's a long shot, but it's worth a try," her eyes lighting up with the possibility.

"What do you have in mind, Missy?" John asked walking to the edge of the painting.

Nina took out her cell phone, shot a couple of pictures, and explained her idea. It gave them a glimmer of hope.

Nina was assisting a customer when Josh walked into the store. After finishing the transaction, she approached him, a confused expression on her face. "What are you doing here? I didn't see a delivery on the calendar for today. Did I miss it?"

"No, I thought you'd be interested in this," he said waving a printed piece of paper and grinning.

"Is that from your sister?" she asked her eyes wide with excitement eager to read it as she reached for the paper. Focusing on the document, Nina read it aloud for John's benefit.

Hey Bro,

Sorry, it's taken awhile to get back to you, but it took a while to trace the deed back to its original owner of the Golden Vein mine, which by the way I did find. However, I am still having trouble tracking down the current owner. It seems there was a break in the chain of title. I do have to tell you I was blown away by what I discovered.

The original owners were John L Smyth and Waylon Parker. Yep, that's right. Waylon was a distant relative of ours, isn't that crazy? It seems that something happens to Mr. Parker, and John was blamed for his disappearance. According to the Shaniko Times, in the late eighteen-hundreds, John returned from his gold mining expedition alone. He tried to explain to the town that he and Waylon had been ambushed and robbed by a gang of outlaws. He claimed to have no memory of the incident due to a bad hit on the head. The people of the town didn't believe him. They shamed him and his family so badly; they were forced to leave town. They took a homestead in a small-town miles away. He changed his last name to Charmington; his wife's maiden name. Now get this, later down the line it was shortened to Charm. Isn't that Molly's last name? I'm not sure they are related, but it is a strange coincidence.

Anyway, tragedy struck the family as John died at the age of 40 with head injury complications. The cause was believed to be from an undiagnosed brain tumor which resulted from the head trauma due to the attack. Medical records show that he had monthly doctor visits for head pain and temporary short-term memory loss. The disappearance of Waylon is still a mystery, and they never found his body. I find this a little sad since he was a relative. Wonder if Mom and Dad know anything about him.

Well, that's about all I have for now. I'll let you know whether anything else turns up. Hope it helps. Let's meet up soon.

Love and Hugs,

Jennifer.

Nina stood in awe holding the letter. "Well that explains a lot," Nina expressed holding her chin.

"What's that?" Josh asked his eyebrows rose in wonder.

"You wouldn't believe me if I told you," Nina said looking up at John for direction.

"You need to tell him," John stressed showing a stern face and nodding his head.

"Try me. Nothing could surprise me after my experience with you at Shaniko."

"Oh, I'm not so sure about that," Nina cringed.

"Nina, I can handle it."

"Okay, but I warned you. I've met the John she's referring to. He's my uncle," she said taking a breath, thinking of a way to start. Deciding the beginning was the best place; Nina told her story and afterward waited with bated breath for Josh to reply.

Josh remained quiet, rubbing his temples, his mind in deep thought as he processed the news. "Let me get this straight, this picture on the wall is your uncle, and he comes to life," he said stepping closer to examine it in detail.

"Yes. I know it sounds crazy," Nina said joining him as he stood staring up at the frozen image. "Hey Uncle J, can you hear me?" she said waving her hand to get his attention, but no response. Great. Josh was going to think she was nuts. Giving it another try, Nina called her uncle a second time, and again no response. "I'm looking like a fool here. Can't you say or do something?" she pleaded, getting frustrated.

"Guess he's having a bad day," Josh commented breaking the tension.

"You don't understand. John doesn't have bad days. He hops from picture to picture. How bad could that be?" Nina exclaimed raising her voice.

"Nina it's okay," pulling her away from the picture."

"You don't believe me," Nina whined with a pout. "I wouldn't believe me either," she cried throwing her arms in the air.

"Well I would," a man's voice sounded from the wall.

"What?" Nina exclaimed with excitement running to the picture, relieved to see the image come to life and by Josh's expression, Nina knew he could see it too.

"I told you," she smirked.

"Hmm," he replied running his hand along the frame looking for cameras or wires.

"You won't find anything. I've done a thorough examination and didn't find a thing."

"Well there must be something causing it to activate," Josh said, with a serious look, his mind searching for answers.

"You don't believe he's a spirit?" Nina said with torn feelings.

"Nina, I don't know what to think," he confessed running his hand through his hair.

Nina stood there taking a stance, her arms crossed over her chest and a stern look on her face. She had to call for drastic tactics, time was running out, and it felt like Josh was slipping further away from believing. Keeping her strong posture, she stated, "Well you'd better figure it out soon, Mr. Parker, especially if you want to go with me to Shaniko. I'm not afraid to go there alone." She lied hoping it didn't come to that. "Also, you should have a vested interest after discovering your relative is involved in this mystery. Maybe we can find out what happened to him," she stated giving him something to consider. "Let me know when you find the answers," raising her head and walking away.

Nina's words and dramatic exit left Josh speechless and shaking his head wondering what had gone down.

"Boy, you sure did it. Nothing worse than a woman's scorn," John commented, offering his two cents.

"I'm not sure what to do," Josh confessed to John. "It's so difficult for me to wrap my brain around this entire escapade. I try understanding it, but logic butts in every time."

"Yes, I could see why you are so confused. Take me for instance; here I am stuck in a picture. I don't know how I got here or how to get out. You think that's not frustrating?" John asked putting his leg on the bench to pull up his boot.

"That must be rough," Josh replied sympathizing with the man. Then, realizing he was having a normal conversation with this image, he expressed. "You are real."

"Something like that," John laughed. "Now, how are you going to fix it with my niece? You can't let her go back there alone. It might not be safe."

"I don't know. But, by the fiery look in her eyes when she stormed off, I would have better luck taming a wild mustang instead," he said causing them to burst into a roar of laughter.

11) LUCIA'S MYSTERIOUS APPEARANCE

Nina, hearing the laughter, hurried to check it out. "What's going on?" she asked in a soft tone.

"Inside joke," Josh answered with a smile, hoping he wasn't still on her bad list.

"With whom?" Nina asked, perusing the area for another person.

"Just a private conversation with your uncle," Josh replied with a smirk.

"You're talking to him? What changed your mind?" Nina asked her eyes wide with wonder. "No, wait. I don't need to know. The important thing is that you are." She tried to hide her smile.

Josh catching the expression commented, "Was I just played?"

"Of course not, would I do that?" Nina replied. She turned her head and pretended to cough.

"Uh huh," Josh said with a frown, not believing her.

"Please be aware," Nina said dismissing his silent accusation, "other people can't see or hear John. So, you do look a little odd talking and laughing in the corner. My last customer mentioned it as she left the store," Nina teased as she giggled walking away.

"You are an evil one Miss Charm. I will see myself out," he called.

"See you tonight," Nina called back, happy on how well that had all played out. A little assertiveness can go a long way. Hopefully, his belief will be enough to allow him into the past dimension. She thought as she organized a cluttered shelf on her way to the front.

Later that afternoon, Nina heard the notification bell. She looked up from her computer surprised to see who was standing in the doorway. "Mom, how did you get here? You didn't drive here did you?" she said glaring at her ready to scold.

"No dear. Dave had some errands in town and offered to drop me off. Wasn't that sweet of him?" Molly expressed, her cheeks glowing. "He will be back in an hour. I wanted to make sure my store was still standing," she chuckled using a walking stick to keep her balance.

Nina gave her mom a half smile over her sarcastic remark, "As you can see, it's all in one piece."

"There was never any doubt in my mind," Molly admitted with a loving smile. "I miss the place, and hopefully I can come back a few hours a week, starting soon." Then she found a chair and sat down.

"I hope you don't mind, I moved some things around and changed a couple of areas to make them work for me."

"No honey, I'm glad you've added your personal touch. Which brings up something I'd like to discuss with you," Molly said with a serious tone in her voice.

"What is it?" Nina asked with curious eyes; a quiet fear probed her mind.

"I want to make you co-owner of the store. Don't worry this doesn't change anything. You can be a silent partner," Molly offered, gauging her daughter's expression.

"Wow, I don't know what to say," Nina said. Her senses numb and the Emotion Department in her mind became overwhelmed and scrambled to find the dominant feeling.

"You don't have to answer now," Molly interjected at the sight of Nina's pale face. "I'll still keep the front lines running. You could create one of your web pages to help draw in more customers. Josh and I have discussed adding a corner coffee bar, and possibly contracting with your company for the coffee and supplies."

Nina's head was swirling, that was a lot to take in. "Mom, you two don't know anything about running a coffee shop." Then red flags started waving, and with a frown on her face, Nina confronted her mom. "This wouldn't be a diabolical plan to get me to move here would it? It's not going to work. I love my life in the city," she said holding her ground.

"Oh dear, not at all," Molly said dismissing her accusation. Josh knows this sweet girl who is experienced with running a coffee shop and happens to be looking for a new job."

"Oh, he does?" Nina asked, twisting her hands nervously; flags down and the jealousy bug taking over. "I imagine you'll be looking at her references and considering other qualified applicants."

"Of course dear, I wouldn't hire her without your approval," Molly replied. "She works at the cafe in town if you'd like to meet her."

"Thanks, I might do that," Nina replied trying not to sound too eager.

"So, what are your thoughts on joining me in this business?" Molly asked hoping to get a response today.

"Well," Nina said with a sigh, "I guess you have yourself a partner. This deserves a mini-celebration." She walked to the refrigerator and selected two bottles of juice. Handing one to her mom, they gave a toast, clinking the bottles to complete the ceremony.

"I'll talk to my boss when I'm at the corporate office about a contract. You're right; a web page will definitely attract more business. I do like the idea of a coffee bar," she expressed taking a sip of the raspberry drink. Nina thought, if I had my way, the barista would be married and have two children.

"Wonderful. You've made me very happy," a smile beaming on Molly's face. "I'll ask Josh if his sister can draw up the partnership papers, and set up a time he can show us the plans for the coffee shop."

"That was fast. It looks like you had this already planned," Nina said with a baffled look; suspicion was lurking.

"Oh we did," Molly admitted. "The addition for the shop was a given, but, the partnership with you was a bonus."

"Ah Mom," Nina said hugging her. The mother-daughter moment broke at the sound of the bell.

"Hi Dave, thanks for bringing mom by," Nina said with appreciation.

"My pleasure. I hate to take her away, but I have a meeting after I drop her off at home. See you tomorrow," he said tipping his hat. Then offering Molly his arm, he escorted her out of the market.

A tear of joy ran down Nina's cheek. Looking up, she said, "Dad, no one will ever replace you. But, I think Dave is close in the running. I know you're watching and want her to be happy. Love you always." Then wiping her eyes with a tissue, she composed herself and started her nightly closing routine. She savored a melancholy moment, thinking soon the store would be part hers.

The next day after work, Nina headed home to change for dinner at her aunt's. Dave had picked up her mom, so Nina was alone in an empty house again, only this time it wasn't the same. Oh no, what if she were getting countrified, Nina feared. "Well that wasn't going to happen," she said aloud. "What I need is a taste of the city to get me back on track." Choosing her favorite clubbing outfit; designer distressed skinny jeans, favorite rock tee-shirt, and two-inch black boots, she got dressed. Tonight she gave a more dramatic style to her makeup. It was much bolder and brighter. A sprinkle of glitter and cherry lipstick completed the polished look. In her hair she added gel and finger styled it, giving it body and lift. After a spray of her best perfume, she grabbed her bomber jacket and was on her way.

Driving over, Nina thought about the coffeehouse, which led to the barista, causing anger to rise inside her. She couldn't believe it. Josh had some nerve having his girlfriend working for her mom. Well, if she has her way that was never going to happen. Then Nina cursed, thinking she'd forgotten to stop by the cafe on her way home.

Josh pulled in behind Nina. His jaw dropped at the sight of the drop-dead gorgeous woman getting out of her vehicle. He'd never seen this side of her and became hypnotized by the way she rocked those jeans. After calming his emotions, Josh stepped from the truck and whistled.

Nina ignored the action as she walked up the steps to the porch. Then with her hands on her hips, she confronted him, "So, you were working to replace me, and I'm not even gone yet."

Josh stopped. Stunned by Nina's outburst, he replied, "What are you talking about?"

"I know all about your plans. Building a coffeehouse and getting your girlfriend to run it. When were you going to tell me?"

"Nina, I am lost here," Josh admitted, running his hands through his hair, feeling confused.

"We don't know if she's even qualified," Nina stated rambling on.

"Wait," Josh said interrupting. Disturbed by Nina's lack of trust, he took a stance. "If you are talking about Chrystal, she is not my girlfriend. She happens to be married to my best friend. They have two sweet young girls, and I was named their godparent. I think Chrystal is more than qualified. She holds a business degree and has been making specialty coffee for over five years. Do I go on?"

"No," Nina said feeling ashamed and embarrassed. "I've dug a big enough hole," looking at the ground. "I'm so sorry Josh; I don't know what came over me. I'll just climb in that hole and bury myself," she cried. "Maybe my uncle has some crow," she said with a half laugh turning to go in.

Josh reached for her arm causing her to stop and turn around. "Don't be too hard on yourself. In a twisted way I could take it as a compliment. Maybe you do care," he said gazing into her eyes. "And for the record, I wouldn't ever do anything like that to a girl I'm falling for."

"Josh," Nina replied, in shock, "I do care about you too. Please don't make our friendship messy and complicated. I'll be leaving soon, and we agreed that long-distance relationships don't work." Nina said turning her head to hide the hurting truth. "Come on let's go inside and check on the family," she added needing to break the tension in the air, leaving Josh stuck in his thoughts.

Josh knew Nina was right, but it wasn't as if his emotions had an on and off switch, or he could wipe her from his mind. He also didn't know if being friends would ever be enough.

Nina entered the house. The scent of Italian spices, freshly baked bread, and cinnamon candles welcomed her into the loving home. Antiques, overstuffed furniture, throw blankets, and assorted pictures gave it a homey touch. One family picture especially touched her heart. It was of her mom, dad, aunt, uncle, and herself. She had a copy of that picture at home. Pulling her eyes from the photo-wall, Nina said her hellos, saving her uncle for last.

She was very fond of him, and always had a special place in her heart for him. They'd always been close, but ties between them grew stronger when her father passed away. To some, with his large size and stocky build, he could seem intimidating. But not to Nina, he reminded her of a big teddy bear. His thick brown curly hair, full beard, and mustache showcased his round face and hid his boyish features. She also admired his love for his country by the flag he proudly displayed in his front yard. She never grew tired of hearing the stories of his years spent in the military.

She found him in their game room, where a pool table took center stage, and a smaller table held his favorite past time, puzzle assembly, on which he was working.

Hearing Nina approach he turned, and with a big smile, he greeted her, "It's so good to see you," and hugged her.

"I missed you too," Nina admitted taking comfort wrapped in his strong arms. He still smelled of Old Spice and looked the same except for a touch of age creeping in. "Thank you for the charm; it's quite fascinating. I bet it has a story too," she said releasing her hold on him. Her attention shifted to the half-completed puzzle of a winter scene, with the single pieces strategically separated by color and shape.

"That it does," he said with a smile, picking up a piece and trying to lock it with another. "I bought it in town at a secondhand store. This older woman helped me pick it out, and insisted I buy it. Then she told me this strange rhyme," Hank said repeating the woman's words. "It holds a secret history that unfolds a sordid mystery. It opens a gateway from the present to the past. So be sure to keep it near, or the magic will not last. It will keep you safe away from any harm, that's all the gifts of this little charm."

"Wow," Nina said stunned by this revelation. A startling chill ran down her spine. Moving away from the puzzle, her attention on the woman's words, she asked, "Was this woman dressed in gypsy-like clothing?" Nina asked, suspecting she already knew the answer.

"Yes, she was. Do you know her?" Hank asked, quietly celebrating the marriage of two puzzle pieces.

"No, but I've seen her a few times. I wonder what the meaning is behind the rhyme," Nina asked, repeating the words in her head.

"I don't know. When I went back to learn more, the store wasn't open, and the building boarded up. There was no sign of the woman," he reported.

"Weird," Nina exclaimed. Then the sound of her aunt's voice, announcing dinner was ready, took them away from the bizarre conversation. They made their way to the dining room. They'd learned long ago never to be late to the table. It was a pet peeve of her aunt's, and it was best to abide by her rules instead of dealing with her wrath.

Nina sighed with relief when Josh held her chair and sat in the one next to her. She was afraid he was still mad at her, and she couldn't blame him. Her actions tonight were so out of character. What had caused her to jump to such irrational conclusions? Why did she care who he dated? It wasn't like they were an item. Sure they had kissed a couple of times and had fun together, but it didn't mean they were in a committed relationship. But what were they? The sound of her uncle giving thanks yanked Nina from her thoughts, bringing her back to the gathering.

Nina took in the warm and friendly sight, as people filled their plates with pasta laid out on a long table, proudly set with her aunt's delicate china. She smiled inside as the room filled with laughter while they ate; exposing harmless gossip, sharing personal stories and, due to another one of her aunt's pet peeves, talk of business was very limited.

After dinner, Nina helped her aunt with kitchen duty. Dave kept Molly company in the living room, while Hank and Josh stepped onto the back porch for a snifter of brandy and a smoke.

Josh bit off the end of his cigar and accepted a light from Hank. Fortunately, he'd never taken up the habit of smoking but appreciated a good smoke on occasion. There was something about the aroma that reminded him of his grandfather. The sweet taste awakened his senses as he inhaled the earthy nectar, and he felt a calming sensation when he slowly released the taunting smoke.

Hank, repeated the ritual himself, releasing the smoke in perfect-sized rings. After taking a sip of his brandy, he asked with a serious look on his face. "So, what are your intentions with my niece?"

"Excuse me?" Josh asked stunned by his abrupt question.

"I can see the way you two look at one another. There is definitely a connection there."

"Believe me, if there were a chance for a relationship, which there is not, my intentions would be honorable sir." Then taking a sip of the liquor and letting the heat warm his throat, he envisioned the beautiful little city-girl getting out of her car tonight. Choosing it was best to put that image aside, he continued, "Nina has made it clear many times, she doesn't care for the country, and long-distance relationships don't work. Tell me something, has she always been a . . ."

"A spoiled city brat," Hank said finishing Josh's sentence.

"I wasn't going to say that," Josh remarked, shocked by Hank's comment.

"Well, it's true. Nina will be the first to admit it," he laughed, taking a long pull from his cigar and then filled the air with a sweet, smoky haze. After savoring another sip from his glass, he patted Josh on the back, "I do have my theory why," he said glancing up at the stars.

"Do you mind if I ask what that is?"

Bringing his eyes back to Josh he replied with a grin, "Sure, after I get a refill. You want another?" he asked safely cradling his cigar in the corner of his mouth, freeing both hands as he reached for the bottle from behind a small outside bar.

"No thank you," Josh answered putting his hand over the glass.

"I shouldn't either, it's very seldom I indulge," he said glancing around. "Please don't tell my wife."

"Man, that's between you two," Josh replied staying out of it.

"Good answer," Hank said nodding. "So this is why I think Nina is bound to big-city life." Then, after he took a pause and a sip, he shared his story. "Nina and her sister were born and raised in Portland. They grew up in a private community in suburbia. Joe had a well-paying job. His income more than provided for his family, and it allowed Molly to stay home with the girls. They made sure they were well educated and schooled in manners and etiquette. Molly was always on the go, transporting them to dance practice, music lessons, and sporting events. She and Joe seldom missed a performance or event. Eventually, the girls went their separate ways. Her sister married and moved away and Nina went off to college. By the way, did Nina tell you she played the piano?" he asked, pausing for a moment as he stubbed out his cigar.

"No, she hasn't mentioned it," Josh replied.

"That's probably because her passion for the music died with her dad," he said quietly. "She'd been gone a few months when her dad received the diagnosis of a terminal illness. The doctors gave him five to seven years," Hank expressed, sadness filling his tone. "He was a good man," closing his eyes thinking back.

"That had to have been devastating for the family," Josh replied offering his sympathy.

"Joe gave his two-week notice. They sold their house and bought a place in a small country town, close to here. I don't have to tell you, Nina was furious. Not only were they moving away, but it was also to a small town, away from all his medical specialists. You never want to see her that angry," he said with a sly grin.

Josh nodded with a smug look and admitted, "I got a taste of that tonight, and I didn't do anything."

"Uh hum," Hank mumbled clearing his throat and eyes looking left, he tried to alert Josh, Nina was at the door.

"Hey guys, I'm taking dessert orders. Can I entice you in a piece of homemade apple-pie a lá mode?" she asked pretending to be a waitress.

"None for me thank you," Josh said patting his stomach.

"I know I can't eat another bite. But Uncle Hank, how about you?" Nina said preparing to take his order with an imaginary pad and paper.

"Nina, that's a silly question. When have you known me ever to pass up a dessert?"

"Right," she said pointing a finger and smiling.

"Tell your aunt I'll be there in about ten minutes. After dessert, we'll meet in the barn, for some dance lessons. By the way, the barn is named The Palace."

"I thought maybe you'd forgotten," she said with a displeased look.

"Nonsense, I'm going to teach you some of my best moves," he remarked. Then he wiggled his eyebrows, and with an imaginary partner, he moved his feet in a pattern, ending with a complete turn; beaming a smile of pride.

"I can't wait," Nina said laughing as she walked off.

After she left, Hank commented, "Whew that was close. I don't think she heard anything," downing his last swallow.

"Yes, but we probably should get inside before they send the posse back to retrieve us," Josh laughed.

"So true. I am almost done," Hank said, and then dropping his voice a level, he continued. "Despite Nina being against their move, she was still supportive and made sure to visit often. Things were going well until Joe's health took a turn for the worse and he died four years later." Then Hank paused for an emotional moment, "I sure miss that man."

"Sorry. He sounds like he was a good man," Josh commented offering his sympathy.

Nodding in agreement, Hank went on. "Anyway, after the service, Nina and Molly had a falling-out. She partly blamed her mom for her dad's premature passing. Stressing, if they would've been in the city, where he was under the care of the specialist, he might have lived longer."

"Wow, brutal," Josh replied.

"Yes, but before she left for home, they had made up. As far as I know, the subject was never talked about again. I think my dear niece still harbors resentments and doesn't even realize it."

"That's quite a hard barrier to break through," Josh commented with a distant look.

"Keep trying my boy," he said patting Josh on the back. "Who knows, maybe you are the one who can do it," giving him hope. "Now let's go inside, my pie awaits."

Nina relayed her uncle's dessert request and afterward decided to go to the barn and wait. She could use the fresh air, and a few moments of alone time to check her e-mails and texts.

She followed the lighted stone pathway. The illuminated flicker from the lampposts felt cozy and inviting. The path wrapped around the yard to the upper barn, close to the house, and then down a hill to the lower barn, which housed the farm animals, feed, tackle, and other farming supplies. They designed the upper barn for events and dances. Nina stood outside the building with the colorful neon sign Party Palace brightly flashing.

Two doors divided the barn. Nina went into the door on the right leading into a room. Nina knew her uncle had designed it for family and friends movie night with a high-tech video and sound system, theater-like chairs, large sofa, and bean-bag chairs for the little ones.

She walked through a connecting door that opened into a large room used for dinner gatherings, large events, and parties. This room had originally been created to host barn dances but has seen so much more. She ran her hand along the smooth oak bar, remembering the last time she had been there. It was for her dad's funeral service. Wiping a tear from her eye and pushing the unhappy memory aside, Nina started moving the tables, clearing a space for them to dance, and being careful not to mar the polished hardwood floor.

Finding a bottle of water in the refrigerator, Nina plopped down in a nearby chair, allowing a few minutes for phone time. Life here had been keeping her very busy, she hadn't noticed her voice-mail was full, and there were ten texts. One was from Rene, wanting the scoop on the cowboy, another from Serena; checking in, and her sister sent her love. She sent a short message, followed by a heart, happy face, and red lips emojis to all three, vowing to reply to the others soon. There were various messages in her inbox, some needing immediate attention, while others could wait. Nina sent a courtesy response to the business-related e-mails and red-flagged the rest for later.

Hopefully, she could find the time tomorrow to take care of them. It wasn't like her to get behind in her correspondences. Laying her head in her hands, Nina thought this country air was turning her into a slacker. Laughing at her quirkiness, she put her phone away at the sound of her uncle's arrival.

"I thought maybe you'd changed your mind," Nina said with a smile turning around. But her expression quickly faded when she discovered it wasn't her uncle.

12) NINA LEARNS THE TRUTH

"What are you doing here?" Nina asked with surprise. "Where's Uncle Hank?"

"He sent me here to get you started. He received an important phone call and will be here shortly," Josh explained.

"Oh," Nina said feeling uncomfortable being there alone with Josh. "I'll wait until he gets here."

"Nina it's only dancing. I promise to be good," Josh replied with a grin.

Rolling her eyes, Nina hesitated and pondered that thought. Then with her arms crossed over her chest, she walked over to him. Offering a cautious smile, she replied, "I guess, but only dancing."

"Got it, I'm harmless," he said opening his arms.

Nina with a frown replied, "Somehow I can't see you and harmless being compatible," She laughed, stepped into his arms, ready for dancing, and made sure to avoid eye contact.

"Funny lady," he smirked. Then lifting her chin, he gazed into her cautious eyes, "relax. Let's start with the two-step and work our way to the swing."

"Whatever," Nina replied.

"All you need to learn is the basics, and you'll be naturally gliding across the dance floor," Josh said in an attempt to calm her fears.

"I don't know about that. I'll be happy not to step on any toes or embarrass myself," Nina nervously chuckled.

Laughing, he commented, "Follow my lead. Slow, slow, quick, quick," he repeated as he navigated her around the dance floor. After dancing around the room a couple of times, Josh commented, "Not bad, now let's try it with some music." Then he walked over and picked out a special song on her uncle's classic jukebox.

"See you are getting the hang of it," Josh said as he two-stepped Nina to the country song. Then he surprised her at the ending of the song with a turn and dip. "You're getting the hang of it," he said gazing into her sparkling eyes.

"I am?" Nina said, locked on his eyes filled with passion.

Then, he lifted her up and brought her next to him. Close enough that she could feel his warm breath on her cheek. Nina couldn't deny the look of desire in his eyes, or the fact she longed to kiss him. But just as the magical moment was about to happen, they were abruptly pulled apart by the sound of Hank clearing his throat.

"Uh huh, doesn't look like you're getting much practicing in," he teased.

"Yes we are," Nina said breaking the awkward moment and taking Josh's arms.

Josh, taking the hint starting dancing, "Quick, slow, quick, slow," Nina chanted in an attempt to remove the smirk on her uncle's face, not realizing she was miserably failing with her effort.

Laughing Hank stepped in, "I'll take it from here. Josh, Becky is trying to get a card game together and needs a partner. Would you please fill in for me?"

"No problem," Josh answered, letting go of Nina. "Watch your toes, she has some treacherous steps," he joked, walking away.

"Very funny, just for that I will make it a point to step on your toes at the dance," she said playfully.

"Okay, where were you?" Hank said, taking hold of Nina while two-stepping around the room.

"I'm doing it," Nina said joyfully feeling confident.

"Yes, you are," Hank said with pride. "Let's change the pace a bit, and try the swing." He selected an upbeat song on the jukebox. Then returned and twirled Nina in place.

After thirty minutes, Nina called it quits. She had the basics down and felt confident she could now appear on the dance floor without making a fool of herself.

"You'll be two-stepping and swinging like a pro," Hank commented. "And you won't be lacking a partner," he smirked.

"Josh?" Nina questioned.

"Yes, you two make such a beautiful dance couple."

"Oh, no, we're not going there," Nina abruptly sounded.

"Nina what are you afraid of?" Hank asked grabbing a bottle of water from the fridge and taking a seat. "Why are you pushing him away? He's a good man." Then taking a drink of the cold liquid, he set the bottle on the table and waited for her reply.

Nina had her guard up as she stood her ground. Putting her hands on her hips, she confronted her uncle. "I am not afraid, and even if I was interested, which I am not, we live miles apart. A relationship like that could never work," she admitted denying the truth.

"If there is a will, there is always a way. Would it be that bad living here?"

"Why should I have to move? I have a career, home, and friends in the city. You don't expect me to pick up my life and move here, and I know he'll never move there," Nina said stating her case.

"Well, I can't blame him. He has deep roots here; you couldn't expect him to give all that up," hoping he wasn't stepping over her boundaries.

"Oh, so you say its okay for me to kiss my life in the city goodbye and come live in the sticks," Nina said with a displeased look. She was on the verge of tears.

"It's not the sticks, dear niece. Could it be that you don't want to move here because you blame the small city life for cutting your dad's time short?" he asked.

"You have no right to say that!" Nina expressed her anger flaring. The tears she was holding back burned her eyes.

"Nina, I didn't mean to hurt you. Honey, I'm sorry," Hank said, seeing her saddened face. He wished he could take back what he had said. He knew he shouldn't have had that second drink; it caused him to have loose lips, and lift the filter from his brain to his mouth. "Nina," he said with compassion, walking over to her.

"No uncle, I can't do this," Nina cried. Running out of the building and ignoring her uncle calling to her, she ran back to the house.

She didn't want to go inside, but her purse and coat were in there. Nina didn't want to talk to anyone; she would say she wasn't feeling well, grab her belongings and leave. And that's what she did, and by the time she made it to the car, the pent-up tears were falling.

"What happened?" Molly questioned Hank as he came into the room.

"I'm sorry Molly. I might have gone a little too far."

"What are you talking about?" she said with a look of confusion on her face.

"We were having a discussion, and I brought up Joe," Hank admitted avoiding the glaring stare of his wife, Becky.

"Oh no! You know that's a tender subject for Nina. We buried that years ago."

"I realize that, but I don't think it was deep enough. It seems Nina is still carrying some unsettled feelings about it. I know it's none of my business, but maybe it's time to tell her the truth."

"I was planning on it, but not like this. But since you opened the door, I'm going to have to deal with it sooner," Molly said with a look of displeasure on her face, shaking her head.

"You want me to go talk to her?" Josh graciously offered, worried about Nina.

She smiled and gently touched Josh on the hand, "Thanks, but this is something I need to do. Dave could you please run me home?"

Molly found her daughter on the front porch swing wrapped up in a blanket. She was holding a cup of steaming tea with a distant look in her eyes. Molly cautiously walked over to Nina. "You want to talk?"

Nina looked at her mom showing her tear-streaked face, "Mom I love you, but please right now I need some space to figure things out."

"I understand, and I will give you as much space as you need after I clear up a few things."

"Why did you guys give up?" Nina blurted out.

"Honey is that what you think?" Molly said with a sigh, sitting next to her daughter and sharing the blanket.

"Then why didn't dad stay and do the treatment?" Nina said sniffing.

"Don't you think I didn't try to keep him there?" Molly said staring ahead, remembering that time. "You know how stubborn your father was. He wanted to live the rest of his life with dignity, not sick from drugs, and I was going to abide by his wish, no matter how painful it was."

"But you could've tried other things, like alternative medicine," wiping her eyes with a tissue.

"Oh, but we did," Molly exclaimed taking hold of Nina's hand. "Your dad tried every natural remedy, drink, potion, and lotion, but nothing worked. It might have bought him a little time, but we never knew that for sure," she remarked. "Giving it one last attempt, we flew to Mexico so he could try an experimental drug. It had a 70% success rate, guess we were part of the 30%," Molly said sadly.

"Why didn't you tell us girls?" Nina asked in wonder.

"We were planning on it, if and when his disease went into remission. He didn't want you to get your hopes up or worry. You were going to school, and your sister was starting her life."

"I wish I would've known about this sooner," Nina said pulling her knees close to her chest.

"I never saw a need for it. Why bring up something we put away many years ago? I'm sorry honey."

"It's okay. I'm so relieved to find this out. Tomorrow you need to call Sara and fill her in," Nina said laying her head on Molly's shoulder.

"I'll make that my first task in the morning. Now why don't we continue this pity party in the house, I brought home some apple pie, and we have some ice cream in the fridge. What do you say?" Molly smiled and patted Nina's head.

"Sounds yummy," Nina expressed standing and helping her mom off the swing.

Sitting at the table, Nina dug into the decadent pleasure in front of her. The blend of sweet flavors exploded in her mouth. She felt a sense of peace after talking with her mom. It had been hard to step back and relive the pain, but it was what she needed to move forward. Feeling better, Nina decided to change to a happier subject, the dance on Saturday.

"Mom do you think there is a place in town that may have the perfect dress, and some bronco-busting cowboy boots for the dance?" she tried to sound western, with unsuccessful results.

Molly laughed at her silly attempt, "I'm sure we can find something. There are a couple of boutiques and a western store in Old Town. I'll see if Dave can drive me to the market in the afternoon tomorrow, and we can leave after work."

"It's a date," making a mental note in her mind. Just as Nina took another bite, her phone rang. Recognizing the number on her caller-ID window, she smiled and decided to let it go to her voice-mail.

"You're not going to answer that?" Molly asked with a curious look.

"No, it's Josh, and I don't want to talk to him. Right now I am enjoying my mother-daughter time," Nina said lovingly. Then she took another bite and slowly licked her fork clean.

Within a few minutes, Nina's phone buzzed again, this time it was a text from Josh. Not able to wait, she opened it. "Hey city-girl, checking to make sure everything is cool. I guess I'll see you tomorrow at the store. Hoping we're still on for Friday, Majestic and Starlet are excited to meet you. Talk later. Josh"

"Josh again?" Molly asked raising her eyebrows.

Nina nodded.

"He sure is persistent. Maybe you should call him. I should get ready for bed anyway," giving her daughter the opportunity to talk with him.

"Thanks but I'll text him later." Nina insisted.

"Can I ask you a personal question?" Molly asked cautiously.

"Sure."

"Why the change of heart about the dance?" Molly asked, taking the last bite of her pie.

"I don't know" shrugging her shoulders and staring into the bottom of her cup, as though she'd find the answers there. "Maybe this country life is starting to grow on me. . . a little," Nina emphasized after seeing the hopefulness in her mom's eyes. "It's not enough to move here, but I am feeling more adjusted and comfortable."

"It couldn't have anything to do with a kind and handsome cowboy, could it?" Molly asked teasing.

"Mom, I do like him a lot, but I am in a quandary. We live in two separate worlds," she expressed scraping her plate, getting every morsel. "Maybe we met in the right place at the wrong time or vice versa." Pondering that thought, Nina cleared off the table and washed the dishes.

"Or it could be that this is the right time and place and you can't see it. Honey, God has a reason for everything that happens," Molly smiled. With that, she walked over to Nina and kissed her cheek. "Good night dear, love you."

"Love you too," Nina expressed, hanging onto her mom's last comment. Could she be right? Nooo! I can't go there now. Way too much emotional baggage for one night she thought and headed to bed.

Before Nina went to sleep, she remembered to reply to Josh's text. "Hi thanks for your concern but I'm okay. When you called, I was hanging with mom getting our sugar fix, a perfect remedy for an emotional overload. Yes, I will see you tomorrow, and I must be crazy, but yes Friday is on. Sweet dreams." Then she finished by adding some affectionate emojis.

Josh smiled when he read the text, looking at his faithful lazy companions, he remarked. "We have company coming Friday, and the house needs cleaning. So what are you guys going to contribute to the chore?" Both animals raised their heads, gave a yawn and looked at one another. Josh laughed thinking that they had some secret code between them. "Right, I forgot your job is to supervise."

Josh didn't know why he felt nervous about having Nina over. But she was special, and he wanted to make a good impression. Also, it was very seldom he ever invited women to his home, but Nina was different. He was aware that he was putting his heart out there, with no guarantee. But in love, there were no guarantees. He shuddered at his last thought. "Where had that four letter word come from? It had to be more like infatuation," he said aloud. "Yes that's what it is," he said battling the feelings.

Fortunately, the ringing of his cell-phone added a welcomed distraction, and he smiled when he saw it was from his sister.

"Hey sis," he greeted. "What's up?"

"Hi, sorry I'm calling so late, but it's the first time today I've had a free moment."

"No worries, I was heading to bed," Josh answered, wondering the reason for her call.

"I'll keep it short," Jennifer commented, "thought you'd like to know the name of the current owner of the gold mine."

"Who is it?" Josh said waiting in suspense.

"Are you ready for this?" she teased keeping her brother in suspense.

"Jennifer!" he playfully scolded.

She laughed, then giving in she answered, "It's Nina."

"Nina? Are you sure?" Josh questioned, sitting down to absorb the news.

"Yes. I'll tell you all about it this weekend. I'm coming down Saturday morning to go to the dance. Is my room available?" Jennifer asked.

"Just like always," Josh assured her. Of course, it would be after he cleaned it. Now he had two reasons to play housekeeper. "Sure you can't tell me more?" he pried.

"Sorry bro, but I'd like Nina to be there, and I would appreciate it if you didn't mention it to her.

"No loose lips here," he laughed.

"Good. I'm going to let you go now. There's an early court date on my calendar tomorrow. Love you and see you soon, mwah," she said blowing a fake a kiss to him over the phone.

"Back at ya, night," he said and then calling to his bed partners the trio headed upstairs.

At 2:00 PM the next day, Molly showed up at the market. Nina took her through the store and gave her an in-depth look at all the changes and enhancements she had implemented. She also gave her a peek at the prototype website of the store. Molly was impressed with most of the changes and offered her opinion on the ones that were still debatable. Nina could tell she was happy to be back in her element; there was an extra gleam in her eyes when she talked about the upcoming changes. At four o'clock, Molly gave Nina the ok to close the store, and then they headed off on their shopping spree.

The quaint little shops were much different than the large department stores where Nina usually shopped. However, she was impressed with the quality of clothing lines they carried. They seemed well stocked with most of the modern styles, and each place had special garments that made them unique. Also, their prices were comparable to the stores she had shopped in the city. But like most stores, there were some fancier items on the pricey side. Between all the stores Nina figured a person could find everything they'd need within their budget; from formal wear to hiking attire. What made the experience extra special was that the clerks and owners treated you like family and you weren't just another sale.

After modeling a few outfits for her mom and the friendly clerks, Nina had selected two pairs of jeans; one skinny and one boot-cut style, a blue v-neck long sleeved sweater, and two pairs of cowboy boots. She also found the cutest dress for the dance. Beige lace draped over a silky slip which hit her two inches above the knee, and Nina loved the flowing flare of the sleeves. It went perfectly with her new tan and black two-tone boots and braided belt. Molly had also found a mid-length denim skirt; Nina surprised her, by purchasing it for her.

Nina dropped Molly off at Dave's on her way home. They were going to dinner. She was looking forward to some alone time to fine tune her website. It needed to be free of errors when she presented it to her boss. The thought of being back at her home and work made her smile. There was also a rumor her good friend Serena might be coming into the city soon. Nina hoped it was true, it had been awhile, and she missed her quirky friend.

John commented the minute Nina closed her computer. "It's about time, I've wanted to talk to you all evening," he smiled as he climbed off the horse.

"Well I'm all yours and thanks for being considerate while I was working," Nina said giving him her attention.

"First, it's good to see you are feeling better; you were very sad the other night," John expressed with compassion.

"Much better now, thank you," she smiled walking over to the picture.

"Love isn't always easy," he quoted.

"What!" Nina shrieked. "Love is not involved, I barely know him."

"My sweet niece, love has no time frame. You can't summon it or toss it away. It somehow appears," he said holding his chin and looking up.

"How do you know so much?" she asked with curious eyes.

"I think I was there once," lifting one leg onto a log and pondering the thought. "In the letter you read, it mentioned I had a wife; she must be the beautiful lady who visits me in my dreams. She has golden tresses of curls falling down her back, eyes that sparkle like a twinkling star, and a smile which shines brighter than a sunny day."

"She sounds very pretty," Nina said picturing the image as she walked into the kitchen to fix a salad and cup of tea.

"Yes she was, at least what I can remember," he said following Nina and appearing in a picture of a haggard looking man, advertising his need for coffee. Then trying to make the man look presentable, he continued. "I must have also been a father because there are two young lads, a younger image of me, standing next to her. What do you think happened to them?" he asked, wading through the fog in his head in search of the answers.

"I don't know," Nina answered doing a double-take at the character he was portraying. "Maybe Lucia will have the answers," putting the tea kettle on the stove and trying not to grin.

"Do you think if I go back, I'll be able to see and talk to them?" John asked with a hopeful look in his eyes.

"We will have to ask Lucia that also," Nina said. "Now Uncle J, I've had a long week, and I want to veg-out, watch some TV, and eat my dinner," she said passing by him with her food, Cassie close by her side.

"I understand," he said, with compassion, now back in the Indian picture. After he said good-night, he tipped his hat and reclaimed his place on the horse.

After Nina finished eating, she curled up in a lap blanket and tried to get lost in a sappy romantic comedy, but images of Josh kept popping up in her thoughts. Not able to follow the film, Nina decided to call it a night. She let Cassie outside, cleaned her dishes, and after Cassie came in, she headed to bed.

Lying down, Nina was hoping to fall asleep quickly, but thoughts kept racing through her mind. Maybe her mom was right, she thought. It was possible she was over-thinking and putting too much energy into analyzing and dissecting a relationship with Josh. She liked being with him, and so far she hadn't noticed many flaws. In fact, he had very many good qualities; his handsome looks and sexy build were an added bonus. Portland wasn't that far, convincing herself. They could take turns making the drive; the road did go both ways. It all sounded so easy and doable, but something still felt off, she just couldn't zero in on it. Best to stay friends she thought as sleep slowly pulled her into the first of many bizarre dreams.

The next morning Nina hit the snooze alarm three times before getting up. She hadn't slept well and felt half asleep as she climbed out of the comfy warm bed. With a head full of fog, Nina rubbed her red sleep-deprived eyes as she tended to her personal needs. Then, dressed in her barn clothes she dragged her body downstairs. After starting a pot of coffee, she and Cassie went to the barn to tend to the animals. She had finally gained the respect of most of the farm crew. However, Gerdy was still standing her guard but was starting to warm up to her. The momma goat, for the most part, ignored her and decided she wasn't a threat. So she allowed Nina to feed her babies. She had found a way to feed the pigs without going into the pen. So as long as everything was fine with the pigs, Nina no longer had to worry about a spa day in the mud.

Molly, glassy-eyed and half asleep mumbled a good morning to her daughter entering the back door. Then she poured herself a cup of coffee and took a seat at the table.

"You shouldn't stay out partying so late," sending her mom a teasing smile, while she fixed her coffee and joined Molly at the table.

"I know, right," she laughed. "After Dave took me to dinner we went to see a movie, and afterward pie and coffee. I think it was midnight when I got home," she admitted covering a yawn.

"Well, I'm glad you're having fun and enjoying yourself. It's about time," Nina said lovingly patting her hand.

"Me too," Molly blushed, and then pointing at her foot, remarked, "I will be so happy to part with this`lovely boot."

"I bet," Nina sympathized. "How much longer?"

"About three weeks and I'll be released to drive, maybe sooner depending on how fast it heals," taking a sip of her coffee.

"Then look out mom. There's going to be a racehorse out of the gate," she laughed.

"Well maybe not that crazy," she said joining in on the laughter.

"And speaking of horses, I'm going over to Josh's tonight. He is going to teach me how to ride."

"Oh," Molly said with a surprised look, trying to picture her prim and proper daughter on top of a horse. "You don't even like horses," looking at Nina over her coffee cup.

"I know crazy huh? But Josh thinks we might have to travel far to get to the mine. He says it will be faster by horseback." Nina said wondering if she was crazy for agreeing.

"Are you sure that's possible?" questioning her daughter's decision.

"I don't know," Nina shrugged, "at least I'll be ready if we can. Well, I'd better be getting to work," Nina remarked, kissing her mom's cheek, bussing the table, and quickly cleaning the kitchen.

At five, Nina escorted her last customer to the door, performed her nightly closing routine, changed into her new sweater and boot-cut jeans. She completed the fun outfit with riding boots, which she had been wearing all day under her long skirt, hoping to break them in. Nina smiled at her image in the long mirror in the back room and said aloud, "Yes, this will do." Then she asked herself what she was going to do with all the new Western-style clothes she'd purchased. Where was she going to wear them back home? Maybe she would take Rene up on the invitation to Wednesday night line-dance lessons. Wouldn't that blow her away? Nina laughed out loud picturing her friend's expression. That reminded Nina to make a note to call her tomorrow and fill her in on life down on the farm, giggling at her choice of words.

Nina arrived at Josh's front gate and wondered if this is what it felt like entering a movie star's estate as she announced her name to the speaker. Then watching the large iron gate open, she drove onto Josh's property. She was in awe as she slowly cruised down the tree-lined driveway. Every tree was placed strategically along the fence line on both sides of the road, and when the house came into view; her eyes grew wide with wonder. It was beautiful, she thought, almost magical. She'd never given much thought to where Josh lived or what it would look like, but she was sure this was not the image. Could she see herself living here? She asked herself. What was with that question? Of course not, she was a city girl. Pushing that notion aside, Nina smiled at the sight of Josh, standing by a beautiful country home surrounded by a bountiful landscaped yard. She swore every bush, flowering plant, and small tree was perfectly manicured. Pulling up next to his truck, he opened her door and offered his hand, as she climbed out of her car.

"Wow, this place is amazing! Don't you ever get lonely out here?" Nina asked taking in her surroundings.

"Nope, inside the house, Whiski, and my cat Moses keep me company and entertained, and at the barn," pointing down a narrow driveway, "the hens are always full of gossip. There's always a guarantee Selma and Louise; the comedian goat duo, will offer a talent show. The cows keep mostly to themselves, except when hungry or on occasion desire my attention." Then pausing a moment, he tossed the ball for the anxious dog dancing at his feet. "And, if I need to get away and think, I choose a horse and go for a long ride. There are miles of amazing wilderness trails to cover here," he said looking at the hills. "When you are comfortable riding, I'll take you there." Then taking hold of her hand, he escorted Nina up the steps to his house.

We'll see," Nina said. "It does sound like you have a full life here."

"Yes, very fulfilling and rewarding," he concluded, when they reached the front porch.

Nina admitted she liked being close to him and the feel of his hand in hers. She wondered though, with all he had already in his life, would he ever have room for someone else, and could she fit here. Oh no! Red-flags were signaling to her that she was getting too close, and the Practicality Board in her mind was luring her back with memories of life in the city. But try as they may, the images were faded. More recent, clearer ones, took their place. Now, what was she going to do? Freaking out, she let go of Josh's hand as they approached the door.

13) THE DANCE

Nina stepped into the foyer, and a large cat was there to inspect his guest. Approval complete, he turned on his motor and rubbed his body against her leg. "So you must be Moses," Nina said squatting to examine the cat. "You are such a big baby," reaching out and petting the feline.

"Now you have done it," Josh laughed. "You've gained an honorary pest for good," also bending to scratch his furry child.

It wasn't long before Whiski noticed the cat hogging all the attention, and barged her way onto the scene. Her action pushed Moses to the side, and at the same time, knocked Nina off balance; landing her on the floor.

"Whiski that wasn't nice," Nina scolded, then laughed as the dog snuggled up to her, offering her wet kisses. Moses, after recovering from the powerful nudge sauntered over to join the party.

"See, how could anyone be lonely with these two clowns around?" he said smiling as he watched the sweet girl on his floor. Her laughter and loving presence filled the room. It was as though she belonged there, Josh thought. Nina was capturing the hearts of his animals and slowly easing her way into his.

"Okay guys, she's had enough of your hospitality," he said breaking up the welcome committee. Then as he was helping her up, she fell into him.

Their eyes locked and hearts racing, the couple turned off the world around them. Nina knew there were many things wrong with this involvement, but it felt right. Luckily the Committee in Charge of Personal Space and Boundaries waved their flags to get her attention. Recognizing the signal, Nina smiled and stepped back. She pretended to brush the fur off her clothes and said. "So are you going to show me your lovely house?"

"Yes, and after that, I have prepared dinner for us," also shaking off the effects of their near contact.

"When did you have time to cook?" Nina asked tilting her head.

"It's not much. I hope you like club sandwiches."

"My favorite," Nina expressed. "Come on take me on a tour so we can eat," grabbing his hand she dragged him along.

When they were through, Nina commented, "you have a beautiful home," following Josh to the kitchen.

"It works," Josh smiled as he prepared dinner.

"What can I do?" Nina asked wanting to help.

"Nothing, sit and relax, I have it under control. If you want, there's beer and wine in the fridge."

"Thanks but I'm going to pass since I'll be riding a horse."

"I don't think the horses will mind, and as far as I know, there's no police riding around in my corral. So I think it's okay if you indulge a little," Josh smirked.

"Ha ha," she said rolling her eyes. "I want to have a clear head when I get on the horse, that's all. I'll stick with water."

"I understand," Joshed laughed. "There's bottled water in the fridge. While you're there could you please grab me a beer? And it's time to eat," he said setting the food on the table.

"Looks yummy," Nina said taking a seat.

"I think you will find all of the four food groups," he said twisting the top off his beer.

"Mmm," Nina mumbled taking a bite.

"Well, are you ready to tear up the dance floor tomorrow?" Josh teased opening up a conversation.

"Oh sure, that's what I'm going to do," she sarcastically answered.

"You'll be fine," Josh said, giving her confidence.

"We'll see," she chuckled.

"Speaking of the dance, my sister called and she'll be down tomorrow. She has some news regarding the mine and wants to tell us in person," he said, taking a pull from his beer.

"I can't wait to meet her and hear what she has to report," Nina replied biting into her sandwich. "Maybe she'll have some information that will help with this crazy mystery." She rescued a piece of hanging bacon and licked the grease from her fingers.

Well, she will be staying with me and going to the dance, so you will have plenty of time to visit." Then noticing a speck of food on Nina's face, he added: "You have something on your cheek."

"Where?" she asked.

Picking up his napkin, he dipped the corner of it in her water and removed the particle of food.

His touch sent chills down Nina's spine and left her face tingling. "Thank you," she blushed, "you can't take me anywhere," adding humor to the tender moment. "So tell me more about your sister and parents," she asked with interest.

"Jennifer is eight years older than me. She's married to a good man, his name is Kevin, and he is a CEO of a large corporation. He recently decided to update and enhance his website to get a stronger online presence."

"Sounds like we would have a lot in common," Nina interjected her opinion. "Please go on."

"She and Kevin are about to celebrate their twentieth anniversary, I think," searching his memory bank to be sure. "They have two daughters; Rebecca; nineteen and Katherine; eighteen. They are both attending college in Corvallis. Such beautiful girls," he said pointing to their pictures on his family portrait wall.

"They are gorgeous," Nina remarked with a sincere smile. "So tell me about your mom and dad. Do they live around here?"

"No, they live in Arizona; the hot weather helps their arthritis. I also think they grew tired of the rain and cold weather here," offering a piece of ham to his very patient furry children. "Dad has a business troubleshooting computer issues and is an on-call fireman for the city. Mom is a part-time bookkeeper and the rest of her time is spent taking care of dad and volunteering at the local food center."

"They sound like some very special people. I see now why helping the community is so important to you," Nina replied.

"Yes, we were raised to give back and always be there for our neighbors," Josh replied proudly.

"Do you get to see them much?" Nina asked getting to know this cowboy on a personal level.

"Not as much as I'd like," Josh replied thinking about them. "I try to go there at least four times a year, and they usually visit in late summer for a month. They divide their time between Jennifer and me. It gives them a break from the intense heat." Then finishing off his beer he said, "That's enough about me. What can you tell me about Nina?" turning the attention her way.

"You already know about me," she replied avoiding the question.

"I'm sure there's much more about Miss Charm I don't know," he said with a coy smile.

"You'll have to wait and see," Nina replied suddenly feeling uncomfortable. "It's getting late, and if we don't do this horse thing soon, we'll have to try this again some other time," she commented jumping up from the table.

"Okay, but we are going to revisit this conversation later," eyebrows raised, making it clear he was serious.

Ten minutes later, Nina was standing in the barn next to Josh as he introduced her to his two horses.

Scanning her surroundings, she commented. "Wow, a person could live down here. Except for a stove for cooking, this place has all the amenities of a hotel."

"I guess it does," Josh laughed, "only the best for my babies, right Majestic," hugging his neck. "And I do believe there is a camp stove in the other shed," he added with a smile.

"He is definitely a big boy," Nina said through gritted teeth keeping her distance.

"Don't let the size be intimidating. He's nothing but a big baby," Josh said assuring Nina while putting the saddle on his back. "You can move closer. I promise he won't bite."

Nina took a few steps towards the animal and reached out her hand. Majestic snorted and stretched his head, startling her and causing her to step back. "I don't think he likes me."

"He likes everyone; come here Nina," motioning her over to the horse. Then taking her hand, he placed it on Majestic's head. "Be gentle," he said letting go of her hand.

"Nice boy," Nina said feeling more confident as she ran her hand down his mane; staying close to the horse while Josh saddled Starlet.

When he finished, he turned to Nina and said, "I forgot their carrots and apples at the house. Will you be okay here with them for a few minutes?"

"Yeah, we'll be fine," Nina answered waving him to go.

After he left, Nina walked over to Starlet, gently stroked her mane and whispered, "you don't seem that wild to me, and I'd prefer to ride you." Then not wanting to hurt Majestic's feelings she added, "Nothing against you boy, it's just that you are so big. Besides, us girls need to stick together, right Starlet?" Then as if the mare understood, she shook her head and whinnied. "I'm glad you agree. Now let's show Josh we can do this. Remember to be easy on me, I'm new at this," Nina reminded the horse as she stepped into the stirrup.

When Nina attempted to pull herself up on her back, she realized Starlet's head was behind her. "Great, not doing so good, girl. I'm pretty sure that I should be facing your neck instead of your behind," she giggled. "Let me turn around and well be ready to go," she instructed. But when Nina twisted to change her position, her leg nudged the horse in the ribs, giving Starlet the signal to go. "Wait what are you doing?" Nina said in a panic. She had both legs on the same side of the horse, and her foot stuck in the stirrup. "Stop horsee," Nina demanded trying to hold on. "Whoa," she tried. "Starlet stop now," she pleaded. And if she weren't already in a predicament, to make matters worse, she'd manage to get her shirt caught in a hook on the reins.

"Noooo, we can't go there, I'm not ready." Then as Starlet headed for the arena, Nina freaked and let loose a loud yell. "Help! Bad horsee," she scolded as the horse started prancing around the ring.

Josh had just entered the stables when he heard Nina's piercing scream. He hurried as he followed the call into the arena. Stepping through the gate, Josh took in the sight while trying to hide his smile. "Trick riding isn't until lesson five, and I'm fairly certain that move is not part of the course," he laughed.

"Oh you think this is funny, well maybe I'm trying out for the circus," Nina snapped with a sarcastic tongue. "Now could you please get control of your crazy horse?"

Josh knew Starlet was only having fun and would never hurt Nina, but by the looks-could-kill expression on the girl's face, he figured it was best to call her in. "Come here

Star," he sweetly beckoned to his horse. Starlet slowed her pace and immediately came to Josh. "Good girl," he praised, rewarding her with a carrot.

"Good girl!" Nina shrieked. "She's a brat!"

"I warned you she was a little spirited. What were you doing on her anyway?" Josh asked working to get her shirt off the hook.

"She looked so sweet and calm," Nina replied as Josh lifted her off the horse.

"Looks can be deceiving," he quoted. "Come on; I'll get you on Majestic, he's much mellower."

"You know," Nina said giving it some thought standing by the mare. "I think I'll ride Starlet."

"Are you sure?"

"Yes, positive."

"Maybe this time sit on the saddle," he teased.

"Such a comedian Mr. Parker," she replied playfully snubbing him.

"Good to see I've made it back into your high graces, Miss Charm," tipping his hat leading Starlet back to the barn.

After they finished, Josh walked Nina to her car. Leaning against the door, she let herself fall into a dreamy kiss, and lingered in Josh's embrace, taking comfort in his strong arms. Even though she was getting off track and heading for complicated territory, Nina was having fun, enjoying the ride, and wanted to explore the detour into fantasy-land. It was obvious her mind was no longer in charge; her heart was driving the train. It wasn't as though she was all in; there were still reservations traveling behind in the caboose.

The next morning Nina awoke with a new perspective. She felt energized and revitalized. Wow, that must've been some kiss, she thought touching her lips. There was still the issue with the long-distance battle, but Nina decided to set it aside. Today was all about the dance, as she moved to the music coming from her music app on her cell phone. She felt like a young girl the day before the prom; nervous butterfly stomach and excitement rolled into a ball of anticipation. Her mom had decided to close the store so Nina could be available to assist her with the preparations for the night's event. She needed to get moving. There were animals to feed, then a shower, and she wanted to devote a couple of hours towards her job. There were emails to answer and tasks needing her attention.

Nina and Molly arrived at the barn close to noon. As Nina stepped through the door, the sound of chatter and joyous laughter filled the partially decorated room. Scanning the area, she zeroed in on Josh. He and three other guys were busy setting up the tables. Sensing her presence, he gave her a sexy smile. Nina smiled back and sent a delicate wave. She was relieved she had decided to wear her new jeans, sweater, and boots instead of her original plan of sweats and tennis shoes, also scoring brownie points for adding a touch of makeup.

"Nina," Molly called to her distracted daughter.

"I was looking at all the tables," she fibbed.

"Well that strong, handsome table has lots of work to do and so do you," she giggled.

Nina remained quiet and gave her a mom a snarly look.

"Let's go and gather the committee together for a short check-in meeting," taking her hand and leading her to a large table.

Nina was impressed as she watched her mom take charge. Within minutes the excited and anxious members were assembled at the table waiting for direction. Nina had to hand it to her, she had everything organized, and after going down the list, everyone went off to tackle their tasks.

Nina had table duty which involved dressing them with linen tablecloths. Then giving them personality, she assembled a flower and candle display then placed it in the center. When she finished and was satisfied with her outcome, she offered her assistance and filled in where she was needed. With everyone working together as a team, the building became transformed. "Looks a like a party is happening here," Nina said surveying the room. "What else is left to do?" she said turning to her mother.

"We're done here. The caterers and band will be here around 5:30 so we can go home now. Give me a couple of minutes," she said, her leg propped up on a small crate.

"Does it hurt much?" Nina asked with a worried look in her eyes.

"Not bad sweetie. I've probably been on it too much today," she admitted. "I'll rest it awhile when we get home. I am ready when you are," slowly moving her leg and standing up.

Molly took a cat nap while Nina spent time tossing the ball for Cassie. The dog needed exercise, and she needed to burn off some of her nervous anxiety. It was a dance, nothing more Nina told herself, but her self-talk didn't even sound convincing. Then she thought about going to Shaniko the next day, and that took her mind to another level of anxiety, so instead, she tried to clear her mind. After her arm grew tired, she went inside to get ready. Dave would be there soon to escort them to the dance.

Nina was in the kitchen, making coffee, being especially careful not to stain her beige lace dress, when her mom walked in. Nina couldn't remember the last time she'd seen her so dressed up. She was beaming in her mid-length purple flowing dress. She even detected a long lost gleam appearing in her eyes again. "Look at you, with the dress off the shoulders; sexy momma," Nina teased.

"You don't think it's too much, do you?" Molly asked second-guessing her choice.

"Not at all," Nina assured her. "Dave won't be able to take his eyes off you."

"Here," she said handing her mom a small gift bag.

"What's this?" Molly asked accepting the bag.

"Open it and find out," Nina commented in anticipation of her reaction.

"What is it?" Molly said, inspecting two strands of shiny beads.

"They're boot bling." Then taking them, Nina wrapped one around each boot and secured it on the inside of the leg. "I know how uncomfortable it is for you to wear that boot, so I thought to add a little decoration to it, might make you feel better."

"They're so pretty, thank you" Molly expressed looking down at the shiny objects, drawing attention to her boots, her eyes watering as she thanked her for the gift.

"Now don't cry, you'll ruin your makeup," Nina said also pushing back the tears.

Molly took Nina hands as she faced her daughter. "Have I told you lately how much I love you and how happy I am to have you here? You look like a goddess in lace; such a beautiful woman. Josh is going to be fighting off all the young men at the dance."

"Oh mom pleeease," she expressed. "Let's get a picture. Sara will never believe, that our mom went out in public showing skin," she giggled as they posed for several pictures. "I'm also going to send these to Rene; she's going to freak."

"Hey, is that the amethyst set dad gave you at Christmas a few years ago?" Nina asked fondling the stone.

"Uh huh," Molly answered followed by a long sigh.

"Pretty," Nina said admiring the stone. "I'm wearing the pearls he bought for me when I graduated from high school," proudly showing them off. "Looks like dad is going with us tonight," she commented lovingly.

"You think he minds me dating Dave," Molly asked with a frown.

Nina smiled and replied, "Of course not, I'm sure he approves. If not, he'd probably find a way to let us know," she laughed.

Their emotional moment was broken by the sound of Cassie's bark, alerting them to a visitor approaching the house. Nina opened the door and greeted the handsome man. Dave arrived dressed in black jeans, a western shirt, and shiny pointed boots. A leather belt with a flashy silver buckle completed the polished look. "Very nice," Nina said giving a friendly compliment.

Dave tipped his hat, "You also Miss Charm." Then he gave a beaming smile as Molly walked into the room. "You look beautiful Mol. Be still my heart," he replied hugging her.

"Oh Dave," Molly said playfully dismissing his comment, but Nina could tell she was enjoying the attention.

"You two are going to be the envy of all the women in the room. And I get the honor of escorting you to the dance," helping Molly with her coat.

"Nina, I remembered the ghost town information," he said pointing to a small satchel on the table.

"Awesome," Nina expressed, "thank you. I can't wait to go through it," picking up the bag as she walked out the door.

When they reached the truck, Dave surprised Molly with a white corsage, and with nervous hands, he pinned it to her dress.

Nina, seeing her mom on the verge of tears, commented, "Where's mine?"

"I'm sorry Nina, I only have one," Dave apologized. "Besides I think that is Josh's job," winking as he opened the door for her.

When they pulled into the entrance leading to the barn, Nina grew more excited as she took in her surroundings. Strings of twinkling lights wrapped around the fence lit the passage, and parking attendants with glow-in-the-dark aprons directed people to their spots. Given that Molly was disabled and the event planner, Dave was allowed to park up front. Nina was moving to the sound of the band as she and Molly linked arms with Dave, as he so gallantly led them to the door.

Nina was impressed. It wasn't like what she'd imagined. A sharply dressed man greeted them at the door, then a young girl in a short dress, all smiles and flirting with a cute cowboy, took her coat. Dave took Molly to a table while Nina stood there perusing the room. She was so focused on Josh, she never noticed all the heads turning when she removed her coat, but Josh had noticed and wasn't happy about their gawking. Wasting no time, he made his way through the crowd. They were all going to know that she was his girl.

"Hey beautiful," he said loud enough for a group with leering eyes to hear. Then taking Nina in his arms, he passionately kissed her.

"Wow," Nina said feeling a little dizzy. "I wasn't expecting that," giving him an affectionate smile.

"The element of surprise," he said raising his eyebrows. "And I have another," he reached into his coat and pulled out a little box. It was a small purple corsage attached to a bracelet.

"Oh, this flower is very sweet," Nina said gazing at the pretty gift. "I love it." She surprised Josh with a kiss on the cheek.

He then wrapped his arms around her waist and replied. "Thought you would. Now I want you to meet my sister," leading her to a table close to the band.

After introductions, Nina sat down at the table and easily fell into conversation, their voices competing with the loud music. After a bubbly waitress took their drink order, Josh asked Nina for a dance. Hesitantly she put her hand in his.

Sensing her fear, he whispered, "You've got this Miss Charm."

Laughing at his comment, she walked with him to the dance floor, joining a line dance already in progress. After a few attempts, Nina fell into the pattern. By the end of two songs, Nina and Josh stepped out of line to dance together. Before long, Nina was starting to relax and have fun. She was a little disappointed when the band called for a break. It would, however, give her time to get some water and use the ladies' room. On her way, she slipped by her mom's table long enough to say hi and meet her friends. After engaging in some small talk, Nina excused herself and continued to her destination.

On her way back, she felt a welcoming breeze from the open door. Deciding to grab some fresh air, Nina stepped outside. But while she was standing by a large tree near the building, she felt someone grab her arm and pull her into the darkness.

"Who are you? And get your hand off me!" she demanded and yanked her arm from his clutches.

"Who I am is not important," a deep voice replied. "Let me assure you. I will not hurt you. I am only here as a messenger."

"What do you want?" Nina asked trying to get a description of the mysterious man. She could barely make out the image. From what she could see, he was wearing a long duster coat and a tall hat.

"I've heard you and your friend have been sneaking around the town of Shaniko," he commented.

"What I do, and with whom, is none of your business," Nina replied with a snarly attitude.

"I'm making it my business. If you're smart, you'll stay away from there from now on."

"Is that a threat?" Nina asked trying to cover her fear as a chill ran down her back.

"Let's say it's a warning," the stranger replied. Then tipping his hat, he walked away.

That was strange Nina thought. She hugged herself as she watched him walk to the parking lot. A shiver crawled down her back as he approached his beat-up pickup truck. She swore it was the same pickup that followed her the day she ventured to Shaniko.

14) THE MINE

After Nina collected herself, she hurried inside to tell Josh what had happened.

"Did he hurt you?" Josh asked with an alarmed look in his eyes. He wasted no time pulling her into a tight embrace.

"No, I'm okay, maybe a little shaken up," she admitted.

Then he closely scanned her body, making sure there were no obvious marks. "I'll be right back," Josh said his face red with fury especially after noticing the red marks on her arm. He gathered a couple of friends on his way to help him search for the jerk.

"Can I get you anything?" Jennifer asked with concern, scooting her chair close to Nina's.

"No I'm fine, thank you. I wonder why that guy was so interested in my trips to Shaniko."

"I don't know, but speaking of which, I have some interesting news regarding the ownership of the mine." Pulling a folder from her large purse, she handed it to Nina.

Before she could open it, Molly and Dave appeared at the table. "Nina dear, are you okay?" Molly asked worry lines showing on her face.

"Yes, Mom, how did you find out?"

"Word travels fast in a small venue," she replied. "What did he want with you?"

Molly listened while her daughter shared her harrowing experience. When she finished, Molly showed her protective nature and gave Nina motherly advice. "I don't think you should be going there anymore."

"I agree with your mom," Dave interjected siding with Molly. "This man, who approached you tonight, could be dangerous."

Molly smiled at him for expressing his concern. Then turning her attention back to Nina, she lectured, "You need to stop your infatuation with the ghost town and the gold mine; they don't concern you," she spoke mostly out of fear.

"Uh, that isn't totally true," Jennifer cautiously interrupted. "I hate to add another level of complication to this mess, but you might want to look inside that." She pointed to the folder on the table.

Nina gave her a baffled look, and then she pulled out a document and started reading. "What? This can't be," she said, a look of shock on her face.

"What is it?" Molly asked lifting the paper out of Nina's fingers. "How can this be?" also blindsided by the discovery.

"I can explain," Jennifer said in a calm voice trying to clear up the confusion. However, before she had a chance, Josh reappeared.

"I couldn't find any sign of him. He must have left, and nobody remembers seeing him," Josh reported, disappointment written on his face. "I did clue in the Sheriff, so he is aware of the situation." He took a seat next to Nina. He felt frustrated.

"You did what you could," Nina said offering a sympathetic smile. "Hopefully the Sheriff will find something. For now we'll have to wait," lovingly patting him on his leg. "You're back in time, Jennifer was about to tell us the history of the deed."

After everyone settled, Jennifer relayed the news. "It seems that your Uncle John and Thomas Parker were co-owners of the mine. If one died, the other inherited the deed. When both were gone, it passed from generation to generation," Jennifer said, taking a sip of wine. "John's children, Amos and Jacob, were the first to inherit it." She paused for a moment as the band reassembled, then she was forced to raise her voice over the music.

"That's when things got a little fuzzy," she said pausing for thought. "It took awhile to find, what we refer to as, a break in the chain of title. After digging into dusty archived boxes,

I discovered someone by the name of Clyde Burton had purchased it."

"What happened next?" Molly asked totally engaged in the story.

"Well, I continued tracing the trail which led me to your dad, Nina. He must have come across it, and after researching the township page discovered it was available and purchased it."

"He must have found it hidden in the frame," Nina concluded.

"Funny, he didn't say anything about that to me. Are you sure it was his name on the deed?" Molly asked with a confused look.

"I believe so. Was your husband Joe Charm?" she asked Molly.

"Yes," Molly nodded. "Wonder why he kept it a secret?" she asked to no one in particular.

"That I don't know. Maybe he didn't think it was that important," Jennifer responded. "I realize that you are all overwhelmed with what I have shared with you today. I am also sorry that it has awakened any hidden skeletons," she said showing compassion to all the eyes full of uncertainty.

Then Jennifer gave her attention to Nina. "Since you and your sister are the next living relatives, you are the rightful owners. I checked, and there are no overlapping rights, and he paid the fees. All you have to do is sign this document, and the Golden Vein Mine is yours," handing her the legal paper and pen.

"What does all this mean?" Nina sent her a puzzled look as she signed the paper.

"Yeah, is there gold in them thar hills?" Josh said being funny trying to break the tension consuming the group.

"I don't know, it closed many years ago, and I'm not even sure you can get to it," Jennifer said, filing the paper away in her satchel.

"How far is this mine from Shaniko?" Nina asked hoping to find out how long she'd be stuck on the horse tomorrow.

"I think it's about thirty miles," Dave answered. "There's a map in the folder I gave you."

"Hmm," Nina said reaching for the folder.

Josh put his hand on Nina's. "This can wait, we came here to dance." He guided the laughing girl out to the dance floor.

By eleven o'clock, Nina was danced out. Not to mention, her feet were protesting and wanted out of her new boots. She was also eager to see what was in the goody bag Dave had given her. So she, Jennifer, and Josh went to his house. Dave stayed with Molly as she met with the three sober survivors of the clean-up committee.

Back at Josh's, the three of them sat in the living room. They were relaxed and sipped tea Jennifer had graciously made, while Nina went through the bag. "Dave was right. Here is a map to the mine," Nina said finding the prize. After studying it a couple of minutes, she passed it to Josh. Then reaching into the bag, she pulled out another piece of history and read a few lines on a pamphlet. She commented, "Quite an interesting little town."

Nina yawned.

Noticing the sleepy-eyed girl, Josh suggested, "Maybe we should call it a day. It's getting late."

"Sounds good to me," Jennifer replied standing up to stretch. "I'll see you in the morning bro, and it was nice meeting you Nina," she gave hugs on her way to bed.

"I should probably get going myself," Nina said gathering her purse and coat.

"I'll walk you out," Josh politely offered, escorting her to the car. "I guess I'll see you tomorrow," Nina said staring into his eyes, "I hope you can step back in time with me."

"I'll try my best," Josh assured her.

"I don't know if I can do it alone," she admitted, her eyes full of doubt.

"Sure you can," Josh replied giving her the courage, even though he didn't want her there without him. "You've got this Nina, there's nothing to worry about, and Lucia will be there to guide you."

Nina didn't know why, but his comment had rubbed her the wrong way. It could've been that her emotions were already raw. Whatever it was, Josh was there, and he had no vote whether she nominated him to be her sounding board. Without warning, she started spewing her thoughts his way. "Really Josh," hands on her hips, "first of all I'll be going back in time, to a place I barely know and most people there won't acknowledge me unless they're green. Sounds perfectly normal to me," she expressed with a sarcastic tongue. "And if that isn't bad enough, the lady driving this stagecoach in this twisted fantasy; my guardian angel, is a lush!" Nina added throwing her arms up in frustration.

"Ah, Nina..." Josh said trying to squeeze in a comment, but with her eyes, ready to shoot daggers his way, he quickly closed his mouth. He kept telling himself she was only venting and not to take anything she said or did personally. He took a deep breath and listened to her.

"Let's not forget; I'm going to be riding a horse I've never been on before, after only one riding lesson," holding up her index finger. "Trusting I find a horse, I will be traveling to a gold mine without GPS. The only thing I will have to guide me is a map that is over a hundred years old and a magic coin. Then, if I make it to the destination, I won't have any idea what is going to happen," shaking her head at the thought.

Josh, finding an opening, spoke his thoughts, "What happened to that strong and independent woman I first met, who tested my patience and rode on my nerves?" he said with a laugh, hoping to calm her down. But his attempt backfired as her emotional gates opened again, and let loose more of her pent-up feelings.

"I'll tell you what happened, Mr. Parker," Nina said preparing her case, "I have been countrified. Yep, that's it," she said strutting around like a proud rooster, impressed by her new word. "Since I've been here, I've been attacked by a maniac chicken, jabbed in the ribs by an overprotective mama goat, and wallowed in the mud with some oversized pigs," sending out a nervous giggle. "I also went to church smelling like a slough and played by a horse that has a spirited sense of humor. And can't forget my encounters with the supernatural, and..." then she stopped in mid-sentence.

Josh watched as Nina's expression changed, and her stance lost its power, she reminded him of a lost child as she reached for the words to finish her thought.

"And... this creepy looking man grabbed me, pulled me aside, then delivered a threatening message to me," she expressed. Then feeling weak, Nina leaned up against her vehicle and slid down the side. Feeling exhausted and drained, she grabbed her knees, covered her head with her arms and collapsed into tears.

Josh was immediately by her side as he pulled the fragile girl into his arms, and held her tightly until she stopped shaking. Then when he felt her body let go, he wiped her eyes. He smiled and commented, "Better?"

"Yes much, thank you," she replied taking comfort in his arms. "I feel very ashamed. I don't have any idea what lit the fuse."

"I would be willing to guess the man in the duster was holding the match. I think he had more of a traumatizing impact on you than you realized," he said offering his assumption.

"Could be" rubbing her sore arm and considering the idea. "I am surprised you're still here with me after my crazy outburst."

"Let's say I'm intrigued by the many facets that make up your personality."

"What my lunatic side?" Nina smirked.

"No, your human side. Nina, everyone breaks down, and after what you've been through, I'm surprised it's taken this long," he said helping her up. "I don't think you're in any shape to go there alone. If I don't make it, I'm calling you back. Your uncle will have to find another way out of his predicament."

"I can't...," but before Nina could finish her sentence, Josh whispered, "Shhh," placing his finger on her lips. "There's no negotiating this one, understand?"

Nina gave him thumbs up and moved his hand, and reaching up; she brushed her lips lightly against his. "Goodnight Josh, and thank you," she said giving him a loving smile.

"Sure, but for what?" he asked slightly confused.

"For being here," she expressed getting into her car.

Nina awoke the next morning with a nagging headache. She blamed it on stress. Hopefully, after an aspirin, it would be a pain in the past. When she went down for coffee, Nina found a note from her mom. "Morning dear, Dave came by early to take me to church; he also was a sweet man and fed the barn animals. See you later, Love Mom."

"Perfect," Nina said aloud. Now she wouldn't have to fabricate a lie on where she was going. With any luck, they'd be home by early evening, and then her mom will never know she went to Shaniko again. Nina should be happy it was working to her advantage; however, the deceit bug was biting her. But how could she explain to her mom something she didn't even understand. Brushing off the thought, she poured a cup of coffee, made a light breakfast and sat down to re-group. When she finished, noticing she was running behind, Nina went upstairs to get ready. She still needed to stop off at the market, hopefully, pick up John, and then be at Josh's by ten. Today is going to be such a crazy day, Nina said shaking her head at the thought.

Thirty minutes later, Nina had dressed in her jeans, flannel, and new traveling boots. After making a coffee for the road and packing a bag of snacks, she gave loving pats to Cassie and headed out.

Down the road, Josh was also preparing for their adventure. He was going over the notes Nina had written for him, things he needed to do and what to expect. After he finished, he walked into the kitchen. Jennifer greeted him with a smile and handed him a cup of coffee, and then went back to preparing breakfast. "Thanks, sis, I could get used to this." he said sitting at the table, "you want to come live here?" he teased.

Jennifer gave him a fake smile, "There's nothing more I'd want to do dear brother than to play housekeeper and cook for you, but I have a job and a husband. You'll have to find another sucker," she said with a laugh placing a plate of pancakes on the table.

"Can't blame a guy for trying," he replied fixing his plate. "Look great, thanks, sis."

"So, what was all that commotion outside last night?" Jennifer asked, sitting down to join him.

"Nina had a small meltdown," Josh answered.

"Is she okay?" Jennifer asked with concern.

"Yes, I think the run-in with that man last night spooked her."

"Poor thing," she said showing concern. "Such a sweet girl. Nothing like the monster you described," frowning at her brother.

"I didn't say that... exactly, besides she's changed," he admitted.

Jennifer, seeing the spark in her brother's eyes, expressed happily, "You're in love with her!"

Josh looked away, as he thought about Nina. "Even if I was, she's never going to move here. I know we should stop it before it gets any more involved, but I can't seem to let go," Josh said looking back at his sister.

"Does she know you love her?"

"No, and I'm not going to tell her, it would only make it more difficult when we say goodbye," he said with determination.

"Who knows, maybe it will work out somehow," she replied with a wink and offering him a loving hug. "Now if you will excuse me I need to clean up, pack, and get going. I told Roger I'd be home early. We're going to dinner with friends."

"Go ahead and get ready, I'll take care of the dishes," he said waving her away, giving thought to her last comment.

Nina parked outside her mom's market. She took a mental moment before going in, and it was clear that today she'd need many of them to survive. Her idea had to work, or there was no use going to the little ghost town. After a couple of deep breaths, she went into the store.

"I thought you'd never get here," John exclaimed as Nina approached the picture.

"Sorry," Nina yawned. "I got in late last night, and I am low on coffee, so give me a little slack here," she said yawning again.

"I heard you come in. How was the dance?"

"I didn't embarrass myself, so that's a plus," she laughed. "In fact, I kept up fairly well. Now I can honestly say, I've been to a down-home country barn dance. I was having fun until I was accosted by a strange man, who creeped me out with his threatening message."

"Oh, Nina, what happened?" John said with concern.

Nina sighed and then briefly shared her story.

"I have to believe this may be my fault," John admitted after Nina finished.

"Why would you say that?" Nina asked with wonder.

"Never should have purchased that mine, it's brought me nothing but problems. It's cursed, I tell you," shaking his fist. "It cost me a good friend, my health, and led to an early demise. Not to mention, I've been kept a prisoner in this picture and only given a selective memory. It left a blank slate in my mind, where I can only see my family in my dreams," he said pacing back and forth with his hands locked behind his back. Then staring directly at Nina with hard eyes, he said, "Now its devious golden vines are pulling you into its trap."

"Really, a curse, Uncle J?" shaking her head. "Don't you think you're a little irrational?" Nina asked questioning his belief. "Besides you're freaking me out, and I'm already stressing. Can't we focus on something positive that has come out of this?"

"What might that be?" John asked with a sharp tongue.

"How about the fact, we've been brought together from two different eras? That is beyond amazing," Nina said with a loving smile.

"There is that. I have found the beauty and glowing personality of my great-niece," he said reciprocating the feeling.

"Ah, Uncle J, I would hug you if it were possible. Now let's put our Zen moment on hold. We need to test out my experiment and get to Josh's," she said reaching into her purse.

"Speaking of the boy, how are you two doing?"

"Fine, good," Nina said, thinking about her meltdown last night and wondering where she stood with Josh.

"Well, I think you two make a lovely couple."

"We are not a couple, Uncle J," Nina confirmed.

"Whatever you say, my lovely niece, I see otherwise" he smirked.

Nina ignored his comment and rolled her eyes. "Let's get moving. Josh is waiting."

"What do I do?" John asked stepping closer to the edge of the frame.

"I made this five-by-seven print of the picture you're in, and I am hoping you can transfer into it," showing John the print.

"You want me to go in there?" he asked hesitantly.

"Yes, and please hurry, we have to go," Nina stressed.

Nina watched as the picture on the wall returned to normal. However, the image of her uncle on the print she was holding, remained frozen. "Uncle J where are you?" she asked searching for him in the other pictures. "Oh no, I lost my uncle," Nina said wondering what to do. Then hearing his voice, she looked down at the print.

"Whew, I made it," John celebrated. "It's not as easy to push my way in."

"Oh Uncle J, you're very tiny," she teased running her finger over his image.

"I feel so small," he said with a bewildered look as he sat on the bench.

"This way you can travel in my pocket. So cute, I have a pocket uncle," she said laughing.

"I'm glad you can find the humor in my diminished existence," he frowned. "You think I'll be able to go back with you."

"Yes, I believe its part of your destiny, and for some reason, Josh and I are along for the crazy ride. You ready to go?" she asked before putting him in her pocket.

"Yep, let's do this," John said and gave a salute.

Josh was waiting by his truck when Nina pulled up. He greeted her with a smile, a friendly kiss and handed her a travel mug full of coffee. "Thank you, I was fading fast," she accepted the cup.

"Me too, I added an extra shot of espresso for the road," he said opening the truck door for her.

Before they left, Nina showed Josh the picture of John.

"How can that be?" He asked, fascinated by the animated image.

"I don't know," she shrugged, "I've learned to accept it, no matter how crazy it is. I am going with the idea that normal is too overrated in this realm," she laughed taking the picture from Josh.

"I'm beginning to agree," Josh stated as they headed out.

Looking into his eyes, she complimented him, "Yes you are, I've seen the progress," she smiled.

On the drive, they discussed their adventure. Nina educated them on some important facts, what they should expect, and might encounter. At times the truck was filled with conversation and laughter. And, at other times silence was a hitchhiker, as they all fell prisoner to their plaguing thoughts of the unknown. Even though the idea of going back was exciting, Nina could feel the tension in the truck almost choking her. By the time Josh pulled into the parking lot, her nerves were on high alert.

"Ok, Josh you know the plan. Don't forget to plug in the recording so that we can get back."

"Yes, it's all ready," he said suddenly feeling apprehensive. What if he couldn't go back? How was Nina going to do it alone fretting the thought?

Sensing Josh's uncertainty, Nina took his hand, "Just believe," pulling him to the edge of the city. "To be forewarned, you may feel a little jerk when you cross over."

While still holding hands, he leaned down and looked into her frightened eyes; he lovingly kissed her softly on the lips.

Nina instantly felt the pull as she had the times before, and again found herself in olden-days Shaniko. Noticing Josh was no longer holding her hand, she concluded he hadn't made it. "Nooo!" Nina cried out at the top of her lungs, frantically searching the nearby area. "I can't do this by myself," she said lost in despair, throwing her arms up in frustration. Then remembering her uncle, Nina took the picture from her pocket; with a slight smile forming at the sight of the moving man.

"You made it," she cheered, relieved to have him along. Even if he couldn't do much in his present state, she'd have companionship on the trip. That was if Josh doesn't call her back. In fact, she wondered why she hadn't heard his voice. What if he went back to a different time and place? Nina thought, causing herself anxiety. Pushing away the scary thought, she pulled herself together. "Let's go find Lucia, get a horse, and do this thing," she said trying to sound brave and in charge, even though fear was swimming inside her.

After guessing on what direction to go, she took a minute to regroup and then started down the road. She hadn't gotten far when she heard, what sounded like a man moaning. She grabbed a post leaning against a nearby building. With her body shaking and stomach twisted in knots, she followed the voice.

15) STEPPING BACK

Nina followed the voice to a small alley and taking care, she crept softly. Carefully she checked out the area for anything suspicious or lurking in the shadows. Only she didn't know what that looked like here. Her first reaction, when she heard the moaning sound again, was to turn and run, but she felt compelled to see what was making that noise. Nina was glad she followed her instinct because there, behind a large barrel, was Josh sitting on the ground, holding his head.

Looking up at Nina with a half-smile, he commented, "I thought you said I'd feel a small jerk. It was more like being catapulted. My poor head," he said rubbing his forehead.

"Josh you made it!" Nina happily shrieked dropping the board and hurrying over to him. "Does anything else hurt besides your head?" she asked with concern.

"Yes, my pride. I think I bruised it in the transition," Josh answered rubbing his backside while slowly lifting himself and brushing the dust off his pants.

As soon as he recovered from the after-effects of his cross-over, they started looking for a place to rent horses and with any luck at all, spot Lucia pushing her wagon, along the way.

"I wonder where she is," Nina said glancing at Josh, who was fixating on his new surroundings.

"I can't believe it! The town does exist," he exclaimed.

"You thought I was making this up?" Nina remarked, putting on her sunglasses to block out the bright sunlight.

"No, not all," Josh admitted. "It seems so much more real seeing it in person," as he enjoyed walking through people and making faces at the strangers.

"You'd better be careful. You might come across someone you know, and they'll be able to see you," Nina warned with a giggle.

Pulling the picture of her uncle from her pocket, Nina faced it toward the town. "Does anything look familiar?" she asked.

John looked around trying to calculate his location. As confusion gave way, his memory surfaced. Thus, allowing him to remember pieces at a time and in short spurts, to not overwhelm his brain. Smiling, he answered excitedly, "Yes, over there." Pointing across the street, he said, "There is the general store. Stan Madison, the owner, is a good person and family man. He played Santa Claus in the Christmas play and needed very little stuffing," he laughed. "Next to him is Sally's Bakery. She makes the best caramel apple muffins; I can almost taste the sweet frosting dripping off the side. And…" John then paused; his expression turned stoic, "I sense an evil presence somewhere nearby."

"Where?" Nina asked stepping close to Josh.

"I'm not sure. But, I think it is coming from the ironworks shop. Let's hurry past it."

"Fine by me," Josh said taking Nina's hand as they sped up their pace.

"What do you think it was?" Nina asked when they had stopped, looking down at the picture; the image suddenly is frozen.

"I don't know," said a voice from behind them, causing Nina and Josh to turn around.

The sight of the man illuminated with a green aura, had Nina almost jumping out of her skin. Looking over at Josh's pale face, she could tell he was also in shock. They stood there with their mouths gaping, staring at John, now in life-size form. "How did you do that?" Nina asked poking at him to make sure she wasn't hallucinating.

John shrugged his shoulders, "I guess in my haste to escape, I pushed out of the picture. It must have something to do with being in this realm because my memory is coming back in stages too. "

"This is too freaky," Nina expressed.

"Yeah, tell me about it," Josh added, still stuck in place, his eyes in a daze while he shook hands with John.

"I'm free," John announced, excitement ringing in his voice. With his arms open wide he called to Nina, "Come here my dear niece so I can hug you."

Nina slipped in her uncle's arms and instantly felt secure and protected. She closed her eyes, and for a moment, she imagined it was her father. Letting go, she shook off the odd sensation that had brushed past her. Then spotting Lucia, she yelled, "You're here."

"Yes I am," John replied lovingly.

"Not you," Nina laughed patting his shoulder, "Lucia, she's over by the saloon, which is apropos. She's probably trying to pawn off some of her healing remedy on some poor intoxicated soul," shaking her head. If Lucia was her guardian angel what were the heavens above thinking? She laughed at the absurdity of the situation.

"Come on Josh," Nina said pulling his arm.

"Uh, sure," he said trying to recover from John's life-size appearance.

"Josh and John, I'd like you to meet Lucia," Nina said giving introductions.

"My pleasure ma'am," John replied tipping his hat.

"Nice to meet you," Josh said repeating the gesture, his eyes glued on her assortment of colorfully filled bottles.

"May I offer you a sample?" Lucia asked noticing his curiosity.

"NO!" Nina stepped in. "But thank you," she added politely.

Lucia smiled, and after taking a drink, she commented. "I see you all made it. It has taken decades to get this combination together. I had faith in you girl," glancing at Nina. "Now you are probably wondering why you're all here."

"The thought did cross my mind," Josh said with suspicious eyes, his arms crossed over his chest.

"Your sarcasm is welcomed here, my boy. It shows character and strength. You need to be strong and alert in these parts," she remarked looking him up and down.

"Could you please explain?" Nina said tilting her head.

"Of course my dear; I imagine this does seem a little confusing."

"A little!" Nina snapped.

"Such a spirited thing," she said with smirk lifting Nina's chin. "I see a little of myself in you, that was when I existed on earth," she winked, and then removed her hand.

"Here is my story," she said bringing them closer. "Long ago I was given an assignment. It involved getting John back here so he could learn the truth of what happened that tragic day at the mine. Then, help him move on," she said pushing wispy strands of gray hair away from her face. "It hasn't been an easy task. To carry it out, I needed to establish the right relationship and connections. Believe me,

I've tried. I had all but given up. That was until you, Nina came into the picture. I had finally found someone tied to John, which was you, Nina. And someone related to Thomas Parker and that is Josh. And when you and he formed a relationship; wallah, my circle was complete."

"That is so bizarre," Nina expressed, digesting what she'd heard. It was clear, by the blank look on her team members' faces; they were thinking the same thing.

"Yes, that may be, but it's how they roll here," she laughed. "Anyway now you know why you're here. Next, I am going to reveal the rules and bylaws to which you must abide by during your visit. It's very important that you follow them or you'll reap the consequences. Is that understood?" she asked with a stern face.

They nodded.

"Nina, you and Josh are responsible for finding out what happened to John. I will take it from there. Also, you may encounter a lesson, or gain insight into, a troubling thought along the way," she expressed staring at Nina.

Nina cringed, a shiver ran down her spine; feeling spooked by Lucia's glaring eyes.

Josh, sensing her fear, draped his arm across her shoulder and pulled her close.

"Now where was I?" Lucia asked herself. "Just my luck I get a woman's feeble mind to go with this disabled body," she remarked shaking her head.

"Oh yes," her eyes lighting-up as her memory kicked in. "I remember," she said putting on reading glasses. Then reaching for a paper containing a long list, she read it aloud. "First, you can't tamper with the past or alter the future. John, my lad, you can watch your family from afar, but there can't be any human contact, and you must not show yourself. If you do, the outcome could be detrimental," she stressed. "You have to realize that in this realm, you can see only one John."

"Next, all of you will be able to talk to people you are somehow related to, or with whom one of the teammates has a connection. I'm sure John will win the popularity contest in this category, since he used to live here," laughing at her witty remark.

"Anyway, you will know these people by the green aura around their bodies; like the one around John," she said informing the group. "However, this does not include immediate family members. That is, and always will be, off limits. I can't stress that enough." Then she scrunched up her face while searching her mind for her next thought. "Also, avoid any contact with people with a red aura. They are dangerous and will do anything to prevent you from discovering the truth." Then, looking at John, she continued, "This is where you come in. Since you are in-between worlds, you can fight off this evil and offer protection. Sorry, you'll be on your own, I cannot help you here," she admitted. "Can you do this?"

After John nodded, Lucia changed the subject as she pointed to Nina. "Did you bring the coin?" holding out her hand to receive it.

"Yes, I did. I knew it was you that gave it to my uncle." Nina commented putting it in Lucia's crippled hand.

"You are a smart girl. I had to find a way to get it to you. Be sure to keep it with you at all times, preferably close to your heart. It has some very special powers," she said grasping the coin between her fingers and holding it up to the light. It was as if she was looking through a magic globe.

"It keeps time frozen while you're here. It's your transportation to get from point A to point B. It's called jumping." Then, looking at the questioning faces, she tried to explain. "Let me show you. A picture speaks a thousand words. One thing I have to make clear is that you had to have traveled the path to the location at least once. You can jump multiple times in the realm, but only once, in and outside of this realm in a twenty-four hour period. However, I don't think that will pertain to you, as I have faith you will solve this mystery today."

"Ah, how would you know that?" Josh asked keeping his guard up.

"Let's see, I am the angel, and you are a mortal, need I say more?" she said with an attitude, and leaving it at that.

"How does it work?" Nina asked trying to hide her smile over Lucia's snide remark.

"I'm getting to that," Lucia said, "you young kids are always in a rush," shaking her head and taking a drink.

"Nina, hold the coin, take Josh's hand and say aloud, a place you've been to around here."

"Okay," Nina replied fulfilling the silly request. "Hotel" she called out.

"What happened?" Josh said standing in front of a large building.

"It worked," Nina expressed with excitement. "Brace yourself, because here we go again," she told Josh. Then speaking into the coin, she said, "Lucia's wagon," and they were instantly back in their original spot. "That was fun, how about...," but before Nina could jump again, Lucia stopped her.

"Missy, that's enough! We still have much more to cover. The big man wouldn't take kindly to me sending you on this journey without being prepared. Besides, your partner looks a little pale. Also, the coin is not a microphone, your touch and words control it," she chuckled, opening a new bottle of the green liquid and pouring herself a glass.

"What's that smell?" Josh asked covering his nose, the pungent scent adding to his queasy stomach.

"Yum, smells like heaven, right? At least this job does come with some perks. Would you like some?" Lucia asked, reaching for a glass.

"Ah, no thank you," Josh politely responded. "My stomach isn't doing well, probably all the bumping around," he admitted resting his hand on his abdomen.

"Oh, but this helps whatever ails you," she said with pride.

"Maybe another time," Josh declined, feeling nauseated. "Would you by chance have some seltzer water?"

"Yes, I can help you with that," she answered with a devilish smile as she reached for a bottle of the clear liquid. She then filled a glass halfway with the seltzer, and after adding a couple of drops of the clear liquid, she handed it to Josh.

He hesitated before accepting the glass, and it didn't help that Nina was giving him that look.

"Go ahead, drink up boy, I promise it's only seltzer," Lucia said giving a boisterous laugh.

After taking a long drink, Josh let out a large belch.

"Well, maybe there was a drop of additive in the bottle," she said with a sly look.

"I do feel better," Josh admitted taking another drink. "What's in it?"

"I'll never tell," then laughing she said, "I think we got off track again," as she searched her mind until she found where she'd left off. "There are clues hidden within the coin, but I couldn't tell you what they are. I was not privy to that information. Can you believe they thought I'd give them away? No respect," she mumbled, adding a drop of oil in her glass.

Nina was getting bored standing around, and wondered how much longer Lucia would be. She figured it must be getting late, so she took her phone out of her purse to check the time. However, seeing a blank screen, she cried out, "its dead," disappointment showing on her face.

Lucia noticed Nina's reaction, and commented, "Modern technology hasn't been invented yet, and cell phones, computers, and other devices will not work here."

Nina frowned as she put the phone back in her pocket. "I figured that, but I thought the clock would be accessible. How are we going to keep time?"

"You need not worry my dear as I said, time is frozen here. However, I should speed this along, as I have other places to be. Anything else?" Lucia said, counting all the points on her fingers. "Oh yes, if you need me, call my name. I will get there as soon as I can," she informed them. "You're not my only assignment. In my other job; I'm a twenty-five-year-old female living in the Florida Keys, watching over a hurricane victim. Quite sad," she said with a sigh. Then bringing her focus back to the trio, she continued. "John you haven't said much. What's on your mind?"

"There's not much to say. I was hoping to hold my wife and children and talk with my brother," he said lowering his head in despair.

"Hmm," Lucia said clicking her nails on her bottle while giving his request some thought. "Let me work on that. There are no guarantees, but I'll see what I can do."

John's eyes lit up, his smile beaming, "I would be forever grateful," he said feeling hopeful.

"Good, now that we have settled that little issue, let's begin with the next part," she said waving her arm. "Now take a look over there," pointing to a covered wagon outside the country store. Watch," she ordered.

Their eyes watched the movie-like image playing out. A man was loading the wagon with supplies while another stood next to a lovely lady and two small boys. Taking her in his arms, he said good-bye and kissed her, and then bending down, he hugged the boys. Tears were seen streaming down the faces of the family.

Lucia waved her arm and froze the action. "Do you recognize them, John?"

"That's Waylon and me," he said. His eyes followed his friend into the store. "We are preparing for our journey to the mine. My wife, Evelyn and my sons Amos and Jacob came to say goodbye," he said with a solemn expression, feeling the sting of the memory.

"Continue watching," Lucia said waving her arm and directing their attention back to the group.

John let go of his sons as another man walked up with his hand reaching out. After the men shook hands and embraced in a hug, the man stood next to Evelyn.

"I know who that is," Nina called out raising her hand.

Lucia moved her arm, and again the image stopped. Glancing over at Nina with a frown she commented, "Nina there's no need for that, but since you've interrupted, would you like to tell us who that is?"

"Uh sorry, I was getting into the mood," she said feeling embarrassed. "That is my Uncle Thomas. I met him on my visit here. You can continue now," shrugging her shoulders.

"Now, if there are no other comments, we will continue," deliberately directing her attention to Nina before starting.

They watched as Waylon stepped out of the store. His arms were full of supplies as he joined John by the wagon. Then after he loaded the wagon, he climbed into the driver's seat while John inspected the horses, and wagon, one last time, before joining the man. Then after he settled in the seat, John took the reins, waved goodbye as he signaled the horses to go. He was unaware of the tears flowing behind him, or his wife leaning on his brother for support. Again, Lucia put the show on pause.

Looking at the saddened trio, Lucia spoke. "John you didn't realize how much they missed you. The fever of gold," Lucia surmised. "You didn't have it as bad as some, but worse than others. I know you wanted better for your family."

"I wish I could go back and change it," John said a tear falling from his eyes.

"Now, enough of that," she said wiping her own eyes. Then, giving her attention to Josh, she commented, "Waylon is your great-uncle, which I assume you already know. I think you look a lot like him," she said mentally comparing their features. But that is neither here nor there," as she made the image disappear. "I think that's it. Remember everything I've told you, abide by the rules and don't mess with the people with a red aura," she said summing up her points. "You're on your own now. You will find the livery stable around the corner. Good luck," she said pushing her cart a few feet before disappearing.

"That's it?" Nina said with exasperated breath. "She's going to send us on our way, and hope we succeed on this crazy mission? I'm not feeling all that confident. What are your thoughts?" she asked her teammates.

"Well I don't know about you guys, but I'm starving. Let's see if we can find a green person in a cafe and get some food," Josh said while rubbing his stomach.

"They are not green," Nina chuckled, "they have a green aura."

"Whatever, I'm hungry," Josh said with a deep sigh.

"That's sound like a good idea to me," John agreed.

"Oh, you guys and your stomachs!" Nina exclaimed. "Josh, a few minutes ago you were complaining about your stomach hurting."

"It was, but that miracle drink fixed it. I feel great now," he said with a wide cheek-to-cheek smile.

Nina, noticing something different about Josh, brought his face close to hers, and squinting, she looked deep into his eyes. "Your pupils are dilated to the max," she announced.

Josh, oblivious to her comment, leaned closer and said; "You are very beautiful," going for a kiss.

"And you are high," Nina giggled and pushed him away. Then she shook her head, disgusted with Lucia for putting Josh in this state. "I should have known that was liquor she'd put in your seltzer."

"Probably White Lightning, I'd say one-hundred-proof," John remarked.

"Great," Nina sarcastically commented through gritted teeth.

"I don't know what it was, but I feel great. In fact, let's find that medicine lady and get a bottle for the road," Josh exclaimed searching the streets.

"I don't think that's a good idea," John said, offering his opinion.

"I agree," Nina nodded. "Uncle J who are you connected with in this town?" reaching for Josh's arm as he started to wander.

"Hmm, I have some friends here, at least I did," he answered taking Josh's other arm.

"Someone in the cooking field would be nice," Nina replied.

"I know of a great spot, it's up the road a little way," he said as they guided Josh along.

"I am so hungry, I could eat a cow," Josh exclaimed almost losing his balance as he leaned into John, kicking up dust.

"And gallons of coffee," Nina stressed struggling to maneuver the intoxicated man down the street.

When Nina walked through the doors of what seemed to be the local cafe, it was as if she'd stepped into a country western movie. Inside, the scent of grease and sugar filled the air. A young waitress with a cheery smile in a long apron greeted them at the door. "Welcome to the Golden Tooth Cafe," then looking at John, she added, "Hi Mr. Smyth, your usual table?"

"Yes, please Miss Belle. How are your folks doing?"

"Okay, I guess. Between school and working part-time I rarely see them," she said escorting them to a table in the corner.

Nina was fascinated as she watched the meet-and-greet between the waitress and her uncle John. It was mind-boggling she thought, how easily he had transitioned into this dimension, and fell so smoothly into his everyday routine. It was like he'd never left. Nina realized this was something to which she couldn't apply any sane logic. The events here were way more sophisticated than the most advanced technology in her twenty-first-century world. Instead, she decided to focus and appreciate the cute little café. The decorations were simple, yet welcoming. She especially admired the embroidered linen cloth draped over the small table, and the candle encapsulated in a beautiful homemade centerpiece, gave it style. After they sat down, Belle listed all the specials and then took their orders. She then hurried off, her long ponytail bouncing as she stepped.

Josh had been quiet since they'd walked in the door, Nina noticed he seemed to be in a word of his own, checking things out, and all of a sudden with a confused look, he turned to face her. "Where are we?"

"We're getting food as you asked. You okay?" Nina asked with concern, noticing his eyes were almost back to normal.

"I don't remember saying that, and could someone stop the room from spinning," he pleaded grabbing his head.

"Here, have some coffee," Nina said pushing the filled cup in front of him. "I ordered you a potato scramble, it has everything in it but the kitchen sink," she smiled.

"Maybe you'll feel better after you eat," she said doctoring her coffee.

"I hope you're right."

"I warned you not to accept a drink from Lucia," she said.

"Remind me of that next time," he said rubbing his head.

"I would like to speak on Lucia's behalf. Do you think she gave Josh the drink to help ease him into the transition? After all, she's here to help."

"I guess that's possible," Nina said contemplating that thought.

"Think about it," John said, "Nina, you've already been here a couple of times, this is all familiar territory for me, but this is Josh's first time, and his entrance into this realm was extremely rough," his said proving his point.

"You could be right with that assumption. I do feel better, even my headache is almost gone," Josh admitted, smiling at the waitress holding their order.

"Even so, I'd be leery of drinking anything off her cart," Nina warned, moving her purse to make room for the plates of food and condiments. Then after Belle topped off their coffee, she went to wait on another table.

While the trio ate, they used the time for discussing an action plan, as much as they could with their knowledge so far. First, they were going to get horses and use the map to guide them to their destination. It would give them a start, and hopefully, reveal more down the road.

As with the waitress at the cafe, John was also friends with the owner of the livery stables. After the horses were saddled and ready for the trip, the owner approached Josh. "Can I interest you in this forty-five, you shouldn't be traveling those roads without some protection, some ruthless men are hiding out from the law," he said showing Josh the weapon.

"Do you think we need that?" Nina asked wearily about bringing a gun along. "Are we even allowed to have one here?"

"Nina, maybe he's right. I only have a pocket knife on me, and that's not going to defend us if we run across any outlaws," Josh said getting familiar with the gun as he held it in his hand before paying the man.

Nina remained silent. It was obvious by the way he looked at the gun; she didn't have a say in this matter.

"Look," Josh said excitedly, the guy even threw in a holster and bullets, I feel like a true cowboy now," practicing drawing the gun.

"Make sure the safety is on," Nina said getting on her horse. Then after the guys mounted their horses, she pulled out the map to plan out their route.

"Do you two mind if we stop by my house? It's only a few miles off the main road, and it may be the last time I see my family," he said with hopefulness in his eyes.

"I have no problem with that," Nina said putting the map away and getting control of her mare.

"Lead the way," Josh stated taking control of the reins.

"Great," John exclaimed, and then gently nudging his horse in the ribs, he led the team out of town.

It wasn't long before they had reached John's property, and found a grassy area away from the house where they hid behind a tall tree. "Isn't she beautiful," John said watching his wife who was outside in the pasture talking with his brother while he mended the fence. "You know Evie begged me not to go. She said even though we didn't have much money, she was happy with her life." John said thinking back, his eyes locked on his wife. "But I wanted to move her to the city, give her a better house and send my boys to a good school." Then facing Nina and Josh, his head looking down, he spoke with sadness in his voice. "I couldn't see it. It took this fool over a hundred years to learn that I already had my gold mine right here."

"Don't be too hard on yourself Uncle J. You were doing what you thought was right. I'm sure Aunt Evie understood," Nina said with compassion, patting him on the back.

"That sounds like my dear wife. She was so full of love and understanding; I don't think I ever heard her complain. You have the same spark in your eyes and fiery spirit."

"Really," Nina said, holding back the tears welling in her eyes. "I wish I could've met her."

"She would've loved you, Nina. Why didn't I see we could've been happy whether we were living in this small country home with barely anything or living in the city basking in luxuries? It shouldn't matter as long as we were together," he said taking one last look at his family. "C'mon let's go, I can't bear to watch this anymore," he said climbing on his horse.

Nina and Josh climbed onto their horses. They were lost in thought as they followed John back to the road, pondering his words of wisdom, and applying it to their relationship dilemma.

After what seemed like forever bouncing along on her riding companion, Nina was more than ready for a break. Her butt felt like jello, and her legs were going numb. Finding a perfect place to stop, she commented. "Hey, guys can we rest here in this meadow for a few minutes? The horses can graze and look, there's even a brook where they can get a drink," she said, dismounting her horse before they could comment on her request.

After tying their horses to a nearby tree close to the water and premium grazing area, they surveyed the countryside, walking to stretch their legs.

"I know this place," John expressed. "I can't recall the reason it sparks a memory, but I sense it has a significant meaning in my life." Then scratching his head, while giving it some deep thought, his eyes grew wide with the recollection, "I know what it is," heading to the water.

16) THE JOURNEY'S END

"Here is where it happened!" John exclaimed, bending down and rubbing his hand along the grassy spot. He became lost in thought.

"This is the place? Are we here already? Nina asked half confused. "Where is the mine?" she said looking around.

"Oh my sweet Nina, this is where I proposed to Evie," smiling up at his niece. "The memory is so very clear. She looked so beautiful in her yellow sundress; almost as bright as the warm sunshine gifting us with its presence," picturing it in his mind. "In her hands, she held a bouquet of wildflowers; the flowing creek and chirping birds set the mood. I was shaking so badly I almost dropped the ring in the water," he said with a short chuckle. Then, staring at a passing cloud, he continued, "When she said yes, I felt like the luckiest man in the world. I believe Nina, that next to the old oak tree you're standing by, is the symbol of the love we shared that day," he said walking over and scraping off the layer of moss to reveal the writing.

"John and Evie Forever," Nina read aloud, brushing her fingers along the carved heart. "Oh uncle you were such the romantic," she swooned.

Looking away, oblivious to Nina's comment, he cried out; "I'm so sorry Evie, my heart is heavy with grief," he confessed, dropping his head and finally mourning her loss.

Nina gently patted her uncle's shoulder and stepped away, as she and Josh gave him time alone to grieve.

"I can't imagine his pain," Nina sighed, watching the ripples in the water, and nonchalantly kicking a rock into the creek.

Josh stepped up behind Nina, put his arms around her and pulled her close. "I think I could," he whispered, turning her around.

"Josh we shouldn't be doing this," Nina said trying to resist the passion burning in his dark eyes.

"Nina, I'm not sure if this is fate or destiny, but I do believe something is bringing us together."

"You're probably caught up in the moment, or your emotions are confused here," she said swallowing and turning her head away from his intense stare.

"I'm caught up in you, Nina!" he admitted, moving to face her. "You blew into town like a raging wind, knocking me over with your big girl city swagger, and blowing me away with your spirited attitude. I knew then my heart didn't have a chance. Even though you challenge me and taunt me with your stubborn streak, you take my breath away every time you look my way." He said staring into her glistening eyes. "I never dreamed you'd brighten my life or capture my heart. I know you don't want to hear this, but Nina I'm falling in love with you." With that, he felt her melt as he lovingly kissed her trembling lips.

After Nina came to her senses and collected her thoughts, she pulled away from Josh, and commented, "Will you please stop doing that?"

"Doing what?" he questioned, showing a sly grin at Nina's flustered state.

"You know very well," sending him a frown, "luring me in with your sexy boyish charm, and sweet talking," she replied.

"I can't help it, you're irresistible," he admitted, raising his eyebrows as he spoke. "Nina you can't deny there is something here between us."

"I don't, but every time you're near me, look my way, or steal a kiss, my mind turns to mush. It's like someone turned off the logic switch in my brain, allowing the emotions to run amuck," she said skipping a rock across the water. "It's possible I am falling in love with you, but I need time to consult my feelings. Maybe it's the distance thing holding me back, or I'm afraid of loving and losing again. Or the thought of love itself, keeping me stuck," she said with a sigh. "I also don't think this is the place or the time for this discussion. I need a clear head to be able to move forward with this mission."

"You think I have boyish charm?" Josh replied.

Nina frowned as she playfully slapped him on the shoulder, "I pour out my heart, and that's all you can say. Just like a man," she quoted.

"What's that supposed to mean?" Josh asked wondering what he'd done wrong.

"If the cowboy boot fits wear it," she said with a sassy tone. Then taking his hand, she added, "Let's go check on my uncle," pulling him along the creek bank.

"Hey guys," John commented, looking up from the map. "I wondered when you'd be back. I was about ready to send out a posse to find you."

"Ha ha, Uncle J, we were exploring this beautiful country."

"Oh, is that what they call it in your era?" he teased.

"Whatever," Nina said with a fake smile; relieved he was in better spirits.

"So how many more miles do we have left to go?" Nina asked. She stretched her legs dreading the thought of getting back on the horse.

"Maybe twelve at the most," he answered folding up the map and stashing it in the saddle bag.

"Eww, that means another four or five brutal hours of bouncing around on this hard saddle. My legs are never going to survive, not to mention my bum," Nina whined rubbing her backside. "If only there were another way," searching her mind for the answer. "Maybe we can use the coin to get us there?"

"The problem is Lucia said one of us had to have been there. That leaves you and me out, and John can't remember," Josh said playing the devil's advocate.

"Oh yeah, that could be a problem," Nina expressed almost giving up hope. "But what if," she said pacing in detective mode, "the memory lives in his subconscious mind, and the coin can detect it."

"It might be a long shot, but what do we have to lose?" John said considering her idea.

"I'm game," Josh agreed.

Nina reached into her left shirt pocket, pulled out the coin, and handed it to her uncle. Everyone stood together holding hands, and John yelled out "the mine." The trio continued holding hands and waited for the departure.

A large jolt tossed them into, what seemed to Nina, like an abyss. Within seconds she was sitting on the ground. Josh and her uncle were in the same position. All of them spaced a few feet apart. She rubbed her dizzy head, feeling disconnected with her body as she took some time to pull herself together. After recovering, she tried to focus on her surroundings. "Where are we?" she asked her teammates who were also reeling from the effects of the jump.

"I don't know," John replied, "It doesn't look familiar," slowly standing and brushing the dust off his clothes.

"What now?" Josh asked jumping up. "We're stuck here in nowhere-land without our horses," raising his arms in frustration.

"Here," John said handing the coin to Nina, "can't we jump back and continue this journey on horseback?"

"I'd rather not," Nina cringed. "There must be another answer," she said rolling the coin in her fingers.

"I wish I could remember," John said, "if only there were a sign or a landmark."

"Where is the gold mine?" Nina said talking into the coin and joking around. Focusing on a tree up ahead and then looking down at the coin, she shrieked, "That's it," excited about her discovery.

"What?" Josh asked with a baffled look.

"The coin shows a building shaded by a big tree. That looks like the tree," Nina said showing them the coin, and then putting it back in her pocket. "C'mon let's go check it out," she said excitedly.

"I can't believe it," Josh said as the trio stared in amazement at the building. It was an exact replica on the coin.

John's expression suddenly turned cold, as he policed the area with his eyes. "Shh, something doesn't feel right," he said keeping his voice low. "You two stay here. I'm going to look in the back."

"What do you think spooked him?" Nina asked hugging her body, her eyes alert.

"I don't know," Josh answered also keeping his guard up.

"Josh and Nina," John called from the back, "come here quickly."

Nina found her uncle hunched over a pile of rocks. A wooden cross marked a grave.

"He's buried here. I remembered now, we arrived at the mine early in the morning, same as every other day. Only this time we had visitors," he said, recalling the memory. "There were two men, both wearing long black coats and cowboy boots. We didn't have a chance. We were ambushed. Waylon tried to stand up to them, but they shot him; showing no mercy. They forced me to bury him at gunpoint, whacked me on the head, and left me," John expressed, his body shivering at the thought.

"That's right, those were my great uncles," said a man all dressed in black, clapping as he came out of the shadows.

"It's him," Nina whispered stepping closer to Josh, "and he has a red aura around him."

"I warned you to stay away. You should have kept your meddling fingers to yourself."

"What are you doing here?" Nina asked drawing on her courageous strength.

"Same reason you are, pretty lady, to claim the mine," he replied with a cocky smile.

"I don't understand," Nina commented.

"I can explain," another male voice said, joining the other man. Dressed similarly, and surrounded by a red aura, he had a gun in his hand.

Josh's finger itched to go for his gun hidden under his long jacket. His eyes glued on the two outlaws.

"My apologies for my rudeness; this here is my brother Wyatt, and I'm Mathew Clyde Burton the third. My friends call me Matt, at least the ones I still have," laughing at his remark.

"We're here to claim what is rightfully ours," Wyatt blurted out with a stern look on his face.

"It's all yours. We don't want it. So you can put down your gun and let us go before someone gets hurt," Josh said standing up to the man, his hand in position to grab his gun. All it would take was for the man to do something stupid and he'd be on him like flies to a cow-pie.

"Sorry I can't do that," Mathew replied, "can't take the chance. How do I know you won't try something funny after you return home?"

"Do we look like funny people to you?" Nina blurted out, her voice cracking.

"QUIET!" Mathew yelled. "I've wasted enough of my precious time. Once you're out of the picture I will stake my claim and all of it will belong to me," he said with an eerie laugh.

"You mean ours," Wyatt added.

"About that little brother, I've changed my mind," he said raising his gun and firing the weapon.

Nina was stunned. She couldn't believe what had happened. That ruthless man had just shot his brother in cold blood. There was no telling what the madman was capable of, she thought. Her heart raced, and her body shook as she stepped behind Josh, who was now pointing a gun at the outlaw.

"Drop the gun cowboy. Nobody's looking for a hero today. You wouldn't want that sweet little girl of yours to be next. And the same applies to you Mr. Miner, no quick moves or the girl gets it. Her fate lies in your hands," he said showing no remorse.

Josh set the gun on the ground. Unbeknownst to the outlaw or Nina, he had purchased two guns in town.

"All of you get over there by the grave," he said waving his gun in that direction separating Nina and Josh. "Now who wants it first? How about you?" he said aiming his gun at Josh.

"Nooo!" John yelled stepping in front of Josh to take the bullet. However, Matthew aimed his gun and shot Nina.

"Foolish man," he smirked after the gun went off, "don't you know you should always protect the women and children first?"

"Nina!" Josh exclaimed. Realizing the deception, he dropped to the ground. His adrenalin coursed through his veins at the sight of her lifeless body. After examining her, he was relieved to find she had a very weak pulse and shallow breathing. He did think it was strange there weren't any blood spots. But he figured there might not be any in this dimension. He felt helpless, as he didn't know how to get her medical attention, and by the looks of her condition, she was living on borrowed time.

"So touching," Mathew said sarcastically.

"You said, you wouldn't hurt her," John yelled out.

"So I lied, sue me. Who wants it next?" Matthew asked, showing no mercy.

Josh stood up. He was raging with anger. His second gun held in his hand, and he aimed at the murderer's heart. "There will be no more," he said ready to fire. However, before he could pull the trigger, Lucia materialized, blocking his view. Waving her arm, she froze Mathew in place.

"Lucia get out of my way. That poor excuse for a man shot Nina, and if she doesn't get the help she needs she could die. He doesn't deserve to live," he stated, standing his ground, holding honor for his lost love.

Lucia stood in place, "Josh you can't go around shooting people here, it would break the rules and believe me you wouldn't want to suffer the consequences, and it's not pretty."

"So what, he goes free?" Josh asked his anger flaring.

"I will take care of him," she said.

"How? Like you took care of Nina?" he asked, questioning her ethics. "And what kind of a guardian angel are you? Why weren't you here to protect her?" his anger lashing out at the old lady. "You must have some potion that can help her," he pleaded.

"Now Josh, the fate of my protégées doesn't lie in my hands. That power belongs to the Almighty himself," she said looking to the sky. "But, with that said, I wouldn't be very credible, and certainly not privileged to wear my wings if I had dead protégées on my record. John, please come take Josh, this hurting soul, to Nina while I deal with this trash." Then waving her arm, she turned Mathew and his brother into piles of ashes. And blew out a breath so strong, it created a whirlwind, carrying their remains into the sky.

When they were through watching Lucia, John followed her request. He took Josh's arm and led the hurting man back to where Nina's body was lying. Then, he bent down next to her and prayed. "Oh Lord I was given the assignment to protect her, and I failed miserably. Please dear God help this child. She doesn't deserve to die. A young man is waiting for her and there is an entire world to explore. She was only helping me. I told her this place was cursed and not to come. Oh, Nina, I'm very sorry."

When John finished, Josh poured out his heart. "How can I go on Nina? I know we can build an amazing life together and raise a loving family. Please don't leave me. What would I tell your mother?" he cried cradling her in his arms, his tears dripping on her pale face.

"Tell my mother what?" Nina mumbled brushing away his tear from her cheek. Then she tried to focus on the faces hovering over her.

"That you have been shot," Josh answered. Then realizing the question had come from Nina he yelled out, "You're alive!"

"Of course I am, and you're both delirious, I wasn't shot." Then as she tried to sit up, Nina felt a stabbing pain in her chest. She freaked as she realized they had been right. "OMG, I was shot!" she screamed, grabbing her chest. But when she touched the sore area, Nina let her anxiety go as she pulled out the coin. "It stopped the bullet," Nina said looking at the bullet lodged in the coin. "That's why Lucia had me keep it next to my heart. She knew how this would play out." Nina said feeling blessed.

"Well, I'll be," John commented with overwhelming relief.

Then shielding her eyes from the bright light, she smiled, "John, look up."

There standing above Nina was Evie, his loving past. She knew they had come to escort him home.

"Oh my Evie," he said standing and swooping her into his arms, hugging her like there was no tomorrow. At the sight of his now grown boys, he pulled them into the embrace.

"He is finally together with his family," a tearing-up Nina whispered to Josh, who was still cuddling her and was not about to let her go.

Nina watched as another man, which she figured was Waylon, patted John on the back. A couple of minutes later his brother, Thomas joined the reunion. After the hellos and hugs, John introduced his friend and family to Josh and Nina.

Lucia walked over to the group. "See John. I kept my word," smiling at the reunited family. "It's almost time to go. Say your goodbyes."

"Please don't send them away yet," he pleaded.

"John my boy, there is no need to worry, you're going with them. Hurry up now, I told the big guy I'd have you back soon, and my time is running out. Hut hut," she said clapping her hands.

Squatting down, he spoke to Nina. "My beautiful niece you were right. I am a lucky man to have had this time with you. I can't thank you and Josh enough for helping me get home. Please don't cry," he said watching her eyes fill with tears. "This is not good-bye. I'll see you again someday, but not too soon. You have a life to live and a special man to share it with," hugging her.

"Josh, you take good care of her. Believe me. I'll be watching," he laughed. "You're a good man. You carry many of the same qualities as your great uncle," smiling at Waylon. "That's why I let you get close to Nina," he confessed.

"No need to be concerned," he said shaking John's hand, "I plan on it. That is if she'll let me."

John grinned, "My niece is stubborn, I'll give you that, but she's smart and leads with her heart. In time she'll come around. I know because I see the way she looks at you with her loving eyes."

"Uncle J!" Nina snapped embarrassed at his assumption.

"Come on, it is time," Lucia commanded.

"Goodbye my sweet niece, I've enjoyed our journey together. Until we meet again, I bid you all a goodbye," tipping his hat and gathering with his family.

Nina gasped as Lucia waved her arm. In an instant, the group had disappeared, and emptiness replaced the spot where they had been standing. Just like the empty void she was feeling in her heart. She was going to miss that crazy miner and wiped her teary eyes.

"It's ok sweetheart, he's going to be fine," Josh said offering her comfort.

"I know, but I'm still going to miss him," she admitted.

"Me too," Josh replied.

"You two ready to go?" Lucia asked sitting down next to the couple, "times a-wasting."

"Yes, but I don't know if I can get up," Nina expressed.

"Oh, you're still hurting, girl. You should've said something. I have a fix for that. I'll be right back," she said running off.

"Josh, I'm feeling very sleepy. Please don't let her give me anything that will make me act stupid." Nina said dosing off.

"What happened to her?" Josh said in a panic to Lucia who had returned with a white tube.

"She's probably in a mild shock. Her body has gone through a traumatic experience. This salve should help," she said rubbing a white salve on the affected area and then giving the tube to Josh. "Make sure she puts this on three times a day, and in a week she'll be as good as new," Lucia instructed.

"How am I supposed to get her home?" Josh asked hoping she wasn't going to leave them stranded.

"Leave that up to me," Lucia answered. "Goodbye sweet girl. If I could, I'd give you a set of wings for your good heart and brave soul," she said kissing Nina's forehead.

"You didn't give me something to make me stupid did you?" Nina mumbled half-asleep.

"No dear, now sleep peacefully," she said brushing her hand over Nina's face putting her in a deep healing sleep.

"Promise you'll take good care of our girl," Lucia said.

"I will," Josh nodded, looking down at the sleeping beauty. Then turning to the old woman, he sincerely added, "I am sorry I doubted you and for my disrespectful behavior. You didn't deserve it."

"No apology needed," she said dismissing his comment. "Given the out-of-ordinary situation and unforeseen circumstances you hurled into, I'm surprised you've handled it as well as you did," she said with a caring smile. "These jumping assignments are so hard," she expressed, "especially when I'm only allowed to give you limited information and direction. Glad this one is over," Lucia admitted releasing a sigh.

"Hey, I don't suppose I could take a bottle of your laced seltzer water with me?" Josh asked with a hopeful look.

"Sorry, can't do that. I'm already twisting the rules by giving you the healing salve," Lucia remarked.

"It's time now," she said placing a hand on his shoulder. "Goodbye, son. Hold on tight. The jump might be a little bumpy," Lucia said waving her arm.

Within minutes, Josh and Nina were sitting on the ground next to his truck. The medicine lady wasn't kidding, Josh thought. He felt like he was bucked off a wild bull and dragged several feet. He was relieved to see Nina was still sleeping and hadn't been affected by their trip back. He put her in the truck and placed his jacket against the window for a pillow.

Before heading home, he took a few moments to stretch and shake off the jump. His mind was spinning, and he was still running on adrenalin. He knew from experience he was going to fall hard when the natural high wore off. Right now, his only concern was getting Nina home and settled, and then he could drop.

When his mind was centered, he climbed into his truck, took a deep breath, and smiled at his precious cargo resting peacefully. An unwanted lingering memory flashed in his mind, and his heart skipped a beat at the sight of the Nina lying still on the ground. He cringed as a void temporarily replaced his sleeping passenger. He shivered, pushing that image far from his mind. Making sure Nina was comfortable, he started for home.

17) HARD DECISIONS

Nina walked into her Mom's dining room and stared at the picture of the Indian. "I'm sure going to miss you, you crazy miner," she said quietly to the still image and feeling a pang of sadness.

A sudden movement caught her eye causing her to step back. "This can't be," she gasped as her curiosity pulled her closer. "Uncle J?" she said half-expecting the Indian to smile and wave.

"Guess again! Pretty lady," an eerie voice sounded. "Sorry about the shooting incident, but it looks like you are recovering well. Hope there are no hard feelings," Mathew said, his eyes dark and void of emotion, giving a cynical laugh.

Nooo! Nina screamed in her head. Then hearing Josh calling her, she tried to run to him, only her legs stood frozen in place. "What's happening?" Nina said starting to panic.

"Nina, Nina honey," Josh said in a soothing voice, shaking her gently to wake her.

"Josh, he's in the painting. We need to get away from here," thrashing her arms, still in the depths of the nightmare.

"It was only a dream. Nina, you're safe here with me," he replied holding her close to comfort her.

Nina wiped her sleep-filled eyes. Then squinting, she focused on her surroundings. There, an inch away from her cheek was the saddest face she'd ever seen and the cutest glistening black nose. "Whiski, what are you doing at Mom's?" she asked reaching out to pet the excited fur baby.

"Nina you are at my house," Josh said. "And that sweet girl hasn't left your side all afternoon."

"How long have I been asleep?" Nina asked, feeling dizzy after trying to sit up too fast.

"About five hours," Josh replied, propping a pillow behind her back for support.

"Oh no!" Nina shrieked. "Mom must be freaking right now," failing at her attempt to stand.

"Girl, please stay put until you get your equilibrium under control," Josh ordered catching her before she fell. "I texted your mom from your phone. She thinks you're having dinner at my house and then we're watching a movie."

"Whew, thanks, Josh," Nina said with relief, rubbing her dry lips together. Then sitting back down, under protest, she tried to relax. "Could you please get my purse, I need my lip balm, and I'd love a drink of water. My mouth is parched."

"Sure, I also made a stew and a batch of cornbread. It's ready anytime."

"Thanks sounds delish, give me a few minutes to wake-up," Nina replied.

"Oh, by the way, you had a call while you were out. It was from Rene, and I think she left a message."

Nina frowned, "That's my assistant and a good friend. She usually doesn't call on Sundays. Her schedule is extremely busy on the weekends. It must be important," then searching her voicemail app, she listened to the message.

Josh returned with the water just in time to witness Nina trying to stand. Rushing to her side, he took her arm, holding her in place until she regained her balance. "Didn't I tell you to stay put?" he stressed. "You're such a stubborn city girl," he said with a chuckle.

Nina ignored his attempt to scold. Instead, with a serious look, she commented, "Rene sounded terrible on the phone. Her voice was very raspy, and I could barely understand her over the coughing fits," Nina replied, feeling sorry for her friend. "I need to go back to Portland. My boss is visiting his daughter and new granddaughter at the coast, so there's nobody at the office. Rene also informed me there are a couple of new contracts scheduled for next month."

"Nina you are in no condition to be traveling," Josh remarked, with an alarming look. "There must be someone else who could fill in."

"I'll be fine. It's my job, and they are counting on me," Nina said moving with care. "I'll be right back; nature is calling," slowly making her way to the bathroom.

Josh hadn't prepared himself for this. He was expecting to have another month; hoping he could spend more time to gain her trust and win her over. Given their bond was premature and weak, he was afraid if she left now, they'd lose what they had.

"Wow, I feel so much better," Nina said entering the room, trying to hide the pain she was feeling.

Josh could see through her facade. The grimace on her face exposed the truth. "Nina, come sit down and let's think this out," he motioned her to the sofa.

"There's nothing to discuss Josh, I'm leaving tomorrow," she replied, keeping the conversation light as she sat next to him, and folded her legs under to get comfortable.

"Just like that? What about your mom? Who is going to be there for her?" he asked using Molly as a crutch.

"She has Dave," Nina answered. "The way he dotes on her, I am sure he'll be hanging at the house a lot. Besides, the doctor said she'd be out of the boot in a couple of weeks."

"What about us, Nina?" Josh blurted out, searching her eyes for answers.

Nina took a breath as she decided how to answer his question. This was a fragile topic, and she knew if she didn't approach it with gentleness, there was a possibility of jeopardizing what they had built so far. "I figure being apart for a while will give us time to think about what we want, and how to make a relationship work."

Taking her hands, he gazed into her sensitive eyes, tasting the nervous sweat on his top lip, he expressed his feelings. "Nina, I don't need time, I already know what I want." Then raking his hand through his hair, he worked on his next thought. "Every time I try to discuss our relationship with you, there's always been an excuse, or you shy away. There always seems to be something more important," he admitted holding in his temper.

"Well excuse me for getting shot," Nina snapped sarcastically.

"You know that's not what I meant. Don't use your anger as a diversion," calling her bluff.

Nina looked away, surprised he had seen right through her. She hadn't intentionally meant to blow up, but she felt like she was being pushed up against the wall. Then turning toward him, she commented. "Josh I am sorry for my bitchy moment," she said offering him a smile. "I don't want us to fight. You knew when I came here, it was only going to be temporary. We also agreed a long distance relationship would be complicated."

"No Nina, you made that decision in your mind," starting to get defensive. "You never gave me a chance to voice my opinion. Sometimes I feel like you don't want this to succeed," he confessed, standing and putting distance between them.

"That's not fair," Nina said in her defense.

"Well life isn't fair," Josh stated. "Maybe if you don't see a future with me, then the best thing for us to do is break it off now," he stated his heart breaking.

"No, you can't mean that," Nina cried out rushing to his side. She ignored the pain in her chest; it didn't compare to the feeling of her shattered heart. "What do you want me to do?" she asked afraid they could be slipping apart.

Pulling away from her, he sadly expressed, "If the answer to that is not clear, then maybe you do need to go back to the city," he said with a heavy heart. Then after a deep sigh, he added, "We're not getting anywhere, why don't we drop this conversation for now, and salvage the friendship we have. How about we eat, and then I'll take you home," he said hiding his true feelings while struggling to keep a positive attitude.

"I'm not hungry," Nina said her stomach in a twisted knot. If only she could throw herself into Josh's arms and give him the answer he was searching for everything would be perfect. Or would it? Maybe for the moment but it still wouldn't fix their problem. "It's been a long day, I think it's time for me to go," she said, grabbing her purse and coat and heading for the door.

"Okay" he replied with a solemn look, "give me a minute and I'll fix you a plate to go, and I'll be ready. I'm following you home to make sure you make it safely, and you have no say in this matter. Please wipe the displeased look off of your face."

Josh pulled up to Molly's house. Before he got out of his truck, he gripped the steering wheel as if it had the magic to give him the courage to let her go. Being the gentleman, he opened her door and took her hand. He breathed in the light scent of her perfume which tried to lure him closer. Instead, he said goodbye and gave her a friendly hug.

Nina wanted to hang on to him tightly and never let go, but she could tell he didn't want that. She asked herself, what had she done to get to this place? She wished there was a perfect fix, but at the moment she was void of any ideas, so with her heart aching she slipped out of his hold.

Stepping away from her, he commented, "I almost forgot to give you this healing salve from Lucia. She said to put it on three times a day," handing it to her.

It was hard for her to find the right words. Nina knew she couldn't make it right, but she was going to do her darnedest not to make it any worse. So after telling him goodbye, she bravely kissed him on the cheek, and softly whispered, "Please don't give up on us." Then she turned and hurried to the porch, afraid to look back, fearful she'd see the pain in his eyes.

By the time Nina had reached the porch, the tears had come rushing in. She licked a teardrop letting the pain of the salty taste, sting her mouth.

Her mom had seen the entire scene and was there to comfort her gasping daughter. "Nina what happened?" she asked holding her while she sobbed.

"I, I, think we broke up," Nina tried to say, her head buried in Molly's shoulder.

"It's going to be okay," Molly assured her, gently patting her on the back. "You want to talk about it?"

"No, yes, maybe, I don't know, it's all so confusing," she said throwing her arms up. "What should've been a simple discussion, turned into a heated conversation. And before long we were aimlessly throwing verbal digs and jabs at one another. It wasn't a pretty scene," Nina expressed to her mom. "Then everything seemed to spiral out of control. It was like a tornado had come into the room; taking all that was good and leaving behind broken wreckage," Nina said mentally drawing a picture of the dispute. "He couldn't deal with the fact I have to go back to the city sooner than I had planned," Nina said and accept a tissue from her mom.

"What are you talking about?" Molly asked startled by her daughter's comment.

"Come on. I'll explain while I pack."

"I still don't understand," Molly replied, sadness filling her at the thought of Nina leaving.

Molly sat on the edge of the bed. While Nina stuffed her suitcases with her belongings, she gently broke the news to her mom. Nina knew another emotional scene would break her, and one was already too many in a twenty-four hour period. To Nina's surprise, her mom was very accepting of the decision. At least she'd done a good job putting on a false front. Then afterward she sat down next to her mom told her what had happened at Josh's, sparing her some of the messy details.

"Ah sweetie," Molly said, placing her hand on Nina's leg, "I wouldn't fret over it. Tomorrow you'll probably kiss and make up, and forget what you were fighting about," she assured her.

"I wish you were right, but I think Josh might be right," Nina replied coming to the reality of the problem. "He wanted a commitment right then and there, and I couldn't give it to him," Nina confessed. "It's possible we are on different pages. If I would've been on the same page, writing the story with him, this decision should've been cut and dry," she surmised.

"Nina, ever since you were a little girl, no matter what you did, it was with gumption; always kicking and screaming. This is no different; you'll find the answer after your head clears and you battle your fears."

"I don't know about this time," Nina replied with a shrug.

"Have faith darlin'," Molly said with a chuckle.

Her laughter was the medicine Nina needed to pull herself out of her funk, at least for a few minutes, hugging her and saying, "Thanks, mom, I'm sure going to miss our mother-daughter talks."

"Me too, we'll have to work on video chat," she smiled.

"I'm down with that," she agreed. "Hey Josh packed some food for me, and there's more than enough for both of us. Are you hungry?"

"Sounds good," Molly said as Nina helped her mom down the stairs.

"You know one thing good that will come out of this," Nina said.

"What's that," Molly answered with a curious mind.

"Dave will be here more often," she teased.

"There is that," Molly blushed.

"I like him, mom," Nina remarked.

"Me too," Molly said with a coy smile. "He's not your father, but he's a different kind of special," she said with a spark in her eyes. "Now what did you say about food?" dropping the subject and making her way to the kitchen.

Dinner finished, Nina cleaned up, then finding her mom in the easy chair she kissed her cheek and headed to bed. She felt drained, and her wound was causing her pain. Before climbing into bed, she rubbed some of the salve on the affected area. Within five minutes she was wrapped in a deep healing sleep.

As Nina slept peacefully in her bed, Josh laid wide awake in his bed, repetitively playing the day's events over in his head, and wondered how it could have ended differently. What had happened? He kept asking himself, only coming up with the same answer. It was possible he had expected too much out of her. Not only had he pushed all her buttons but he also overloaded her emotional circuits.

He had acted like a complete jerk. Nina hadn't done anything wrong. All she wanted was a little time to figure things out, but when she announced the news of her returning to the city so soon, he had lost it. The truth was, the thought of her leaving terrified him. He was afraid she'd go home and slip back into her comfortable and safe city routine, forgetting about him, and brush off their relationship. That is why he had wanted a commitment of some kind before she left. Realizing he had been wrong, Josh sat up and looked at a sleepy-eyed Whiski, who was probably wondering what her crazy human was doing at 2:00 AM in the morning. "Whiski girl, tomorrow we are going to Molly's, and catch Nina before she leaves and make it right." With that decision, Josh was able to drop the stress holding him captive, and finally get some sleep.

The next morning, Nina awoke early, slipped into her farm attire, and for the last time, fed the barn animals. She was going to miss them but not the barnyard aroma. She also took a melancholy moment and smiled as she thought about her first time; rubbing her hand where Gerdy had left her marks. Then, the memory of Josh standing by the chickens, flashed through her mind, causing Nina a pang in her stomach. She imagined more memories of that man were going to haunt her for awhile and figured the best way to handle it, was to feel the sadness and move on. Now all she had to do was convince her Heart and Soul Department, she thought walking back to the house.

When Nina reached the back porch, the sweet smell of maple bacon lured her hungry stomach into the house, where her mom happily stood at the stove cooking breakfast.

"I thought I'd feed my daughter breakfast before she got on the road," Molly said her eyes tearing up.

"Mom, please don't cry. I promise I'll visit more often," she said washing her hands.

"You'd better. Now sit down and eat before it gets cold."

By nine-o'clock, Nina was in her leggings, sweatshirt, and traveling tennis shoes. She was all packed and standing outside her car. She bent down and petted the loving Cassie. After giving her mom one more hug, she kissed her cheek, said goodbye, and got into her car. She wiped a stray tear from her eye before pulling out of the driveway. She left with all the memories of Josh riding as a passenger, and as she passed by his road, she wondered what he was doing and if she was on his mind. Unbeknownst to her, he was pulling into her mom's driveway at that moment, wondering the same thing.

18) EPILOGUE

Nina had been back at home for over two weeks and was still dragging around a wounded heart. Sitting at her desk, she let her eyelids close over her sleep-deprived eyes as she asked herself age-old questions. Why does love hurt and how can she heal her broken heart? She tried everything and still hadn't been able to get Josh off her mind. He was with her twenty-four hours a day. Every time she tried to dump him somewhere, he found his way back. Nina hated that she missed him so much, that he could have such a hold on her, and he wasn't even here.

"Why don't you just call him?" Rene said, pulling Nina from her thoughts.

"Call who?" Nina asked playing innocent.

"Your cowboy, it's obvious you miss him. All you do all day is mope around and sigh. I've had a better conversation with my fish this week than I did with you. At least he moves his lips," she teased, hoping to bring Nina out of her funk.

"I'm sorry. I'll try to step up my game and work on being better company," Nina replied with a half-smile. "It wouldn't do me any good to call him, he probably doesn't want anything to do with me," Nina admitted, digging in the file cabinet for a specific document. "Besides we're still in the same predicament; I don't want to quit my job and move to the country, and he can't give up his ranch to move here. Neither is right or wrong, and no one is to blame. It's how it is," she said pulling out the paper. "I'll get over him soon. I hope," Nina said trying to sound convincing.

"I have an idea." Rene said with a large grin, "Let's go out this weekend. We could go to a couple of bars and kick up our boots on the dance floor," she said doing a quick-step routine. "You mentioned you wanted to try line-dancing. I thought maybe this would be a perfect time. I'll be able to wear my new designer jeans and show off my new hair color," she said tossing her reddish hair to one side. "It might even help clear your mind of what's-his-name."

"Josh," Nina corrected. "I don't feel much like dancing," she answered showing very little enthusiasm.

"Okay, how about we go mall shopping? Retail therapy cures everything," Rene said trying to convince her friend.

"Nah, I think I'll pass," Nina answered.

"Maybe you'll change your mind by Friday. If not, then I'm going to show up on your doorstep with a half-gallon of toffee ice-cream and two spoons."

"That I might go for," Nina said trying to sound upbeat. Then she put their conversation on hold and answered a phone call from her boss. After ending the call she looked over at Rene, "I wonder what he wants," she said, as she grabbed her notebook and coffee cup on her way to his office for an impromptu meeting.

"Nina, please come in," Mike said politely. "Take a seat; there's something I need to discuss with you," pointing to a plush chair.

"So, it's good to have you back. We've missed you. I take it your lovely mom is doing better," he said with compassion.

"Yes, she hasn't stopped going since she became boot free," Nina laughed, admiring a recent picture of Serena and her family. "How was your visit?" Nina asked picking up the framed photo.

"Great, he sure is growing like a weed, referring to his grandson in Serena's arms. "I'll tell you, Nina, I thought the greatest gift was raising children of your own, but now I believe it's the grandchildren that make life worthwhile," he said showing his pride for his family.

"So sweet," Nina expressed smiling at her boss. "I was hoping she would be here this week."

"She was planning on it, but the baby had a sniffle, and they decided it would be best to wait until he was feeling better. She has 'first mom' syndrome," he laughed. "I know you're busy, so let's get down to the reason I called you in," he said, figuratively putting on his boss hat.

"First of all, I want you to know that when Serena suggested we promote you, I had to admit I was a bit skeptical. But I trusted her judgment and I am so glad I did.

You have gone above and beyond my expectations. I couldn't be more pleased with your work," he said proudly, giving her praise.

"Thank you," Nina responded, subconsciously twisting her hands, feeling a little uneasy as she wondered where he was going with this talk.

"I have noticed lately that your mind has not been fully focused on your projects. You seem a little distracted," he said with concern, shuffling some papers in front of him.

"I'm sorry," Nina said her voice cracking.

"Nina, I can't help to think it has something to do with your trip to your mom's," he said handing her a glass of water for her dry mouth.

Nina accepted the glass, and took a long drink, as she processed her answer. "I met this guy, but we agreed a long distance relationship was too complicated, so we called it off," Nina said, turning her head to hide her painful expression. Then taking a deep breath, she added, "Believe me I'm trying to get over him," Nina admitted. "I promise to keep my personal life outside of work," suddenly feeling anxious.

After Mike cleared his throat, he replied. "Nina, I think you should go back."

Nina stood up in shock as she approached her boss, "Are you firing me?" a mixture of fear and confusion tugged at her...

"Of course not, now sit back down and let me explain," he said in a soothing voice. "You're mom called me last week, and we got into a lengthy discussion regarding the new coffee shop that she's putting in her market.

"She did?" Nina asked with a perplexed look on her face,as she returned to her seat.

"Yes, I looked at the proposal you submitted and was very impressed. Molly's agreed to sign a contract with us for coffee and supplies, under one condition," Mike said with a grin.

"What is that?" Nina replied interested to hear her request.

"She wants you to oversee the project, and I'm in total agreement with her decision. You know what is needed to start-up the shop and what is involved in maintaining it," he said giving praise.

"Wow, I don't know what to say," Nina said holding in her excitement.

"Wait, there's more," he said picking up a document. "I also received this from a woman named Jennifer, who lives in Bend," handing Nina a signed contract. "She is planning to open a coffeehouse in her building, and has especially asked for you to manage the operation, that is until the business is off and running."

"I can't believe she did this," Nina gasped placing her hand over her mouth. Her heart swelled as she looked at the proposal.

"Do you know her?" Mike asked pouring himself a glass of water.

"Yes, she's Josh's sister."

"Sounds to me like both families want you back," he said offering a caring smile.

"What about my work here?" Nina asked challenging the offer.

"You'll still be employed here and keep your title. You'll need to train Rene and be available for support. I also expect you to report to our monthly meetings. If you can't make it, we'll set up a live conference call. We'll set you up in an office in Maupin. In fact, I have a realtor looking into it as we speak," showing her a few possible prospects. "Hopefully, we'll have you moved in and ready to operate early next month. You'll be able to manage both businesses from there. I also imagine, with your drive and determination, you'll have a couple more on board before the year finishes," he said with a laugh.

"I don't know what to say," Nina said looking at the documents, overwhelmed by the news.

"What's it going to be?" Mike said anxiously awaiting her reply.

"Yes! Yes of course," she said jumping up to hug him. "Thank you so much. I won't let you down," Nina exclaimed, ecstatic over the opportunity and breaking into a happy dance.

"Good," Mike said laughing at his employee's quirkiness, "I was hoping you'd say that. I'm happy for you and look forward to the extra income from the added business. But, I have to admit, I'm going to miss your friendly smile and bubbly personality. You always bring this office to life," he admitted showing gratitude.

"I'll miss you too," Nina expressed trying not to get overly emotional. "You gave me my first job and took a chance on a young girl out of college. I am grateful for everything you've done for me," tears welling up in her eyes.

As she reached for a tissue, she caught sight of Rene trying to catch her attention outside the glass window. Excusing herself for a moment, Nina stepped outside the office door. "What's up?" she asked wondering what was so important it couldn't wait.

"Uh there's a man in the lobby asking for you," Rene said relaying the news.

"What does he want? Find out if he can wait for a few minutes," Nina commented.

"I don't think he can," Rene said. "He says he has some important business to discuss and has made it very clear, he wanted to talk to you. I think he's a new client."

"Rene, I trust your judgment to handle it. You might as well get used to it," Nina said on her way to the lobby.

"What?" Rene said with a baffled look.

"Talk to the boss," she said smiling at Rene and pushing away the urge to blurt out the news.

When Nina reached the lobby, her face lit up like the brightest star, and her smile beamed with happiness. There, checking out the magazine rack, was the man about whom she had dreamed. He was in a dignified three-piece business suit. She had to laugh inside at the cowboy boots and hat. "Uh sir, you're not from around here are you?" she teased, remembering the first words he'd said to her.

"Why is that?" he said playing along.

Smiling, Nina replied, "Because men around here don't dress like that," she laughed rushing into his arms.

"Josh what are you doing here?" she asked, her heart racing.

"I came to see my girl," he stated. He picked her up and spun her around. Then, after they shared a respectable kiss, Nina introduced him to Rene and excused herself. She needed to get back to her boss' office, so she left abruptly.

"He's here," Nina said busting into the room, hardly able to contain her excitement. "I want you to meet him," practically dragging Mike out to the lobby.

After she introduced Josh to Mike, they spent a few minutes in small talk. Nina then escorted him into her office.

"Josh, what are you doing here? Don't get me wrong. I am very glad you are here."

With a sexy grin, Josh answered her question. "I do believe you owe me a scenic tour of your city," he said removing his hat and placing it on the coat rack.

"You think so?" she flirted.

"Yes, people in my town always keep their word. I hope it's the same here," he said pulling her into his arms. "I've missed you so much," he whispered raking his hands through her hair. "My life hasn't been the same; I needed to see you, even if it's only for a couple of days."

"I know I've missed you too," Nina admitted. "A day hasn't gone by when you haven't been on my mind," looking into his passionate eyes. "But you know my views on long-distance relationships. I can't do it," she confessed. Then seeing the hurt and disappointment on his face, she added, "That's why I'm moving to the country," laughing at his changed expression.

"I don't understand," Josh stated. "What about your job and your glamorous city life?"

"Let's say mom and your sister offered me opportunities. I couldn't refuse."

"How's that?" Josh asked with a confused look.

"I'll explain later. Right now I have a sightseeing date with a sexy cowboy. I need to get my city fix in before I move to the sticks," she teased.

"It's not too bad," Josh said laughing at her comment.

"Yeah, but I'm still going to be keeping my house here, so I don't become totally countrified," she said giving him a coy look.

"We wouldn't want that to happen, would we?" he grinned.

"Seriously Josh. Something Uncle J said made me realize is that it doesn't matter where we are as long as we are together. And I want to be with you Mr. Parker; wherever that might be. I love you so much," she said gazing into his eyes.

"And I love you too, Miss Charm," pulling her into his arms and sharing a passionate moment; giving meaning to a real hello kiss. Then as they turned to leave the office, Nina hid a smile as she noticed her uncle wave to her from the framed photo of him on her desk.

DON'T MISS:

HISTORIES AND MYSTERIES:
RED WINE AND BLACK ROSES

THE NEXT BOOK IN THE
HISTORIES AND MYSTERIES SERIES

BY LINDA K. RICHISON

Maggie never imagined her life any other way until a mysterious stranger leaves a glass of red wine and one black rose on her table, and a hard to refuse job offer on her voicemail.

Tempted by a large sum of money; enough to fuel her dreams, Maggie accepts an unusual assignment and finds herself living in an eerie stone manor, under the same roof as the most gorgeous and sexiest man she'd ever seen.

Playing along at the request of Mr. Sexy, she pretends she can communicate with spirits. When the twisted charade grows deeper, Maggie discovers something about herself that could be a life changer.

As the chemistry heats up between her and Mr. Sexy, so does the fury fuming inside the spirit. Finding herself caught in the middle of a family dispute, Maggie must decide to do what's right and lose the money or keep her promise and risk betraying the man holding her heart.

ABOUT THE AUTHOR

Linda Richison resides in Salem, Oregon. She believes in living life to the fullest as she balances work, spending time with family and friends, dancing, writing and puppy cuddling. She also enjoys outdoor activities as she loves connecting with nature.

She is continually working to maintain a healthy lifestyle. An ever-changing goal of keeping physically, mentally, and spiritually fit is always a challenge but is so rewarding as it allows her to keep doing the things she loves.

Made in the USA
San Bernardino, CA
31 May 2018